CHRYSALIS CORPORATION

T.A. VENEDICKTOV

DSP PUBLICATIONS

Published by
DSP PUBLICATIONS

5032 Capital Circle SW, Suite 2, PMB# 279, Tallahassee, FL 32305-7886 USA
www.dsppublications.com/

This is a work of fiction. Names, characters, places, and incidents either are the product of author imagination or are used fictitiously, and any resemblance to actual persons, living or dead, business establishments, events, or locales is entirely coincidental.

Chrysalis Corporation
© 2015 T.A. Venedicktov.

Cover Art
© 2015 Anne Cain.
annecain.art@gmail.com
Cover content is for illustrative purposes only and any person depicted on the cover is a model.

ISBN: 978-1-63476-171-0
Digital ISBN: 978-1-63476-172-7
Library of Congress Control Number: 2015909598
First Edition November 2015

Printed in the United States of America
∞
This paper meets the requirements of
ANSI/NISO Z39.48-1992 (Permanence of Paper).

Annette: To our fans on DeviantArt who encouraged us to take *Chrysalis Corporation* to the next level. To our families, to our friends, and lastly to Requiem, for always reminding us that nothing is impossible. Thank you.

Trista: There are so many people I need to thank, but this first book is for my mom and dad, Ivy and Louis, for always telling me that I could do anything I put my mind to. For raising me on a bookshelf, letting me read whatever I wanted to (even if it involved my elementary school principal handing them an *Elfquest* comic book in a paper bag), and for never stifling my imagination. Thank you for being the best parents anyone could ever dream of.

And also to my coauthor, Nette, because without her this book and the ones following would never have been born. For fifteen years we've been dreaming up ways to get our characters into trouble. Let's try and make it another fifteen more, plus some.

Acknowledgments

Without Tammy's editing, this book would have been submitted looking like crap. Thanks for taking our rough-draft edit and polishing it into a gem.

Prologue—Damion Pierce Hawk

Mars Recruitment Center
0726 GMT (Greenwich Mean Time)

DAMION HELD one bag. One bag that contained his entire life—nothing more than a few chips full of pictures and vids, as well as Stim cigs, spare clothing, and enough money to get him here. Chrysalis Corporation Military Recruitment Center. He was standing in line for the second day with countless other candidates, waiting their turn to sign up and get physically assessed before being approved for entry. The Recruitment Center only took in a certain number of candidates a day, and yesterday he had arrived too late. Today he made sure to arrive before sunup, and despite that, he was still behind twenty people.

The Chrysalis Corporation brand displayed one long wing stretched outward from a perfectly cut crystal. Damion had seen it everywhere since he was a child. He assumed it was supposed to inspire hope, which was appropriate since this was his only hope to get off Mars. The Corporation kept their primary boot camp here on Mars, but if Damion made it through the ninety-day brutal treatment, he'd then be transferred to another planet for more training.

The idea of going off planet was surreal. Damion had never been off world before. No reason to, since his entire family was here and they didn't have enough money to rent out a shuttle to take them all. Despite his mother's constant trips to the temple and laying offerings to Ploutos, they had never been blessed with riches. His family had settled on Mars before his father was born, and they made a meager living off the dangerous mining of Red Ore—the ore that was used in all spacecraft engines. His mother's family had been part of it, Damion's brother was part of it, and his sister would also be when she was older. However, he didn't want to follow the family trade. The mining hazards included cave-ins about once a year, frequent equipment failures, and for many, a progressive lung sickness from breathing in the red dust. They lived near starvation, on the precipice of hope that their situation would become better over time. Damion knew it never would.

When Damion left home, he knew that feeding two children instead of three would be easier on his family. And if he graduated from boot camp, he would be able to send his mother part of his military pay, which would make up for the lost wages the family was out since he quit the mining job. His father had told him not to worry about it, but Damion knew that meant the old man would just work ten extra hours a week trying to make up for the gap in the family income. His mother worried more about him being killed, even if there was no true war going on at the moment, only skirmishes against rebels who attacked numerous colonies across the solar system and, from the media coverage, continuously attacked Corporation shipments. The rebels would steal supplies, ships, and at times people. The rebel propaganda Damion had come across urged people to turn their backs on the Corporation. Damion, as well as many other people, considered that suicide. The rebels' habit of putting innocent civilians in the way of their attacks was not gaining them favor.

Damion's gaze lifted higher, past the tall building, toward the stars. He let his mind wander away from the sweat pouring down his back and chest. Each star was supposed to be surrounded by planets, and Damion's heart raced with the awe-inspiring thought of seeing different colonies.

The sound of a large speeder roaring to a stop behind the long line of hopeful recruits broke his introspection. It appeared to be a private transport from the sleek look and lack of red dirt on the sides. He couldn't quite make out who got out of the speeder, but he wasn't a naturally nosy person. Damion Hawk had one person to worry about… and that was Damion Hawk.

He let out a small sigh of relief as he passed through the doorway and into the climate-controlled building. The air inside was easier to breathe and the temperature a good twenty degrees cooler. Corporation Infantry soldiers stood at attention, barely moving a muscle, their stances rigid. Living on Mars, Damion had seen the infantrymen get away with a lot of shit. He had a great distaste for the way they used their affiliation with the Corporation to break the most simple laws in his colony, such as night curfews and alcohol consumption on working days. Their presence would be tolerated by the locals as long as Red

Ore was flowing from the mines and there was a chance of a rebel attack on the Corporation's main source of clean engine fuel.

Damion had no desire to join the Infantry. He wanted to be a pilot. He had seen the vids of ships chasing off rebels since he was a kid. He had no clue how to fly a spaceship, but he would do anything to learn.

He stepped forward, and the man in front of him stepped to his right as they were ushered into different lines. At the end of each was a desk, and behind that desk was the person who decided if you continued on or went home. Damion stepped onto the scale. There was a small beep and a full-body examination scan rotated around him. His future was determined by his interviewer and the computer currently scanning his entire history. Damion was certain he would be allowed in since he wasn't overweight, didn't have any diseases, and had no record of breaking the law. He was confident, but that didn't mean he was going to get past that woman behind the desk.

Her suit looked perfectly pressed, and a medal Damion didn't know the meaning of was pinned to her right sleeve. Her nameplate stated that she was Lieutenant Orion.

Damion stepped forward, dropping his bag in front of his feet.

"Family name."

"Hawk, Damion Pierce."

"Age." She typed on the transparent keypad, the monitor she focused on obscuring half of her face.

"Twenty-six."

"Do you have any other markings on your body besides the tattoo on your arm?"

"No, just that one." A crystal Earth with wings coming from behind, protecting the home world of all humans. It was the only body art he had ever put on his skin. His father had been upset because, in his opinion, Damion had ruined his body.

"Do you have a history of disease, including childhood or venereal?"

"No."

"Do you have surviving siblings?"

"Yes."

"Do you or anyone in your family own a loan against a Corporation Banking System?"

"No."

"Do you have any children?"

"No." Damion said a silent prayer of thanks. He couldn't imagine having children in the near future.

"Do you have family currently employed by the military?"

"No."

"What is your aspiration for joining the Chrysalis Military?"

"To be a pilot." Damion pulled back his shoulders and straightened his back.

"Clarify." An intonation of boredom entered her voice.

"Oh, ah, to be a Spacecraft Fighter."

Damion felt these questions were rather mundane and asinine, considering the Corporation had most of this information on file from his application. However, he was ready to answer a hundred more if it meant getting him inside. The woman continued to look at the computer screen, moving her hands every five heartbeats or less.

He swallowed a lump forming in his throat as the briefest seed of doubt began to eat at his gut. There really could not be any skeleton hiding in his past preventing him from enlisting. Neither his father nor his mother ever told him about any long-lost rogue pirates in the family line. They would have warned him before he headed out of the house.

Right?

"You've been approved."

The words seemed surreal until the lieutenant's dark eyes tore away from the computer screen to glare at him. "Mr. Hawk. Please move to your left and go through into the medical clearance area."

"Yes, ma'am."

He picked up his bag in a daze and walked past two more Infantry guards.

The next five hours were a complete blur. Snapshots of events. The military police who monitored them and watched them their entire stay allowed Damion enough time to use the lavatory and head down to the mess hall to be served a meal by local workers. His clothes had been taken by the Recruitment Center's LADDS—Laundry and Decontamination Dry-cleaning System—and he'd been issued a standard black suit that had his last name on the left side of his chest, along with matching black boots. Damion's arm felt sore from the twelve shots the medical team gave him after clearing him. They said he would need another five rounds if he passed boot camp.

Then he was stuck at a computer and forced to take the longest test of his life. Math, reading, problem-solving puzzles, and a few questions Damion had no clue how to even categorize. Thankfully, his mother had made sure he and his siblings went to school the entire time until they were eighteen, even though it wasn't required on Mars. Damion knew his father could barely keep the budget and let his mother do it, since she had been able to attend school until she was fifteen versus his father leaving school after he turned ten years old. So he wasn't completely lost, but it certainly droned on. If he had to pass the test to continue on with boot camp, he would do it.

Taking a deep breath, Damion prepared himself for a long day and buckled down to finish the test.

He was finally getting off Mars. He was going to see the stars.

Prologue—Core 47

Saturday March 12, 454 MC
Destroyer Class Flagship Zeus
2043 GMT

CORE 47 managed not to wince as Alpha Fighter Morales, the man Command had assigned him to, roughly slammed him against the closed door to Morales's new Alpha quarters. This was yet another assignment for the Core, or Corporation Organic Robotic Entity. Despite telling the Creators that 47 knew who his Fighter was, they had yet again gone against protocol and assigned him to a Fighter not of his choosing for the third time.

He was bred by the Creators, a singular group of scientists who lived on ship and were rarely seen by lower personnel, for the purpose of strengthening the Alpha Zodiac spacefighter systems. The Fighter whom 47 had chosen was coming soon. Damion Hawk. 47 had been tracking him for a little less than two years, ever since the Fighter's initial training test scores had come into the system. And he had not been disappointed, because the Fighter continued to improve as time and training went by. He had known since then that Damion Hawk was the Fighter he wanted to fly with, for 47 was the best Core the Chrysalis Corporation had, and he deserved to be assigned to the best. Together 47 and Fighter Hawk would be able to achieve great things for the militaristic Corporation, as well as further advance their technology and battle tactics for the battle against the rebels, which would protect the colonies.

Another teeth-rattling slam against the metal door shook 47 out of his thoughts. The shooting pain up his spine and into his head forced him to pay attention to the present instead of his future plans. The fingers digging into his shoulders and holding him harshly against the door tightened and were accompanied by the nasty voice of 47's newly assigned Alpha Fighter—Riviara Morales: a man who was an undiscovered murderer and a mediocre pilot. 47 was also aware, from performing a check into the pilot's background, that Morales was cruel to his Cores, his last one having been taken away and plugged into the *Zeus*'s main control system since his body had been too damaged to walk again. All this would have caused any normal human to be terrified of their fate, but 47 was a Core and didn't have the ability to be afraid.

"Are you even listening to me, you little shit?" Morales growled as he shook 47 so hard that again 47's teeth rattled, his head hitting the door. But 47 didn't raise his gaze from where it had focused on the zipper of the Fighter's black flight suit, nor did he answer. The Fighter's right hand left 47's shoulder, only to grab his throat. Using his thumb under 47's jaw, he forced 47's glacier blue gaze to meet the anger in his chocolate brown eyes.

"You are mine now. Crow and Luco may not have been smart enough to keep you under control, but I promise you that I won't have that issue." The Fighter's thumb dug painfully into the soft space right beneath 47's jawbone, so much so that it pushed his tongue up in his closed mouth and forced his head back farther. "I'll bring you to heel quickly and to the point that you'll be so respectful of me that you won't even think about offing me like you did those two pilots. That's why the Commander pressured the Creators into giving you to me. He knew I could control you and beat that rebellious and holier-than-thou attitude right out of your machine brain. Do you understand me?"

"Core 47 understands your words, Fighter Morales," 47 replied in a monotone voice as Morales's grip loosened. His gaze locked with the tanned man's.

He said this, and he did understand the man's words completely, but he would never submit to this Fighter's commands because he was not 47's Fighter, the only person, besides the Creators, from whom 47 would take commands. While he could bond with Fighters whom the Commander matched him with, he would not with this man. He would go through the motions without forming the connection. Cores were made to merge with the Zodiac systems, including navigation, life support, engine performance, and programming high-response protocols for the Zodiacs. The bond aided the Core to modify those systems to suit the individual Fighter. The bonding process allowed the Core to sense the Fighter within the system. It made them able to recognize the way their pilot worked within the Zodiac. 47 would be his Fighter's key to unlocking optimal performance.

"Glad we have an understanding," Morales said with a smirk, his massive ego showing through. "I have no idea how a weak-looking thing like you got the best of two other Fighters. You'll be a good little dog soon enough." He yanked 47 away from the door by his throat before throwing him toward the bathroom door. 47 managed to catch himself with his hands on the floor before his face smashed into it, and he stayed there, knowing better than to get up without permission. 47's body had been modified since his creation, but he still bled from his nose and mouth as a normal human would. Bleeding was apparently not enough for the Fighter, though, as the swift kick in the ribs that flipped 47 onto his back showed him. He kept his gaze lowered, locked on the boot that had nearly cracked a rib, his face expressionless, not even showing the pain throbbing through his neck and chest.

"Get up and strip. Your first lesson is going to be how to please me, and I need a shower. You're going to wash me as well as make sure my cock is properly drained. I don't care how long it takes or what I have to do to you, as long as I am satisfied in the end. Do you understand me?"

"Affirmative, Fighter Morales, I understand you," 47 said clearly, getting to his feet and beginning to unzip his flight suit.

Oh yes. This man was going to join his former comrades. This man, who was *not* his Fighter, was going to die.

Chapter One

Tuesday March 22, 454 MC
Destroyer Class Flagship Zeus, 1208 GMT
Damion

THE MESS hall was crowded and loud. The *Zeus* was the largest ship in the Chrysalis Corporation fleet, an immense combined battle cruiser and scientific transport of nearly thirty levels. Ten of those levels were strictly military controlled and housed the Fighters. The *Zeus* was a colony in and of itself. It held everything from a local market to a missile that could destroy an entire planet. It was a majestic vessel that seemed to extend forever as it floated through limitless space. At this point in the day, there were nearly a hundred people in this common area, from all ranks and of differing ages. The hall was cacophonous with all the voices echoing off the shiny steel walls.

Damion was dark-skinned, as most Mars-born were due in part to the UV lighting used in the tunnels, but not nearly as dark-skinned as Mercurian men and women, who were generally so dark that their skin contained blue highlights. He was also taller than the average pilot, since the Corporation had stipulations on maximum and minimum height, but the rule could be overlooked for skill. And Damion definitely had the skill.

He ate with his fellow Beta pilots. Sammy and Dulton were the seniors at their table. They were there to get a bead on the rookies, find out who were the troublemakers and who had potential to go further up the ranks. They had asked Damion where Juni had run off to, and he told them Juni was choosing sleep over chow, again. Damion didn't care about the loud vocalizations, because the more he listened to all the bullshit flying around, the more he was able to sift through it and pick out what was real and what was fiction.

In the short time he had been listening, one subject stood out: whoever the Core named 47 was, he seemed to like killing his Alpha Fighters. As he listened to the story unfold, Damion hoped he never crossed paths with him. The stories seemed to be more fiction than fact.

However, the first parts came from Dulton, who appeared to not be one to bullshit. The senior Beta pilot told Damion that the Alpha Fighters had all died on their first mission with 47. They all suffered from unexplainable life-support failures within their pilot chairs in the bow of the Zodiac.

Except for the last one. According to Dulton, the last one had a feeling what his fate was going to be based on the Core's previous two Fighters, so he had tried to kill 47 three days ago while out on a mission. According to the reports, as soon as the Fighter's hands wrapped around 47's throat, the boosters activated and the unfortunate Fighter was thrown against the hull, crushing his head against the hard metal. Dulton said he had seen the bruises from the Alpha Fighter's fingers on Core 47's throat, telling of the Fighter's obvious abuse of him.

Then Sammy stepped in and continued telling the tall tale of the evil, homicidal Core to the table. Damion half paid attention while determining if he should eat the protein offered on his plate or the baked goods his mother had sent him last week instead.

Sammy's deep voice caught his attention. "Generally within the Chrysalis Corp, Cores pick their Fighters. It seems to work better that way since a more positive working bond forms between them. But in 47's case, he had repeatedly refused to select a Fighter since he arrived on the *Zeus* about two years ago. He held off, telling the Creators and Commander Sandrite that he was waiting for the best and wished to experiment on different weapons systems for the Zodiac spaceship. But they didn't believe him, so they went with a default protocol to reassign a Core when one refuses to make a choice and assigned him a Fighter—or rather, several Fighters. I'm sure they're kicking themselves now."

"They should just kill him," Tethis spat in disgust, shaking his head. "No Core could be worth that much trouble."

"Why would the Corporation or the Creators put up with that?" another Beta asked from farther down the table.

"I don't know," Sammy answered. "Everything I get about them is from a friend who is dating a sister of one of the Alpha pilots. For some reason what they do is super hush-hush, and unless you get picked, you don't get told shit."

Tethis frowned. "But we need to wait for one of the disturbing bastards to pick us to get a spot."

"Well, technically we need to wait for someone to vacate an Alpha seat." Sammy winked and pointed a finger at Tethis.

Damion did not have an opinion on the matter—at least not in the open space of the mess hall.

"One of the Zodiac Cores was overheard telling his Alpha Fighter that he heard 47 mumbling 'He's here. He is finally here' a few days ago." Dulton tossed his head back and drank down the last of his ration of water before changing the subject to maintenance schedules and away from murdering Cores.

"Well shit," Dulton blurted.

"Speaking of the demon spawn…." Tethis groaned.

Damion half turned his head to see whom the men were cursing about.

The Core strode through the room, his gaze in their direction and apparently not bothered that the mess hall was becoming quiet. A silence similar to the void of space descended in the large hall.

Damion would have known immediately what the Core was by the suit he was wearing even if Sammy hadn't pointed him out. It was a typical black flight suit with the Chrysalis Corporation brand of the crystal and wing. There weren't many differences between a Core's suit and a Fighter's except for the holes. All along the back of the Core's suit, strategically placed cutouts fitted over the ports installed in all Cores' skin; ports that allowed them to access the system.

"Fighter Damion Pierce Hawk, please come with me."

Everyone at Damion's table stopped eating, staring at the Core behind him. The dark color of the attire made everything else about the Core stand out. Pure white hair that was nearly see-through hung slightly haphazardly around the almost severe features. The only thing that didn't make the Core's face angry-looking was the softness around his jaw, his slightly pointed nose, and his full pink lips. Those made him handsome. Not that Damion often looked at other men, but this one drew his attention. From the white hair to the pale-as-snow skin, it was obvious the Core was of Plutonian descent. But what drew Damion in completely, almost compellingly, were the glacier-bright blue eyes that had fixed on Damion. They were like two chips of aquamarine that shone brightly but without any life in them.

Damion cleared his throat and spoke as authoritatively as he could, "Why? What is your number?" He didn't think that pilots, no matter how low in rank they were on the ship, were supposed to take orders from Cores. But honestly, he didn't know much about the modified, emotionless beings. He was only a grunt—a mere Beta pilot.

"I am 47. You have been chosen. You need to accompany me so that you can receive your reassignment from Beta to Alpha class as well as begin to familiarize yourself with your Zodiac-class vessel." The Core tilted his head slightly to the side, his expression blank, his voice a monotone as he added, "Is that sufficient information?"

"A little weird, but yeah, sure." At the moment he couldn't produce a witty reply if he wanted to. Uranus's ball sac, this was just his luck.

Damion put his utensils down and stood up, motioning to Dulton to take care of his tray. The men at his table looked as surprised as Damion felt, not to mention as confused. The evil Core swooping in on his chow time to take him to the Commander's office was nothing to laugh about, especially considering Core 47's history. Damion's best friend and roommate, Juni, wasn't going to believe any of this, and of course this was the day Juni had decided to skip mess to nap.

"Let's go, Core."

The Core didn't say anything as he turned and swiftly walked out of the mess hall and into the corridor. He didn't stop until he reached the elevator at the end of the corridor and called it to their level. He waited for Damion to enter it before himself, then pressed a button to take them to the fifth floor—the floor with the Commander's office.

"We will be reporting to Commander Sandrite to have your assignment made official and also to retrieve your room access card and pass for the Zodiac vessel." The Core announced the orders in a monotone voice. Typical for a Core, or so Damion had heard. This was all completely new to him. His brow furrowed in confusion. He'd been working hard to eventually achieve command of "his own" Zodiac, but he hadn't expected it to be so soon or to be receiving one in such a manner. All junior pilots had aspirations to be assigned to a Beta ship that they would share with other pilots before finally working their way to Alpha status and a Zodiac-class ship of their own.

Achieving Alpha rank so quickly was unheard of. Until today.

"A bit soon, isn't it? I haven't even met any other Cores, and I've only become part of the Beta squad." Only top pilots—the Alphas— were paired with Cores. Ten Alphas were in command of a unit of twenty Betas each, along with working as a unit with ten other Alphas. This brought the *Zeus* attack fleet to a total number of 210 ships available for deployment. Unless there was a large battle or they had to practice maneuvers as a unit with their Alpha leader, Betas generally stayed on the ship and worked with simulation units, which had proved boring to Damion so far, Although that didn't mean he was ready to become an Alpha.

"You do not need to," the Core replied without looking at him. The doors opened, and the Core waited until Damion exited first before doing so himself. "You have already been chosen by a Core. Therefore there is no need for you to meet others. We are the ones who pick our Alpha Fighters. The Fighters do not pick the Core. It is not 'a bit soon,' as you say, for one such as yourself."

The Core began walking down the corridor beside Damion, obviously leading him but not walking in front of him.

"Right, but how can I be chosen if none of the other Cores have met me?"

Damion was starting to feel even more unbalanced than before. He felt as if he were talking to a wall or a computer console, but knew that if he were truly going to be an Alpha, he would have to adjust to the way Cores spoke, no matter the frustration. If the Commander didn't laugh him out of his office first.

"You were chosen before you arrived on the *Zeus*," the Core stated as if it explained everything. He paused at Commander Sandrite's gray office door.

Damion sighed as he pulled on the edge of his uniform to straighten out any remaining wrinkles. "I hope you're not being extremely obtuse on purpose."

The Core finally turned to him, his odd-hued eyes meeting Damion's through a length of bangs. "What do you need me to explain? I assumed I was being clear."

"You didn't answer my question," Damion replied, glancing at the door. A hint of excitement joined the nausea in his stomach. "There is no way someone can choose me if they haven't met me. It's impossible."

"Nothing is impossible, and anything deemed such should be proven otherwise," the Core stated matter-of-factly, some essence of almost emotion flashing in his eyes. He turned to the door himself. "As I have just proven."

When the Core pressed the door chime beside the metal entrance, a buzz was heard inside the room and a gruff voice bade them enter. The Core walked forward and the door opened automatically. He stopped in front of the door sensor and waited on Damion to follow.

"Obtuse." Damion gave a small glare at the Core before he marched into the office. He made sure to keep his eyes facing forward, stepping only a few meters into the room before giving the Commander a formal salute.

The office was large for a destroyer class ship but befitted the Commander's position. Directly in front of Damion and his Core was a massive wooden desk. The Commander sat behind it with a console in front of him and an intership communicator off to his right.

"Reporting as requested, sir." Damion spoke in a clear, strong voice.

The Core stopped slightly behind and to the right of Damion, gaze lowered to the ground in a submissive pose that was unlike his previous almost commanding attitude.

"So you're the one he's been waiting for? I sure hope you were worth the three fucking lives that 47 went through to prove his gods-be-damned point." The Commander was an ex-Alpha Fighter with a no-nonsense air about him. His watery pale-blue gaze rose from a comm tablet to look first at Damion and then at the Core before looking back down.

"Excuse me, sir?" Damion looked behind him at the silent, expressionless Core before directing his attention back at his Commander. "I don't understand. I never met this Core until ten minutes ago."

The Commander looked up again, his mouth pinched in a frown. "Let me give you a bit of advice for free, Fighter. Never try and understand a Core. What they do, how they do it, and the decisions they make are nothing we will ever understand. They're trained and modified from birth to be nothing more than breathing computers with a pulse. They also give our Fighters an edge in combat when they merge with the Zodiac flight systems, making them a pivotal element to our forces."

Damion had always felt, from the moment he first saw the Commander, that this was definitely a man who wouldn't take any shit and would give more than he got if pressed. He was middle-aged, with salt-and-pepper hair, and he was in a position he had obviously earned instead of kissing asses to get there. Damion had not overlooked the height difference, having noted before that the Commander was a full hand shorter than him, but the man made up for it with a stocky stature that commanded attention.

Grumbling under his breath, the Commander finally put down his tablet, placing his elbows on the desk before lacing his fingers in front of his chin. "That particular one especially. He's gone against his programming and isn't the perfect little toy that the Chrysalis Corporation or the Creators want him to be. But he's so fucking good, they won't wipe him and plug him into the *Zeus*'s system. No, they let him get away with killing my goddamn Fighters, because they wouldn't listen to his reasons as to why he hadn't chosen yet. He's been here on my ship for over a year now. When he said he'd chosen but his Fighter wasn't here or ready yet, they decided to go against protocol and force him to pair with different Fighters. He's too good to waste on idleness."

The Commander's voice was rising, getting agitated as he slammed his hands on the desk loudly and stood, glaring at the bowed head of the Core. "When asked why, his only explanation was that he deserved the best! So—" He paused, turning his angry gaze back to Damion. "—you better be the fucking best, or you'll be just as dead as the other three. Do I make myself absolutely fucking clear, *Fighter*?"

"Yes, sir!" Damion answered automatically, but it was a knee-jerk response and not what he truly felt. He didn't understand for one damn moment why this Core had killed while waiting on him. He also knew that if the Core didn't kill him, it seemed the Commander wouldn't mind throwing them both out an airlock and into the nearest sun to be rid of the Core. It had started out as such a good day, too, and now it had turned to shit. "I will either prove myself or obviously be killed by this Core trying to."

"That's all we can really ask for, I suppose. Hopefully it will be different with you," the Commander growled, taking one last moment to glare at the Core before sitting back down.

He took three items off his desk and held them out to Damion. "This is your assigned room passkey along with your security clearance and also your Zodiac. You're assigned to the *Ares* Zodiac. It was specially outfitted under this Core's direction and has already been modified to accommodate your height and body shape, since you're so damn tall." Sandrite glared again at the silent Core. "He had the maintenance crew modify it three months ago. How he knew you were coming, I'll never know and won't attempt to guess. Why he didn't tell me you were his chosen before today also goes into the increasing 'I don't understand this Core' pile. If he had given us a name, perhaps he wouldn't have been matched to the last Fighter, but I can't waste time waiting on one rogue Core's opinion. I had an Alpha seat to fill, and I filled it, damn it.

"Moving on, that piece of paper contains your official assignment. You'll start exercises with your Core tomorrow so that you can become better acquainted with each other's styles and complete the bonding process. Any questions?"

"No, sir."

Like hell. He had a lot more questions but didn't want to be thought insubordinate. He also doubted Commander Sandrite would answer them. Hopefully he could keep up the front that he had his shit together and hide the fact that his state of shock was slowly wearing off. Of course, this meant his heart wasn't beating as hard as before.

Damion didn't even know what you did with a Core. Sure, he had heard the men talk, but most of the Fighters now with Cores had been regular or Beta pilots for years until chosen by a Core and becoming an Alpha. A Core did have the ability to bond with different Fighters, in case a Fighter died in combat, was reassigned, or failed to perform to expectations. Damion reached out and took the items held out to him before giving the Commander another salute. "Permission to leave, sir?"

"Yes, yes. Get him the hell out of here. He's your responsibility now. Good fucking luck." The Commander flapped a hand at him, dismissing them.

The Core was already at the door, waiting to follow Damion out of the office.

Damion read the room assignment, and as he expected, it was on the upper floor with the higher-ranked Alpha Fighters. "47, show me to my room."

If there was one thing he had picked up from his talk with the other pilots, it was that the Cores had to do anything asked of them by their Fighters, and most of the time they complied. But this one had a record of refusing orders, and killing three of his Fighters in the process. Damion figured he had better test out the waters now, rather than risk his life in open space.

The Core merely turned back toward the elevators and pressed the up button, waiting yet again for Damion to get in before entering and queuing the elevator for the seventh floor. The command and control offices were on the fifth floor because it was the center of the ship and most protected from outside attacks. The officers' quarters were on the tenth, while the other floors were scattered with different offices, Medical, mess, and general quarters. The seventh floor was for the senior Fighters, the Alphas.

Once they reached it, the Core followed Damion out and led him to the right, passing a dozen doors or so until he came to one marked 256. Pulling out his passkey from a chest pocket in his suit, 47 scanned it and the door hissed open. He waited for Damion to enter before following him inside. The entire time the Core was silent, his expression blank, emotionless, cold.

The room was twice the size of the quarters Damion had shared with Juni until today. It even had a private toilet instead of a communal one for each corridor. Damion tossed the cards and assignment on a small table that had two thick Fighter manuals on it. He saw the full-size bed against the right wall and the recessed closet to the left. Hell, his duffel didn't hold more than three uniforms and a few odds and ends—there would be plenty of room left over. Room for what, he didn't fucking know, since he hadn't planned on any of this.

Damion couldn't recognize the last piece of furniture until he stepped closer and inspected it. The odd, egg-shaped bed (if that was what it could be called) was partly recessed in the floor and the back wall. It looked like that was where the Core would plug himself in for any number of reasons that Damion couldn't begin to fathom.

The Core. Damion turned back to take in the pale man… kid… computer… whatever he was. Cores were something you heard about as a grunt in the Infantry and saw in flight school from far, far away. They were with their Alpha pilots, a constant silent, yet observant, shadow, and it did not help that the Alphas refused to share many details about their Cores.

Cores. They fought side by side with the Alpha Fighters to make them faster and better than any other seeded pilot, they obeyed, and they were for the Elite—the rich citizens in the private class. They didn't kill and they didn't scheme. Juni had mentioned seeing them on Lunar, but Damion was from Mars, and his colony didn't have anything as high value as a Core. But now Damion himself had one and was stuck with him.

"47. Why did you kill those men?" Damion had to know what they had done so he didn't follow in their footsteps. Or rather, their graves. He didn't think he was the best—not yet—but damn it all to hell if he was going to just let someone kill him.

The Core still stood by the closed door, his gaze following Damion as he looked about and explored their quarters. "They were not whom I picked. They were assigned to me and were inferior to the one I had already chosen."

"They were still your Fighters. They were human." Damion crossed his arms. "What did they do to deserve death? Did they harm you? Threaten you?"

The Core tilted his head to the side briefly, seeming to consider the question. As he did so, it exposed part of his neck and showed stark bruises that wrapped around his windpipe in the shape of fingers.

"They were not the best. They were not whom I had chosen" was all he finally said. And he said it in a way that meant he deemed the question answered to its conclusion.

"You're always like this, aren't you?" Damion asked. He felt about ready to smack the back of the Core's head. Perhaps there was a magical restart button back there, along with a "don't kill my Fighter" button too. "You haven't even seen me before. Why did you choose me and how?"

"I found you within the system two years ago. The top of your class, you had test scores above and beyond all your classmates in piloting and weapons. You were required to study two fighting styles, but you studied five. Your reaction time is also above average and beyond what the Corporation has seen in over twenty years. In addition you've shown yourself to be superior in battle tactics and leadership in all your simulation flights and in the reports from your days in the Academy. You are the best. I will accept no less." The Core tilted his head again. "Does that sufficiently answer your question?"

"You picked me out by my test scores? I think I'm more worried than before." Damion had other questions, but talking to this… being was stressful. He needed to move around and attempt to work through the whiplash of excitement and fear warring inside him. "I need to get my gear. Shit, I haven't even been in a frontline pilot simulator since placements. Now I have to get into the real thing in less than ten hours."

Damion picked up his new passkey and slipped it into his pocket. "You follow me. Tell me about your first Fighter. I want his name and how many missions you flew with him."

As they stepped out of the room and into the corridor, they met a small crowd obviously waiting for them. Alpha Fighters with their Cores surrounded them. Damion was taller than all of them by a good fifteen centimeters, but he wasn't stupid enough to think they couldn't kick his ass as a group.

"One," said the Fighter who was standing at the head of the group. He had short-cropped hair and a pissed off expression to go with a muscular body that spoke of more brawn than brains.

"Excuse me?" Damion's brow furrowed in confusion.

"The three of them were able to fly once, and they barely made it to the battle before that broken piece of shit killed them," the Fighter spat. "He should be plugged into a trash compactor and forgotten, not plugged into a Zodiac and bound to an Alpha."

Wonderful. It was obvious that the Goddess of Luck, Tyche, was not with him today. First he was promoted and assigned the angel of death as his Core. Now a small mob was ready to kick said angel of death's ass—and maybe Damion's as well.

Dear Mom, life isn't fucking fair.

Chapter Two

Damion

"THEY WERE not my Fighter," the Core said, his gaze once again directed toward the floor.

He had stopped right outside the door, his hands behind his back, leaning casually against the access console for the door to his and Damion's quarters. "First, Keith Matthew Crow expired due to system malfunction in his air supply. Second, Gabriel Sebastian Luco expired due to unexplainable atmospheric pressure. Third, Riviara Ricardo Morales expired due to being out of his control seat during a sudden burst of acceleration. He was crushed against the bulkhead."

The Core relayed these facts quietly to Damion since it was what his Fighter had asked and he was required to do anything his Fighter requested. His words were uncaring as he spouted off the names and how they died as if he were quoting atmospheric conditions instead.

"They were good fucking Fighters, and you killed them!" the blond shouted, and the crowd behind him stirred. The man, whom Damion identified as Arkin by the name patch on his flight suit, took a few paces forward, shouting, reminiscent of a five-year-old—a very large five-year-old—having a tantrum. "You're a murderer, and you shouldn't be allowed near another Fighter!"

"Look…." Damion wasn't happy with 47's answer, as there was a lot of "why" left out of it, but he'd defend his Core if he had to. And as much as he might dislike the fact, the Core was his responsibility now. He kept his gaze on the fuming Arkin, trying to figure out if there was any way to get out of this situation without kicking some ass and ending up disciplined right on the heels of his promotion. "I just found out about him being my Core, and I know he's killed the others, but you can't mob him! The Commander obviously wanted him to pick another Fighter and that Fighter is me."

Damion refused to hide in his room or run away. As he stepped in front of 47, he didn't stop Arkin from grabbing the front of his jumpsuit. His gut told him to punch the hothead and get the ass whopping—his, probably—over and done with. It would be easier to get knocked out until tomorrow and have this weird shitass day over with. He instead kept his arms to his sides, palms out to show he was no threat.

"Like hell we can't! Are you really worth three of our Alphas?" Arkin spat, and even if he was smaller than Damion, he had the upper-body strength to push him back against 47, effectively pinning the Core against the wall and access panel. "*He* fucking isn't, that's for sure! There are dozens of other Cores out there able to take his place. Best, my ass! Do yourself a favor and get out of our way, rookie, and I won't send you out the airlock with him."

"Listen to Arkin! Just let us deal with the little freak!" another Alpha in the back of the group shouted.

Damion could see over Arkin's shoulder that the other Cores had moved to the other end of the hall, not responding to the Fighters threatening 47's life. These human computers did not even seem to care if another of their kind was threatened.

"You can't take this into your own hands! That's treason!" Damion started some screaming of his own, letting his gaze meet Arkin's. If he had learned at least one thing while talking with the other pilots, it was that the Cores were items, tools, and property that belonged to the Corporation. While not as bad as murdering a Fighter, you would get a court-martial if you went after the Corporation's expensive human computer property. "If the Commander, for some reason, wants me to make his death look like an accident, fine, I'll do it, but only under direct orders from him. You can't act like a group of dirty rebels."

"Big talk from the little murderer's chosen *best*." Arkin spat the last word out in complete disdain.

47's monotone voice emerged from behind Damion. "For two thousand credits, three years before he joined the Chrysalis Corporation, Fighter Crow left a girl carrying his unborn child in the hands of organ farmers. Fighter Luco participated in illegal drug trafficking, resulting in seventeen overdoses, including a thirteen-year-old girl's. Fighter Morales killed four Cores prior to joining the Corporation but was never convicted because the Justices could not locate all the body parts and no witnesses were willing to come forward. Passable pilots, unacceptable people."

Damion had a feeling 47 had turned his gaze to him. "Shall I continue by communicating the history of the Alpha Fighters present or inform them that Security will be here in 1.49 minutes?"

Arkin growled at the Core. "You little bitch."

"I think you're upset that he outsmarted you." Damion smirked out of habit, not out of any form of happiness, since he doubted this would be the last they heard from Arkin and his cronies. "But if you don't leave willingly, I'm sure the Commander will gladly arrest you."

"Fifty-nine seconds," 47 stated. "The security team will arrive first. They are armed for an assault."

"Fuck you." Arkin released Damion's jumpsuit with a push. As he and the rest of the pack retreated down the corridor, Arkin called back, "Just wait. He'll kill you next."

"I'll take my chances." Damion kept his smirk as they marched away, making a hasty retreat.

As soon as they were out of sight, 47 turned back toward the panel, letting a cord slip out of his hand. After a few seconds, it retracted and the panel closed completely.

"Order canceled," he reported to Damion before turning back to him, raising his gaze. "There is a 99.9 percent chance that I will not kill you. You are my chosen Fighter. It would be illogical."

"Thanks." Damion wasn't sure if that made him feel better or not. However, in the long run, it was better than the odd little Core saying he would kill him. "People try and kick your ass often?"

"I have my ways of avoiding them." 47 motioned toward the console he had used, and a hint of what might have been a frown crossed his brow. It was gone as quickly as it had appeared. "This time I was… preoccupied. I apologize for the confrontation. It will not happen again."

"Not your fault, I guess." Damion didn't know what was going on, but if his fellow Fighters had it out for him, it was going to be hell keeping them both alive. "All right, let's try to get back to Juni again."

"If it is any consolation, they would have merely incapacitated you. You were not their target. I was. As soon as you were unconscious, they would have terminated me but would have left you alone." The Core followed Damion to the elevator. "I have been able to escape them in the past and have suffered minimal damage because of my tactics."

The Core paused a moment, waiting for the elevator doors to open. "It would have been more logical for you to let them take me. Why did you not?"

"I am not saying you don't need your ass kicked, but they would have killed you. That is something completely different." Damion sighed, lowering his head and rubbing the back of it, feeling a headache already emerging. "Is all that info you said about those Fighters true?"

"It is truth, and yes, they would have terminated me, but doing so would not have affected you in any way. In regards to, as you say, getting my ass kicked, they have already done so on a few occasions. It would not make any difference."

47 waited for Damion to exit the elevator before he did so.

"You're not getting it." Damion sliced his left hand in the air in front of them. "There is a thin line between breaking the rules and taking justice into your own hands. What happened back there, that was treason."

The Core paused his walk so that Damion's determined hand movement did not hit him. He cocked his head to the side like a bird's, looking like he was trying to understand.

"I apologize, but I still do not comprehend. It is logical to assume no one would care if I were terminated. And since you are the one that would benefit the most were that to happen, I do not understand why you would care."

"How would I benefit?" Damion asked, walking forward again.

"Your survival would be secure. Not that I plan to terminate you, of course." 47 followed. "The other Fighters would cease to antagonize you because of my existence."

"I also would lose my chance at being an Alpha Fighter and piloting a Zodiac-class ship." Damion shrugged and let his mind wander back to the fact that he had just been promoted to an Alpha Fighter at the whim of a walking machine. "I don't think I'm the best, but I think I can prove myself."

"You are the best. I will only bond with the best," 47 stated as they came upon Damion's previous quarters. "I have modified the *Ares* Zodiac since I was placed here. It was designed around specifications that will only match with you. Your reaction time and abilities were factored into the modifications and therefore only you can fly it."

"*Only* me?" Damion asked in surprise. He now had to make certain his performance in the new craft never dropped or he could possibly be 47's next victim.

"Because of that, you would not lose your Alpha station. You would be quickly chosen by another Core, but many modifications would have to be made to allow that Core the ability to sync with the *Ares*. Port plug-ins would have to be removed, and the computer reconfigured. It is the Core's responsibility to make your commands to the Zodiac flawless as well as predict what you will need during battle and modify the Zodiac accordingly. But the Zodiac is yours. Only you can fly it. I denied requests from my former Fighters to reconfigure the *Ares* to fit them."

"Thanks. I think." Damion would have to decipher this new information later.

Damion opened the door to his now old Beta quarters. As he expected, Juni was in the room, watching vids instead of being in the gym where he should have been.

As soon as Juni noticed Damion, he shut the vid off, turning to look at his roommate. "Hey, what happened—oh! He's still with you? The Betas woke me up and told me you were whisked off."

47's gaze was once again directed toward the floor. It seemed that the only person he would look up for was Damion. He stayed silent, standing to the right of the door, near the console control.

"Yeah, he's my Core. 47," Damion informed his now former bunkmate.

"Nice knowing you."

"He promises not to kill me." Damion reached into the tiny closet at the back of the room and pulled out his duffel. "I also start Alpha training tomorrow, and a group of them almost mobbed us."

"Juni Saint Mathis will be picked by a Core in the near future and join the Alphas. The chance of it being within the next two weeks is currently at 56.6 percent."

"Is he serious?" Juni looked at the Core, then at Damion, his eyes wide in disbelief.

"He hasn't lied to me yet." Damion scratched his head, looking into the closet before his gaze slid to Juni. "Look, Juni, do me a favor and snoop around about a guy named Arkin. 47 has his reports, but I want to know what other pilots think. Hell, even the maintenance crew if you can find out."

"That would be unwise," 47 piped up, his voice quiet but still monotone, his gaze on the floor. "Arkin's Core, 92, is inferior to me but still skilled in riding the system. In fact, he is trying to observe us now, but I am holding off his view. Once we leave he will continue to monitor Beta Mathis."

"I meant by talking to other people," Damion explained. "Not through the computer system."

"They really have no clue about human contact." Juni sounded more interested and amazed than frightened by 47 and his information. Damion had to remind himself it was because Juni was Lunar-born and had seen Cores from time to time at his homestead. Also, Juni didn't have the good sense of when to be scared that most humans had.

"I did not mean through the system. There are cameras everywhere, through which 92 can observe anything at Arkin's order, as well as the Cores who were in the hallway with us previously."

"Okay, that's just creepy." Juni gave an uneasy chuckle. "Don't like to think someone is watching me jack off in the middle of my shower."

Damion shook his head, ignoring his friend's crass words because he had heard much worse in training and in the mines on Mars. "It's better to know your enemy than not. I think this whole day went from normal, to weird, to great, and suddenly turned really shitty."

"If you order it, I can block 92's feed," 47 offered after a few moments of silence. "Beta Mathis would be safe to question others. Tracking persons who are not our Fighter is considered a breech and my block would not be reported as the Fighters would not want to be penalized."

"Then why didn't he just suggest that to begin with?" Juni whispered in Damion's ear.

"You're asking me? I've only known him for thirty minutes." Damion rolled his eyes. "Go ahead and block it for a day. After that, let them have it back. Got that, Juni? You'll only have twenty-four Earth hours to snoop."

"Sure, a day of no one watching me take a piss. For some reason that makes me feel a bit better. On the other hand, you're asking me to be your mole, O high-and-mighty Alpha Fighter."

"As you command." 47 turned around and opened the console, and he pulled out a cord and attached it to the port at his wrist. He closed his eyes and went silent as he worked.

"What's he doing?" Juni whispered again, his blue eyes trained on 47 in a manner that led Damion to believe his friend expected the Core to spring into song and dance.

"I don't know," Damion hissed back. "And why are you whispering?"

"I deduce that the Beta pilot thinks that I cannot hear him if he speaks in a lower tone," 47 replied, right before he went rigid.

The wires around his fingers turned red hot before fading back to their normal multicolor casings. 47 pulled his fingers from the wires and hid his hand behind his back as he turned toward Damion.

"92's video access has been disconnected for twenty-four hours, along with his access to any other communication links."

"Ah." Juni stared in amazement at 47.

"Why don't Cores have names?" Damion asked 47 suddenly. It had been a constant question on his mind ever since he first learned about Cores. They were never referred to with names, only numbers.

47 had been looking at the floor, but at Damion's question, he looked up at him, careful to avoid eye contact with Juni. "Cores are not given names. We are assigned a number sequence according to when we were conceived or found viable within genetic testing, the date we were retrieved by the Creators, and the day we are given over to the programmers. Names create emotion and familiarity, which we do not require."

"But that's three numbers, and you have two," Juni pointed out with a bit of a smirk.

Damion wondered for a moment if his friend really had placed in the upper 5 percent in the IQ testing, as he had boasted while they were still in boot camp.

"A few of us were placed in the unknown factor for the date of conception and therefore only have two numbers with which we are branded. It assists with telling Cores apart."

"You have a brand?" Damion raised an eyebrow. "Thought that was just talk."

"You are supposed to think many of the truths are merely rumors," 47 replied with another birdlike tilt of his head, once again showing the stark bruises that dappled his neck. "But that one is a truth. We are branded with our numbers and have chips surgically implanted in our brains before we are put in the sensory deprivation tanks as infants."

"Wow," Juni breathed out.

"On that note," Damion said, "I'm going to my new bunk. I need to brush up on the protocols so I don't look like an idiot tomorrow."

He knew he should be happier with the answers 47 had given him, yet everything he didn't know and now had to learn astounded him. 47's answers brought new questions to the table.

47 turned and pushed the button for the door to open, following Damion out of the room with his gaze cast down and his hands still behind his back.

"You better not forget about me!" Juni yelled out the door after them.

"You're like a bad venereal disease, buddy. Nobody can forget that."

"Screw you, Hawk!"

Once they had entered the elevator again and the door closed, 47 finally looked up. "Did I say something inappropriate?"

"No, not really." Damion shook his head. "It's just very real, very soon."

"I do not understand," 47 replied as they exited the elevator once again.

"All right." Damion tried to think of a way to explain it to someone who couldn't fathom emotions like a normal person, but more like a child, or idiot savant. "Just think of your one ambition, your one dream suddenly coming true, but you're not ready for it. So when it happens, you feel like you're treading space wake."

"I have no ambitions, nor do I dream." The look on 47's face let Damion know he truly believed this statement, but Damion wondered if it were the truth. Obviously 47 had ambition, or he wouldn't have waited for the one Fighter he construed as the best. "This must simply be one of the things that a Core is not meant to understand."

Damion shrugged. "I suppose it is just to improve your performance," he said as he entered his new, larger, living quarters, not attempting to explain any more. "I wonder where I get my new uniforms."

"They are in the left side of the closet," 47 informed him before answering his first question, once again standing by the door. "Yes, it is. It is felt that Cores should not have any emotions, attachments, or anything that will impede their connection to communications and the Zodiac's control systems. We integrate with the systems of the Zodiacs and the Zeus to research and find ways to improve the ships. The Cores who are with the Fighters are given clearance to walk around the Zeus with or without our Fighters. We follow orders without question from those who have the clearance to give them to us. Primarily our chosen Fighter. Precedence given to those that enhanced us—the Creators— and the Commander."

Damion wasn't sure what to do with a slave. Really, that is what he thought of the situation. He had heard of wealthier Earth-and Lunar-born having maids, servants, and the occasional personal Cores, and there were Cores on Venus and other pleasure colonies that were used strictly for sex. Those were rumors. The books the Academy had given them at flight school glossed over Cores and their functions, stating they were primarily for support systems and were to be approached only by Alpha Fighters or the Creators. Damion had the idea from rumors and Academy books that the Cores were modified humans with the ability to access the system. A chosen servitude. However, this was very different. "I really don't need you to do anything," he said because he felt the Core waiting for him. "I need to read my assignment log to see when to report."

Core 47

47 MOVED farther into the quarters and went to the closet embedded into the wall. It was on the right side, near his capsule, next to the bathroom door. He waved his hand and the action opened the left side of the closet that contained his Fighter's uniforms. There were eight of them in total—one for every day of the week, including one for the day the others would be sanitized. 47 had the same number of uniforms, but his had to be specially dealt with since they had more holes for port entries than any other Core's.

47 had not been boasting when he said he was the best. He had altered himself, installing more ports in his skin to better access the

ship's system. The more ports he had, the quicker he would be able to access information as well as transmit into *Ares*.

47 turned, indicating the uniforms before going into the bathroom and closing the door. There he ran water into the sink to wash his hands. Looking at his fingers, he dispassionately noted the angry, blistering lines of burns like tangled wires that crisscrossed the fingers and the top of his hands. The fight through the communications systems against the other Core had been more difficult than 47 had estimated, but he wouldn't make that mistake again in the future. He was better than the other Cores and would continue to be so by increasing his own abilities. He took a moment to wash the burns on his hands before he spread antibiotic on the livid wounds. After he was done, he pulled out a pair of cotton gloves from the pocket on the leg of his suit and pulled them on before turning off the water with his elbow. Then he walked out of the bathroom to see what his Fighter was doing.

Damion

DAMION SAT at the desk, looking through his new schedule. He thought the Core was acting strange, but he didn't know what a Core acting normal looked like. He should be scared that this Core was still going to eject him out of the ship during their first run together as he had done with all his other Fighters, but Damion couldn't worry about that and focused instead on learning what he needed to. Death could come at any time for any person, so dwelling on it was pointless.

Damion looked over his shoulder and saw the Core merely standing in the bathroom doorway, waiting for orders. The Core had never had his own Fighter before, aside from those the Creators had ordered him paired with, and he hadn't obeyed them because they had not been his chosen.

How a Core should behave for their chosen Fighter was programed into 47. Damion felt the Core would live up to the programming.

After a good ten minutes of being creeped out by the silent Core, he finally asked, "Why are you just standing there?"

"You have not ordered me to do anything else," the Core stated in his matter-of-fact way.

"Don't you have things you want to do?" Damion asked.

It was definitely going to take a day or two for Damion to get used to this. Possibly longer. Or never.

The Core was silent for a moment. "If you do not have any orders for me, I could jack in to the capsule and finish my last modifications for the *Ares*."

"All right." Damion nodded. "Go ahead and do that, then. I'm just going to read these for a while before heading to bed. Um, you sleep in that capsule too, don't you?"

"Yes, that is correct. Resting in the capsule keeps Cores connected with the ship and the monitoring systems. What the Creators wish to know about Cores, they find out when we are sleeping. Anything they perceive as needing repair within our neural cortex is also done while we are jacked into the system."

"Tell me a bit about the Creators." Damion had heard the term but was unsure what and who these men and women were or did—aside from manage Cores.

"They are a group of high-clearance scientists. They oversee all Core production, integration, experimentation, and assign each Core to their specific specialty."

"And your specialty is Zodiacs?" Damion asked.

"Correct. I was given the assignment to produce a workable Zodiac with advanced weaponry and defense systems. I was also given permission for unconventional experimentations on the Zodiac and myself."

Damion raised an eyebrow and wondered if the freedom the Creators programmed into the Core was the reason he was capable of breaking rules. "Having free rein to experiment isn't the norm for Cores that are assigned Zodiacs?"

"Not to the extent of, as you call it, the freedom that I am permitted."

The Core moved to the metal capsule and sat on the edge, lifting his legs over to the inside of the sparsely padded white device. There he paused for a few moments before speaking. "May I ask a question?"

"Sure," Damion answered, hearing the surprise in his voice.

"I apologize for my boldness, but I wish to understand. Why did you ask me if I had a name? I perceived that it was common knowledge that Cores were not given what is called a traditional name."

The Core's back was to Damion, but still in a rigid, perfect posture, allowing the cables to connect to his spinal ports through automatic biometric tuning. Damion could see the numerous holes in his suit along his spine where jacks would enter the ports under his skin. He could also faintly see port access bumps behind each ear, and when he looked carefully, one at the base of the Core's skull. The how or why so many ports were desired by the Core was a question Damion wouldn't pose to him at this moment.

"Most stories about how Cores are made are just that—stories. Really no one talks about how or where they get people to become Cores," Damion said and almost wished he could see the Core's face. "I didn't know if you had a name before becoming one and really—" He hesitated before speaking the truth. "—I feel a bit uncomfortable calling another human being by a number even if I know Cores are not raised normally."

"Uncomfortable? I do not know what that is. No one else has ever asked me that question, which is why I am trying to understand. As for how Cores are produced, more than 90 percent are altered from infancy, and 10 percent are above two years of age. The origin of our bodies is not disclosed." The Core finally turned, twisting around so that his glacier-colored eyes could meet Damion's. "If you have more questions, I will answer them."

"I figured you would." Damion had a feeling his new Core—and slave—was programmed to be more than only helpful. "I'll have more, I promise, and you'll be able to tell me all the answers." He paused, his gaze moving to the floor as something sparked in his mind. "Wait, I just thought of one. How old are you?"

The Core tilted his head, the shadows of the room hiding his bruises. "If my calculations are correct, I am twenty-four years, ten months, and twenty-three days of age. My date of birth is not exactly known, so my calculations may be incorrect by a few days."

"I think twenty-four is close enough. What month?" Damion didn't really care, but hell, knowledge was power, or so they had told him growing up. Of course, his father also told him that drinking before work helped the day go faster and with less aggravation.

"Approximately the middle of the second week in November," the Core replied, looking slightly perplexed as to why it was relevant.

Damion nodded. "Can you make sure I'm up by 0600?"

"Affirmative," he answered from the capsule.

Damion went back to reading his manual for a while at the desk before carrying it to his much softer, bigger bed for the night.

Core 47

47 WAITED until Damion lay down and made sure that his Fighter was distracted by his reading before 47 activated the plug-in. He gasped softly, forcing his body still as the input jacks slid through his skin and into the ports beneath the regenerative layer. Jacking in to access the *Zeus*'s system wasn't a pleasant feeling, particularly the five ports in his skull and the ones down his spine. But the aftereffect was what made it worth it. He let out a quiet sigh and closed his eyes, saying hello to the only friend he had ever known.

The ship itself.

A FEW hours later, 47 noticed Damion had finally fallen into a deep REM sleep. He released all the jacks but one from his ports, separating himself from his capsule except for the line still in his left wrist. He walked the short distance from his pod to Damion's bed and gazed down at his Fighter.

47 knew he was incapable of feeling, yet he couldn't deny the strong urge to complete the bond that would bind him and Damion as Core and Zodiac Alpha Fighter. He sat down on the edge of the bed with utmost vigilance to make certain he did not disturb his Fighter's rest. He reached up with both hands and touched the very tips of his fingers to Damion's temples.

The mild electrical current from the cable in his wrist traveled into Damion's body, and 47's fingertips received the current back into his own. 47's mind ignited from his Alpha Fighter's electrical patterns. A web of blue-and-white energy surged suddenly from Damion's mind. 47 gasped and his back straightened as he assimilated the biophysical patterns and fed the information needed back into their Zodiac ship. He began to feel changes in his physical response to the bonding. Respiratory and heart rate increased, as well as an unfamiliar hunger to retain connection to Damion's bio patterns indefinitely.

47 decided to end the connection before subsequent problems arose from the enormous electrical feedback.

Damion's eyes opened after 47 released his head. Damion had goose bumps all over his arms and up his neck. It was a fascinating reaction—as was the obvious erection tenting the sheets.

Damion

"WHAT WERE you doing? Trying to electrocute me?" Damion asked in a bewildered tone as he slid away from 47 and closer to the wall, needing to put distance between them. He frowned as he saw the cord plugged into one of the strange ports—this one in the back of 47's hand. The same hand that had been touching Damion's head.

"I believed it would be more relaxing for you if the bonding process happened while you were asleep, since many Fighters find the reaction to the process unacceptable."

"Bonding? Huh? Wait, what does *bonding* mean? The material I read on Cores didn't explain other than it helps us pilot. What did you do to my body?" Damion sat up and pulled the sheet up to his hips to hide his erection.

"I assure you, I did nothing that would cause you harm. Your body's reaction to the bonding process is not unusual," 47 stated calmly, placing his hands on his knees. "I apologize if I alarmed you, but I needed to expedite the bonding process so that we are better prepared when you pilot the *Ares* Zodiac for the first time. As for what the bonding is, I will attempt to explain as clearly as possible if you wish for me to continue."

"I'm not sure I want to know, but it would be nice to be sure you're keeping to your word of not killing me."

"I cannot lie to you, Fighter Hawk. Breaking my word would be akin to lying, so therefore I am unable to make a promise to you that I could not keep."

"Don't do anything like that while I'm unconscious ever again." Damion lay back down with his gaze fixed on 47 in suspicion.

"I will not need to," 47 replied. "I apologize for causing you discomfort. Completing the bonding process was necessary. It was pivotal that I become educated in the electrical signals that you emit.

By doing so I can better serve and protect you. I will be able to adjust the Zodiac as you fly so it can anticipate your reactions, as well as monitor your biorhythm to assess how much stress you are under during battle."

"They should give a class on you guys," Damion grumbled, turning on his side so his back was to the wall.

47 shook his head. "A class would not be beneficial as only 3 percent of the colonial population would ever be in knowledgeable contact with a Core. The Creators deem our existence should be kept as quiet as possible."

"What about Beta pilots?" Damion countered. He wished someone had prepared him better for having a Core.

"There are currently twenty-five unassigned Cores aboard the ship. They will not be assigned a Zodiac here unless a Core is terminated. There are only ten Zodiac Fighters on the Zeus. There are presently two hundred Beta pilots as the Zeus is at full battle readiness. Information on Cores would not benefit their self-piloted vessels," 47 replied.

"You saying people don't need to know about Cores because they probably won't see or have a Core? But you just said knowledgeable contact meaning you guys are planted all over? We're not supposed to know you're there? Who came up with that theory of bullshit?"

"The Creators."

Damion blew out a long breath and rubbed his eyes. He knew 47 would have an equally frustrating answer to all of his questions. Well no one had ordered him, yet, to keep his mouth shut. Still it was best to follow the lead of the veteran Alphas since he was new.

"Do you need assistance with anything?" 47 inquired, standing up.

"No. Stay in your pod until it's time to get up."

"As you order, Fighter Hawk." There was another small pause, as if 47 was really trying to make sure that Damion wasn't angry with him or that his actions hadn't caused a rift between them. "I apologize again for making you feel in distress. Are there any more questions you have for me at this time?"

"Tons. But I need to attempt to sleep because I must be focused tomorrow." Damion let out a long sigh before closing his eyes.

"Affirmative, Fighter Hawk. I will wake you at 0600." 47 walked back to the capsule. The cord still plugged into the back of his hand retracted as he got closer.

"Right. Stay there," Damion muttered, shifting as he tried to get comfortable with his odd, and inconvenient, hard-on. "No more… electrical stimulation."

"Again, I apologize. I did not mean to make you uncomfortable," 47 said, slipping into the capsule. "Hence why I was attempting to bond with you while you were resting. I promise you, I did it so that I can perform and protect you more efficiently."

"We'll see after our flight tomorrow."

"Affirmative, Fighter Hawk." 47 activated the capsule. He let out a soft gasp as the input jacks snapped into his ports, and Damion saw 47 shudder as he settled into the cold, metal-lined coffin. The only padding inside the capsule was under 47's hips and behind his shoulders. "Good rest."

"Good dreams," Damion grumbled before he fell back to sleep.

Chapter Three

Wednesday March 23, 454 MC
0701 GMT
Damion

DAMION WALKED into the docking bay, but on the upper level that held the Alphas' Zodiac ships instead of the lower where his Beta C-19 vessel was now empty and awaiting a new pilot. Despite what the Core stated, Damion only felt slightly better from 47's promises not to kill him and his inability to lie. Damion would be on his toes during their flight. He didn't want to be the fourth victim. He already felt off being on the Alpha level, as if he were doing something he would get in trouble for… but then he looked at his new spacecraft.

His.

Damion flexed his hands and hoped the fit inside that magnificent ship wasn't too tight. He was much taller than the average pilot, but he had learned to adjust in his C-19 Beta fighter. However, that didn't mean it had been comfortable.

Last night Damion had tried to get up-to-date with his new starship model, learning all he could from the manuals. The Zodiac-class ship *Ares* was one of the more recent designs, modified to the fullest with the latest technology. Although only built about five or six years earlier, within that time span it had constantly been updated. Just like the Command ship *Zeus*, the hull was midnight black and sleek to better hide within the depths of space. The engine output was clean due to the synthesized Red Ore. The hull was lined with a material manufactured from the crystal byproduct of the amalgamate of Red Ore fuel. This made the Zeus blend into the background, making it harder to find on long-distance radar. This was all possible due to the many forms of Martian Red Ore.

Faintly birdlike wings arched out and back from the main body. A window in the front of the ship went almost halfway along the side, and a seat could be seen inside the view window. Immediately below the window sat a track that the main gun ran along so that the Fighter inside could turn his seat and control the gun for a full 180 degrees.

The hatch into the *Ares* was on the top of the ship. A metal roll-up ladder leading up to the entrance draped down the side. Damion had to drop down into the ship instead of going in from the side like the Beta models. Corporation engineers had changed that feature on the newer models since too many ships had blown apart because of damage to the door, resulting in the vacuum of space pulling the pilot out of the craft. In battle the spacecraft had a higher chance of receiving direct hits on the sides than directly above.

"Is the *Ares* to your liking?" 47 asked softly from behind Damion.

"Yes." Damion nodded, continuing to marvel at the Zodiac, admiring all its curves as he practically drooled on himself. "I want to fly her. Now."

"The *Ares* is ready for immediate takeoff whenever you wish to board. As I have said, it has been modified for your exact specifications, abilities, and physical needs," 47 said as he returned from the flight preparedness station.

"I need clearance. They haven't said I can take her out yet." Damion rubbed his gloved hands together. Even if it was just a sim—a simulated attack in open space with computer drones—it would allow him to open the *Ares* up and get a feel for the ship before a real battle. The ammunition used wouldn't cause any true damage to the *Ares* or the drones. Sims were also a necessity to keep pilots on their toes between long periods of real battle. Now he would do his first sim as an Alpha, and no matter what, this Zodiac was his, and hopefully 47 wouldn't kill him.

47 tilted his head and then moved toward the *Ares*. "I will get you clearance." He climbed up the ladder like an agile cat and dropped into the ship before Damion realized what he was doing. Damion climbed to the top of the ladder and peered down. He was curious how 47 fit into the spacecraft.

Inside, as he slid into his padded seat, 47 ignored the faint bloodstains that remained from the scrub team on the inner hull, but Damion saw them clearly from his perch. The leather-covered throne had a pattern of holes that lined up precisely with his ports. Putting his identification code into the panel embedded in the throne's arm, he leaned back as the reclining seat turned slowly until it faced the rear of the ship. The way it sat meant that 47 and Damion would be back-to-back while flying. The seat clicked into place, and 47 pressed in another sequence of numbers. As soon as his hand gripped the end of the armrest, he gasped as the jacks on the chair slipped into his body. His eyes remained open but flicked back and forth, viewing something only he could see.

"Where did you…?" Damion looked down at the empty platform before suddenly hearing the announcement that he was cleared to start his sims. "47?"

The only answer he received was the sound of the Zodiac powering up.

"What are—? Never mind." Damion shook his head in minor frustration before dropping into the top hatch. As the ladder automatically retracted, he slipped into his seat and pulled the helmet off the console that would recognize his presence. After putting his helmet on, he extended his legs until his feet slipped into a comfortable crevice, his eyebrows rising in surprise. "My legs actually fit."

"I informed you. The *Ares* was modified for your exact needs." The voice was 47's, but it didn't come from the wide-eyed man in the chair—it came from all around them, out of the ship's comm system. 47's lips never moved.

"What the hell is that?" Damion turned his entire body to be able to look behind him at the reclining 47. "You doing that?"

"There is no other Core connected with the *Ares*," 47's voice replied as if that answered everything.

"This is my first time flying with a Core, remember?" Damion shook his head and put his hands on the controls.

"But not your last. When connected with the *Ares*, I can control its guidance system and speak to you through the comm. I have access to all of the ship's controls, save the weapons system, to monitor their levels as well as take over if something happens to you. Do you have any questions that I might help you understand better?"

"If you do all that shit, what am I supposed to do?" Damion frowned, wondering why he spent two years in flight school if a computerized machine was going to do his job.

"Do what you do best. Fight. Cores can show you where the enemy is, but we cannot fight them. We can warn you of dangers, but we cannot protect you against them except by giving you the knowledge you need to defeat them. We can tell you the best route to fly, but we do not have the instinct that you do to maneuver the ship in the most efficient and safe way. Cores are the informers while the Fighters are the saviors. Fighters are the ones who protect the Command ships, such as the *Zeus* and *Hera*, the colonies, and the planets. Cores are merely tools to help the Fighters accomplish their goals." 47's voice was dispassionate, not even wavering when he called himself a tool. "Fighters have the emotions to render the correct judgments, evaluate a situation, and make decisions. If the Zodiacs were given completely to the Cores, we would kill everything we viewed as an enemy.

"An experiment called the Core Incentive was done thirty-three years ago, to try to eliminate the loss of human life by leaving Alpha Fighters and pilots out of the battle equation," he continued. "The incident was masked by the Corporation, which controls all the media in the colonies, and the truth became a guarded secret only shared with Cores. When a raider ship escaped into an open colony hangar bay, the Cores destroyed the whole colony, deciding it was the most efficient way to dispose of the enemy. Millions died before the Creators could deactivate the Cores. That is what Fighters are for."

"All right, then," Damion muttered under his breath, looking at the opening hangar-bay doors. As the metal parted, he could see the protective shielding that kept the bay pressurized and gravitized. The shield shimmered in an almost imperceptible silver grid that separated the bay from space. "I guess we should start running the simulation."

"Simulation download begun. Simulation start time in twenty seconds. Nineteen... eighteen...." 47 counted down, and Damion's weapons systems powered up with a flicker of blue and red lights over the flat-panel screen in front of him.

Damion eased the *Ares* out of the hangar, quickly realizing that the controls were more responsive than he was accustomed to. If he wasn't careful, he could spin them out of control with too much thrust. When 47 finished counting, small drone spacecraft began appearing on Damion's screen as they flowed from over the top of the *Zeus* and toward them.

Damion swerved the Zodiac left and decided that he would try to dip down below the drones first, hoping he could get an advantage over their superior numbers by surprising them.

"There are fifteen drones within the immediate vicinity and fifteen more out of view. All have full shield capabilities. They are limited in speed but have 25 percent more agility than Zodiacs," 47 reported. "All systems are at maximum levels and working at 100 percent."

"Thirty?" Damion exclaimed sharply in disbelief. "I thought this was supposed to be an easy gods-be-damned sim!"

Damion rolled them to the right and saw three of the drones pursuing him, so he increased their speed and raced toward the small craft above and in front of them.

"It is my belief that they are testing you beyond the other Alpha Fighters because you are the one I chose. They are wondering what you have over the other Alphas," 47 stated as they performed a perfect 360-degree rotation. "The drones' weapon systems are powering up. Six seconds until they fire."

"Then let's start firing first," Damion said through clenched teeth, rolling the *Ares* and targeting the two drones in front of him before banking left past the third. "How close are they behind us?"

"They are approaching at ten kilometers per second and will be within optimal targeting range in sixty seconds. They are closer than the five approaching the bow of the *Ares*." 47's gaze flicked back and forth even faster in his supine body as he kept track of every enemy. "May I suggest a full flip movement, dispatch the enemies toward the stern, return to current position, and do the same to the enemies aft in under five seconds?"

"Five?" Damion let out a bark of laughter as he turned the aircraft around within a second. "You really do have high expectations!"

At least it was only a sim, but Damion didn't want to die even a fake death. It wasn't about pride. It was the fact that if he could die in practice, he could die during the real fight, and Damion had never had a death wish.

"My expectations, as you call them, are merely based on your logged skills and reaction times," 47 said as Damion destroyed the three drones previously behind them.

Damion tensed to invert the ship again, and 47 silently asked the computer to boost the thrusters so that they flipped faster.

Damion was edgy and wired by the time they had dispatched the first ten drones and there were still twenty more to go. *Fuck.* "I need to put some distance between us so we can try and lose them."

"Would you like me to activate booster fire?" 47 asked, helping maneuver the ship into a spin to avoid the stun fire from the drones.

If they were hit, the stun fire would impact the *Ares*'s hull and be noted by outside sensors to alert 47 that he and Damion had been "destroyed" after frequent direct hits or to simulate certain system losses.

"Yes, I'm going to bank right and use the *Zeus* to buy us some distance." Damion turned the *Ares* and began swerving around the much larger ship. The *Zeus* was massive, and it took more than a few seconds to navigate around the multiple lighted decks. Around a thousand people, having no idea what was happening, were only meters away from them.

"Activating sub boosters now." As soon as 47 ended the last word, the ship put on speed, pressing Damion back against his seat as they shot off. "Sub booster shut down in five seconds."

"Fuck!" Damion wasn't used to the speed that this craft held, and had to struggle to keep the *Ares* straight. "They following?"

"Affirmative, but at a much slower speed. However, there is a new, unauthorized opponent that has entered the battle area," 47 informed him. "It is the *Hephaestus*, Fighter Arkin's Zodiac."

"Son of a bitch. Why would Command let him out now?" Damion suspected the Commander might want 47 dead, but this was going a bit too far. "All right, we need to sweep out the drones quickly. If they want to play dirty, let's see if we can steer some of these stupid drones to run into his ship."

"Unofficial authorization was given. The drones were not reprogrammed to attack the *Hephaestus*. Only the *Ares*." The Core reported his findings unemotionally. "May I suggest the Cube technique to get rid of the drones?"

The Cube technique was well known to any pilot, but only a very few could pull it off. It involved very precise piloting skills that not many pilots, including Alphas, had the skill or the reaction time for. If performed correctly, the drones would not only run into the *Hephaestus*, but also each other. Damion had run it once in flight school, impressing a lot of people but also ending up with an earful from his sergeant. There was some crazy shit that looked good or remarkable but didn't always work. Although Damion was a brand-new Alpha and the maneuver was difficult even for the Elite, he knew he could do it.

"You better be as good as you say you are, then," Damion said through clenched teeth. *He* had better be as good as 47 thought he was too if this was going to work. "All right, let's go under first, then swing left."

"As you order."

47 took control of the sub boosters; he activated them in short bursts, one at a time to correlate with Damion's control on their maneuvers and weapons. The first three drones crashed into the *Zeus* when they dove under. As they banked left, Damion shot straight down to avoid the two drones approaching them from opposite directions, causing them to crash into each other.

"Nine drones remaining. *Hephaestus* approaching from above the *Zeus*."

"Fuck," Damion cursed, banking hard up and back to flip and spin the spaceship completely around again toward the drones. "In about three seconds, I need some more speed."

"If I may make a suggestion, fly away from the *Zeus* and let the *Hephaestus* follow you."

The Core would generally use the sub boosters for tight maneuvering and short bursts of speed. Using the main boosters could make them fly faster, but it was hard on their bodies and the hull integrity if used for too long. But Damion had to trust 47 would activate them long enough for Damion to complete what he needed. "Firing main boosters."

"Why do I want him to follow me?" Damion wasn't against hearing suggestions since he was running out of ideas.

"Currently, he is at full capacity while you are at approximately 50 percent stamina. We have already been fighting, while he and his Core have not. The best course of action is to dispose of the *Hephaestus* quickly. While we would still achieve victory, our chance of doing so with limited damage drops the longer we wait," 47 stated. "And I wish to perform an analysis of a modification that I have not yet been able to test."

"Oh, well, don't want to stop your research there, 47. Shit, I hate using a number for you." Damion was babbling, but he was also trying to circle about and make sure he had the *Hephaestus* on his tail without getting said tail blown off.

"Bank starboard," 47 instructed as he gauged the distance. "The *Hephaestus* is powering its weapons. Their ammunition is superior to the drones."

Damion didn't question; he just reacted. He suddenly realized that he had to trust 47 if they were going to make it out of this situation alive. Space streaked by outside the window.

"Activating the Impulse Barrier, test one point zero. Subject: nine simulation drones and the *Hephaestus* Zodiac." The words echoed around the inside of the Zodiac as a high-pitched whine came from 47's control chair powering up.

"Activating what?" Damion screamed.

"Core going offline for fifteen seconds," 47 informed him as a shot from the *Hephaestus* grazed their hull.

The thrum that had begun from 47's chair and spread to the ship suddenly hit a crescendo, a loud, bass boom bursting from inside *Ares* and rattling its occupants. A circle of crackling light exploded outward from the *Ares*, passing over the nearby *Hephaestus* and drones, sending them all into uncontrolled spins as the light hit them. Leather creaked and a thump could be heard as 47 collapsed back into his chair, panting.

"Fighter Hawk has approximately thirty seconds remaining to dispatch the opposition before all enemy systems come back online."

The voice over the comm system sounded weak but confident.

"Holy fuck! I don't know what you did, but thirty seconds is more than enough time." Damion was a little scared and confused by whatever his Core had done but also excited as hell, adrenaline ripping through him. He began to eliminate everything in his path—except for Arkin's Zodiac. He made sure all the remaining drones were out of the way so that the *Hephaestus* would be dead in space without killing him.

Damion heard Arkin's scared and fury-filled voice over the scratchy comm. "What the hell are you doing? What was that?"

"Surviving your cowardly attack." Damion smirked. "I should just kill you."

"There is a 78.3 percent chance that Fighter Arkin will attack us again in the future. It would be wise to terminate him now," 47's weak voice advised through the comm speaker in Damion's ear.

"My Core tells me to kill you now and save me the trouble later." Damion half agreed with 47, but he refused to be a coward like Arkin and kill a man in a disabled ship.

"You don't have the guts!" Arkin snarled, his obvious false bravado evidenced by the hitch in his voice.

"Righhhhht," Damion drawled before shooting at the stern boosters of the *Hephaestus*. Even when the Zodiac came back online, it wouldn't be able to go anywhere without assistance.

"Fifteen seconds until the *Hephaestus* comes back online. Core 92 will not awaken by that time. He has taken permanent damage to his cerebral cortex from the Pulse. Enemy Zodiac's booster capacity disabled, life support at 49 percent and falling since Core 92 went offline," 47 reported. His voice over the comm was becoming stronger.

"You killed my Core!" Arkin must have noticed his Core's unresponsiveness.

"Maybe if you ask nicely, the Commander will send a crew to come get you." Damion turned the *Ares* around and headed back toward the upper hangar bay of the *Zeus*. "47, you okay?"

"I am still at an operating capacity," 47 stated, not really answering the question. "Core 92 is not terminated, merely disabled. The effect the Pulse had on him was an unexpected variable that I did not consider. It is one of the things that I will have to take into consideration when I make additional modifications."

When they arrived back at the *Zeus*, the bay doors failed to open at first, and Damion worried whether they would be permitted to dock. He let out a sigh of relief when the doors eventually did part to admit them.

"Command, this is *Ares*. It seems there is a Zodiac outside. An unauthorized one." Even though there was no response from Command, which was suspicious, it didn't affect Damion's mood. He had been grinning since the docking doors had opened, but the smile quickly faded once he set eyes on 47 as they exited the *Ares*. "You look like hell. What did you do?"

47 was obviously attempting to pretend he didn't need to use the *Ares*'s hull to remain upright, but Damion suspected he did to avoid collapsing onto the cold metal of the catwalk under his feet.

"I have not been able to determine how to install an additional energy supply specifically for the Pulse yet. I routed it through me so it would not take away from any of the *Ares*'s other systems. The energy the *Ares* uses is electrical, and the normal human body has electricity constantly moving through it. Cores have an increased electrical charge because of our body modifications at birth and our input ports. I merely had the Pulse take the energy from me instead of the *Ares*. It was my first test of the weapon. I will have to modify it with the results gathered from the deployment."

"I'm not sure if trying out experiments in the middle of a firefight is the best of ideas." Damion sighed as he went over and helped 47, wrapping an arm around his thin waist. "I bet there are a lot of disappointed and pissed off people on the bridge right now, so we better stay in our quarters until we get further orders."

"It was not something I could test within the *Zeus*. I ran many simulations and scenarios. There are only so many analyses that you can perform before you need to test out the real thing. That was my first opportunity." 47 hesitated for a moment before wrapping an arm around Damion's waist. It would have been more helpful around Damion's neck, but then 47 would have been on his toes. "Fighter, I do apologize for bringing you into a hostile situation. It was never my intention."

"Don't call me Fighter. Besides, we survived. Now we just have to get you fixed."

Damion was walking down the catwalk toward the exit when the Commander marched out from the main door. His face was red and Damion could see the obvious irritation.

"I do not require medical attention, merely to rest," 47 replied quietly.

As the Commander strode toward them, 47 bowed his head and went silent. Damion could tell that at this point it was taking everything in 47 not to fall asleep.

"What the fuck happened out there, Hawk?" the Commander growled, stopping approximately two meters away and crossing his arms over his broad chest.

"Sir." Damion stood straight and gave a salute—a bit sloppy, but a salute. "I was going through the simulation exercises when another Fighter joined the battle against me. He was firing live rounds at my Zodiac, so I had to defend myself. I left him alive, but his Core was damaged and his Zodiac stranded."

"And how in the hell did you damage his Core?" The Commander's gaze flickered to 47's limp form. "And what the hell is wrong with him? He try and kill you yet?"

"It seems an EMP—an electromagnetic pulse—swept through the enemy vessels. My Core protected my life, shielding me from it," Damion lied, partly because 47 did save his life and now was drained as a result. And because he really had no clue how the Core had achieved the EMP, even though 47 had explained it to him.

The Commander was silent for a few moments, glaring at the top of 47's bowed head. "You're telling me that after he killed three other Fighters, he suddenly decided to save your ass? That makes no sense, Hawk."

A sound from across the bay distracted the Commander, and he moved his look of death from 47 and Damion to out over the bay. Arkin's Zodiac was being towed into the bay by hauler vessels. They could see the man's glare through the Zodiac's window even from where they stood.

"You had better be tellin' me the truth, boy, or your Core isn't going to be the only object of my ire."

"I'm sure it's also not true, sir, that you authorized Fighter Arkin to try and kill me. I trust you far too much as a superior officer to believe you would attempt such an act." Damion bowed his head for a moment. "Request to be dismissed so that I can take my Core to Medical, sir."

The Commander stood there for a long moment, grinding his teeth. His fists clenched in anger before he answered. "Get the fuck out of my sight, Hawk, and try to stay out of it." The big man strode off toward Arkin's disabled Zodiac.

"Yes sir." Damion saluted awkwardly again and then walked out the exit with his Core next to him. Arkin would not have been able to head out there without clearance. Arkin was a cocky son of a bitch but he wouldn't risk his Alpha status. He had to have permission to go out there from the Commander.

They were in the elevator on the way to Medical before he spoke to 47 again. "He's going to be pissed for a while. I can understand why he might be peeved with you 'cause you killed those other Fighters, but I'm starting to suspect, with his reaction there, that he wants you dead for more reasons than that."

Could Damion prove it? If the Commander was out to end 47 because of his past actions, would Damion be able to stop it? Would he have any support in proving the man in charge of planned homicide? He doubted there were many willing to put their necks out to protect a Core.

"I really do not require medical attention," 47 said quietly, with his head resting against Damion's shoulder. Damion was certain 47 was on his feet and awake by strength of will alone. "And who is going to be… pissed?"

"The Commander. It's not good when the guy who hands out assignments wants you dead." Damion blew out a long breath. "And yes, you need to get looked at since you've never done that before. How do you know you didn't blow something in that crazy brain of yours?"

"The Commander does not want you dead," 47 attempted to assure him in his not very encouraging monotone. "I did not, as you say, blow something. The Pulse merely pulls on the electromagnetic waves in my body to produce enough electricity to activate the Pulse. Therefore I merely require rest."

"Sure, I believe that you have it all figured out, but since it's never been done before, like I just said, let's just have them plug you in and check."

Damion shook his head at the stubbornness of his Core. For someone who was supposed to follow his commands, 47 did have an opinion on just about everything.

"As you wish," 47 replied after a moment. Damion saw 47's eyes widen, trying to stay open, but Damion had caught him closing them a few times.

Finally, he was too tired to keep awake anymore. "Apologies," he managed to murmur, before falling into an exhausted sleep against Damion's shoulder, going limp in his grasp.

Cursing under his breath as he took on 47's full weight, Damion picked up his Core easily and carried him to Medical, handing him over to the first person he saw. He described what he had observed during the flight—which was nothing—and watched them drag 47 into one of the special Core pods that they used for scans. He could only hope that 47 had been telling the truth and that all he needed was rest… or it was going to be a very short partnership.

Chapter Four

Core 47

IT WAS only an hour later when 47 awoke with a gasp. He attempted to sit up quickly but immediately was jerked back when the cables plugged into his ports wouldn't allow him any more movement. Heart pounding and eyes unfocused, it took him a few moments to figure out where he was. Once his vision cleared and 47 realized he was in Medical, he sank back into a supine position while beginning to take an internal diagnostics check. He was still tired, but not as much as he could have been, thanks to the electrical pulses through the cables that renewed his internal reserves. For a human it would have been the equivalent of drinking twenty-four cups of coffee in an hour. It would take true sleep to completely heal him, but for now it would do.

"Hey there, 47."

His brows knitted together as he saw Damion. He then experienced a rush of numbness, which preceded momentary confusion. "You are still here."

"Needed to make sure no one tried to kill you in your sleep," Damion said with a shrug and a small smile. "I did run back to my room, but I returned here within twenty minutes. I figured typing out the sim report would better serve us if I got it done early rather than letting the Commander make it up for us."

47 was silent for a few moments, staring at his seated Fighter searching for something. "Logical," he finally stated. "May I go back to our quarters now?"

"If you think you're ready and the med girl thinks it's all right." His Fighter's shoulders rose and lowered again. "She said you were drained pretty bad."

"A negative side effect of activating the Impulse Barrier. Next time we enter battle, I will attempt to have the modifications in place so that it will not happen again. I apologize for the inconvenience. I do believe I am ready to leave." He hesitated for a moment before continuing. "I do not find the medical facilities… personally acceptable."

"You don't like them? I can understand that." Damion smiled. "I don't care for them much myself. As for the Impulse… let's not do that again unless we really, really need to."

"You do not approve of the Barrier?" 47 tilted his head to the side in his questioning, and the jacks plugged into his temples and behind his ears pulled against their moorings in the capsule.

"I don't approve of you killing yourself."

Damion reached out and began to gently pet the top of 47's head.

"If I were terminated, you would be free to be chosen by a Core not suspected of possibly terminating your life prematurely. Is that not agreeable?" 47 was surprised to find Damion's hand on his hair… pleasant.

"I'd have to wait to be rechosen. And you're forgetting that more than likely they're now trying to kill me along with you." Damion chuckled. "Basically keeping you alive and me alive is one and the same."

"Logical in some ways. It would not take you long to be rechosen. Once I was deceased, the Commander would provide you with accolades. With all the evidence provided, you still attempt to keep me functional. Why?" 47 was being bold, seeing how far this kindness would go. He'd never had anyone touch him with anything other than malicious or clinical intent before.

"You didn't kill me," Damion answered simply, as if it were the only answer needed. And to Damion, 47 deduced it was. Damion was a good pilot, but they both knew it was their cooperation and working together as partners that finally saved them from being killed.

47 was confused, and it was something he was unfamiliar with. He was never confused. Inquisitive, yes; confused, no. But ever since he met Damion, he seemed to be feeling this… repeated emotion. Damion attended to him in a way no one else ever had. He treated him as… something other than a tool, a computer, an inanimate object. Damion treated him like what he really was—something living. Human. "I do not understand at this time. But I will try to in the future. May we leave now?"

"Yeah." Damion turned and called over the attending nurse.

She typed for a short while on the console next to 47's head, then looked up and spoke directly to Damion. "He's free to go. We'll continue monitoring him through his daily rest periods."

She stepped around and stood at 47's side, and with a wave of a hand over another screen, she retracted the connectors.

Unable to help it, 47 gasped as the jacks drew back from his input ports, feeling his world go almost dark again. He was in one world now, instead of two, and he felt the loss of his friend, and without the constant feed of energy, the weight of exhaustion took over. His body and mind were tired again, but he wanted to go back to his quarters and his familiar capsule. The ones in Medical did not contain enough plugs, since he had twenty-two in total and the typical Core had ten.

Placing his hands on the sides of the pod, 47 pulled himself into a sitting position. "Thank you."

Damion helped him out of the capsule and walked beside him as they headed back to their room.

"Tomorrow we have another sim, hopefully without the murderous Fighter on our tail."

"I do not believe it is enough time to modify the Impulse Barrier's electrical draw feed," 47 stated, wondering if he had available opportunity to accomplish his work between now and the next day, since he found his final conclusion on the Barrier lacking. "There is a 42 percent chance that we will be attacked again."

"I think we'll be fine." Damion smiled, and it was obvious his Fighter was attempting to calm 47's alarm over the recent events, which 47 did not share. "They won't try it again, not until they can figure out what you did. And honestly, no one else can do what you did."

"There is approximately a 98 percent chance that no Core will be able to copy the Barrier and an even higher probability against deducing how to prevent it," he replied confidently.

"Then they won't try. Trust me. My gut feelings tell me we'll be okay for a while." Damion smiled once again. "Hungry?"

47 couldn't understand what Damion meant by "gut feeling," but he felt that he had already asked too many questions for the day. "I do require some sustenance, yes."

"I'll go down to the mess once you're safe in the room." Damion frowned. "What do you want to eat?"

47 didn't want to tell Damion that being in their room did not guarantee Damion's safety, much less his own.

"The Cores are only allowed the food exclusive for us. If you tell them that you are retrieving food for your Core, they will give you the appropriate sustenance. Though they will find it strange that a Fighter is collecting rations for his Core since it is usually the other way around."

"I don't mind being different." Damion shrugged but seemed agitated by 47's words. "And it gives me a reason to stop by and see what Juni's found out about Arkin."

"You have always been different," 47 said casually as they arrived at their quarters and he scanned his passkey. "I will watch you through the security system and therefore know if you are in trouble."

"Even if I am, keep your ass here," Damion commanded sternly.

47 opened his mouth to protest, but just as quickly shut it. He strode into the room, toward his capsule. "Core 47 will obey." It was the standard monotone reply in the words that many Cores used in response to orders given. Perhaps Damion wasn't that different from the other Fighters.

"I hate that number crap." Damion had shown increased discomfort using 47's designation, and it seemed to be agitating him further. "Just stay here. I'll be back soon. Maybe Juni found out more about Arkin."

"Affirmative," 47 replied without looking back toward him, then slipping into the capsule.

"You don't have to say 'affirmative.'"

Damion shook his head and left.

"Affirmative," 47 mumbled under his breath as he lay down and punched in the code to activate his jacks. It was still a while before he could fall asleep, no matter how tired he was. Though when he did, he kept tabs on his Fighter, as he had said he would. Even if ordered not to leave the room, it didn't mean that he couldn't do anything if something happened to Damion. 47 had chosen him and would stick with him, no matter what his personality turned out to be.

Traveling the communication and security system, 47 saw Fighter Micco enter Arkin's quarters, telling him Damion's whereabouts. Listening in, 47 caused the cameras to rotate around the room, and a feeling he had never experienced before entered his chest as he spotted Arkin's Core. 92's unconscious body was in the closet, limp against the back wall and partially obscured by the hanging clothing. Even only being able to see part of him, 47 could see blood staining the dark gray uniform. He idly compared 92's form to a picture he had once viewed of a marionette whose strings had been cut. The feeling in his chest increased, and he noted that he would have to ask Damion later what it was he was experiencing.

"How you holding up after that last round?" Micco asked with arms crossed.

"Fine. My Core, though, is worthless. Not responding to shit." Arkin spat. "He'll be in Medical, and I'll need another."

"Man." Micco shook his head. "How the fuck do you keep getting new ones? I'm not the only one thinking about that."

"You go ahead and keep thinking." Arkin smirked. "I may break them, but the Creators love dissecting them. Whatever that freak Core has come up with, they're going to want to test it, and they won't care how many I break."

"They're expensive…." Micco countered.

Arkin growled. "What's your damn point?"

Micco held up his hands and took a step back. "Nothing, man."

"I've been on the Alpha team the longest, kid. All the rest have either been transferred out or killed. You are all new to me, but the *Zeus* and the Commander go a long way back. That enough for you?" Arkin stepped forward with a finger pointed at Micco's chest.

"Yeah, it's enough. What do you want me to do?" Micco cleared his throat. "You want to deal with Damion, right?"

"That lucky-ass bastard has to have a trick. I want to know what, or I want him out of the Alpha squad."

It looked as if Arkin was about to leave his quarters to find Damion. 47 sent commands to the system, Arkin's door locked, keeping both him and his friend in. When Arkin went toward his console, 47 shut it down so he could neither access it nor call for help. Arkin went into a rage, screaming at the room around him and at his comrade until his gaze fell on 92. 47 disconnected from his view of Arkin's quarters, running from what he was sure was going to be a brutal scene as he switched camera feeds to look for Damion.

Damion

DAMION STOPPED by the mess hall first. He received looks—lots of looks—but he couldn't find Juni. When he asked for 47's food, he was not impressed by the sight, smell, or color of it. Of course, when he asked for his tray, his food didn't look much better and that was an Alpha meal plate, but the Core food seemed overly, if not completely, synthetic.

Although Damion knew it would cause more talk, he sat with Dulton until the man finished his food. Damion doubted he would see the man often now that their positions were so different. Damion never saw himself as the type to forget the people he once shared food with, but being an Alpha was busy work. Soon, with all the simulations and constant scouting missions, he'd not be able to see his old Beta squad outside of the cockpit. He didn't worry about his own food or 47's becoming cold. The food was naturally served at room temp.

Damion was scrambling for normalcy. He was also curious as to how people around him would react. He had spotted a few other Alphas walk in to pick up their food. Alphas were distinguished by the two red stripes on the right arm of their uniform. They paid Damion no mind. He hadn't had time to get to know the other Fighters who were not in Arkin's mob. He only hoped they weren't all assholes.

Two trays in hand, Damion headed back to his old bunk and his old bunkmate. Juni greeted him warmly, and Damion told him about Arkin and what had happened during sims. Juni was stunned at what Damion said 47 could do, but Damion could see the anxiety in Juni's demeanor. Juni had learned that Arkin was one of the top Alpha Fighters on the *Zeus* and had a loyal following. Whether said following was due to admiration or fear or both, Juni didn't know. What he did find out was that Arkin had the most kills and was the longest-surviving Fighter, but was also on his fifth Core.

"That is because he kills them when they are no longer useful."

47's tight voice came through Juni's console speakers, causing the men to jump in surprise.

"I apologize for interrupting like this, but I just sealed Arkin in his quarters with Fighter Micco. He has some of his supporters tracking you and reporting your every movement to him. He was about to go after you despite being confined to quarters. The Fighter is currently very angry and… distracted. I deemed it wise to warn you."

"Shit, that Core is creepy as hell," Juni grumbled. "But it sounds like you should get back to your room."

"47, you really are creepy sometimes." Damion repeated Juni's words as he stood. "All right, I'm heading back."

"I apologize for being, as you say, creepy. I will not do it again," 47 stated. "Also, Beta Mathis, you had a virus eating away at your console. I have gotten rid of it. If you wish to avoid more in the future, do not download anything more from hotbodsfrommars.gal."

Juni turned bright red and muttered about nosy, creepy Cores while Damion chuckled. They spoke for another ten minutes before Damion left and made it back to his room—with just enough time to think about 47's words and how to handle the new situation.

"I didn't mean to say you have to stop being creepy," Damion told 47 when he returned, setting both trays down on the very small table. "But yeah, speaking suddenly through a personal console does tend to throw people off."

By now 47 had unplugged from the capsule, and with his feet on the ground and hands gripping the edge, he sat looking down. "I did not know how else to contact you." His voice sounded strained, even through its lack of emotion. He rubbed his chest. "I will send another apology to Beta Mathis."

"No, don't. At least not right now." Damion shook his head. "Trust me, he'll forget about it. Why are you so stressed?"

"Is that what I am feeling? Stressed?" 47 asked, looking up at Damion.

"Uh, I don't know." Damion sat down in one of the two chairs and focused on his Core. "Only you know what you feel."

"We were taught and programmed not to have emotions and are continually given chemical supplements to suppress them." 47 motioned toward the food as he slipped off the pod and walked toward the table, sitting in front of the gray, gruel-like concoction. "Therefore I do not know what I am feeling. It began when I viewed 92. After I sealed the door and cut off his console, Fighter Arkin became… irritated, and it appeared as if he was going to do bodily harm to 92, which it appeared he had previously done. Core 92 was discarded into the closet at the time of my viewing, unconscious and wounded. I can no longer reach him in any way."

"Aren't there rules against that type of abuse?" Damion couldn't believe the Corporation didn't have some restrictions in place to protect the Cores, since they were such valuable assets. "Is there not supposed to be an investigation every time a Fighter's Core is terminated?"

47 picked up his spoon and pushed the gray mush around its bowl. "There are rules, a lot of them, but many feel that they are made to be bent or broken. Or they perhaps feel that the rules do not apply to

them. In the end Cores are...." 47 paused, his gaze rising to meet Damion's. He was contemplating if it would be wise for his words to be spoken out loud, before looking back to his food and continuing. "Cores are tools, machines, and are meant to be used as such. When a tool, as with a toy, is broken beyond repair, one merely throws it out and gets a new one. At least that is the belief that I have observed many Fighters having."

"I guess I was wrong."

Damion was hungry and dove into his food with gusto. He had been too busy talking with Juni to eat when he visited him and also hadn't eaten much in the morning before the sim. After surviving another close brush with death, it made even synthesized food tasted better... but the dinner conversation was rather depressing.

"I thought Cores were rare," Damion continued. "There must be more than enough Cores for them to not enforce the rules. I don't understand the recent push to recruit really, since there haven't been any big wars in over a century. We're really here to protect the colonies against the rebels."

"We are fairly rare because we are expensive to make and not every infant they receive to create a Core survives the process. Approximately 70 percent die. Some Fighters, such as Arkin, do not care. When Cores die, the Creators study the body to see how they can make them stronger, more adaptable, harder to kill. Yes, Alphas use the Cores for stress relief, be it in the form of sexual intercourse or physical aggression, because it allows them to study how it affects the Core. They need to build Cores so that the Alpha's treatment will not result in traumatizing the Core in such a manner that they can no longer work in a Zodiac."

Damion came to the silent conclusion from 47's explanation that although Cores were rare, the Creators valued experimentation over the cost of production. Fun group. He thought the tales of the demons of Hades were scary, but they had nothing on the Creators. Damion looked at 47's plate and then his own. "Want to try some of mine? Don't think it's much better, but watching you eat that gray gruel kills my appetite."

47 looked over at Damion's meal, and Damion could tell he was slightly curious by the faint expression on his normally guarded face.

"I do not know how taking your sustenance will affect me, nor do I know what would happen if I did not eat my assigned meal." 47 stood up, taking his bowl and walking toward the bathroom. "I will eat in here so that you may get your appetite back."

"That's not what I meant." Damion groaned and shook his head. "Damn, you could drive a man to drink. You can eat with me, and I don't think a bite of my dehydrated meal will hurt you any more than the stuff you eat."

47 stopped and turned, looking down at his bowl before walking back over to the table "Very well, I will try your meal," he said, sitting down. Damion knew 47's pod would not be able to replace the necessary energy lost after what happened today. Even modified humans needed food.

"Thanks." Damion shook his head again, cut off a piece of his protein, and handed it over to 47. "Is it true they can disconnect Cores?"

47 inspected the food for a few moments. "Disconnect in what way?"

"Like an automatic shutoff. Is it true?" Damion resumed eating.

"If we are plugged in, then, yes, it is possible," 47 replied after a moment's consideration. He took a tentative bite of the food that Damion had given him and looked at his fingers, then at his own food, then back at the bit of protein.

"It has been done before, after the Core Incentive incident. Every Core involved in the incident was either wiped or remotely terminated by detonating the chip in their cerebral cortex." 47 took another small bite of the food.

"You want more?" Damion laughed as he pushed his plate closer to his Core. 47 had the perfect chance to kill him, turn on him. Instead he had, in some odd way, determined Damion was worthy of survival. Had it been the bonding? Or was this new trust part of the process toward becoming one of the best pilots?

Trust.

47 eyed Damion's plate and then looked up to Damion. "I should not. You need your sustenance, and we are required to eat our prescribed food." He popped the remainder of what he already had in his mouth. Damion pretended not to hear the small sigh of pleasure as 47 ate.

"I could go back down to the mess and ask for another tray." Damion grinned as he watched 47's reaction to the food. "Don't tell me that gruel is that much more nutritious."

"Not much. But it is meant to have no flavor to tempt us, nothing in it to make us feel... curiosity. It also contains vitamins and chemicals to keep us alive, in top health, and to make it easier for our bodies to take the abuse of jacking in."

47 paused for a moment. "As well as help the Creators control the Cores. It contains a supplement that we have received since birth." He spooned a portion of the tasteless gruel into his mouth and swallowed.

"And that means no." Damion stood up, "Finish it all, mine included. I'm going to go back down and demand that they give me another Alpha tray and watch the lady handing them out refrain from jumping the counter to kick my ass."

"I cannot. If I eat your food, I will not be able to eat my own and therefore not digest my daily regimen." 47 looked up at Damion in confusion. "I thank you for your… consideration, but I cannot."

"Hm." Damion slowly sat back down. "I guess I don't want you to get in trouble. Do they check your stomachs too?"

"No, but they can tell what we have eaten when we enter the capsules and port in. The chemicals they give us help…."

47 paused again, apparently considering Damion's words. Putting his spoon down, 47 sat back in his chair, his gaze on the tasteless oatmeal-like substance he had apparently eaten his whole life.

"The chemicals they give us help them monitor and control us. They keep us placid—block our abilities to feel emotion and other distracting derivatives of such. They also help bond us closer to our chosen Fighter so that we must listen to that person no matter what. It is only when the bonding is complete with our Fighter that a Core attains maximum efficiency and becomes comfortable in that state."

"But you don't listen to me. Well, in the *Ares* you did, but not really. You already have your own mind." Damion had seen a light in 47's eyes, unlike the other Cores he had come across, who looked blank and completely dead inside. "Yet you haven't been deactivated."

47 seemed momentarily surprised by Damion's astuteness. He lowered his gaze and rose from the table, leaving the rest of his meal untouched. "With your permission, may I resume my rest?" he asked submissively.

"I would rather you answer my question and try some more of my food." Damion frowned at 47's desire to leave the table. "Unless you're feeling uncomfortable."

47 slowly sank back into the chair at the request, still keeping his gaze downcast. "You did not ask a particular question for me to

answer," he stated quietly. "And I feel nothing, therefore I cannot feel… uncomfortable."

"I'm just attempting to get past the fact that they want to kill you, and now me by association. And yet they haven't terminated you in your sleep, which probably means you have something they want." Damion ate more of his meal out of the need for a distraction more than anything else. "Why wouldn't they be able to just pull what they want out? Would it damage you?"

"The Commander or other Cores cannot just terminate you. The Creators are not regulated by any entity within the *Zeus*. They would be displeased if our progress to further develop the *Zeus* were to stop. The reports they receive from the Commander can differ from the ones they receive from us and they determine when intervention is needed. They monitor our treatment and find ways to improve Cores' development from how we fail our Fighters. We are considered replaceable despite the cost it takes to produce one unit.

"You and Beta Fighter Mathis were not aware of our full capabilities even after being admitted into the Corporation fleet. There is no one who speaks for our physical beings. Cores are kept away from the general populace. The Creators block the truth about our lives. No. They would not terminate you because the Creators are vested in the *Ares*'s success. Forceful extraction could damage my ability to adapt to the system, which they will not risk at this time." 47's gaze drifted toward the capsule. "That, and there is something they want. Me. Completely under their control and yet still be able to think independently. Until they deduce a way to do so, they will not attempt to terminate me. There are some who do not agree. Those are the ones currently attempting to disable me."

"Then you're going to have to tell me when you notice things, even if you are creepy when you do so. You'll also have to trust me and maybe listen to me a bit more." Damion sighed and pushed his plate away before standing and walking over to his bed, then sitting down. "And first… take another bite of my meal before you finish your gruel."

"I do not see how your first sentence correlates with what I have told you."

47 picked up Damion's fork and took a bite of the Alpha meal. He let out a small sigh of pleasure.

"As long as they're trying to kill or experiment with you, then I'm in danger too. I don't want to die. Not now, nor in a few years." *And I thought having a Core would make things easier.*

"They will not kill you as long as the Creators do not suspect that I have told you what I have. And they will have no inkling since I am initially programmed to be unable to speak about Cores in this manner," 47 told him around spoonfuls of his tasteless meal. "If they do succeed in killing me, you will be chosen again. If they establish the control they wish over me, you will have the perfect Core. Arkin was not completely incorrect when he called me broken. I am flawed."

"You're just the right level of fucked up." Damion smirked, removing his boots before lying on his bed and closing his eyes. "Just don't overdo it tomorrow. Nothing flashy."

"I do not understand your terminology or your meaning." 47 tilted his head in his unique way.

"Don't stand out. Nothing new. For the next few sims, we're boring, got it?" Damion opened his eyes and looked at him. "And I need to call you something else."

"I understood your order, Fighter. It was the first part I did not." 47 finished his meal and stood, then walked toward his capsule, sat on the edge, and eased down. "Nor do I understand your aversion to calling me by the number assigned to me."

"47 doesn't sound right, and if we're going to be a team for the next few years, you need something unique, because you're nothing but. Just give me time to think on it." Damion knew 47 had to mean more than birthing tanks or dates of conception or what the hell else. He had to mean something more to Damion than a numbered tool.

"As you wish. Do you need anything more from me?"

"Unless you know how to get the knots out of my upper back, then no, you can plug in and do whatever it is you do." Damion turned onto his side. "I'm exhausted—too tired to undress. Wake me up an hour before sims, and I'll sort it out then."

"I have been trained in the techniques of massage." 47 turned to look at him over his shoulder. "If it would please you, I will attempt to ease your discomfort."

Damion questioned if he should allow 47 full access to his body, and it set an alarm off in his head. "You wouldn't lie to me, would you?"

"I am incapable of lying to you," 47 replied honestly as he turned his back toward Damion once more. "But I can sense your apprehension. You still believe that I might terminate you."

Damion *was* still a bit apprehensive, but it had only been one day since he was assigned a Core. Well, a day and a half. Either way, he wasn't completely positive that 47 didn't want to kill him. Damion had survived their first taste of combat together, unlike 47's previous Fighters—but that didn't mean he'd make it past the second.

"I shall wake you an hour before sims as you ordered," 47 stated as he ran his hands over the sides of the capsule almost lovingly.

"Thanks." Damion rolled onto his back once again. He knew he wouldn't have to wait long to feel the pull of exhaustion due to the new, intense physical and mental activities in his life.

As he fell asleep, his thoughts were of what to call his new partner.

Chapter Five

Tuesday March 29, 454 MC
1333 GMT
Core 47

47 ONLY used Damion to help him walk along the hallways back to their room because of minor dizziness. 47 had used the Impulse Barrier against another assault from Arkin in the sims. Arkin's new Core was unable to modify the *Hephaestus* against the Barrier. How Arkin continued to be chosen by Cores so quickly, 47 did not know. While Damion was vehemently against the use of the Pulse, 47 had needed to test it out again since he had installed the new energy drain into the *Ares*. The purpose of it was to supply the Impulse Barrier with the energy it needed to work without draining him.

Unfortunately he hadn't installed a large enough conduit and they had needed to stun more enemies this time around, since Arkin slipped an ally into the battle with him. So the energy drain had run out and the Pulse had looked for its next source, which was 47. But it wasn't nearly as bad as previously, and 47 was merely weakened instead of downright exhausted.

"Damn it," Damion spat.

47 knew Damion didn't like the Pulse—well, Damion liked not dying but didn't like the attention it drew, and they were both becoming exhausted from Arkin's attacks. It was also becoming a stress factor within the Alpha ranks. The Commander would have to address the attacks soon—it just wouldn't be today. After this round of sims, they were supposed to be given assignments or wait until the first rebel raid or uprising to go back out.

"How bad are you?" Damion asked.

"I am merely having an imbalance of equilibrium at the moment. I shall be acceptable in about seven minutes' time."

"Right." Damion looked over his left shoulder at the other Zodiacs being dragged in by maintenance haulers. They were all without power and their Cores more than likely stunned. "Let's get the hell out of here before the Commander appears again."

Damion walked a bit faster. Most of the people they passed didn't even pay attention to them since they had to drag in a few downed Fighters, and some Cores needed assistance. 47 suspected Damion had an easy goal: their quarters.

47 was silent as he contemplated the Impulse Barrier. He needed to install a larger energy supply for it to drain from. He looked back and saw Arkin's new Core, 108, being pulled from the ship. The dark-skinned Core's body was rigid, his gray eyes open in a sightless stare. He was still alive but… 47 looked at Arkin, supported by his comrades as he glared at his disabled Core in disgust.

47 turned away, allowing Damion to help him onto an elevator. Once the doors closed, he had a confession for him. "I have… reservations about using the Impulse Barrier against other Zodiac ships."

"Why?"

47 tripped, then straightened out as the world spun for a moment. "Arkin will terminate 108, blaming it on the Barrier. I am doing harm to the other Cores."

"No others need to die because of that bastard. There has to be a way to stop him." 47 was relieved that Damion had held back his usual derogatory diatribe. "Why does he get chosen? The other Cores have to know that he's been through so many."

"He is one of the better Fighters. Not as exceptional as you, but good. The Commander wants him to remain an Alpha. While most of the time Cores choose their Fighters, sometimes they are forced to pair with the ones the Corporation wants on the field. The Creators want me to use the Impulse Barrier and Arkin is an Alpha willing to attack us with no reservations. They did the same with me, except the other Cores have no way of fighting back. So they die."

47 closed his eyes to try to push back some of the dizziness. It helped until they had to exit the elevator and start walking toward their quarters.

"Screw the Commander." Damion looked happy to see the door to their room. "Lie down for an hour or two and then try and find 108. Maybe they'll take him to Medical before releasing him to Arkin."

"As you order." Once Damion sat him on the edge of his capsule, 47 slid down into it. He wouldn't rest yet. He pushed in the code to activate the capsule and gasped as the jacks entered his body, sagging into the embrace of the system. Following the circuits throughout the *Zeus* like the pathways of an underworld, 47 emerged in the Medical Bay. He searched each pod before coming to 108's and slipping into the feed. He sent out an inquisitive pulse toward the unconscious Core.

There was mute surprise at first and then acknowledgment.

While Cores might be bonded to Fighters and forced to fight one another, they had no negative feelings toward one another. They were a silent community, helping and watching over one another through the system when they could and when it wouldn't go against any order given. It was the only way to help each other since they couldn't do so out of the system.

47 asked 108 if he was okay, and 108 reported that he was acceptable. He inquired about Arkin, and 47 felt something he had never experienced before—fear. Overwhelming fear. Emotions shouldn't transfer over the cold circuits, but the burst of energy that pierced 47's mind was enough. He pushed 108 back toward calm and then further into sleep. He wanted to keep 108 there, in the Med Bay, for as long as possible. But he knew that Arkin would take his Core, whether or not he was unconscious, as soon as possible. After saying farewell, 47 quickly made his way back to his own mind and awoke with a gasp.

"You okay?" Damion had changed out of his flight suit and into jeans and a plain black T-shirt. "Did you find him?"

47 sat up, the cables falling slack. Tired of having the standard-length cables, which tended to pull at him, he had made the ones in his capsule longer. He blinked blearily at his Fighter, swallowing as he tried to get moisture back in his mouth.

"Affirmative. He is in the Medical Bay. I pushed him into a deeper sleep and sent a message from the medic terminal stating a flux in 108's Norepinephrine levels to try and delay Arkin's collection of him, but I do not believe it will work. And 108 is… *scared.* He believes that Arkin will claim him whether he is conscious or not."

"47, think." Damion leaned down so they were almost face-to-face. "What would keep a Core from being claimed by his Fighter? Other than being near death. Coma? Poison?"

"A Core is a possession, not a person. If a Fighter is insistent enough, nothing can keep him from claiming his Core except the

Commander or the Creators." 47's gaze met Damion's unwaveringly. "The medics assume that a Fighter would know his Core best and therefore would do the best for his Core's recovery. The medics fear the Creators' ire if they interfere with their experiments. How far a Core is pushed despite the repression of emotions to stimulate those emotions, even fear, is an ongoing experiment. It allows the Creators to refine their development techniques."

"Except this bastard wants to find one to be better than you, and there isn't one." Damion closed his eyes and let out a long breath. "Hack into the medical computers. I don't care what you come up with, but make up something that would make Arkin unable to pick 108 up for at least an hour. I want you to stay here and keep plugged in while I go talk to Juni. Hopefully this won't get us tried for treason."

47 was silent for a moment as he thought, and then a faint twitch of his lips betrayed a very quick smile. "Delanor space seed. 108 may have gotten it on him while exiting the *Hephaestus*. It would be fathomable it attached to the inside of one of his ports as it attaches to the outside of the craft. If the scanners sensed a sudden outbreak, the computer would close down the Medical Bay for quarantine. Will that be acceptable?"

Damion spoke with a large grin "You're a genius. I heard about one outbreak while in training. Bay scanners missed it because it was tucked into a pilot's helmet somehow. I'm just glad it's fake and we don't have to worry about gigantic hives and respiratory failure." He ruffled the top of 47's head. "I'm going to see how anxious Juni is to get his own Core. Remember, you stay here and lock that door after I leave in case Arkin comes looking for you or me."

"I will observe Arkin and proceed to warn you if he or any of his associates approaches," 47 promised, pleased that his Fighter was happy with him. He sank back down into a supine position, launching himself into the circuits again.

Damion

DAMION DIDN'T waste any time getting down to the lower decks. This would piss Arkin off more and delay him getting another Core, but he couldn't stand by and watch it happen again. The other Alphas'

Cores were used, some badly, but only Arkin was getting away with multiple counts of manslaughter. Damion would need to investigate if these actions were solely contained to *Zeus* or if they were found on the other flagship, *Hera*. He prayed it was only this Commander and group of Fighters that treated such amazing people with indignity.

He found Juni in the exercise room. Damion gripped the front of Juni's shirt and pulled him roughly off the workbench where he was doing sit-ups, then led him to the side of the room. "You want a Core?"

"What?" Juni's blue eyes widened in surprise at both the question and the near manic expression on his best friend's face.

"Look, Arkin's been killing Cores. I'm not sure how many they have on this ship, but right now there is one that he'll probably kill within the next twelve hours. They may have a supply of Cores on this ship but I'm tired of sitting here doing nothing," Damion explained in a low, hushed tone, making sure no one could hear him.

"Um, I don't know what the hell you're going on about here, buddy." Juni frowned, and Damion could tell that he wasn't sure if Damion was telling the truth or had gone completely off the deep end. "Is this even legit?"

"Probably not." Damion shook his head and then dragged Juni by the upper arm out of the workout room and away from others. "Look. You'll be saving a life, and I'm not making that fucking part up. Plus, we get to piss off Arkin."

"If I get dishonorably discharged, I'm kicking your ass." Juni yanked his arm free from his friend's bruising grip and followed Damion.

"That's it?" Juni's quick agreement surprised Damion.

"You're either crazy, drunk, or I'm just insane enough to trust you. We'll figure out which one it is in a few minutes."

"Just be quiet, follow me, and don't make a sound."

Damion knew a few other people in the corridor would start to notice they didn't belong within the area, so he used his Alpha-status badge to purloin the Elite elevators to Medical. He trusted 47 to gain him access even if Medical was now in fake quarantine.

Once Damion and Juni were in the elevator, 47 spoke through the speaker system. "I apologize if I am being 'creepy' again, but deemed it necessary to report. Medical is fully sealed under quarantine. No one is present except for 108. The other Cores were already claimed by their

Fighters since they were not as affected. Arkin has been confined to his room, also under quarantine. I have impressed your plan onto 108 and implemented the beginning of the bonding process between him and Juni. He was never fully bonded with Arkin, and he agreed quickly."

"Bonded, huh? Isn't this supposed to be done after we're chosen?" Juni looked at Damion in obvious confusion.

"By the power invested in me and my incredibly talented Core, you've been chosen. Think of it as making a best friend in about five seconds." Damion had no other way to describe it, since Fighters didn't go through the bonding process in the same manner as Cores. All Damion knew was that 47 had initiated the bonding while Damion was sleeping on the night 47 chose him. But Damion had trusted the strange man ever since, even finding himself liking and enjoying 47's company more and more over the week that he'd known him.

"Is he broken? Why the fuck are we going into a quarantined area?" Juni was beginning to panic.

"It's fake, the quarantine—47 can do that. But no, 108 is fine for being a Core. No one will think anything other than 108 is a bit of a fickle ass. He's lucky, because Arkin is good but not as good as us, and this time Arkin got real damn close to blowing us into space vapor— something he's never been able to do with his other Core. I think 108 will be even more exceptional once he's out of Arkin's control." Damion tried to sound excited for Juni, but really he wanted 108 out of Arkin's hands.

"Won't Arkin get a new one in a few weeks?" Juni asked as the elevator doors opened onto the Medical corridor.

"Shhh." Damion waved his hand to shut Juni up and looked around. He wasn't going to take any chances. Happy that the hallway was empty, he ran. He followed the green, open doorways to find the Core Diagnostic section in the Med Bay where 108 would be kept, knowing 47 wouldn't allow him to get lost.

Once Damion and Juni were inside, the doors closed behind them and the lights turned red. 47's voice came over the comm system.

"I have stopped all the sensors from indicating a disturbance, but I will not be able to hold it for long before someone recognizes a loop. I'm bringing 108 out of stasis now."

A few seconds later, 108's eyes fluttered open. They were steel gray, a color only found in the eyes of those Saturn-born. The rest of him—the dark tan skin, ebony hair, and fine bone structure—were also traits from the same planet. Those eyes met first Damion's and then Juni's.

"He will not be able to communicate for approximately two hours due to the stun from the Impulse Barrier. I have already changed records to show that 108 has chosen Fighter Juni."

"Why did I have to come?" Juni asked, looking down at the rather skinny young man in the pod.

"Here." Damion went across the Diagnostic room and dragged a chair over to the side of 108's pod. "Sit."

He pushed on Juni's shoulders and Juni had no choice but to sit down quickly. Then Damion took his hand and put it on 108's. "Let him bond to your electromagnetic waves and a bunch of other stuff I don't get, so that there is no chance in hell that Arkin can dispute this."

"Okay, sure. Damion, you sound like a crazy man." Juni frowned but kept his hand on the Core's. "Arkin wanted you dead before. Now he's going to want me dead too."

"When we're done with this, we're going to go have a nice chat with Arkin," Damion said in a dark voice as he walked over to one of the computer stations. "47, give us a four-minute head start before the system comes back up, but keep Arkin locked in his room. Then I want you to secure a path for us to the air locks down by the trash collectors on the seventh floor starboard area. Just in case we need them in an emergency."

"As you order," 47 confirmed. "You have approximately eleven minutes before I can no longer hold the systems." A diagram of the areas Damion had spoken of appeared on the medical screen in front of him, an arrowed path appearing on the map. "This is the route you will need to take so that I can keep you secure."

108's gaze seemed to be riveted on Juni's. Hearing 47's voice, his steel gaze flickered to the monitor and then back to Juni.

"Forgive my interruption, but 108 is still… afraid. He is worried that Fighter Mathis will treat him just as Arkin did. For all my attempts to tell him otherwise, I deduce that he only might start believing it if you told him the truth."

"Juni, hurry things up, tell the Core that you're not a raping, abusive asshole." Damion looked over at his friend, sighing with impatience.

"You serious? Wait, never mind, you and your creepy Core go ahead and keep plotting your crazy schemes." Juni shook his head and stood back up so he could look down at the Core. He kept hold of 108's hand. "Is my arm supposed to buzz?"

"Juni!" Damion hissed.

"Eh, hey, I'm Juni. Juni Mathis. I've never hit anyone in my life—well, not in the way Arkin hit people, only the people in bars who try to steal my date. I don't really have much interest either in other guys. No offense. I sort of dig the tits-and-ass type to keep my interest."

Damion rolled his eyes. "Classy. And I thought you Lunar-born were Elite citizens."

"It's the damn truth!" Juni exclaimed, and then he must have realized 108 was still there because he winced when they touched, as if the Core's arm was extremely cold. "Hey, I don't know what's going on, but I'm not an ass. Wow. His arm's really cold!"

108 continued to stare at Juni for a few more long moments before his eyes closed. The cables retracted from his ports, and he let Juni's hand go so that he could use the sides of the capsule to push himself to his shaky feet.

"He has agreed to be your Core. Fighter Mathis, 108, direct your attention to the monitor in front of Fighter Hawk," 47 said before a full diagram of the Zeus appeared and then narrowed as the escape path on the schematic began blinking. "I will help guide you if you become confused on the route. You have six minutes before I must turn off the warnings. I can continue to keep Arkin contained until further notice. Is there anything else I can do for you?"

"Just stay in your pod." Damion grinned almost maniacally. "The rest is something I've been looking forward to."

Damion and Juni helped 108 to Juni's quarters and gently placed him in Juni's bed so that he could rest. Beta quarters didn't come with a Core capsule, so it was the only place comfortable enough for 108 for now. Medical would be pissed and worried about contamination, but by the time they started accusing Juni of kidnapping, 108 would be able to tell them through the uplinks that he had gone with Juni willingly.

In the meantime Damion took Juni with him to Arkin's quarters. Damion knew 47 was following them through the ship's cameras. The array of talents 47 owned was truly impressive. Damion could see why the Creators would not want to terminate him just for being annoying. He waited for 47 to unlock Arkin's door before he knocked. The ignorant blond bastard was cursing as he opened the door. Damion punched him—hard—before the door had completely slid open.

Arkin yelled out in surprise and pain as he fell back into the living quarters, crashing into the small table. As soon as Damion and Juni stepped into the room, 47 closed the door to prevent anyone from disturbing them.

"What the fuck, Hawk! Not only do I have to deal with your freak of a broken Core, now you have to burst into my fucking room and attack me?" Arkin watched the blood pool in his cupped hand from his broken nose. "The Commander will hear about this!"

"You're lucky that all I did was break your fucking nose, since I've had at least two clear opportunities to kill you during simulations." Damion grabbed the front of Arkin's shirt and easily picked him up, slamming him against the wall. "You want to know why I didn't?"

"I do." Juni didn't look comfortable being part of the beating, but he wasn't against it either, nor was he moving to stop it.

Damion punched Arkin in the stomach after blocking the bleeding man's pitiful kick. "Because of the Cores. They don't ask for this, but they keep following us. I actually feel sick knowing how many you've killed."

A rumble started in Arkin's chest that soon turned into a roaring laugh. Arkin looked almost demonic, cackling laughter with the mess of blood running down his face.

"You feel sorry for the fucking slaves? How pathetic!" Arkin grinned up at Damion with teeth stained red. "Your Core been feedin' you sad stories? Telling you this shit to lead you into a false sense of security, to pity him and let down your guard so that he can kill you just like he did the others? The only difference is this time he's playin' with you before killing you outright.

"You know what CORE stands for? Corporation Organic Robotic Entity. *Robotic Entity.* They're just a computer with a human body— toys. That's what Cores are for—to do whatever we fuckin' want. Whether it's to feed us dinner, bend over to be fucked, or to die when we want them to. They ain't human. They're fucking machines. Who the fuck cares if they die? There's always another one waiting to take its place."

The console from which 47 had been talking was oddly quiet, almost dangerously so.

"They are not machines." Damion's large hands moved quickly to Arkin's neck, easily contracting the cartilage and blood vessels. "They are *human*. Even if 47 is trying to kill me, it would still be a human killing another human."

Juni finally moved, putting a hand on Damion's shoulder. "You're not going to kill him, are you? I thought you were going to kick the shit out of him."

"What does it matter? He doesn't learn. He never fucking learns." Damion squeezed the thick neck harder. "How many of your Cores did you do this to? Or did you just beat them to death? Coward. Dirty *fucking* coward."

Arkin's hands flew to grasp Damion's wrists, his eyes widening in fear and popping at the lack of air as he struggled to get free. Even if he wanted to respond, he couldn't speak from the pressure around his neck. He kicked out in retaliation, connecting with Damion's legs, but it didn't seem to have any effect as Arkin bucked his body.

The console was silent for a few more minutes until Arkin started to lose consciousness. "Fighter Hawk, your termination of Fighter Arkin in this manner is unwise. I apologize for my boldness, but may I suggest releasing him?"

"Listen to the creepy man." Juni tugged at Damion's arms, trying to coax him to release Arkin.

Damion allowed Arkin to pull free, his hands still shaking with fury as he watched Arkin sputter and fall to his knees. A cold emotion filled his stomach, almost making him sick. "I had planned to drag you to the trash chute and push you out the air lock, you asshole. You have a Core to thank for me walking out of here without killing you."

Arkin took deep shuddering breaths and coughed as he rose to his hands and knees.

"Now I see. Instead of the slave following your orders, you've become a slave to the machine. Is that it?"

"He doesn't control me!" Damion went to punch Arkin again, but Juni stopped him by grabbing his forearm.

"So it wants you to think. But it does all this crazy shit, and you don't wonder what *other* shit it can do. Come on, you naive bastard!" Arkin coughed and swayed on his hands and knees. "I used them the way they're meant to be used, and once they outlived their usefulness, I got rid of them. And you should too, before that crazy tool decides that you aren't useful anymore either!"

Arkin continued to laugh as he sat up straight and then braced himself against the wall to stand.

"Don't!" Juni shifted the same instant Damion moved to hit Arkin again "Don't kill him yet!" Once again, Juni strained to hold Damion back, using all his strength to keep the stronger man from slaughtering Arkin.

"Stay away from any Core for the next few weeks, Arkin, or I swear I'll finish what I just started." Damion turned to leave, knowing if he didn't go now, he might kill the asshole.

"Oh, I'll stay away from them, but it doesn't mean they will stay away from me. They love what I give them, every second," Arkin replied, snickering as he moved along the wall toward his console. "Maybe I'll get my hands on your Core. I'm sure he'd love me trying out that sweet ass. I've heard he even cried for Morales. Of course, that's just a rumor, but I'd love to see if it were true. You'll have to let me know." Arkin reached his console and with one quick punch had it sparking into pieces. "Now spy on me, you fucking freak of a trash compactor!"

Juni had to stop Damion, once again, from attacking Arkin. With a firm grip on Damion's bicep, he yanked him out of Arkin's quarters, waiting for the door to close behind them before speaking. "Man, breathe. We don't have long until they find that Core missing and search the entire ship for him."

"I should have killed him," Damion muttered, wiping sweat from his forehead with the back of his sleeve.

Core 47

BACK IN their room, 47 gasped and sat straight up in his capsule, stifling a groan as he cradled his head in his hands. The backlash from Arkin breaking the console had almost knocked him out. 47 had seen the fist coming and pulled out at the last second, but not quickly enough. He was relieved Damion wasn't in the room to see his weakness. His skin burned at every input port in his body, and he knew he couldn't go back into the system right now. With blind fingers, he found the keypad. His head was pounding and he needed to get it under control before his Fighter came back. As soon as he was free, he pulled himself up to sit on the edge of the pod and tried to breathe. 47 hated being blind and not knowing exactly where Damion was, but that was the way it was sometimes.

Damion

JUNI ESCORTED Damion straight back to his quarters. Damion was relieved to see 47 was still in the room, but not happy to see him looking so pale. Before he was able to ask what was wrong, there was a sudden alarm and announcement, telling everyone to return to their bunks for lockdown.

"Juni, go quick. They're going to start searching each room for 108. When they show up, tell them he came to you by himself."

"108 will confirm your story. The trauma to his body from the Impulse has allowed him to distort his programming. The Creators will not be able to find this distortion for quite some time, as long as 108 is meticulous in his actions. He is officially your Core. There may be a small investigation, but nothing will come of it. It has not been announced, but Fighter Traynor is resigning his Alpha post to take a promotion with the Academy. Fighter Traynor's Core was reassigned due to low performance and a query into a replacement was placed within the Creator database for an appropriate match twenty-two hours ago. The *Hermes* will be your Zodiac. 108 will begin adjustments as soon as he is capable," 47 supplied, pushing himself to his feet. "He still will not be able to communicate for approximately twenty-four minutes. They will not search your bunk for another thirty-six."

"Great. Damion, you okay?" Juni backed up toward the door.

"No," Damion snarled. "But I won't attack the bastard again. At least, not right now."

"You and I need to have a talk about your temper." Juni left swiftly, but he still looked uncomfortable.

47 walked over to the miniature kitchen. It was nothing more than a small fridge and a coffee producer, but it was enough to get them by.

After opening the fridge, 47 took out a beer and walked over to Damion, handing it to him before going back to sit on the edge of his capsule. "I apologize for requesting that you not terminate Fighter Arkin. I know it was not my place. I understand that by doing so I increased the tension of the situation." His words were quiet, tired.

"It was the right choice." Damion took off the seal and began drinking his beer. "I want to kill him, but if I did, it wouldn't make me any better than him."

"Yes, it would. He was also under suspicion with Fighter Morales for the murders I informed you of. Murders they committed before they were recruited, even if he did abuse Cores. Arkin did not cease murdering, only slowed his pace. You would have been terminating him to keep others safe, while he killed out of malice." 47's gaze was on the toes of his boots.

"Did Morales rape you?" Damion asked in a tight voice, not sure if he wanted the answer.

47's gaze flashed up to Damion's face and then back down to his boots, almost too quickly to track. "What Fighter Morales did with me during the time we were paired was in perfect compliance with what is acceptable for a Fighter in situations where stress would need to be dealt with in the form of sexual release. It is beneficial to the Corporation Alpha Fighters who are consistently in high-stress situations. If they limit their sexual needs to their Cores, they would not push those needs on other personnel," he replied evasively, standing and walking toward the bathroom.

"Damn it, 47! I am not in the mood!" Damion stalked forward and caught 47's upper arm. "Yes or no?"

47 did not flinch as Damion's large hand grasped him tightly. He was silent for a few minutes, not looking at Damion. "According to the statute, there is no such offense when it comes to such behavior between Fighters and Cores. So no—" He paused, his gaze on the floor. "—but according to my own rules, yes. According to my research, that is what it is called."

Damion nodded and let 47 go. He wasn't sure what he was feeling at the moment, now that his suspicions had been confirmed. "Arkin won't stop."

47 took a small step away from him, closer to the bathroom, standing in the doorway and taking small covert glances at him. It was

as if 47 was waiting for Damion to come for him like Morales and the others did. "No, he will not. If my analysis of his personality is correct, he will only increase his efforts to defy you."

"He needs to be stopped, but the Commander won't do it since he, and Arkin, want you dead for killing the other Fighters. The rape would just be covered up before I could even get it to the Ethical Boards, that is, if they would be brave enough to confront the Creators. I suspect the Commander fears the Creators and losing his cushy job and that's why he hasn't put a bullet in you. However, my gut says this all feels as if it's a distraction, but I can't say why, which is about as helpful as Red Ore in my coffee." Damion tossed his empty bottle into the trash receptacle with more force than necessary, drawing satisfaction from hearing it shatter.

47 was silent for a few minutes, reaching out to grip the bathroom doorframe. "Do you really believe what you stated about Cores? That we are human?"

"Yes." Damion answered without hesitation. "It doesn't matter if you were grown in a lab or taken at birth from a whore. It doesn't change anything."

"Most are born, like you, and only modified in a lab. Only a few, like me, are grown." 47 was quiet for a few minutes more. "I could do it if it would please you."

"Do what?" Damion asked warily.

"Terminate Fighter Arkin," 47 replied softly, still not looking at Damion.

"No, you shouldn't." Damion glared at him. "You've killed enough, and those men attacked you directly. Arkin has only tried to kill us in simulations… so far."

"Yes. Only us." 47 sounded close to normal, but a bit colder. He walked into the bathroom and shut the door.

Damion rested his head in his hands, wondering how long it would take the Creators to do their checks and find 108 gone, and then how long until Arkin went to Medical looking for some drugs to take away his pain and to collect his Core.

He would give anything to see Arkin's face when he found out 108 had bonded with Juni. Damion wished he could go to the gym, find it in him to watch a vid, read a book, to be able to think of anything but 47 being sexually and physically abused.

Core 47

NORMALLY 47'S showers were quick and efficient, enough time to clean himself according to the top hygienic codes. But today… today he stood under the hot water longer. His whole body ached from the backlash and his head was still pounding, but the heat helped ease his discomfort. Unfortunately, it did not help deter him from thinking about Damion's words and obvious anger about the previous abuse of 47. 47 did not understand why Damion cared when no one else did.

Shaking his head in wonderment, he turned off the multiple jets and stepped out of the shower, wrapping himself in a towel. The chemical rinse was devoid of color or smell and simulated water. The creation of this invention was something 47 had pondered the full logistics of in the past and found no answer. Looking about, he realized he had made a tactical error and forgot to bring his clean uniform into the bathroom with him. That was odd; he never forgot anything. Perhaps he had taken more damage from the backlash than he had suspected.

After drying off, he grabbed a robe and stepped out of the bathroom. He retrieved his clothes from his side of the closet and went back into the bathroom to change. In the room again, he could hear the repeating alerts telling everyone to stay in their rooms. Avoiding looking at Damion, 47 retrieved another beer for his Fighter, and then sat back on the edge of his capsule.

"You think you can check in and see if Juni is doing okay?" Damion asked.

47's gaze met Damion's for a second or two before they slid sideways to avoid Damion noticing any emotion showing in them. "I apologize but… I cannot. Not for approximately ninety minutes. Perhaps more."

"What? Why?" Damion immediately appeared concerned, not mad in the least.

"I am… I received minor damage when Fighter Arkin demolished the console I was riding in," 47 responded regretfully. "I apologize for my inadequacy at this time and the inability to follow your orders. If you wish, I will still attempt to contact Fighter Juni."

"No, no it's fine." Damion shook his head and waved dismissively in the air. "It sounds like you need to rest. Between the Pulse and getting 108 out, you're probably exhausted. I made a decision while you were cleaning up. One I want you to try and respect."

"I am adequate should you need me. I have learned to push aside the need for rest." 47 tilted his head, looking at Damion from underneath his hair. "Core 47 will obey."

"I'm giving you a name," Damion said with a firm voice, he didn't let 47's gaze move from his.

47 moved his head so that he was looking at Damion without his hair impeding his vision. "This is the decision you speak of that I must respect?"

"Yes. Meaning once I give it to you, I want you to respond to it and not ignore it. All right?" Damion gave him a tight smile.

"Affirmative. Do you also wish me to respond in the instance that others use it?" He did not understand this insistence of something as menial as a name, but if it was important to Damion, then it did not matter whether or not he himself understood.

"If you want. That is your decision." Damion stood and came over to hold 47 gently by the biceps. "If you hate it, tell me, and I'll think of another."

47 looked down at Damion's hold on him and then back to his face. "I will respond to you by any designation you give me, but I do not believe I will answer if anyone else uses it."

Damion smirked. "I'm not surprised. You love being in control and hate when others try and take it from you."

Damion took a deep breath and wrung his hands. "Requiem."

47 tilted his head again, blinking as he contemplated his new name. "Requiem. A mass for the dead, a chant, or music for the deceased. If you do not mind my asking, why Requiem?"

"It just seemed… fitting. You don't like it?" Damion frowned.

"I do not have the ability to like or dislike it." Requiem's gaze fell again to Damion's hands on his arms, and he was intrigued that he did not mind the almost consuming touch. It was not anywhere near the same as the others who had touched him. It did not contain any… maliciousness, and he could get away if he wanted to. "But if it pleases you, I approve."

Damion's smile stretched ear to ear. "Yeah, it pleases me. Now go rest, because I'm going to talk to the Commander and see if I can explain this mess before Arkin gets to find out about 108. Then I'll check in with Juni to make sure he's okay."

47… no, Requiem now, to Damion, found his lips twitching in response to Damion's smile, almost as if they were making an attempt to match it. But finding the feeling in his facial muscles strange, he stopped, and his face went back to its normal passiveness. "As you wish." His gaze fell yet again to Damion's hands holding him.

"Great," Damion said and released Requiem's arms to ruffle his hair gently. He then went to the bathroom.

Requiem turned. His gaze followed Damion as he shut the door, then rested on the capsule. A name. His Fighter had given him a name. How… intriguing. Requiem had never come across any records where this had happened before.

Another strange feeling entered his chest, causing pressure, but not a disagreeable one like when he witnessed Arkin's abuse of 92. No, this one was… pleasant. Not understanding it, Requiem climbed into his pod and lay down, weariness taking over his limbs. He gasped in mild pain as the jacks entered his input ports, but he was able to ignore it. Fighter Damion Hawk was definitely… interesting.

Requiem shut his eyes, almost immediately falling into a deep sleep.

Damion

DAMION SLUMPED down in Juni's quarters.

"What's wrong?" Juni came and sat by him.

Damion kicked at the table leg, then groaned. "The Commander is letting Arkin slide again."

"You're surprised? Really?" Juni shook his head. "Arkin's nose is so far up the Commander's ass I'm surprised he can detach himself long enough to fly."

Damion dry washed his face. "Arkin was there—right there in his office. The Commander said he's willing to overlook *my* insubordination if we stay away from Arkin. The Commander expected we were behind 108 disappearing and must have suspected that I'd go and see him. They both really don't give a shit about Cores."

"But… can 108 stay here with me?" Juni glanced at the unconscious Core in his bed. "And the whole Alpha thing?"

Damion nodded. "So long as I tell 47 to steer clear of Arkin, the Commander said he'd overlook your sudden enlistment." He patted Juni's leg and found enough happiness for his friend to smile at him. "Welcome to the Alpha level. Don't expect a welcome party from anyone. I've hardly been able to talk to the other Alphas. They avoid me because of 47."

He wouldn't call 47 'Requiem' in front of other Fighters.

Juni's bright smile in regards to the news diminished as he spoke. "And Arkin? Was he ordered to stay away from you? Will he get another Core?" Juni cast a worried glance at 108, concerned for any Core given to Arkin.

Damion scoffed. "The Commander *advised* Arkin to stay away. Politely. And Arkin *loved* that. As for another Core? Arkin's been put on a four-month waiting list."

"Well that's something at least, right?"

"Maybe. The Commander also altered the rotation so we wouldn't be on shift together. Time will tell." Damion stood up and paced the small quarters. "This can't go on."

"Hey. It's four months. Gives us time."

Damion frowned at Juni. "Time for what?"

"You might not be able to talk to the other Alphas because of 47, but they may talk to me and we can help change your rep."

"Change my rep? I'm not a politician," Damion reminded his friend.

Juni's face broke out into a toothy smile. "Let me work on it."

"May Athena watch over you." Damion raised his arm to the sky and then made a small bow.

"Trust me. If Prometheus could steal fire from the gods, I can work on getting you in with the other Fighters."

"Damn," Damion said. "I almost believe you."

"You should. And since I'm not getting a party, you get to help me move my shit when they give me my new room!"

Damion laughed. "I'm not getting near your nasty ass boots!"

They talked for a few more minutes before Damion went back to his room. Despite the events in the Commander's office, he had Juni as an Alpha. Damion was happy he had another Alpha he trusted implicitly for partner sims and in real battle. He also was heartened by Requiem, who appeared to enjoy his new name, and that pleased Damion. Arkin would be without a willing victim for months. Juni would be there to watch his back. He went to sleep that night feeling content for the first time in weeks.

Chapter Six

Monday August 1, 454 MC
2251 GMT
Core 47

REQUIEM SPLIT his time between his own experiments, alterations to the *Ares*, and helping 108 adapt. 108 was still very skittish around Juni and other Fighters, as was understandable. To help with this, Requiem had 108 assist him in finding out what exactly had happened to Cores who were in the ships hit with the Impulse Barrier. Silently, they went through possibilities and hypotheses based on 108's experiences when the wave hit. They sat on the edge of Requiem's pod, each with a jack plugged into the inputs at the base of their skulls, and communicated through the system.

While they did this, Damion and Juni would talk and trade stories and experiences themselves.

Juni leaned back with Damion on the bed, watching a vid. "You think they even know we're in the room?"

"Probably… I don't know. All this time, and I still couldn't tell you entirely what they do when they sit there like that for hours." Damion shrugged and sipped his beer, looking at the two Cores only for a moment before concentrating back on the screen. "Maybe it's selective hearing."

"I finished up my simulations this week. Thank the Gods." Juni sighed. "I was killed twice."

"They make it hard so you learn." Damion frowned as a sudden thought crossed his mind. "Twice? That just doesn't make sense here. You should be doing better than ever. Maybe you need to learn to rely on your Core more."

Requiem's ears perked up a little more at hearing Damion mention the word Core. It was one word that could get his attention while he was in the stream with 108. He found it beneficial to learn what Fighter Juni thought of his Core, specifically so he could help 108 improve upon those points. He supposed he had become a bit of a mentor to the shy and withdrawn 108, but Requiem also discouraged 108 from relying on him too much for answers.

"He's great... but, um...."

"But what?" Damion prompted Juni.

"I don't know if he likes being my Core." Juni frowned and swirled his beer around the bottle.

Requiem mentally nudged 108 through the system, pushing his mind back into the forefront and warning him to stay silent and still, as if they were still engrossed in the system.

Damion laughed. "I'm not sure if they have likes and dislikes much."

"He just... I don't know." Juni shrugged, and it was obvious that he was having trouble finding the words he needed to explain further.

"They don't show much emotion," Damion said with a smile and a small shake of his head. "Don't expect any offers to share a beer or hang out with you in the exercise area."

"When we fly, he just seems to be holding back." Juni's thin lips turned into a deeper frown. "I'm not blaming him for anything, but it's like he's not using all his skills. Like he doesn't trust me."

Requiem's eyes flicked to 108's steel gray ones, sending a question through the system. 108's gaze slowly lowered to the ground followed by a nearly imperceptible nod. Requiem's lips twitched in a momentary frown. Another question. *Why?* The answer came back hesitantly but truthfully.

Of course, there was no way to lie through the system.

Requiem asked 108 to delve back into the system and practice the exercises that he had asked him to do. 108 immediately complied and soon was out of hearing—he hadn't quite gotten the hang of being both in the system and listening outside his body at the same time.

"108 is holding back. He deduces that if he refrains from displaying his full potential then you will not punish him when he fails, as you would be unaware of his complete set of abilities," Requiem finally explained.

"Why would I punish him? Oh...." Juni knew the answer to his question immediately after expressing it, but it seemed to upset him more. "Look. I'm not Arkin."

"He's not saying that, or I don't think he is." Damion finished his beer and tossed the bottle into the trash chute. "108's just playing it safe. Give him time. He's not going to let you die."

"Fighter Arkin was not 108's first Fighter. There was one before him who treated 108 with even more malice than Fighter Arkin. The Fighter had an obsession with testing how much pain 108 could tolerate before tears were produced. He ended up in the Medical Bay every three months for the first year of their partnership. The Creators were interested in the fact 108 could still produce the reaction. 108 was able to halt the reaction after the third trip to Medical. 108 was this Fighter's Core for three years before the Fighter was terminated in a confrontation over gambling debts during leave on one of the entertainment colonies. With both Fighters, 108 nearly terminated himself several times," Requiem explained, tilting his head slightly. "I have done what is within my capabilities to strengthen his… trust of you. While he can neither like nor dislike you, he is learning that he is safer being bonded with you than his two previous bondings."

Juni groaned and pressed his left palm into his left eye. "It's like having a girlfriend."

"Worse." Damion chuckled as he gave Requiem an approving smile. "They don't even comprehend what they do to us."

Requiem tilted his head, his chin-length bangs covering one eye. "I do not understand what you mean. Please clarify."

"I don't think I could." Damion laughed and Juni did as well. "Maybe one day when you know more about relationships."

"Ah, your little girl is growing up." Juni sniffed and wiped an imaginary tear from his eye.

"He's definitely becoming mouthier."

"Those rebellious teenager years."

Damion grunted. "All those years remind me of is girlfriends and how there are no women on this entire ship who will come near me right now."

Damion and Juni began a conversation about the female sex for a few more minutes, or really the lack of "available" women or those who didn't seem to be carrying some sort of space venereal disease.

Requiem clenched his teeth against asking another question and turned away from the Fighters by putting his feet in the pod, his back to them. It was fine if they chose to mock him. It was their right and a particular habit that all Fighters seemed to have. Even his own, whom he had thought was above that type of pettiness. He did not understand them, and they did not understand him. It was the way it was and the way it was supposed to be. If Fighter Damion thought Requiem was being… mouthy, then he would only speak when spoken to.

Ever since Damion had taken over retrieving his food from the mess hall, most of his mandatory provisions had ended up down the trash chute and Damion had somehow gotten a reputation for having a massive appetite. Requiem had tried to protest, but Damion had quickly told him to eat his food and keep quiet. He did so while still ingesting a small amount of his rations per day so that he did not go into withdrawal, and he understood this brought more emotions to the surface.

Juni stood up and walked over to the two Cores, placing a hand on 108's shoulder and shaking him gently. "You awake?"

108's eyes snapped open, immediately going to Juni's face, and the trace of panic could be seen clearly. Requiem silently soothed him through the system, letting him know that Juni wasn't a threat, and that he wasn't going to hurt him. 108's eyes went back to their normal blankness, and he nodded to Juni.

After reaching over, Requiem placed a gentle hand right underneath the skull port and then grasped the cable with the other to twist and pull the jack, releasing the cable.

As 108 stood, Requiem unplugged his jack, letting both cords retract back into the capsule.

Damion waited until Juni and 108 left before speaking to his own Core. "What's wrong?"

"Everything is acceptable," Requiem replied, flipping open the programming panel to reset the capsule for one instead of two.

"You have that scowl that you use when you think something is not acceptable." Damion tugged at the back of Requiem's hair gently.

Requiem blinked at the pull, but he had gotten used to Damion's random touches. "I did not know my face betrayed anything. I will work on improving on that problem."

"You don't have to." Damion sighed. "It's more comfortable for me to know that I can understand you just a little bit."

There seemed to be no real way to respond to that, so Requiem went back to changing the settings again. He wondered that if Damion could read some emotion on his face, who else could too? But perhaps Damion's ability was only due to the fact that they were together constantly.

"You didn't answer the question." Damion crossed his arms over his chest in apparent exasperation. "Or do you just not want to talk about it?"

"I answered that everything is acceptable. I am trying to avoid being 'mouthy' since you appear to disagree with it."

Requiem rubbed at the input port at the base of his skull, trying to massage feeling back into it and also stretch the tight muscles without looking like he was doing so.

Damion let out another sigh. "I don't mind that you're… mouthy. I didn't mean it as an insult. You seem comfortable enough around me to voice what you want. I enjoy it."

Requiem was silent for a moment, his attention fixed on Damion's face. "Your personality type gave favorable feedback on my being able to speak with more liberty than if I were paired with a different Fighter. That is why I have given detailed information to you that no other Fighter would be privileged to. I apologize if my apparent reaction displeased you. As a Core I am used to being the object of less than favorable conversation but have gotten out of the habit of acting accordingly."

He finally stood, discreetly stretching his stiff shoulders.

Damion snorted. "You have an odd way of making me feel lucky and a bit sad for you at the same time."

"Lucky? Sad?" Requiem tilted his head. "I do not understand."

Damion gently gripped Requiem's shoulders and began to rub them, having probably noticed the subtle stretching despite Requiem's attempts to hide them. "I know."

Requiem tensed at first but then began to relax as relief flowed out from his stiff shoulders and down to his sore back. His eyes slowly drifted closed, and he let out a barely audible sigh of relief. "Explain it to me, please?" he inquired hesitantly, quietly.

Requiem was uncertain why his Fighter was silent. He opened his eyes and glanced over at Damion. The Fighter's mouth was twisted. Requiem had noticed this was a movement that showed Damion was collecting his thoughts before speaking.

"I didn't have such a bad upbringing, so your experiences evoke sadness. I still feel honored you chose me to be your Fighter."

"So you no longer believe that I will terminate you?" Requiem looked through his bangs at Damion. "Do not concern yourself with my past or the pasts of other Cores. That is why it is the past and nothing can change it. I thank you, though."

"There, see. That is more normal for you to sound like." Damion grinned. "You're helping 108 out? You seemed a bit tense."

The massaging of Requiem's muscles felt… pleasant and helped him relax. "I am trying to help him bond more closely with Fighter Juni. Trying to make him understand that Juni will not harm him. Unfortunately, some things are hard to reteach. As for being tense, even though we are medically and electronically enhanced, we still have some of the same limitations as normal humans."

"You push yourself too hard and too often." Damion frowned down at him in disapproval. "I wish you wouldn't take so many chances."

"That is another thing Cores are for. To take the chances that Fighters should not." Requiem was reluctant to give up Damion's hands but wanted to continue on his projects for the *Ares*.

"I don't want you to take chances. There. That clarify?" Damion shook his head.

Inwardly sighing, Requiem looked toward the ground, stepping away and out of reach of Damion's hands.

"What are you doing now?" Damion asked, watching him.

"If you have no need for me, I was going to go work on the *Ares*."

"You could just sleep." Damion let his arms fall to his side since Requiem was now out of reach. "It's late."

"We have a sim in two days. I want to be ready to test the energy draw for the Impulse Barrier by then. I am also designing a new defense mechanism, and I would like to see how it will fit into the system by initiating some tests," Requiem stated, his head still bowed. "Of course if you do not wish me to go, I will obey your orders."

"I hate that Impulse Barrier," Damion growled as he sat at the small table. Even if their lives had been saved by it, Damion had voiced multiple times that he didn't like his Core using himself as a battery. "Just… don't take long."

"I am attempting to remove myself as an energy draw option. For that, I need to increase the actual draw port power so that it will not revert to me when it runs out." Requiem looked up and tilted his head slightly to the side. "What is an acceptable time frame?"

Damion had learned better than to deter Requiem when he was set on a goal. "Thirty minutes?"

Damion sat back and continued to watch the vid he and Juni had been watching. Requiem knew he wouldn't follow him, which was a good thing because Damion would be bored to tears and would slow him down.

For a few seconds, Requiem merely looked at him, but then finally turned and walked toward the door. "As you wish," he said. The door slid open, allowing him to leave the room. He didn't know what Damion expected him to get done within those time parameters, but he had to listen. He may have time to start a diagnostics check.

Once outside, Requiem started toward the flight bays, walking quickly. The faster he arrived there, the more time he had to work. He thought of, assessed, and disregarded or accepted many trains of thought—including, briefly, his Fighter's strong hands. He could only hope that Damion would give him another massage in the future and maybe trust Requiem enough to return the favor. It would honestly improve Damion's fighting if his muscles were loose and easy to move.

Requiem's mind was on the tests he wanted to run and the modifications he wanted to make, and he was not paying attention to his surroundings.

He was nearly to the flight bay when he heard a noise behind him. Stopping, he turned, his gaze flicking back and forth through the empty corridor. Damion had been correct: it was fairly late and most people would be sleeping right now. But something didn't feel right. He started slowly backing up toward a door console, his hand edging upward as he continued to search the hall, listening intently. The tips of his fingers were about to drift away from the console when someone grabbed him by the wrist. Requiem immediately dropped to the floor, hoping his weight would force his captor to release him, but the grip only tightened, grinding the bones of his wrist together as he was dragged into a dark, open doorway.

Twisting about, Requiem saw his attacker's face.

Arkin.

Chapter Seven

Requiem

"WHAT WERE you doing, huh?" Arkin asked with a cruel, cold smile as he shut the door with his free hand. "I don't know why everyone is so fucking scared of you."

"If you do not fear me yourself, why do you attempt to terminate me?" Requiem questioned as he used Arkin's painful grip on his wrist to raise himself to his feet. He quickly looked around and realized his stupendously grievous error. To get to the flight bay, he had used the corridor that passed right by Arkin's quarters. Now he had to try and figure out how to escape from a situation caused by his own stupidity.

"I won't kill you tonight." Arkin used his superior strength to turn Requiem toward him. Using the momentum of the pull, he raised his fist and punched Requiem hard. "I'm going to remind you what you really are: a tool. I'll show that stuck-up bastard how to really use you."

Requiem's head snapped to the side from the hit. Pain flared through his jaw and cheek and he fell to the ground. But he didn't make a sound, he wouldn't. He needed to get to an outlet, a panel, the pod—something so that he could call for help. Damion didn't want Arkin dead, but Requiem wasn't going to die tonight either. He knew he couldn't defeat Arkin, but he might be able to outsmart him. Getting to his hands and knees, Requiem ignored the blood trickling from his mouth from where his teeth had cut into his cheek. He couldn't open his right eye, but he did use his left to gauge distance.

"You do not even know how to use a Core properly," he said, trying to keep Arkin distracted from his slow movements toward the empty capsule.

"I know *exactly* how to use you." Arkin grabbed the back of Requiem's hair, yanking him up by the strands so that he was standing once again. "Where do you think you're going?"

Arkin kept his grip on Requiem's hair while he let loose a flurry of punches that drove him back down to the floor. Arkin hit him in the ribs, stomach, face, and many other places that Requiem couldn't keep track of after a while.

Requiem attempted to curl in on himself as much as he could against the tight grip Arkin had on his hair. He knew two things. One: a capsule was the closest outlet to him and it was still two meters away, and two: in ten minutes, his thirty minutes would be up and Damion would come looking for him. Requiem was always, always right on time. He needed to live long enough for one of those two things to happen.

In a momentary pause in Arkin's attack, Requiem lashed out, kicking upward and out to connect with Arkin's pride and joy, his reproductive organs.

Arkin screamed and let go of Requiem out of shock, grabbing his groin in pain as he bent over. "You'll pay for that, you broken bitch!"

Requiem didn't reply. As soon as Arkin let him go, he lifted his pain-filled body to his hands and knees and crawled quickly to the capsule. As soon as he reached it, he flipped open one of the repair panels and grabbed the wires tightly in his hand, reaching through the system. He was in too much pain to put his voice through the system—it was too distracting. Hoping that Damion was still awake, Requiem grabbed Damion's vid screen and flashed one word on it.

Arkin.

Arkin recovered quickly, and once he caught his breath, he strode a few steps over to Requiem and kicked him viciously in the side, and away from the pod. He crouched down, punching him again in the same side.

The pain dragged Requiem's mind back to his body as his connection with the pod was torn away. Agony flared through his chest as something gave way in his ribs, and he lost his breath, falling to the side. He couldn't open his eyes anymore, fear for his good eye keeping them tightly closed. His face and body were a mass of agony, but he still didn't let Arkin have the satisfaction of hearing him scream. He hoped that Damion had received his message. He also hoped that he had placed his trust in the right Fighter and that he was going to live long enough to be proud that he had listened to Damion's orders not to kill again.

Damion

DAMION WAS flipping through a book he had read five times already and looking at the digital readout on the wall beside his bed, wondering if Requiem would walk in at the exact second once again. Then he noticed a flash—his vid. What he saw made his stomach clench and his anger flare. He grabbed a pair of pants without worrying about zipping them, running out into the hallway at full speed and down to the bastard's room.

It didn't take long to reach Arkin's quarters. He banged on the door once, figuring Arkin would be arrogant enough to leave it unlocked. He was right.

He walked in, and Arkin stood up with a sneer on his face. Damion had surprised him.

Damion watched Requiem attempt to slide away along the floor, back toward the pod.

Damion's hands clenched tight at his sides as Arkin reached for the top of Requiem's head and grabbed a fistful of white hair. He put one foot inside the doorway, but stopped as Arkin pulled Requiem to his feet and put Requiem in a choke hold.

"You stupid motherfucker." Damion was going to kill him this time if he could get away with it.

Requiem

REQUIEM WAS alarmed when he felt the Fighter's forearm wrap around his neck, tight against his windpipe. Arkin was going to use him as a hostage. Great.

"Coming to rescue your bitch?" Arkin grinned savagely toward Damion. "How sweet of you. Too bad you'll have to sit and watch while I fuck his sweet ass."

"Like hell!" Damion growled, his shoulders rounded forward, but he didn't step any farther into the room.

Here Requiem was again, getting Damion into trouble. He really needed to find a way to avoid this in the future. Requiem looked to his Fighter with his one good eye, still having trouble seeing him through the blood that dripped down his face from a cut on his forehead. Assessing the situation, he wasn't sure how he was going to be able to help if he couldn't get near anything electric to tap into the system. His whole body throbbed with pain, especially his face and chest. So he decided to do the next best thing. Taunt.

After spitting out a collection of blood that had pooled in his mouth, he concentrated on Damion's face. "Do not be concerned, Fighter Hawk. He will do nothing to me. I have already damaged his reproductive organs fairly severely."

"I wouldn't say I am unable to satisfy a whore like you." Arkin licked the side of Requiem's face in a slow, wet drag, from chin to temple.

"Don't touch him," Damion commanded. "What do you want, Arkin?"

"Isn't it obvious?"

Out of everything, the wet feeling of Arkin's tongue on his skin caused Requiem to wince. He lowered his gaze from Damion's face to the floor, not wanting Damion to see the brief flash of disgust in his expression. Finding some strength, knowing it wouldn't do him much good but needing to do something—anything—Requiem elbowed Arkin in the ribs with one arm, hard.

Arkin let out a small grunt that sounded more of annoyance than pain. "You little bastard!" He raised his fist to strike again, but Damion's shout stopped him.

"Don't! Let him go and fight me!"

"And miss watching you in pain as well when he begs me for mercy? I think not."

"Is that why you torture Cores? To hear them ask you to stop?" Requiem asked quietly, unable to take deep breaths because of the flare of pain from his ribs and the grip on his throat. "Then I am not the right Core for you. I will not beg nor scream. So you achieve nothing by attacking me. Fighter Hawk will not feel any pain by seeing me hurt other than remorse that I will not be fit enough for sims for the next few days. You gain nothing." He raised his good eye long enough to meet Damion's gaze, hoping that Damion would see that Requiem knew his words about him were not true.

Damion appeared hurt until he recognized the flash of silent understanding in Requiem's gaze. "You will piss me off, but he's right. He is replaceable."

"You really feel that way?" Arkin eyed Damion suspiciously.

Damion nodded and shrugged nonchalantly as if the thought truly didn't bother him. "Look. You know what Juni's been saying about me, right? I know your friends have been goading him for info about 47 and me. All I want to do is keep my Zodiac and we need to resolve our shit for the squad."

Requiem had directed his gaze back toward the floor, momentarily fascinated by the pool of blood forming on the metal from the drops from his face. He could only hope Damion looked as convincing as he sounded. "You see, there is no satisfaction in harming me further. I will not give you the excitement you want from screaming, and Fighter Hawk will not give you the satisfaction of caring beyond the inconvenience it will cause him. You do not benefit in any way."

Arkin looked between the two, Fighter and Core, as if trying to gauge if either one of them was lying. "You won't care, then, if I fuck him, as long as he comes back alive?"

Requiem swallowed and then coughed as liquid clogged his throat and new blood trickled from his mouth. This was not an answer he could give. Arkin's question was for Damion and Requiem could only hope that he wouldn't let his emotions get the better of him.

"I would only object because I haven't been able to fuck him yet myself." Damion waved a hand in the air. "I didn't want him to kill me, so I held back."

Arkin used his free hand to squeeze the front of Requiem's groin over his flight suit. "That is your loss, then."

"It doesn't have to be." Damion stepped into the room and smiled cruelly and with complete conviction. "We could share him right now. I will hold him while you do him first, then you hold him for me."

Somehow Requiem managed not to move while Arkin's hand squeezed him and ran up and down his crotch on the outside of his suit. He wanted to struggle, to push away, but it would undo what Damion had said and what he was supposed to be. "There is no need to hold me down. As my Fighter commands, I obey."

"You going to obey?" Arkin sneered with disbelief.

"Core 47 will obey if that is what Fighter Hawk orders," Requiem replied quietly, after spitting out the blood in his mouth. He let his head fall as if defeated, Arkin's forearm tightening against his neck from the movement.

"You're just going to let me fuck him first?" Arkin obviously did not trust them, which only meant he might be smarter than they'd thought. But not by much.

"As long as I get him next." Damion spoke as if he didn't have a care in the world.

Wanting to take a deep breath but unable to, Requiem raised his head so that his good eye could focus on Damion, amazed at the uncaring expression that adorned Damion's face. As he raised a hand to the tab of the zipper at the top of his suit and pulled it down, Requiem hoped it was all just an act. "As my Fighter commands."

Arkin slowly released his grip on Requiem, but his cold eyes still moved wildly, searching for any betrayal. "He might kill you."

"I wouldn't allow him the chance." Damion gave a tight smile, shrugging again.

Requiem nearly fell to the ground as his weak legs took his weight again, but he managed to stay on his feet, slowly turning toward Arkin, with the zipper to his flight suit opened to his waist. He couldn't move too fast while Arkin was still wary and Requiem was within grabbing range. He had to bring Arkin's guard down.

Arkin licked his lips and reached out to wrap both hands around Requiem's already bruised neck. "You like to be fucked like the tool you are. Tell him I'm right."

"I only listen to orders from Fighter Hawk," Requiem stated as he stared at Arkin.

He was really starting to dislike objects around his neck. What was it with Fighters wanting to choke him anyway?

Arkin sneered, and his hands squeezed tighter around his neck. "You still have a smart mouth on you."

"Let him get undressed first." Damion walked forward again, now only a few meters away from them. "He doesn't need to talk anyway."

Requiem couldn't help gasping for breath. Dark spots appeared in front of his eyes and his lungs burned for the few moments before Arkin released him. He didn't cough or try to take large amounts of air into his lungs, just stumbled back a step. Trying to take slow, short breaths, Requiem pulled down the top of his unzipped suit, pulling an arm out of one sleeve and then the other. His hands went to where the suit was sitting on his waist, but instead of pushing it down, he dropped bonelessly to the floor, giving Damion room to move quickly in the area above him.

"What the fuck are you doing, you stupid—"

Arkin didn't get to finish his sentence before Damion tackled him to the ground and began to deal out everything Arkin had done to Requiem—and more.

Requiem couldn't do more than lie there, crumpled on the ground for a few minutes, listening to Damion pummel his fury out on Arkin's flesh.

Requiem's body burned, his mind swirled, and it hurt to breathe. He was finally able to gingerly sit up, crawling slowly over to the pod while remaining unnoticed by either Fighter. Reaching into the pod, he pulled out one of the retractable cables as far as it could go. Once Damion rolled Arkin close enough to him, Requiem stabbed the jack into Arkin's hand and signaled the pod to let out an electrical charge, the voltage sufficient to knock out Arkin. Then Requiem gripped the side of the pod, trying to stay upright.

Damion let out a loud curse as he received some of the backlash shock from Arkin's skin.

"Requiem." Damion stood up, nearly tripping over Arkin's collapsed body, in his haste to help Requiem up. "We're going to Medical. No arguments."

Requiem stifled a scream as Damion pulled him to his feet, Damion's every finger hitting a bruise. "Damion, no Medical. Please."

"You need to see a doctor." Damion's voice was stern. He moved them as quickly as he could into the hallway; his focus was on the elevator and keeping Requiem from collapsing. "You could have some dangerous injuries."

Requiem knew he was right, but "I dislike the immersion tanks," he whispered softly, unable to help the small whimper that escaped as a spike of pain went through his chest.

He hoped Damion could support him as far as it would take to get to their destination. "It can't be helped. Not this time." Damion stepped into the elevator and then called for it to take them to Medical before he bent down and picked Requiem up effortlessly in his arms.

The moment the elevator's doors opened, people in the corridor stared. Requiem was half-naked and bloody, and Damion had his own small wounds from the battle. Damion was also half-naked, since he had only had time to put on a pair of pants before bolting out of his quarters.

"This is not wise. We are drawing too much attention," Requiem whispered in Damion's ear from where his head lolled against the Fighter's shoulder. His breaths were short and gasping, blood trickled from his mouth and numerous other places, and blackness crept in on the edges of his vision.

"Let them talk." Damion nearly ran to the Medical Bay. One of the nurses immediately gasped in horror at the state of Requiem. "He needs help. He was attacked," Damion said urgently.

The tallest of the orderlies gently but quickly took Requiem from Damion, but Requiem grasped Damion's arm before he could be taken too far away. "Do not leave me?" he begged, his voice barely audible and a deep tone of pleading in it.

"I'll be right here. Don't panic. You're safe."

Requiem was able to process that Damion was attempting to console him with a soft tone and smile.

Requiem looked at him for another beat of his heart and then released Damion's arm, resulting in his own falling limply as the orderly took him away to a glass tank that dominated one corner of the Intensive Care Unit.

For physical healing that needed to be performed in emergencies, immersion tanks were used. This one was already filling with a gelatinous liquid that Requiem would float in as soon as he was prepped.

Nurses placed Requiem on a metal table and began working on him. His mouth was pried open and a breathing apparatus, used while in the tank, forced its way between his teeth. At the same time, the nurses plugged monitors into his chest and next attached some cables to his head ports, allowing them to document his life signs. The rest of his suit was quickly removed, leaving him in only his boxers. As soon as he was ready, they lifted him up again and, with the help of two orderlies, gently lowered him into the tank.

Requiem's good eye stayed focused on Damion until the tank was full. He distantly heard a hiss through the liquid, and as much as he didn't want it to happen, he couldn't help but close his eye as he was forced toward sleep by the dissolving gas. Through a haze, he felt his chin droop to his chest before unconsciousness took him completely.

Damion

DAMION SIGHED, very happy that his Core was dead to the world for at least the next hour. He sat heavily on the metal table Requiem had vacated. He did not know where to go from here. If he made a report, would the Commander still turn a blind eye to the damage done by Arkin? Did the truth have any value in a world where they turned men into machines?

One of the nursing aides offered him a sedative to help him sleep, but he declined. He wanted to be here for Requiem when he awoke. He had a feeling his Core would not leave his side if he were injured. He figured that sort of loyalty warranted a cold ass and a stiff back.

Chapter Eight

Requiem

REQUIEM CAME to consciousness slowly, his eyes fluttering as they opened. He was alarmed for a moment to see how blurry everything was and then remembered he was in an immersion tank. Figures rushed back and forth beyond the glass, and then one walked up to the tank. It took him a minute to recognize Damion placing his palm against the tank, fingers splayed. Still groggy, Requiem moved his hand slowly through the gelatin, eventually placing it on the glass, matching Damion's. There was a tug from above, and he was pulled from the liquid. He noticed a male doctor walk into the unit and take a small data pad from a nurse.

Damion tilted his head up to look to the top of the platform and gave Requiem a small grin. "Hey, Sleeping Beauty. You feeling better?"

The nurses brought Requiem down, laying him on a table so that they could dry him off and assess his injuries. He glanced up at the polished backside of an overhead light. His reflection showed bruises still covered him, though now they looked as if they had been healing for a few days—still blue and purple, but with greens and yellows interspersed around the edges. Both eyes could open, but his right one was bloodshot. And he was very sore, but not in agony.

"I am… acceptable," Requiem finally replied in a hoarse voice as soon as the nurse removed the mouthpiece.

"Acceptable, yes, but not well enough for duty," the doctor said as he walked up with a clear portable console in one hand. Words scrolled across the screen. "You had a concussion, three broken ribs that punctured your left lung, a fractured jaw and cheekbone, and your spleen had ruptured. Not only that, but some of your input ports were damaged." The doctor looked up at Damion, his face serious. "What the hell happened? Did he get hit by a transport truck?" His expression showed he blamed Damion completely.

"Arkin," Damion said simply, giving the doctor a glare. "I responded a bit too late." He came over to the examination table and touched the top of Requiem's damp head.

A tension that Requiem didn't know he had been holding released, and he let out an inaudible sigh and opened his eyes. "Your response was in acceptable parameters from the time I contacted you. It was my tactical error that brought me within range of a subject I knew to be volatile."

The doctor frowned. "I don't know why they keep giving that man Cores. It seems like every other week I'm repairing one or examining one for cause of death. I've submitted many reports, but they're ignored every time because of Arkin's fighting skills. That man makes me sick. He's psychotic. If the Creators and Command weren't so damn adamant in having him stay in the Alpha squad I could have filed a motion for dismissal."

"I wouldn't be surprised if Arkin pushed too far this time." Damion scowled as he kept petting the top of Requiem's head.

"And killing five Cores,"—the doctor's irritation was clear in his tone—"Almost six, is not already pushing it too far?"

"I know, the Commander won't stop him." Damion responded, and Requiem would hypothesize Damion's arms were also crossed. "How long will he be down? He will lie to me if I ask him. His pain tolerance is too high."

"His pain tolerance is what kept him standing for that long. It's extraordinary," the doctor said, his eyes full of possibilities as he looked down at Requiem.

"I cannot lie to my Fighter. I can merely work around the truth," Requiem mumbled, showing that he was not asleep.

The doctor shook his head. "At least a week. We've repaired most of the damage, but the tissue and bones are still soft, so he must rest for that long so that the body can heal his remaining injuries naturally."

"Looks like we are out of the sims this week, and you shouldn't work on the *Ares* either."

Requiem turned his head at the second command, looking directly at Damion. This time the sigh was audible as he closed his eyes once again. "As my Fighter commands."

"You shouldn't even jack in for a few days. Let the ports that were damaged repair. I've already sent in my report to operations, so they know that you won't be in the system for a few days. They were reluctant, but I was determined," the doctor said. "I was amazed to see the number of input ports that were installed on his body," the doctor continued. "Was this something you had ordered for a particular reason, Hawk?"

Damion snorted. "No. I haven't even seen them all. Is there something different about them from other Cores?"

"Other than he has more, no. They're the same, but while the typical Core has about ten or eleven, he has twenty-two in total if my count was correct. I've never seen a Core with so many input ports."

Requiem felt the doctor smooth a thumb over one of the ports in the back of his bicep. His eyes opened again, watching the doctor with a blank expression.

Damion frowned. "Who puts the ports in?" He eyed Requiem critically.

"I did. Or rather, requested the Creators to install them," Requiem whispered after a few moments of that penetrating stare. "They help me get deeper into the system to better assist my Fighter."

Damion rubbed his left temple. "Let's go back to our quarters."

"I don't think that's wise at this time," the doctor protested. "Core 47 did take an extensive amount of damage to many of his internal organs, and while they're healing I would like to continue monitoring him."

Requiem's gaze stayed connected to Damion's. "Back to our quarters. Please."

"That's what I said." Damion gently helped Requiem off the examination table.

Requiem's legs were still shaky and very weak. He clung to Damion while trying to appear as if he were standing under his own power.

The doctor followed them toward the door. "I really must protest against this. Core 47 should stay in Med Bay for at least another day so that we can do some tests to make sure he's healing correctly. If you take him out of our care now, we don't know if you'll be able to get him back here in time if something goes wrong."

"No offense, Doc, but I won't leave him anywhere Arkin will have direct access to."

"You think we can't protect him here? Med Bay is under constant surveillance." The doctor's voice rose in anger, following them out the doors. "If you take him from my care, I won't be responsible if something happens because of your neglect!"

"Why does he think I would be negligent in watching over you?" Damion looked at Requiem and frowned. "Okay, he has a small point since I let you be attacked."

A mumbled "Stupid Fighters" came from the doctor before he stomped back into Med Bay.

"You did not let me be attacked. It was my own error that took me past Arkin's quarters and therefore put me unattended in his sights. I am the only one at fault for my injuries," Requiem replied quietly, his voice strained. He knew Damion wouldn't argue with him.

"The doctor also wants to study you."

"Probable. I have avoided the Med Bay and any doctors for this reason as well as others until now." Requiem found himself very sleepy all of a sudden. It was becoming more and more difficult to put one foot in front of the other. "If I may offer some advice, please warn Fighter Juni of the assault. I think it would be wise to inform him so that 108 does not travel alone, as I did, and therefore avoids Arkin."

Damion effortlessly picked up Requiem once again as the elevator opened to their floor, "Damn, I feed you, but you don't gain any weight. Don't worry. I'll tell him everything once we get you comfortable."

"I am not worried. Just cautious." Requiem's voice was strained from the pain of being picked up, his many bruises and half-healed wounds becoming apparent. He was silent for a few minutes as Damion carried him. "I must admit to not knowing what to do since I cannot jack in to my capsule. This has never happened before."

"You can sleep in my bed."

Damion's tone wasn't joking or sarcastic.

"That would be unacceptable. Where would you rest?" Requiem paused for a moment, leaning his head on his Fighter's shoulder. "I have never retired outside of the capsule. Nor have I ever slept while not plugged in."

"It's big enough for both of us as long as you don't kick. I think." Damion narrowed his eyes at Requiem, expecting a challenge.

"I… do not know. Being plugged into the system is similar to being in a cryogenic state. A Core's mind is not fully within his body, but instead in the system," Requiem explained, another unfamiliar feeling clutching at his chest. He thought it might be called… *anxiety*. Maybe *worry*. He didn't know.

"You'll be fine. It's just until you are healed enough so you won't blow your synapses up or whatever happens when a port gets damaged." Damion's shoulders relaxed as they made their way to their quarters. "I won't leave your side tonight."

"It is highly improbable that Arkin will attack me in our quarters. It would be tactically unwise. There is no reason why you should keep surveillance over me all night. I am certain Fighter Juni would appreciate your company and the warning you will bring to him and 108 concerning Arkin."

"I can send him a wave through the comm in the room. It will do." Damion let out a tired breath as he looked at the back of Requiem's arms. "You always have to push things too far. Why do you have so many ports?"

"I have already explained. It helps me enter the system deeper, therefore I comprehend more and control more. It also helps me conceive what I need to do to create new defensive and offensive weaponry for the *Ares*. It lets me make the impossible possible." He kept his eyes closed so that he did not have to look at Damion's face. He knew Damion was upset with him for many different reasons, and he regretted being a Core that was a hindrance to his Fighter, instead of a help.

Damion was silent the rest of the way to their room. Once they entered it, he set Requiem carefully down on the bed and gave him a firm look. "Stay in the bed unless you need to use the shower or toilet."

Requiem looked at him for a moment before lowering his gaze. "As you order." He wrapped his arms loosely around his chest and tucked his knees up as far as his injuries would allow. Being clothed in nothing but boxers in front of anyone except himself in the mirror caused an interesting feeling, not to mention a chill that ran through him, which was something he wasn't used to. It was possible his body temperature was below normal parameters.

Damion gave a few pets to the top of Requiem's head before moving away. He went to his drawer and pulled out one of his of duty shirts. It was quite a bit larger than Requiem needed.

He handed the shirt to Requiem. "I'm going to wave at Juni now."

Requiem blinked at the clothing before pulling it on over his head. He was swimming in it, but he felt better now. Suddenly tired but not tired enough to sleep, he eased down in the bed, making himself small against the wall as he laid his head on the pillow. He was intrigued at how much more comfortable the bed was compared to his pod. Although he didn't feel physical discomforts as much when he was in the system, so he supposed the relative discomfort of the pod didn't matter.

Damion turned on the comm and told Fighter Juni what happened. First Juni was surprised, then cursed about Arkin, and finally showed concern for Damion and Requiem.

Damion sighed wearily, rubbing his eyes with thumb and pointer finger. "We'll be fine. Just don't let 108 out by himself."

"I apologize for being the cause of so much strife," Requiem said quietly as soon as the comm connection ended. "I did not hypothesize that this would happen."

"You have to stop apologizing," Damion grumbled as he turned in the chair to look at him. "Seriously, you can't control the future."

Requiem sat up, leaning against the wall. "Nothing is impossible. I should have done a logical hypothesis of the situation when I terminated my previous Fighters." He bowed his head, looking to the side. "I just did not see any other choice."

Damion shook his head. "We aren't meant to know the future."

"But we can hypothesize," he replied. "Through proper situational analysis we can identify certain alternatives to various encounters. I just… did not have time."

Damion gave him a warm smile. "It wasn't your fault."

"You cannot say that because it is not true," Requiem said as he finally looked up. "I did kill those other Fighters. For many different reasons, but in the end, I did terminate them. That is the catalyst for the chain of events that have caused you so much strife up to this point. So yes, it is my fault." He paused, looking down again for only a moment until he raised his gaze again to meet Damion's. "And if you ordered me to, I would also terminate Arkin."

"You killed to protect yourself. That is called self-defense." Damion sat next to him and sighed. "As for Arkin, I want him dead. I should be the one to kill him, but if they catch me, we'll both be terminated."

"I could kill him." Requiem tilted his head slightly, making sure his full attention was on Damion while he made this offer. "It would be… appropriate."

Damion's mouth twisted into that tight line. "You hate him just as much as I do, I know, but I don't want you risking your life."

"I do not hate Arkin. I just do not see any benefit from his continued existence. He does not bring anything productive to the Chrysalis Corporation or the *Zeus*. He is more a hindrance and a danger," Requiem stated logically, finally easing back in the way he was sitting and stretching his legs out in front of him. "I… do not have to get near him to terminate him."

"That sounds like hate to me," Damion pointed out. "How can you kill him if not in person?"

Requiem was confused. What he said had been logical, not emotional. He would think more on it later. "If he were near any electrical object—the pod, an access point, his terminal—I may be able to electrocute him. Or I can trap him in the shower while he is bathing and dial up the heat too high. Any number of ways. I could even get into the *Hephaestus*'s systems, but I do not know if Arkin will be flying his Zodiac without a Core until I access those systems."

Damion flinched a bit at Requiem's cold and clinical way of talking about death—about murder. "You've thought about this… a lot."

"I anticipated this situation," Requiem replied after a moment, looking down at his hands so that he didn't have to see the look in Damion's eyes. "I surmised that you would not be able to terminate Arkin yourself, so I began to think of ways to keep both of us safe."

"I think I feel a bit more worthless now, but what you said is true. We need to take care of him." Damion rubbed his forehead. "How do you want to do this?"

"In the end, it is up to you," Requiem said quietly, then closed his eyes as he took a deep breath. Pain shot through him as he released the breath from his still healing lungs. "I will not be able to do anything for a few days until my input ports are healed."

"You should never rush to kill." Damion moved so he could pull Requiem close to his side with one arm around his shoulders. "Now you rest."

Requiem's eyes widened for a split second, barely perceptibly, before he smoothed his features again. He was tucked under his Fighter's arm, his head on Damion's chest. He hesitated for a moment before releasing the tension in his sore body. Slowly moving an arm to wrap around Damion's waist, he closed his eyes. It was an interesting feeling, being held by someone. Warm and… safe.

He was quiet for a moment or two before speaking again. "I mean no disrespect when I ask you this, but... I am... intrigued as to why you treat me with such... kindness."

Damion turned his gaze on Requiem and a chuckle escaped. "You are my Core."

"But many others have Cores and do not treat them like you or Juni does. It.... I suppose the word is confusion. It confuses me," Requiem mumbled, weariness dragging at him. "Explain please?"

"We treat you like human beings." He tilted Requiem's chin up and looked at him.

"That does not explain why," Requiem replied softly, opening his eyes as soon as he felt Damion's gentle fingers on his face. "As much as we are told otherwise, we Cores know that despite all the modifications to our bodies, we are, in truth, human. But you are the first non-Core I have ever met who also believes so."

"Everyone should still remember you are indeed a living person. Even if your modifications make you special, it doesn't change the fact that you deserve to be treated equally."

Requiem blinked as his Fighter's warm breath tickled his skin. And then Damion's lips were on his own slightly parted ones, firmly pressing against them. Requiem knew there was a meaning to this that wasn't aggression. The last Fighter he had had before Damion had done the same but violently, forcing Requiem's mouth open so that the man could thrust his tongue inside, nearly choking him. This was different. This was... nice, and Requiem didn't feel threatened in the least. He also didn't know what he was supposed to do or what Damion meant by it.

Damion blinked and pulled away. "Sorry. I—I shouldn't have done that. We should sleep."

Requiem tilted his head slightly, momentarily confused. "I... did not mind. But you seem to have."

"I should not have done that." Damion rolled his shoulders forward and put his head in his hands.

"Then why did you?" Requiem questioned softly, sounding much like a child, but he didn't understand. "I am yours to do with as you wish, yet you have never forced me to do anything I did not want to do. I... am grateful for that." He paused for a moment, licking his lips, intrigued by the momentary difference in taste. "I did not mind what you just did."

Damion shivered as he turned his head and watched the tip of Requiem's pink tongue run along his lips. "Because I shouldn't use you for sex. You should only have sex that is consensual."

Requiem unconsciously frowned, still very confused. No one had ever asked him if he wanted to have sex. The Fighter usually took it as a benefit, another service that a Core was supposed to provide. It had only happened to Requiem twice, and he knew that if he had protested either time, he would have been disciplined by the Fighter or Creators. He had no aspiration of staying in the Creator Medical Unit for a week for programming modifications or to be beaten needlessly when it was easier to submit. So he had lain there and tried to ignore the pain until the Fighter was done. This idea that he had a choice in the matter of sex confused him, and he could not understand why Damion would not just take.

Damion

"CORES DO not have that liberty. We provide whatever service a Fighter wants, to make his life easier. I do not comprehend how sex is different… how it is a… consensual idea."

"That's why I shouldn't have done that and confused you." Damion didn't know what had come over him, but he was determined to not let it happen again. "When you figure out what consensual is, then perhaps you'll understand."

"I know what the word means," Requiem replied, almost snappishly, looking up at Damion through his bangs. "I just do not know how it applies to a Core. Are you saying that a Core has a choice to… have sex… willingly?"

"Yes. That's it." Damion nodded quickly.

Requiem was silent for a moment, looking into nothing as he thought. "Why… why would anyone want to?" he finally asked quietly, his head falling back to rest on Damion's chest. "It… it is painful."

"It's not supposed to be." Damion felt like he was having this talk with a prepubescent, which, in the scope of social experience, at least, Requiem was. Damion had been taken by his older brother to a local bar and hooked up with a woman nearly ten years older than him. There was a lot to the theory an experienced lover was better than an inexperienced one. From there on out he had no problem hitting up his own dates. His father passed on few words of wisdom other than to be respectful. Requiem had no brothers to hook him up or go to with questions. He mentally kicked himself—again—for the actions he had taken to cause Requiem's confusion.

"Then why has it always been that way? What way is it supposed to be?"

"Because that was rape." Damion didn't know what else to call it, and the conversation was awkward enough as it was.

"I understand. But I still do not understand how else it is supposed to be. From my understanding the word rape is used for nonconsensual sex that is painful, correct? What do you call sex that is consensual?"

"Uh… good sex." Damion pinched the bridge of his nose, feeling a headache brewing behind his eyes. "Some romantics call it making love. There is a goddess and god who are in charge of that shit."

"Love is an emotion I am not familiar with," Requiem stated and then sat up slightly. "I am making you uncomfortable with my questions. I apologize. I will stop. I am only trying to understand better about the subject and also attempt to comprehend what you think you did wrong."

"You don't have to be apologetic. I just don't know how the hell to explain a few things. Since we were raised differently and you don't… you don't *feel* your emotions the same, it's like the square peg, round hole problem."

"I do not have emotions. At least I and the other Cores are not supposed to. I find lately that…." Requiem eyed him warily before confessing, "I find lately that I am having… feelings that are unfamiliar to me within my chest. I do not understand what they are, but they are there. I appreciate your attempt at trying to help me understand. Maybe it is beyond my abilities to do so."

"Maybe, maybe not. Right now I think we both need sleep." Yes, escaping into unconscious bliss and away from the talk of sex when he wanted… well, Damion didn't quite know *what* he wanted.

"Affirmative. I am very weary," Requiem agreed, punctuating it with a yawn. "I do admit to having some reservations about resting outside of my capsule." He eyed his usual bed with a look of regret. But it didn't last long, as his previous ordeal finally caught up with him and he drifted off to sleep.

Chapter Nine

Requiem

DAMION HAD stayed next to Requiem the last five days, and Requiem was about ready to climb the walls from not being able to plug in. "Are you doing all right?'

"I am acceptable," Requiem mumbled from where he was sitting on the bed, back against the wall, staring at his capsule like it was a long-lost lover that he couldn't touch.

Damion had ordered him to stay in bed when he wasn't in the bathroom, and he had followed those orders to the max. But he was… screamingly bored. And uninformed. He hated not knowing what was going on in the system and around the *Zeus*.

"Command is going to talk to Arkin, but still won't do anything to him, even with the attempted rape." Damion explained as he sat next to Requiem and handed him a small sweet piece of protein bar. "Although he's under house arrest, I think they're ready to give him another Core now too."

Requiem's hand paused on its way to take the bar. He moved his gaze to Damion's face, asking him if he was serious. Letting out an inaudible sigh, he took the bar, suddenly lacking an appetite.

"Then another will be terminated," he finally stated, the bar hanging limp between his fingers.

"Not if we take care of it," Damion said slowly in a low voice as if afraid someone would hear.

Requiem's gaze shot up to meet Damion's dark eyes, an intelligent mind working furiously behind them. "I obey your orders," Requiem stated just as quietly, a type of maliciousness appearing in him as well. Not out of pure viciousness but protection and revenge for his fellow Cores, and for himself.

"What do you need to do the job from here?" Damion had said he wasn't sure if Requiem was ready to plug in yet, and it was their best chance to avoid suspicion if he did not plug in for another few days. Neither the Creators nor anyone else would expect him to, therefore they would not be looking for him. The Commander would have a difficult time accusing Requiem this time of murder since he would not be in physical contact with Arkin or in the same room as him. The Creators wanted Requiem to improve the Impulse Barrier. They would be far busier attempting to figure out how he had performed the task than to reprimand him.

"I have everything I require in the capsule," Requiem replied, finally unwrapping the protein bar and taking a bite. He blinked once, looking at the bar and chewing slowly, cataloging the taste and finding it appealing. He savored it as he looked back up at Damion. Every day his Fighter brought him something new to try, and he had yet to find something he disliked.

"Where does he need to be?" Damion began to pet the back of Requiem's head slowly, as if he weren't aware of his actions.

Requiem's eyes closed as he sighed softly in contentment, swallowing the sweet bite. "It depends on what particular scenario you wish to approach the situation with."

"Something that leaves no chance for them to track it back to us, but the bastard dies a painful and much-deserved death."

"I can block any tracking methods, making it impossible for them to see that I jacked in, especially since I am not cleared to do so at this time. That will be easy. Is Arkin still under house arrest?" Requiem took another bite out of the bar, his appetite reappearing as he considered their options.

"As far as I know, until he's let out for his meeting. I don't know when that is, though," Damion admitted. All he knew was what Juni and 108 had found out.

"Then we had better expedite the process." Requiem finished the rest of the bar, licking the remnants from his fingers as he shuffled out from underneath Damion's gentle hand and off the bed. He was once again wearing only his boxers and one of Damion's shirts. The doctor had advised against him wearing his suit, saying that the open areas that surrounded his ports might irritate the damaged jack points on his body. "If we do not act quickly, there is a possibility that after his meeting he will be free from house arrest." He moved toward his capsule, placing the empty wrapper in the disposal as he walked.

"You're going to do it now?" Damion asked, sounding surprised, but moved with him off the bed. "How?"

"Jack in, search the system for Arkin's location, and receive a visual on the possibilities of termination." Requiem started to step into his capsule and realized that he couldn't access the jacks in his current attire. Without pausing, he pulled Damion's shirt over his head and threw it toward the bed. His boxers wouldn't get in the way, but the shirt would have. He lowered himself into the capsule, his mind working furiously to push away the small pains his body didn't want him to forget.

"Don't push yourself. That's an order," Damion said in a worried tone.

Requiem paused, still sitting, his hands on both sides of the capsule. "Damion, I am the only Core with the ability to achieve what I am about to do. I reached this point by pushing myself to the limit. If I cannot push myself, then I cannot do what is required of me at this time."

"You don't have to make it sound like I'm being unreasonable." Damion crossed his arms over his chest. "Fine. Do what you have to do, but still… don't fuck all your healing out the window."

"You are not being unreasonable, merely overcautious. You needed to know clearly what I intend to do and how I will achieve it. That is all I was explaining. I will do my best to achieve your orders."

Requiem lowered himself into the capsule. His fingers flipped open the control panel and he punched in his code to activate the jacks. The plugs slammed into his input ports, and it was the first time he could ever remember it being so painful. He struggled to breathe, his spine bowing as he entered the system. The pain disappeared as his mind expanded, flitting across the circuits and bypassing the energy pulses that flashed past him, lest he get caught up in their attractive power.

He went straight for the observational systems and followed the circuitry to the monitor in Arkin's room, looking for him.

Fortunately for Requiem, Arkin was sitting on the edge of the Core capsule making preparations to receive his new Core in the near future. The look of malicious glee in the man's eyes caused Requiem to nearly lose his concentration when he felt his own… heat. Was this *anger*? It was possible. He would have to investigate the feeling at a later time. But for now, he had to concentrate on the task at hand. Looking closer at the capsule, he discovered something that would have made his blood turn cold if he had concentration to spare.

Arkin sharpened one of the smaller knives he owned. The Alpha obviously knew he would receive a new Core in the next few days.

There was the rust color of dried blood in the bottom of the capsule; next to every hole where a jack would exit was a small blade.

Trying to push it out of his mind, Requiem switched from the observational circuits to the inner workings of the capsule, pulling in power from it. He could feel his body take a deep breath as he prepared to do something he had never done before: manipulate the jacks. Storing energy for a minute or two, he released it all at once so that the jacks used the freed power to spring out of their resting places and wind around Arkin's form, dragging him into the capsule. The jacks wouldn't be enough to kill him, but they would cause him quite a bit of constricting pain before Requiem went on to his next action.

Arkin began to scream in both panic and pain, struggling against the electrical cords binding his arms. "What the fuck is this?" He flailed side to side, the arm with the knife trying to hack into the half-centimeter-thick cords.

Requiem's body took another deep breath inside his capsule as he split his consciousness through the circuits. One part stayed tentatively within his body, the other within the capsule that Arkin was flailing in, and the third to the comm system on the wall of Arkin's quarters. "Fighter Arkin, I suggest that you cease struggling. Doing so will not help your current situation."

The bindings around Arkin became more numerous, holding him tightly so that he could not move his arms.

"What the fuck is this, you insane piece of shit!" Arkin didn't stop fighting; he struggled harder against his restraints. "Let me go! Let me go *now*!"

The more Arkin fought, the tighter the cords became. The whole event had to seem like a freak accident in case there was an investigation.

"The chances of that happening are highly improbable," Requiem said over the comm unit. "Nor do I follow your orders or any other Fighter's but my own. This is what you Fighters would call… justice. I am receiving justice not for myself, but for the five Cores you terminated for no plausible reason and for 108, who suffered at your hands. I'm disposing of an inadequate Fighter as well as preventing you from harming another Core. My… hand is merely carrying out the unofficial sentence."

"You're a murdering freak! Puppet bastard!" Arkin was sweating profusely as he realized he couldn't get free. "I killed five? Who fucking cares? You killed three! You're scared. Scared that you're like me!"

"You forget, former Fighter Arkin, I do not feel fear. Nor do I feel guilt. I feel nothing," Requiem said as he gathered more energy from the circuits. "I am nothing like you, for there is a very distinct difference between us. You have terminated five innocents, Cores that could not defend themselves and were programmed to not go against their Fighter's orders. You took advantage of that fact. You have killed five innocents, while I have killed three guilty."

There was a distinct pause, and a hum, increasing in volume, could be heard from the capsule that Arkin was currently trapped in.

"I apologize for my miscalculation. Make that four guilty."

With those words, Requiem released the energy. An electrical panel beneath Arkin exploded in unseen sparks, conducting power through the metal knives embedded in Arkin's body with maximum voltage, electrocuting him.

Arkin screamed as bodily functions began to shut down, secrete, and then relax until there was no more movement from his body.

Requiem retreated from the communication systems, covering his tracks by smoothing over the circuits, almost as someone would hide their footprints in the sand. He also left signs of capsule failure. It was rare, but electrical surges and equipment faults had occurred in the past, damaging Cores and—at times—the Fighter in the room. He did this all the way back to his capsule. Once there, he looped the system time stamp as if he had never jacked in, then pushed his consciousness back into his own body.

Requiem came back to awareness gasping, eyes shooting open as his fingers groped for his control panel. With a shaking hand, he punched in his code again and disengaged the jacks. He nearly screamed as they aborted from his ports, pain ripping up his spine and head from his damaged inputs. Requiem lay there for a moment, catching his breath before reporting, "Mission complete."

"I knew you could do it, but what damage did you take?"

Damion had not left Requiem's side, and he leaned down and picked up Requiem, who was shaking uncontrollably, to carry him back to the bed.

Requiem stifled a groan. Blood leaked down his pale skin from three damaged ports in his back. "Minimal. I did what had to be done." He paused for a moment, closing his eyes and resting his head against Damion's shoulder. "He had installed knives in the bottom of his Core capsule. One above each port."

"Sadistic ass." Damion sat Requiem on the bed and then grabbed a discarded towel to place against his wounded ports. "You're sure he's dead?"

Requiem couldn't help the hiss of pain that escaped his parted lips. "Positive. Before I retracted I checked all vital signs." He attempted to sit up. "I will go into the bathroom so I do not bleed on your resting place."

"It's fine, just sit." Damion dabbed gently at the ports. "Should I take you to Medical?"

Requiem turned and gave Damion a look, pinching his lips in pain. "If you take me to Medical, they will know that I jacked in, defeating the whole purpose of covering my trail."

"I know, but I don't know how bad these wounds are. Remember, I'm a Fighter, not a medic." Damion smirked, but it seemed more worried than full of humor. "At least take some analgesics. We have some in the bathroom."

Requiem nodded wordlessly, his body throbbing. Even though only five ports were damaged, it felt like one big pulse from head to toe. "I will do as you order. I was not ready to jack back in, but saw no other choice. If we did not act now, there was an 87 percent chance that Arkin would have been freed and given another Core to torture." He slid to his feet to get to the bathroom.

"I'll get them—you sit." Damion gently pushed down on Requiem's shoulder before heading to the bathroom.

The regular medicine wouldn't kill the pain much, but Requiem hoped it would help enough.

He eased back onto the bed with a sigh, making sure the towel was underneath him before lying down and closing his eyes. "There is only a 0.001 percent chance they will deduce that it was not an accidental death. And an even less percentile that they will figure out it was me. Even if they do, if most of the Medical staff has the same mentality as Doctor Condo, they will not say anything. Especially after they see what is in the bottom of the capsule."

"They won't find out. You're too good." Damion handed Requiem three pills and a small cup of water. "Here, try this."

Requiem gave a brief hint of a smile. He took the pills and the water. "I appreciate your confidence in my abilities. It seems as if since I arrived on the Zeus all they are being used for is to terminate unworthy Alphas." He put the pills in his mouth and swallowed them with the water. "Thank you."

"You were saving lives. All those Cores who would have died and the ones he would have tortured. You also did what I ordered you to do."

"Both points are true. I do not regret what I have done. But it was not what I… hypothesized doing with my advanced abilities when I decided to upgrade myself." Requiem turned onto his side so that he could see Damion better and to take pressure off his ports. "I want to help not only myself but other Cores, and in the process help the Chrysalis Corporation become better equipped to engage in battles with our enemies. That is what I had planned."

"You'll do all that and more." Damion smiled as he took the cup back and put it on the table. "I believe you are a man with limitless abilities."

"Nothing is impossible. It simply takes some work to find the possibilities," Requiem said, his voice a bit of a mumble as his eyes fluttered closed. Between the damage done to his body and the fast-acting pills Damion had given him, he was suddenly very sleepy. "Once those possibilities are found, it merely takes a little more work to make them possible for all."

This bed dipped as Damion sat down. "You keep saying that, and I know you believe it, but every one of us has our limitations. I hope you don't push your limits to the point that they lead to your death."

Damion

DAMION GENTLY stroked Requiem's cheek until he fell asleep. He sent a wave to Juni and tried to act normal. They talked about their upcoming week of leave, and Damion made a point of saying that Requiem seemed to be healing well but was a bit upset about not being able to plug in. He was in a state of shock. It took him about two hours to understand what he was feeling. He had always known taking a life was not only a possibility but also a likely eventuality when becoming a Fighter. Damion had never expected one of those deaths to be another Alpha Fighter. He knew Arkin had deserved the justice he was dealt. But did Damion step over a gray space into a dark realm the Commander and Creators occupied?

Requiem slept for about sixteen hours straight, and when he did wake, he was still groggy and seemed confused about what was going on around him. The moment he looked at Damion, it was as if his eyes wouldn't open fully. He could finally speak, but it was a mumbled comment. Something about wishing to be clean as he struggled to untangle himself from blankets and get to the bathroom.

Damion was waiting with a towel when Requiem came out. He wrapped Requiem into the stiff material and briskly dried him off. "You feel any better?"

"A little more awake, yes. Thank you. I apologize for resting for so long." Requiem lifted the towel, drying his hair, not self-conscious in the least as the cloth fell away from his body where Damion had wrapped it. "Is there any intel on the Arkin situation?"

Requiem

DAMION NODDED, leaning back against the doorframe of the bathroom and crossing his arms over his chest. "They found him around an hour after he was supposed to be at the meeting. They already ruled it an accident."

Requiem let out a breath of relief, tension he didn't realize he was holding in easing from his shoulders. "Excellent." He gingerly walked to the closet to grab a pair of boxers. "Fighter Juni and 108's reactions?"

"I can't read 108 well, but I'd say it was a bit of happiness with a dash of suspicion." Damion smirked. "Juni said we should hold a party while on leave."

"I have never been on leave. It was unwise to do so without a Fighter because of the kidnappers."

Who wouldn't want a human who would obey your every order or merely lie there silently to be beaten or raped? Cores were perfect for black market brothels, and if one was left unguarded for too long, they could be taken and used for such purposes. The kidnappers had become very adept at tearing out or deactivating the tracking device that Cores had implanted at birth, and they didn't care much if it hurt the Core or even permanently damaged them—the implants lay too close to the spine and brain stem to avoid injury. Some smarter kidnappers had even managed to override the tracking devices so that they answered to the kidnappers and not the Creators or Corporation.

Requiem sagged down to sit on the bed. All the muscles in his body ached. "What do you do on leave?"

"Most go home to their families, others go get drunk, high on drug stimulants, or worse. Others don't even leave Corp areas." Damion explained, watching him closely. "Do you need Medical?"

"I am acceptable." Requiem lay down on his stomach. "What will you do?"

Damion shrugged casually. "I don't know if I should head home or not. I don't particularly miss my small town, plus I'm not sure how they'd take to meeting you."

"Meeting me?" Requiem repeated Damion's words. He looked at him from where his head rested on his arms. "Why would you want them to meet me?"

"You're my Core. It's a big deal." Damion waved his hand through the air as if erasing Requiem's words. "I mean, I put my life in your hands."

"You are adapted to Cores and the way we are. I am sure that my presence will be… disconcerting to your family unit," Requiem stated. "May I suggest that you travel to see your family? I will remain here."

"No." Damion shook his head quickly. "Let's go with Juni to Lunar. When we were talking about our break a few months back he said his family would put us up for the week."

"Is 108 accompanying him?" Requiem had hoped Damion would leave him on the *Zeus*. If he did, and without the looming threat of Arkin, Requiem could work on the *Ares*. He shifted his position on the bed, withholding a wince. "When will we depart?"

"Yeah, Juni isn't about to leave 108 behind, because where he is from, Cores are a big sign of making it. As for when we leave, probably in a few days. Have you even been off the *Zeus*?"

"Yes. I was originally in a Core Lab and then on the *Hera* for training. It wasn't until approximately three years ago the Creators assigned me to the *Zeus*. I pushed through an unofficial order to have me sent here because I knew that you would eventually be assigned here. But I have never been in what you refer to as 'the outside world.' I have never been planet side."

Damion looked at Requiem with some concern. "You also have nothing considered normal clothing, but we can fix that when we get to the relay at Venus."

"You are correct. All I have are my uniforms. I never had any need for anything else." Requiem looked at Damion, tilting his head so that he could see his Fighter better. "What is wrong?"

Damion sighed, shaking his head. "You just look exhausted. You want anything from the mess?"

"I do not require food at this time. Thank you." Requiem watched his Fighter, knowing that Damion was not completely verbalizing what was wrong.

"What's the first thing you want to do in the outside world?" Damion asked curiously as he sat on the bed and gently grasped Requiem's hand, looking down at it.

Requiem thought about it for a minute, somewhat intrigued that Damion had asked him. "I do not know. I have never given it much thought."

"Just stay near me. We'll try and dress you and 108 normal enough so that people won't think you're Cores simply by the way you look." Damion turned Requiem's hand in his own. "How do the ports feel?"

"They are…." Requiem paused, looking at his hand in Damion's and the port on the back of it. "They are unacceptable. As much as I do not… like the prospect, I cannot jack in for a while."

"Is it addicting?"

Requiem thought about it for a moment, his fingers curling and uncurling in Damion's. "Imagine being blind and the only time you can see is when you plug in to the system. Not only can you now see, you can see everything, know everything, and gain knowledge. So yes, it is addicting."

"What about the real world? I know on this ship it's boring, but outside of this, it's rather, well, depressing at times, but also amazing." Damion gave him a small smile.

"I have only seen pictures of the outside world, so I really have nothing to compare it to." he rolled onto his side with a minimal wince. "Being integrated into the system, being a part of the system, is my world."

"Well, there is another world out there for you to explore." Damion patted Requiem's hip casually. "I will buy you all sorts of sweet treats."

Requiem blinked slightly. "Treats? What are those?" he inquired, slightly confused. Damion had become more tactile with him and he did not mind the feel of his Fighter's hand on him. "And there is always more to explore. The system is never ending. There is always another pocket to discover."

"You know, you can say I'm right from time to time." Damion stood up and went over to grab the extra blanket off the chair that he had asked Requiem to request from Supply.

"I never said you were right or wrong. I do not have enough data to say otherwise. I merely provided another point." Requiem's gaze followed Damion intently. It almost seemed as if Damion was keeping himself on pins and needles since he had kissed him, and Requiem wanted his carefree Fighter back. "And you still did not answer my question. What is a treat?"

"It is smaller than a dessert, but it is as sweet—except sometimes it can be savory. There are many types." Damion put the blanket over Requiem, making sure to cover his shoulders. "I think you will like it."

Requiem tucked the edge of the blanket under his chin and cocooned himself in the rest of it without seeming to pay attention, being quiet for a few minutes. "I believe it may be wise for me to resume eating my allotted food from the mess hall. While I have been intrigued by the food you have brought me to try, I am starting to experience the… effects of not ingesting the vitamins and chemicals over a long period of time."

"Your stomach hurts?" Damion laughed softly, shaking his head. "Sorry."

"No, that is not it exactly. Although I have experienced some initial abdominal discomfort. The problem seems to be that I am starting to… to *feel*, I suppose. Feelings and emotions that I do not understand and have never experienced before. It is… disconcerting."

"I want to show you that feelings are good."

"Feelings and emotions are compromising. Feelings have no place within the system, and therefore having them makes the system harder to understand," Requiem replied clinically, but he believed those words.

"You're human. You don't have to rely on the system all the time." The Fighter let out a long sigh, verifying what Requiem had known the whole time—that the system was very addicting to Cores and that it was hard for a regular human and a Core to connect.

"It is all I know." Requiem turned on his back again, only to wince slightly and turn back to his stomach. "It is similar to me asking you to stop feeling."

Damion didn't argue that point. "Just rest, there is no one out to hurt you."

"There are many people out to hurt me. You are the only one I trust not to." Requiem closed his eyes.

Damion smiled warmly at that and watched Requiem fall asleep again as he wondered if he could risk leaving. He was getting too attached to Requiem in a way that was dangerous for both of them.

He stood as soon as he was sure that Requiem was deeply asleep, and Damion headed to the mess hall. He was happy to see Juni there and immediately went to sit by his friend.

"You by yourself?" Juni looked surprised, searching behind Damion as if he were waiting for Requiem to appear.

"Yeah. He's asleep, and I just needed space." Damion scratched his temple and looked around the room.

"Something wrong?" Juni asked, frowning slightly.

"Ready for the leave." Damion needed to get away and be around normal people.

"Have a girl lined up?"

Damion snorted. "No."

Juni laughed before he took a sip of his drink. "Need me to arrange a girlfriend experience?"

"I don't need a hooker." At least not at that moment. Not unless his confused feelings toward his Core became worse.

"What's wrong, Damion?" Juni asked, and in that moment, Damion was happy to have one friend.

He may not get along with the other Alphas as well as he had with the Betas, but he had Juni.

He unloaded all his confusion at Juni's feet. He tried to keep his voice down so no one overheard. "I'm not sure how I feel about 47." He tugged at his hair.

"Feel how?" Juni frowned.

"I mean I can't decide half the time if I wanna choke him out or if I want to kiss him."

Juni was quiet for a few minutes. "Kiss? You not getting the girl feelings for him."

Damion punched Juni in the shoulder, hard.

"Son of a bitch!" He yelped and a few heads turned to look at them. Damion beating Juni up was not a new sight and they went back to their meals. "Don't take your sexual frustrations out on me."

"I'm serious." He snapped as he looked at his open palms. "What is wrong with me?"

Juni rubbed his shoulder. "You need to get laid."

"That's it, huh?" he muttered.

"Damion, you've been in a ton of shit the last few months. We both have. When was the last time you got off with something other than your hand?"

His lack of reply was enough for his friend.

"See?" Juni sighed and crossed his arms over the top of the table. "Look. There is a reason why they're made to obey. They've said that it's one of their functions, but you and me, we're not going to do that. My dad always supported my screwing around. He said a man's sexual drive was equal to the factors in that man's life. He said we wouldn't have gods dedicated to sex if we weren't supposed to have it. There are plenty of women here on ship, but you run the risk of one of them spreading gossip about more than your lack of skill in bed."

"I'm fine in bed."

Juni raised his hands. "I'm not offering."

Damion pushed at Juni's shoulder, this time almost dumping the man on the floor. "I'd rather fuck a computer terminal than your ugly ass."

Juni laughed as he clung to the table so not to fall to the floor. "See?"

He shook his head. "See what?"

"You need to get out. When we get to Lunar I'll take you out. We'll drink and find girls to take to some hotel, maybe two apiece, and we'll both feel better. You'll get all of this out of your system." Juni sounded very calm and certain. "And you shouldn't get too attached.

They're waiting for you to slip up, Damion. I get that he may be a friend, you want to protect him, but keep it there."

"All right. Thanks."

"Sure. I am highly educated." Juni winked.

Damion stood up and smacked the back of Juni's head. "You're an idiot."

Damion felt better after his talk with Juni. Maybe his friend had a point. He was only horny, and finding yourself getting too attached to another person could be dangerous. Although Juni had tried a little too enthusiastically to convince Damion that his attraction and feelings toward Requiem were the result of sexual frustration, and it seemed a little unwarranted. Maybe this was merely something Fighters with a bit of a soft spot went through. Or perhaps he could order Requiem to let Damion fuck him stupid, but only once, to get it out of his system.

He felt guilty as shit even thinking about that as he walked slowly back to his room. There would be no way in hell he'd ever be able to ask that of Requiem and then look himself in the mirror the following day.

Requiem

REQUIEM DIDN'T sleep for long, and when he did wake up, he was slightly confused as to why he had done so. It took him a few minutes to realize it was because Damion wasn't there in the room with him. He sat up, the blanket still wrapped around him, and he blinked blearily around the empty space. His gaze fell upon the capsule, and for a moment he entertained the thought of jacking in and finding his Fighter. He pushed the idea aside. For one: Damion had every right to go where he wanted without taking Requiem with him or even letting him know where he was going. For two: he knew that Damion would be very, very angry with him if he came back and found Requiem as debilitated as he might be if he abused his ports even more.

He slowly lay back down, planning to wait with everything but his eyes covered by the blanket. It was then that he felt something he had never felt before, but he could guess what it was.

Loneliness.

Damion

DAMION ENTERED his dark quarters with a long sigh, rubbing his eyes as he tried to get his thoughts back in order after his walk back from Juni. He sat down on the bed to remove his boots and was surprised when he saw the blankets move. "You're awake?"

"I have been in a state of awareness for a while now, yes." Requiem peeked out of his cocoon, his gaze meeting Damion's.

Damion was unable to help the laugh that bubbled out of him at the sight. "You look like one of those odd insect pods they grow on Lunar for the silks. Are you feeling okay? Cold?"

"I am fine," Requiem replied, his gaze intent on Damion's face. He shifted until he was in an upright position, still somehow making it look graceful even while he fought the blankets. The fabric slipped from his head, revealing his shock of white hair standing up in nearly all directions.

Damion reached out and combed Requiem's soft hair back from his forehead. "You feel any better or still tired?"

"Both," Requiem admitted after a moment, his eyes closing. He moved his head to follow the movement. "I do not feel as tired as I did before."

"That's a plus. Tomorrow you'll almost feel normal, and after a while you'll be able to jack back into your computer." Damion touched the port on the base of Requiem's skull. "You can look up what treats are and such. If you don't like the leave to Lunar, then I won't take you off ship again, deal?"

Requiem opened his eyes a mere slit for a moment to look at Damion silently before closing them again. "If that is acceptable to you. I am your Core, to do with as you wish. If you wish for me to leave the ship with you again, I will accommodate you," he said.

A barely audible sigh left Requiem as Damion moved his fingers through Requiem's hair.

"I don't want you to be bored." Damion continued petting him. "You still not hungry?"

"As long as the capsule remains in my possession, I will never be unoccupied with things to do." Requiem didn't notice that he was relaxing more and more and because of that, drifting closer to Damion until he was nearly leaning on him. "I do not require sustenance at this time, thank you."

"All right." Damion took his hand away slowly, reluctantly. "Let's lie down so we can get some rest—or more rest, in your case."

Requiem's eyes blinked open, glancing for a moment at Damion's hand and then up to Damion's face, and nodded. "As you wish." Requiem unwrapped the blankets from his body and smoothed them over the bed so that he didn't have all of them, and then lay back down, close to the wall.

Damion smiled as he pulled off his shirt and boots. Requiem still acted like a child at times, always waiting for his approval. Damion was now getting confused. It would be natural to want to protect his Core. The rest of his feelings were purely pent-up from not having any time with girls lately. He stripped down to his boxers once he was sure he wouldn't embarrass himself with his previous unwanted desires. As Damion lay down and rolled to his side, he gave Requiem another small smile. He wanted to protect him and that was what was provoking this… need. Nothing else.

Damion tucked the pillow under his head, then opened his arms. "Come here, I'll keep you warm."

Requiem hesitated for a moment before obeying, sliding under the blankets and into Damion's arms while facing him. He was smaller than Damion, and it was easy for him to curl up into Damion's hold, resting face to chest as an arm around his neck helped keep him close.

"Are you positive that you are comfortable? I would not want to be an inconvenience to your sleeping pattern."

"Stop asking if it's all right so often," Damion chided in a low voice. "If you're doing something I don't like, I will tell you. We're both comfortable and warm. Now just relax. We'll be on leave before you know it."

Requiem nodded silently, arms curled against his chest, and relaxed further against Damion. Damion was happy that Requiem felt safe in his arms. He watched Requiem carefully until he drifted off to sleep.

Chapter Ten

Saturday August 20, 454 MC
Relay Station, 0953 GMT
Damion

DAMION WAS used to picking out clothing for himself but not others. As he stood in front of a rack bursting with all cuts of pants and jeans, he felt overwhelmed. The relay station was always busy with people traveling to this planet or the next. Juni, though, was right at home and had 108 already in a dressing room trying things on.

"You ever wear jeans?" Damion asked his nervous-looking Core.

They were getting more stares than Juni and 108 since Requiem had an albino look that usually only appeared in the residents of distant Pluto. It was more because of that than the fact he was a Core. Plutonians were rarely ever seen, since the planet was not only small and cold, but primarily held a combination of several research facilities. The scientists who resided there were hermits, introverts more interested in their work than traveling or interacting with the other galactic residents. To see one was rare. A Core from there was a complete anomaly.

Requiem, to say the very least, was extremely out of his element. His ports had still not completely healed, so he couldn't wear his uniforms, and even if he could have, Damion insisted they were out of the question and Requiem left them back on the *Zeus*. He had borrowed a set of Juni's clothes since he and Juni were more similar in size than he and Damion, but they were still a little baggy.

"Jeans? No. I have only worn my uniforms or other materials I have been given to wear by the Corporation."

"I have no idea what size you are either. Do you know your measurements?" Damion picked up a few different styles in the smallest sizes he could find in waist circumference. "Let's start with these. Go into the rooms there, and I'll try and find you a few shirts."

Requiem shook his head and took the pants slowly, clasping them to his chest as his gaze flicked first to the dressing room, then to

Damion, and back again. "Negative, I do not know my clothing size," he replied softly before turning and walking into the dressing room to try on the pants given to him.

Damion was still looking for shirts when Requiem exited the dressing room.

"They all fit appropriately. Although these are a bit too long." Requiem kept his gaze toward the floor as he held out the two he spoke of to Juni. His gaze was almost always focused toward the floor. Unless he was walking, and then he kept them as far down as he could without walking into anything.

"That's great!" Juni smiled, turning to 108. "I think 47 might have a bit more weight than you and even be a bit taller, 108. You sure you're not spliced with a girl?"

"That isn't funny," Damion snapped at his fellow Fighter.

"Damn, man, calm your tits." Juni huffed. "It was a joke."

"Not funny. He's—they—are both men." He turned, handing Requiem a few shirts. "Go find one to wear for now. Are you cold still? Do you want a jacket?"

"It's not cold once we leave the relay station and land on the colony," Juni announced proudly. Despite Damion's original thoughts and judgment when they first met in basic, he had since learned that Juni was not the type of person to consciously flaunt his wealth or family status, but he was proud of where he came from. It was a thin line between the two, but the bright, outgoing man never made you feel lower than him. If anything, Juni's clumsiness made him seem below his Fighter title.

Requiem's gaze flicked up to Damion. Damion was easily shuffling clothing around so that he could grab a shirt. Requiem seemed to be trying to ignore the stares that he was receiving from civilian shoppers. "If it is not an inconvenience, I would appreciate a jacket," he said quietly so that only Damion could hear him.

Damion noticed Requiem's shoulders curling forward and his head bowed lower. He realized Requiem was trying to make his presence as small as possible in a crowd of people who crossed his path and stared at his exposed ports.

Damion reached out and ruffled Requiem's hair affectionately. "Hey. It's all right. Just go put on a shirt, and I'll be right back with a jacket."

"He's skittish," Juni said as they watched Requiem head off. Juni gave a look to 108, who appeared tense as well. "Or they are, I guess, a bit."

"They'll be fine. They've probably never been off ship before, unless they were being transported to another ship."

Damion waited for Requiem to come out of the dressing room. When Requiem walked out and stood next to 108, he was wearing a shirt that was the same color as his eyes. Damion was positive Requiem had no idea how tightly it clung to his chest and arms. The shirt served its purpose and covered his skin and ports. Or at least most of them.

108 looked as wary as Requiem himself, but dressed in black slacks and a matching shirt, oddly tight on his dark frame as well.

"I like it. Wait here." Damion turned and left them for a moment.

After searching the racks, he came back with a light synthetic jacket and handed it over to Requiem. "Give me what you have in your arms there so I can buy them."

"Let me buy it all," Juni offered. "It's coming out of my allowance, and most of that's been saved since we don't spend much on the *Zeus*."

"I can buy him clothes." Damion frowned. "I'm not that poor."

"You can't take money with you when you croak." Juni took out his ID card, which was linked to his bank account, and waved over the happy-looking clerk.

Requiem handed the clothes to Damion.

Damion and Juni continued to argue as the clerk rang up the two Cores' clothes. Damion had a feeling it would come to this, but luckily he could charm the clerk more than Juni.

He was able to pick up most of Requiem's new clothing and almost felt bad for the two Cores standing together, looking so lost. Most other people would call Requiem and 108's expressions bland and even say they were expressionless, but after spending nearly every waking moment with his Core, Damion knew better. The tightness around Requiem's lips and eyes showed unease.

Damion waited for Juni to grab his bags before waving at the Cores. "Let's go. We need to get you two fed before we catch the midday Lunar transport."

"What do you want to eat?" Juni asked 108 as they exited the store. "There's some good and insanely spicy Mars cuisine."

108 lifted his gaze to meet Juni's before looking over to Requiem and then back at Juni again. "Whatever you wish to consume is fine," 108 answered softly, barely heard over the voices of the crowd.

Requiem and 108 were walking in between Damion and Juni, which the Fighters had insisted on for their Cores' protection. Not every eye that looked upon them was curious; some were calculating, looking first to the Cores and then the Fighters who accompanied them, as if judging them and their strength.

There was a small, though lucrative, underground market for Cores.

So the Cores walked in the middle. Requiem was as close as he could get to Damion without actually impeding his movement as they approached a large area that primarily contained restaurants. There were fifteen different self-serve areas and four clerk-run vendor stations, those were more expensive, and the one large full-service restaurant and bar. Juni had the credits and patience to deal with the crowd of people who would be inside there. Juni said it was spicy, and while Mars was known for spicy food, Damion knew there was more taste than heat when his mom cooked. It was the media and food market that produced it far spicier than the meals his mom cooked in her kitchen.

Damion noticed most of the self-serves were offering local favorites. There were a few names Damion recognized from home on the signs. One sign was *Matchellos* and even had a clerk. He had picked up a habit of eating at those counters when he lived back on Mars. It was self-service at home. He wondered if the food was different if someone handed it to you.

"You can go to that restaurant if you want," Damion told Juni. There was a low roar from the crowded room so he spoke louder, "but I am not going to let that stuff rot 47's guts." He knew better than to have Requiem eat something extra spicy. It would just hurt his stomach later. "I'll pick up a few sandwiches from a vendor. I can smell the grilled bread from here."

"Please do not change where you wish to receive sustenance on account of me. I am not all that hungry as it is," Requiem mildly protested, but only Damion would hear it as such. Anyone else would merely assume he was trying to appeal to his Fighter's good side in that monotone voice.

"Juni likes to burn the lining of his stomach off all the time, but that doesn't mean we have to as well." Damion gave Juni a look. "Meet you at the docking stations?"

"Sure. Only thing I can smell is that curry and peppers from inside there. Won't take us long to eat. Twenty?"

"You better make it fifteen, or they may leave your ass behind," Damion teased as the pairs split ways once they entered the large food court.

Requiem

NOW THAT he didn't have Juni and 108 on the other side of him, Requiem made sure to always be touching Damion in some way, as if Damion was his security blanket. He kept his gaze down through the busy hallways of the relay station. It was full of people he didn't know, in a place that was completely and utterly alien to him. So yes, he was a little on edge. Not to mention he was worried for 108 even though the other Core seemed to be taking the whole experience in better stride than he was.

Damion reached out and took Requiem's hand and nearly dwarfed it in his own. "Do you like chicken?" He did not wait for an answer. "Never mind. I'll just order."

Requiem held on to Damion's hand tightly, keeping himself partly hidden behind him and not speaking until Damion had finished ordering. "I do apologize. It seems I do not quite have the aptitude for leaving that which I know. Perhaps it would be easier for you if I took a transport back to the *Zeus*. I do not want to be a burden during your leave. This is not exactly a situation in which you will be able to relax." His voice was quiet and hesitant.

Damion shook his head. "No, if I left you on *Zeus*, then I would only worry. I'm used to you by my side." He coughed and cleared his throat. "Continue to stay close, and it will all be fine."

"Why would you worry? I resided on the *Zeus* without you for approximately three years and rarely had confrontations."

Even saying those words, Requiem knew it had become increasingly difficult for him to be separated from his Fighter. And with his current state of health, although it was improving, he still wouldn't be able to jack in to the computer system and work with projects that would keep him distracted.

"Do you hate spending time with me that much?" Damion teased as he handed Requiem the bag of clothes. "Here. I need to carry the food."

Requiem blinked, eventually releasing Damion's hand so that they could each take what they needed to. "I do not hate, so that is not a possibility. I have no reluctance to being with you in any way."

"Then stop asking to go back to the ship." Damion walked toward an open two-person table. "We will eat and then put up with Juni's babbling all the way to his parents'. I heard him say they had a community pool."

Requiem took a tentative bite of the chicken that Damion had ordered for him, and then, finding the taste agreeable, took a larger one. "I apologize. I was merely trying to make your leave more relaxing for you." He paused, thinking about what else Damion had said. "Is this pool large?"

"You never been to a pool? Well, I hadn't either until I joined the Corp, but it's a large hole with clean water, and it's rather fun," Damion explained between large hungry bites.

"I will have to take your word for it." Requiem ate slower than Damion, savoring the food and the flavors in it. "I must admit that I have an... aversion to being submerged in water."

He couldn't stand to be surrounded by water in a tub, let alone anything larger. It brought back fragmented memories of his childhood that he'd rather not remember.

"I saw that you were stressed in Medical that one time in the tank." Damion had become patient in waiting for Requiem to eat and to speak throughout the time they had been together. "Why?"

Requiem's gaze flicked up to Damion's and then back down to the food that he was now pushing around with his fork. "When Cores are young, mere infants, we are put in sensory deprivation tanks to help us along the path to cease feeling. Feeling emotions, feeling senses, anything. It helps us connect with the system better if we can ignore what is going on with our bodies. To most, there is no lasting effect. For me... there is. I am no longer comfortable in small places and with liquid surrounding me."

Damion nodded. "That's why you hate going to Medical. That, and the doctors keep wanting to run experiments. I understand, but a pool is much larger, and you may enjoy it. You can swim, can't you?"

"That is exactly why Medical is a place that I am wary of visiting," Requiem replied, continuing to push around his food. "No, I was never taught how to swim, nor was learning encouraged. It is not an activity the Corporation approves of us participating in."

"I think you will catch on quick since you're smart. Try and get a few more bites down before we have to leave." Damion reached out and ruffled Requiem's hair. "Please. You're already too skinny."

Requiem briefly closed his eyes under the hand but reopened them as soon as it was absent. He pierced another piece of chicken with his fork. "I am of acceptable weight for my body type," he insisted before taking a bite.

"Not to me, so eat up." Damion chuckled warmly. "I don't want you to be so skinny, and I'm your Fighter, so you're supposed to listen to me."

"As you order, I obey."

"Uh huh." Damion smiled as he sat back.

Requiem followed the orders and finished his meal. While doing so, he wondered why the Fighter worried overly so. Damion wasn't only worrying about his health so that he could stay at peak performance levels to function as a Fighter's Core—he genuinely cared about Requiem's well-being.

After his last bite, Requiem took a sip of water to wash it down, and then did something that Cores were well known for if they thought they could get away with speaking—being blunt. "Forgive my forwardness, but why do you care so much? Beyond official protocol, that is."

Damion looked up, eyes wide and jaw dropped. "I ah… don't know."

"If you do not know, then why do so? It is illogical." Requiem wiped his hands on a napkin before looking up at Damion, meeting his gaze.

"Life isn't like a computer." Damion fumbled for the correct words to explain. "I just feel the way I do, and I can't help it."

Requiem continued to look at him for a moment. Finally, he looked down to his empty plate, cleaning everything up so it fit on one tray, and then tipped it into the trash compactor attached to their table. "The transport is leaving in approximately thirty minutes. I advise that if we wish to arrive in time, we leave now." His voice was cold and mechanical, his gaze on the table.

"You're probably right there." Damion stood, took Requiem's clothes bag, then offered his free hand to Requiem.

Because it was as good as an order, Requiem took Damion's hand in his own, but pretty much his whole body had gone rigid. It was as if the life had gone out of him, like he had reverted back to what he was before Damion came into his life. After all, for all intents and purposes, he was a computer. A living, breathing computer, and that was his purpose. He wasn't supposed to feel, have emotion, or anything else that generally brought out natural humanity and life in other people. This was who he was, or at least what he was meant to be.

Chapter Eleven

Requiem

DAMION WALKED with Requiem to the waiting platform. They ignored all the odd looks people gave them. Whether it was merely the sight of a Core or of Damion holding his hand, Requiem didn't know or care. He was not surprised to see Juni running in with 108 only seconds before the boarding bell rang.

"How can you let him be late?" Damion asked 108 jokingly.

108's gaze flicked to Requiem before it lowered to the ground. "I informed Fighter Juni of the deadline, but he insisted that his pace was acceptable. I believe, despite my warnings, that he lost track of time."

"Ah, don't blame him! I was showing him the cool vids they play in the bars." Juni laughed and nudged his Core forward as the line to the ship began to move.

Damion rolled his eyes. "You mean you were getting drunk before we left."

"Fighter Juni consumed approximately three bottles of the high alcohol content Butterfly beer in quick succession before we left the establishment," 108 reported as he shuffled forward.

The two Cores were again between the Fighters, with Damion in front, still holding Requiem's stiff hand. 108 was behind Requiem and Juni was at the rear. Requiem kept his head down, letting Damion's movements lead him.

"You're not supposed to nark on me," Juni bemoaned as they moved forward.

"You should know better," Damion said. "Or at least brought me one, you bastard."

"You know we're not allowed to have drinks in public except in bars," Juni said to Damion's back. "Though these two would be fun drunk."

"We are not allowed to consume any inhibiting substances," 108 said quietly. Requiem had ceased all communication. 108's words were hesitant but informative. "As for 'narking' on you, per se, if Cores believe that our Fighters have put themselves at less than full capacity, we are encouraged to report it for safety's sake."

"We're not going anywhere to fight, nor are we expected to," Juni answered petulantly

"I think your Core is smarter than you," Damion teased. "Let's just get to our cabin."

"Yeah, and nap the rest of the way!" Juni seemed excited for a long sleep, but after eating and drinking, it wasn't a big surprise to anyone.

They finally made it to their rooms, which were small, but big enough to hold necessities for two people to sleep.

"It is true that you are not scheduled to fight, but not everyone is here on leave and the potential threat of being attacked is 15 percent. It is wise not to drink, currently," Requiem whispered, only loudly enough for Damion to hear as they entered their room. His eyes stayed focused on the ground, hidden by the fall of his shock of white hair, but he was still very observant even through the thin barrier.

He waited until Damion walked into the room first, letting Damion lead him by the hand.

Damion yelled out the door for Juni to keep his ass in his own room for the rest of the trip, before letting go of Requiem's hand. "What's wrong?"

Requiem didn't speak for a moment, his head still down. He couldn't lie to Damion—it was almost physically impossible—but he knew the truth would only start an argument. So he gave him truth without really telling him anything. "You will not want to hear it. It will only make you angry." He walked over to sit on one of the beds without looking up.

Damion rubbed his hands through his hair and sat down on the small bed next to him. "Requiem, please, it's been a long day already for both of us, and it's not over with yet. But ever since we ate, you've been different."

"Then I shall not make it longer by making you upset," Requiem retorted quietly but coldly.

"Stop that!" Damion snapped and glared at him. "Talk normal, damn it! When you sound like that, it… it gets on my fucking nerves."

Requiem finally looked up. "And that is the point. I do not talk in a way that you perceive normal because I am not that way. You feel, because that is who you are, how you are. I do not, because that is how I am, who I am. I am the computer that you are not. Therefore I do not understand why you feel the way you do, nor could I ever. You do not seem to understand that. Unlike others, yes, you do see me as human, as living and breathing, and you do not understand how I cannot feel or have emotions the way you do."

He lowered his head again, breaking the hold his gaze had on Damion's dark, warm eyes. "So perhaps you are at a disadvantage that other Fighters do not suffer from. You see me as human, and it makes you confused because you do not understand the way I am. While others treat Cores accordingly: as the computers and machines that we are."

This could as well be one of the longest speeches Requiem had ever given.

"You're not a computer! I treat you like a human because you are one! You do have feelings!"

Damion was probably yelling because he truly felt that his Core was a flesh and blood human being and not some tool. Damion was disgusted and angry at Requiem for not taking a stand and insisting on his own humanity.

Requiem couldn't help but wince at the fury in Damion's voice, and he leaned slightly away from him. "You said yourself that, for you, life is not like a computer. For me, it is. It's all I know and all I have ever known and probably all I ever will know. The feelings I may have currently are marginal, and even I do not understand them, nor was I ever meant to. You cannot change the way I am, just as I cannot change the way you are."

"I'm sorry. You're right." Damion still sounded angry, but his posture relaxed. "You're right, we are… what we are."

"I am sorry that I am not what you wish me to be," Requiem replied quietly, relaxing as he realized what had cooled Damion's fury. Even if he didn't understand it, he could see the hurt in Damion's eyes from Requiem's ingrained reaction. Requiem tentatively licked his lips, lowering his head even more. "I also do not wish to hurt you or make you feel pain. I… know you will not cause me harm, Damion. My trust is something that I am working on and will try and expedite the process."

"You're fine. It's not you." Damion dry washed his face. "You're the best. I'm only trying to force you to be something you're not, and maybe it's time for me to stop that."

"I am not helping the situation either. I wish to understand you and your emotions, and perhaps that is not something I should be attempting to do. You are only doing what you perceive to be the best for me, while I am looking out for both of us." Requiem leaned forward for a moment, hesitated, and then continued until he took Damion's hands in his own. "I belong first to the Creators and the Chrysalis Corporation. I am completely owned by them, and while my loyalty is to them, my primary loyalty is to you. This in itself is dangerous enough. I am able presently to suppress these changes. If I start to experience a full array of emotions, start to act even more different from other Cores than I already do, they will take action. Not only will you be reprimanded and ejected from service, I will more than likely be wiped and installed into the ship's systems."

A knock on the door interrupted anything more that Requiem might have said.

"Everything all right in there? We heard shouting, and 108 is as jumpy as an acrobatic cat on a trampoline."

"We're fine." Damion patted Requiem's hands. "Sorry. Just arguing with him about sports. Go to bed, you drunk."

"Right. Sports," Juni replied. And then from farther away Damion heard "Sports, my ass" as Juni left.

Requiem tentatively tried to pull his hands away, his gaze flicking to the door and then back to their hands, but knew that Damion wouldn't give up what he had achieved.

"Requiem." Damion said his name in a low voice. "I won't let them kill you. It makes me a bit happy you actually worry about me, but remember I can take care of myself."

Requiem looked straight into Damion's eyes as he said the name Damion had given him. Requiem could see the seriousness in his eyes and he knew that Damion truly meant what he said. "I know you will not let them do anything. But they will do it nonetheless. Besides that, it is part of my function to… worry about you. As I am your responsibility, you are mine." He paused, licking his lips unconsciously, his gaze not breaking from Damion's. "But I do not just… *worry*… about you because it is my function. I wish for you to know that."

Damion had a smile from ear to ear. "That makes me even happier to hear. Then we can just act normal the rest of the trip."

Requiem tried to make his lips mimic Damion's but failed. The facial motions weren't familiar to him, so he stopped after a moment. Seeing Damion's grin caused an odd feeling in his chest that he wasn't familiar with. "That depends on your perception of normal. My normal seems to upset you."

"Ah, but you're my Core, so I don't mind." Damion let go of Requiem's hands. "Now let's rest. I think you'll be overstimulated when we land."

Requiem opened and closed his hands, feeling as if he had lost something for some reason, and his gaze dropped to them in puzzlement. He spoke in a low whisper. "Damion… could I request something of you? I know it is not my right, but…."

"No, it's fine, go ahead." Damion's eyes were open.

Once again Requiem licked his lips. It was becoming a small nervous gesture, and while he was aware of it, he couldn't stop doing it. He looked up, his eyes and face hidden by the fall of snowy hair. "I do not have the right to ask this, but… whatever happens, please… do not leave me and… and protect me to the best of your abilities. Please do not allow them to take me away from you. Whether the reason is my own miscalculations or a machination of their devising, protect me, and I will attempt to protect you in my own way."

"All right. I'll have to keep you around until I'm killed either in battle or protecting you," Damion said with an air of happiness, but also with seriousness.

Requiem stood, going to the bag of clothing to pull out a pair of sleep pants Damion had bought him. They were very soft black cotton pants that looked stark against his pale skin. "That is the only length of time I would ask of you, for if you die, I will die as well." He stripped out of his current clothes without any hint of modesty and folded them neatly, placing them back in the bag before pulling on the sleep pants.

"Why would you die if I die?" Damion asked.

"Because it is the truth. For example, if you die in battle, I will more than likely be with you. Therefore we will both be terminated. Another, if you perish while I am not around, no matter how valuable my knowledge may be, I am considered a liability to the Corporation. While my body may still be kept functional, my mind will more than likely be wiped and I will be connected to the ship's main server, never to regain consciousness. So my consciousness will be terminated." Requiem turned back to Damion, his arms relaxed at his sides.

"That doesn't scare you at all?" Damion frowned at Requiem.

"I do not feel fear the way you do," Requiem replied, walking back over to sit next to Damion on the small bunk. "I am not afraid, as you say, to die. I think I am more… *afraid* of merely existing. Existing trapped within my own mind or not having any mind at all. Of being a drone, a true computer to be used and thrown away. But death, no. Not at all."

"What is your goal in life?" Damion threaded his fingers behind his head and lay back, looking at the metal ceiling above them.

"My goal?" Requiem parroted, blinking as he looked over at Damion. He was silent for a few minutes, thinking about it—or really thinking about how to put it into words. "To be the best and continue being so. And not… and not follow along blindly. To not be a victim because I do not know any other way of life. And continue to think independently and create, understand, and invent devices to make myself and all other Cores safer whether they know it or not." His gaze flicked to Damion's face nervously, gauging his reaction, wondering if he had overstepped his bounds.

Damion chuckled, rubbing his neck. "That sounds like something you would say, but it's a lot nobler than mine. I want to survive. Isn't that sad? I didn't want to do the Corporation's bitch work on my home planet, so I decided to do their dirty work instead. I guess shooting down rogues and pirates really isn't dirty work, but I can't say I don't see where they're coming from either."

"You are a hero. You protect the planets and the colonies from rebels and would-be warlords who would exploit them and harm them. With your skills you will save many innocent lives. And you can leave once your term is up if you feel it no longer suits you. You have the freedom to do so, but when you leave, you will return to your home a hero. How is that not noble?" Requiem pointed out, lying down across the width of the bed, his feet still managing to touch the ground.

"Hero? I'm not sure about that, and where would I go if I left the Alpha Fighters? Back home? Work in the mines?" Damion shook his head. "No. Besides, if I left, I'd have to leave you too."

"You could go anywhere with the skills you are developing and your high IQ. Many are proud and honored to have a Fighter come home and work for them. And your skill set qualifies you to make higher wages. You have many options."

Requiem, however, did not have many options. He was born by Corporation medical advancements, lived by Corporation regulations, and expected to die as property of the Corporation. His only escape from them would be his death, but he'd already made it another goal in his life to make the most of what he had. He turned on his side, his gaze fixed on Damion's face. "And I am not your life. You should not live it according to how it will affect me."

"Kind of hard to think of when my life is heavily dependent on you almost every day." Damion sighed and sat forward to pull Requiem into a hug. "You're like a little lost brother, except unlike my real brother, you don't steal my girlfriends."

"I did not mean to put such a burden on you, and I apologize for making you feel as if I had. I felt as if I needed to be honest and so I was," Requiem replied, losing his balance as he was pulled into the other man's arms. After a moment of stiffness, he relaxed into the warmth, sighing in a previously unknown contentedness. "I would never steal anything that belongs to you. I do not know either what it means to have any siblings, so I do not know what you're referencing."

"You need to stop apologizing so often." Damion gave him a sad but warm smile. "None of this is really your fault. It's just fate."

Requiem opened his mouth to apologize yet again but then closed it, tucking his head under Damion's chin and against his chest. "But it is. I chose you. If it were not for me, you would not be in this situation. I made it happen. So yes, it is my fault. But even if you wanted me to, I would not let you go. That is one order I will not follow."

Damion chuckled. "A bit possessive? If I didn't know you better, I'd be a little worried. We could go back and forth for at least an hour blaming each other, so let's just rest like I suggested."

"I am realistic, that is all. I fought for my right to choose you. If I decide to fight for something, I tend not to let it go," Requiem said quietly, his arms wrapping around Damion's waist awkwardly. "But rest. As you wish."

Chapter Twelve

Saturday August 20, 454 MC
Lunar
Requiem

THEY WERE awake before the transport landed, but Damion had passed the remaining time finishing up the book he'd downloaded before they left the *Zeus*. Of course Juni wasn't awake, and Damion even had to knock on the door and tell 108 to wake him up. Damion didn't know where Juni lived and told Requiem he wasn't about to get lost in the busy city.

While Damion read his book, Requiem had kept himself occupied on the terminal provided in the room. His gaze scanned the console quickly, reading about Juni's satellite and the colony that they were visiting, trying to learn all he could. Despite that, he was still quiet and withdrawn when they stepped off the transport, sticking close to Damion's side.

This particular area was known for the rich and well-to-do. A type of people that, despite Juni, were known for not being kind to those below their station and to those they didn't deem to be proper. While they did not keep slaves because it was illegal, servants were kept for a minimum wage. People who were merely trying to make a living were seen as little more than insects under the foot of the Corporation.

Cores were less than that.

Cores were created—born for a purpose.

They had different purpose within the lives of the rich, even though some of the wealthiest had personal Cores only as status symbols. Quiet dolls, there to serve as personal walking computers for entertainment. Because of that knowledge, Requiem's palms were sweaty, his heart was beating like a hummingbird's wings, and his mouth was dry. He had no idea how to make his body cease its reaction.

When it was time to finally exit the shuttle, Juni yawned and groaned the entire way out of the ship, but the moment his feet touched the docking bay, he was wide-awake and smiling as normal. "Ah! Fresh air!"

"It's still filtered and generated by scrubbers," Damion muttered as he watched well-dressed men and women greet other well-dressed individuals and people overlooking their new "workers."

"Yeah, I know, but it's where I grew up. Come on, Mom will be waiting for us with a big meal. But don't worry—she didn't cook it. Woman can barely open a protein pack." Juni laughed good-naturedly. "She'll be happy to see you."

"Then shut up and move."

108 and Requiem stayed close to their Fighters, keeping their heads down and their mouths shut. Some people, mostly workers, looked at them with curiosity, and one girl even gave them a shy, warm smile. But then there was the upper class that made up a large portion of the population in the terminal. Requiem tried to ignore the glares, turned-up noses, and jealousy in the eyes of passersby. There were mutters and people quickly stepping out of the way so that they didn't have to touch the Cores, even though they were in between Juni and Damion.

If this was humanity, Requiem wanted nothing to do with it.

Juni waved down one of the public transport vehicles, and the driver got out to load up their three bags. It was tight in the vehicle, and the Cores were sitting in their Fighters' laps, but it was only a fifteen-minute ride to the front of the family apartments. The accommodation block was clean, shiny, reflective steel made so that as Lunar cycled through its thirteen-day rotation and the surface heated up to past 695 degrees Celsius , the heat that wasn't collected by the protective dome would bounce off the buildings. During the thirteen and a half days of night when the temperature dipped down to negative 240 degrees Celsius, the dome would release the heat that it had collected during the two Earth weeks of day to keep the colony warm.

Juni got out, handing the man a few credits before Damion and the others followed, grabbing their bags. "They're on the tenth floor."

"It's busy," Damion commented, looking around the crowded streets and airways. "Noisier than I thought it would be."

"The buildings dampen most of the noise," Juni explained as he led them forward. He pulled out his citizenship ID to get past the scanner in front of the desk and the automaton that sat behind it.

Requiem's gaze flicked up and then back down, taking in everything in a split second. Without really thinking, he reached out and ran slightly shaky fingers over the ID scanner, almost lovingly. The feeling of electricity and the familiar buzzing of circuits jumping back and forth in the system beneath his fingers helped ground him and made him relax marginally. Despite that, he walked close to Damion, practically stepping on Damion's shoes.

108 was stiff as he walked but seemed to have put his complete trust in Juni to keep him safe. And Requiem was sure that Juni had talked about his family at length to 108, helping allay some of his wariness. Requiem merely had Damion, who did a quick debrief on Juni's family. The Fighters gave the impression this interaction was common and simple.

They stepped off the elevator, and Juni led them to one of the only four doors on this level of the building. He happily rapped against the door, and it quickly opened. An older woman, probably in her early fifties, stood there smiling. He had heard of women, and men, taking part in expensive skin treatments. Her face showed that her years had been spent serving instead of living in the lush seat of higher citizenship and so she would have been unable to afford such treatments.

"Master Juni, welcome home."

"Hello, Matha." Juni dropped his bags and hugged her tightly. "Is Mother home?"

"Of course. She is waiting for you and your friends in the study." The servant laughed, giving Juni's back a small pat. "You've grown strong."

Juni let her go and took a step back. "Yeah, they kicked our asses in boot camp."

"Language, master." She frowned at Juni and picked up the bags he had dropped. Then she offered to take Damion's as well.

"Hey!" Juni frowned.

She turned her attention to Juni and raised a brow. "I cleaned your backside when you were just a babe." Then she redirected her attention back to Damion and extended her arms to accept his bags.

"Ah, no thanks." Damion shook his head, holding on to his and Requiem's luggage. "I can get it."

"She's stronger than she looks!" Juni laughed at Matha's frown before reaching out and taking hold of 108's hand. "Come on, don't you three stand here like you have red rocks in your shoes."

Juni tugged 108 forward and led him into the large apartment. The place was huge. It had at least five bedrooms, a study, a full kitchen, a dining area, and right when you walked in through the door, there was a large living space.

Damion blindly stumbled after Juni through the immense apartment.

There were thick, vibrant area rugs with patterns, which had originated in the Venus Artistry Institutes. Requiem had done research and such patterns were not available in the open markets on Mars, or Mercury, or even Saturn. As they all followed the excited Juni through the apartment, they passed the kitchen. It was three times bigger than Damion's entire bunk and had a real cooktop and even an instant food fabricator for produce.

"Juni! Juni Mathis! You're home!" a high alto voice shouted from inside the room ahead of them.

Juni let go of 108's hand and laughed as he hugged and spun around a woman who didn't appear a day over thirty, Requiem judged. Either she had had Juni at a young age or she partook of some of the new antiaging surgeries and supplements. Requiem noticed Damion's smile and deduced that Damion found it rather endearing how tightly the woman in the thousand-dollar outfit clung to Juni. Juni had his mother's light blonde hair—the one thing that didn't look altered on the older woman—and even her height.

"You're so thin!" She patted Juni's chest before pushing her hair back, looking as if she were expecting something more from her son.

"They don't serve good food there like Matha cooks us." Juni kissed the top of her head. "And they keep us busy."

His mother tsked. "All that hard work. You should have gone to work with your father or at least taken a station as an officer."

"I'd be bored, Mother." Juni's happy face turned sour for a moment, and then he looked over at the other three people in the room. "Oh, Mom, these are my friends. This is my mom, Daulee." Juni went over and put an arm around 108's shoulders first. "This is my Core. He flies with me in the *Hermes*."

"Oh dear." Daulee wrinkled her nose. "I mean, how nice. I'm sorry. I didn't know you were going to bring home your servant. I thought you were bringing home a girl."

"He's not a servant, Mom. He's my Core," Juni said in a near-chastising voice. "This is Damion and his Core, 47."

"Hello, ma'am." Damion bowed halfway, feeling awkward. "Thank you for letting us stay in your beautiful home. It is more than generous."

"Well, Juni has talked a lot about you since he left." Daulee brushed back her perfectly done hair in a flirtatious manner, seeming to suddenly forget about the Cores.

"He helped me get through basics." Damion stood up straight and gave her a smile.

"Him? He basically carried me through the flight simulations!" Juni laughed, still not letting go of 108's shoulders.

"Well, go settle in. Your father won't be home for another few hours, just in time for dinner as always." Daulee sighed, folding her hands together and looking back and forth between Juni and Damion.

"As always." Juni stepped forward to kiss the top of his mother's head again. "I'm going to give them the tour. Go back to your primping."

"The study is not for primping." Daulee giggled to cover up her embarrassment and tucked her manicured hands behind her back before stepping sideways to block their view of a tall bottle of wine and an automatic cosmetic bot on the floor.

"Of course not." Juni winked and then turned 108 around, waving a hand for Damion and Requiem to lead the way out of the room.

Requiem was silent until the door closed behind them, and then he leaned closer to Damion. "I do not think it was wise to bring 108 and myself here," he stated at a volume only Damion would be able to hear. "Our presence is disturbing to his mother."

Juni was too much in the land of happiness to even attempt to hear Requiem's words, but 108 must have caught them because he looked toward him, nodding slightly. They continued to follow Juni down a long hallway with expensive paintings and other priceless collectibles adorning the walls. But scattered throughout were painted portraits of the family who resided here, giving the home an aura of warmth and not the usual professional-decorator coldness that was common in so many other homes of the wealthy.

"He told me it would be fine. I forgot the part where he can be a complete idiot," Damion agreed.

"I do not say that I understand how normal humans think. But perhaps he was merely too excited about the thought of his family meeting you that he repressed the fact that his family may not want to meet 108 and me. I am not saying that Fighter Juni is a selfish person, merely that this time his own emotional wants got in the way of sense," Requiem replied softly, stepping away from a doorway quickly but elegantly as a servant exited it.

"Yup, sounds like him. At least they don't seem like complete snobs."

"This will be your room, Damion. Uh, yours too, 47." Juni opened the door right in front of them. "There is a full-functioning drink replicator, and you have your own bath and vid screen—"

"Holy shit." Damion's jaw dropped open.

Requiem remained polite. "This will be more than adequate. Thank you, Fighter Mathis, for your hospitality." Requiem bowed his head slightly even as his gaze stayed on the openmouthed Damion. "However, are you quite sure we are welcome here? Your mother did not seem pleased."

Juni shrugged. "Mom will be fine after she moves her things into the bedroom and gets herself cleaned up. They might come off as a bit, well, stuck-up, but really they're not that bad."

Damion put his bag down on the huge bed, still looking around in amazement. "She seemed surprised to see the Cores."

"She wants me to get married." Juni sat down on one of the extra chairs and gave a full-body sigh. "They don't understand why I joined the Armed Forces Division of the Corp. And after they figured I wasn't going to change my mind, they sort of gave up."

"I'm surprised they didn't threaten you or cut you off. I've heard of some people breaking away from their rich families and losing all support. I didn't have any financial support to lose in the first place." Damion patted Juni's shoulder.

"I think Dad thought about it, but I'm the only child, so Mom probably talked him down." Juni turned to the table behind him, and to Requiem's startlement, shouted out, "Make me a Hairy Balls."

Juni smirked at Damion's raised eyebrow. "You can teach the Drinkologist 250 to make whatever you want and then name it too." Juni chuckled and picked up the drink the moment he heard the beep of completion.

"What's in it?" Damion asked as he walked over to look at his friend's idea of a unique drink.

"Would you believe me if I told you I forgot?" Juni laughed, handing Damion the glass tumbler before asking the computer to make another. "I was plastered after one of my dates, and I thought it up."

Damion looked down at the liquid. "Looks red and fizzy." He pulled in a sniff of the drink and cleared his throat before speaking. "I believe you, sadly, and it just smells like it would burn my throat."

"I dare you to shoot it down." Juni sipped from his glass.

"I won't take that dare, and I think you're crazy." Damion sighed, shaking his head and looking at the Hairy Balls in his hand. "I suppose it's better to have some social lubricant in me than none at all, since I'm bound to put my foot in my mouth eventually."

He took a sip of the drink, he tensed, and he sucked in air through his teeth.

Juni laughed before turning to give 108 a warm smile. "Want to taste?"

108 sniffed the drink and all but wrinkled his nose. "No, thank you. I will leave you to enjoy your beverage on your own."

Damion went over and ruffled Requiem's hair since Requiem still seemed a bit tense. Both of the Cores did. "Just stick to the golden rule: stay close to me and it will be okay."

Requiem leaned into the warmth and security of Damion's touch. "I trust you, so I believe in your words. And I will do as you ask." He took solace in Damion's warmth.

"Think you can make it another week without being plugged in?" Damion asked seriously.

"We don't have… pods here." Juni looked at 108. "Will that be a problem? I guess I should have thought about seeing if one could be installed. No way are you two going to be by yourselves in another room. You'll just have to sleep in my bed. Don't worry, it's big enough to share. Uh, unless you're not cool with that."

"That is not a problem," 108 replied smoothly, his gaze fixed on Juni's face.

108 had transformed from the broken man who had been afraid of being abused.

"If I have need, I do not require a pod to jack in to the system." Requiem looked almost longingly at the console in the room. His input points had come a long way in healing but were still a bit raw.

"It won't be as long as you think." Damion was attempting to distract him, futilely.

Juni was already halfway through his drink and still swiveling around and around in his chair. "If you want, after dinner we could go out to the bars and try and get a few itches scratched."

"I don't think I want to go back to the ship with an 'itch.'" Damion sighed. "When did I become so boring?"

"They're clean! I mean, well, they should be for what they cost." Juni laughed, but stopped when he saw 108's bland look. "Uh, guess we'd have to leave you two here, though, since it would be rather dangerous to go out with you to bars."

Requiem didn't quite know what they were talking about except for the fact that Damion was leaving him here. By himself. In a potentially hostile environment. He looked over at 108 and saw that the other Core wasn't particularly pleased with the thought either. But he knew that it would come down to his decision. If he told Damion that he did not want him to leave, Requiem knew Damion wouldn't. But he wouldn't be the one to hold Damion back from having a good time while he was on leave.

"Of course. It would not be wise. 108 and I will be acceptable here by ourselves," he stated, stepping away from Damion to sit in a nearby chair, separating himself from his Fighter to prove to himself that he could. Even if it was less than a meter away. "I am sure we can find something to occupy ourselves."

"I don't know, Juni. They will be in danger here too." Damion gave his friend a small frown.

"They are safe here, I swear on it," Juni said with firmness and perhaps a little hurt in his voice, holding up his hands in a placating motion.

Damion put down his unfinished drink. "I am not trying to insult you. I am just saying they're targets."

"And we haven't been laid in months!"

Requiem leaned forward, reaching out to grasp Damion's hand tightly, making Damion meet his gaze. He was careful to make sure his true feelings were hidden. Damion had become too adept at reading him since they had paired. "Fighter Hawk, 108 and I will be fine. We truly wish not to be a burden on you or Fighter Mathis. You promised me that I would not affect your enjoyment while you were on leave, and that is exactly what you are letting me do. If you wish, please go. We will lock the door after you, and I will alert you if anything is amiss."

"I guess it couldn't hurt to at least go out. I mean, I've never been to an upscale bar before," Damion said slowly. He turned and fixed Requiem with a stare. Requiem was curious why, in the past few weeks, Damion had stared at him for prolonged moments of time far more often than before.

Damion glanced away from his Core and spoke to Juni. "All right, all right. I'll go out with you. However, I make no promise to help you get any girls."

"Like I'd need your help." Juni snorted, rolling his eyes at the absurdity of Damion's words. He turned his head, giving 108 a small smile. "You'll be okay a few hours by yourself, right?"

108 looked to Requiem, who could see his true feelings— nervousness, confusion, and a bit of hurt. But all that was completely gone when 108 let his steel gray eyes meet Juni's. "I will be acceptable. I will stay here with 47 if that is your wish."

Requiem's reasons for not wanting Damion to go were perhaps more selfish than the Fighter could realize. The thought of Damion's hands touching another with the same warmth they touched Requiem made him feel... well, he didn't know *what* he felt, but he didn't like it.

"Let's go see what Matha has cooking." Juni suggested the distraction as he stood up from his chair. "We need to have dinner with the parents tonight yet anyway."

"Do you wish for myself and 108 to stay here so as to not disturb your evening meal?" Requiem inquired, more an extreme suggestion rather than the plea it was.

"You two need to eat as well." Juni shrugged. "Besides, I want to show 108 my room too."

Requiem opened his mouth to protest once again, but closed it as he saw the look on Damion's face daring him to say something against consuming a meal. He knew it was a battle he could not win. "If my Fighter commands it," he said without emotion.

Juni nodded to Damion and Requiem. "I'll come get you two once the old man gets in, so stay here and chill until then." He took 108's hand and walked out of the room.

Chapter Thirteen

Requiem

REQUIEM SAT there silently, his head still bowed until long after the sound of the door sliding closed completed. Only after that did he stand. "May I get you anything?" he asked his Fighter.

Damion shook his head. "You don't like not being plugged in. You're going to go crazy if I leave you alone for a few hours." Damion went to check out the large bathroom.

"You being here will not hold off the need I have to jack in any more than if you are not here," Requiem replied honestly after a moment, staying in the same spot that Damion had left him. "I have the console if it becomes… too much. And you promised me you would not let me become a burden." He watched Damion's movements from underneath his hair. "Of course, if you allow me to do so, I have no say against it."

Damion came out of the bathroom with a frown etched into his face. "I am not saying I wouldn't like to go out, but you worry me."

"I do not mean to do so." Requiem bowed his head even more. And it was the truth. Even if he could lie to Damion, it would have still been the truth. It was the last thing he wanted. "I will work harder at not causing you to worry."

"That won't happen overnight." With a long sigh, Damion sat back down in the chair next to where Requiem sat. "I'm not trying to make you feel guilty. I don't want to put you in danger. I trust Juni, but I want you to swear not to open that door for anyone."

Requiem looked down at Damion, unnerved at the viewpoint of standing over a Fighter as a Core should not. "If you order, your Core will obey," he said softly. This was one order he had no problem agreeing with.

"I don't want to always order you around," Damion explained in a huff. "But by being on that ship and around you nonstop, I'm starting to feel… different."

Requiem blinked as he looked at Damion. Not able to handle it anymore, he knelt next to his chair. "You've never acted, spoke, or felt the same as any other Fighter to begin with. Perhaps that is the difference you feel."

"Maybe. I really don't know." Damion put his head in his hands. "Even surrounded by luxury, you can confuse the shit out of me. I know by being a Fighter nothing makes us normal to begin with, and with me being an Alpha Fighter, we'll be under even more stress sooner than we realize." Damion looked at Requiem. "Do you even feel... need?"

Requiem tilted his head.

"Need? In what capacity do you speak of this?" Requiem shifted so that he wasn't on his knees anymore. He sat to the side, mostly leaning against Damion's leg.

"Lust? Sex? They've taken all of that out of you, but me... I'm... not nineteen anymore, but damn if Juni wasn't right, and I think I might be overreacting because I haven't, well, you know, had sex in a while." Damion let his head fall back on his shoulders. "Gods."

"Why have you not?" Requiem asked. But before Damion could answer, he added, "As for that category of needs, no, I do not have them." Requiem thought about it for a moment, trying to remember the past. "That is incorrect. I did, when I was younger, but did not understand them. I was still contained in the laboratories then, too young to be assigned to a ship or a Fighter. Myself, and other Cores of a similar age, all felt the same thing and were... confused. When we presented the inquiry to the Creators about it, they placed us in the tanks. Eventually the feelings dispersed and they started us on another diet, which contained a suppressant. Something that we continue to consume to this day. I have not had full access to my emotions since. Not even when the other Fighters ordered me to."

"What will happen now that you'll be off that food for over a week? Nothing? Has it melded into your body?"

Requiem shifted so that he was facing away from Damion, leaning against the side of the plush chair, one knee held to his chest. "The chemicals and medications they give us do eventually become a permanent part of our bodies' functions. And I have continued to eat at least a bite of our regulated food at least once a day, as has 108. We have even brought some with us. We do not know what will happen to us if we are away from those chemicals for too long. It has been a steady part of our diet since practically the day we were born and brought into the Corporation. We cannot afford to become ill because of the lack of it, and the possibility of going into withdrawal without it is quite strong."

"You mean it's almost like an addiction? Or something similar to that? Next leave, I'm just going to sleep."

"Perhaps. But since we are unaware of how it will affect us precisely, we choose to be cautious instead. I am no use to you if I become ill or perhaps even perish." Requiem was quiet for a moment, weighing his options. "You did not answer my question. Of course you have every right to choose not to. Why have you not participated in sexual contact?"

"It seemed like a pain on the ship. Most of the girls were trying to suck up to a higher-ranking officer. Don't get me wrong, a few years ago I wouldn't have cared, but then I was promoted and we were so fucking busy, and the rest of my time…."

"The rest of the time you were picking up the pieces of the messes I left behind or created," Requiem finished for him. They weren't the words that Damion probably would have liked, but they were the truth. "Forgive me for saying so, but Fighter Mathis is correct. Going out with him tonight is a wise idea to relieve stress." Although that didn't mean Requiem had to like it.

Damion reached out and touched the top of Requiem's head again. "Yeah, and you two don't seem like the type to enjoy bar hopping and girl chasing. At least I could see Juni get turned down a time or twenty."

Requiem's eyes closed and a contented sigh eased out of him. He relaxed. "And you would not be able to enjoy yourself if I was there with you. You would be too tense and worried about my safety. No, this is for the best. You do not need to be by my side at every moment, and I'm sure you will appreciate some time spent away from your vexing Core." Even if Requiem would not.

"I've become rather accustomed to you being by my side." Damion chuckled. "But yes, a few hours attempting to be a normal citizen might help clear my head."

"Normal. That word again." Requiem slipped out from underneath the comforting touch on his hair. He was starting to realize that he felt like one of the old Earth pets called a dog—a creature that was willing to do anything for the warmth and kindness of its owner's hand. Requiem kept his back to Damion, his head bowed. "May I take a shower before the evening meal?"

"Yeah, sure, you could swim in that white-coated circle they call a bathtub." Damion looked over at the huge vid screen. Finding the control tablet on the table beside him, he punched in the code to dial out to his parents. "Going to see if I can send a wave home."

"I prefer showers," Requiem said softly, walking toward the bathroom. "Enjoy your communications with your parents."

Damion

"CONNECTION COMPLETED," a generic voice said from the control panel.

Damion's mother came into view less than a second later. It had been a few months since Damion had sent her a wave. Since then, her hair seemed to have grown grayer where it interwove into her dark ponytail.

"Hey," he began simply, as he did more often than not—most likely due to the odd sensation of feeling five every time he saw her.

"You look good." She smiled, and Damion chuckled.

"You always say that even when I've been bruised up. Are you receiving the money still? No more problems with the transfers?"

"Yes, we're getting it, and it's drivin' your father crazy how much you're sending. Tell me you're leaving yourself something to live on."

She was always concerned he was sending too much money. If he had still been a Beta pilot, it would have been too much. The transfer to Alpha had increased his salary, and since he did not have a wife and children to support, he and the other single Fighters had more money than most of them knew what to do with—Juni notwithstanding.

"I'm fine, Mom. Seriously. They provide most of our meals, not to mention I wear my uniform nearly every second of the day. So in my downtime, I'm still wearing clothes I brought from home. Well, the pants, that is. The tops I sorted through."

"As long as you're livin' a li'l."

Her concern always made Damion smile, even though he hated that he made her worry with his profession. Even if he died in the next encounter with the rebels, he had signed up for the Chrysalis Corporation's life policy. His family would get a year of his wages outright as long as he died fighting.

"I'm on Lunar, actually." He felt his smile widen as her heavy, wrinkled eyes grew. His mother was always baffled by the small satellite being bestowed its own title. After the mass colonization of what was formerly the Earth's moon, the ones who were pouring money into the venture demanded a proper label. So, Lunar it became.

"It isn't wise to lie, son."

"I'm not!" He laughed. "My friend Juni, he hails from here. Only reason I can afford it is because he's putting us up, and he paid for half the private transport fee. He's generous, and he doesn't have a lot of friends."

"If I believe half of what you say about him, it's because he's pretentious and has a mouth faster than your brother's bike engine." She sighed and shook her head. "Still, be wary when people offer things for free."

"I know, Mom. I know. I'll take a lot of pictures, and I'll send you a gift."

"What about your father?" Her dark eyebrow arched upward.

"He's not one for trinkets, Mom. If I see anything useful to him, I'll pick it up, though. Promise."

Damion never wanted to make promises to his mother, as he never wanted to let her down, but the enormity of her desire for him to include his father produced a strong urge to please. His father rarely kept items that were not of use in the day-to-day activities of a miner. Damion had learned that living simple was not merely a way of life, but a choice for his father. If he sent him some statue, he'd hock it for money to buy a new tool. It served Damion best just to outright buy the tool and avoid sentiment.

"Good." She nodded and then pursed her lips. "Son, you said 'us.' Are you seeing someone?"

"Oh." He straightened up as he began shaking his head. "No, no, not like that, Mom. Just me and my Core."

"You took it with you? Why?" His mother's frown was of undeniable reproach. "We are not a slave-keeping family."

"Mom"—he cut off her tirade—"it's not like that. I swear to Hera it is not. He belongs to me, yes, but also the Corporation. I need to keep him safe, and the best way to do that is to keep an eye on him."

"I don't like those things," she said in a hushed voice.

"He's not a *thing*, Mom. He's a person. He didn't ask to be a Core. I can at least treat him well. You always told me to treat men with cautious civility. Mom, 47, he won't hurt me. He physically can't, and I think it's civil for me to make sure no one hurts him."

"You make him sound like a dog." Her nose wrinkled as she flapped her hands. "No, no, we're not going to discuss this while you're on your leave."

"Okay, Mom." He rubbed a hand over his face. "I, uh, love you, and I'll send you a wave as soon as I can."

"You mean as soon as you remember." She let out a small bark of laughter that was very unladylike and completely endearing.

"Yeah." He laughed and waved. "Goddess bless, Mother."

"May the gods protect you, Son."

Damion was closing the call as Juni returned, announcing that his father had arrived home from work and they would sit down to eat in the next ten minutes. Damion was not looking forward to this dinner and hoped this would be the only meal he was obligated to attend.

Requiem

REQUIEM WRAPPED a towel around his waist before he came out of the bathroom since he hadn't taken any clothes in with him. Generally, when it was he and Damion, he didn't bother since Cores didn't have a problem with modesty, but he didn't feel right being bare in front of his Fighter's friend. Keeping his gaze down, he went to the bags and opened them, pulling out the first thing he found before scrambling back to the bathroom to change. He could hear Damion's and Juni's voices drifting through the door.

Requiem saw Juni shaking his head and grinning as he disappeared into the bathroom.

"He shy?" Juni laughed.

Damion sounded amused as he spoke. "Not usually. We will be down for the dinner, don't worry."

"And after?"

"Yes, I will go out to the bars with you." Damion sighed. "But you're buying!"

Requiem came out a few minutes later, completely dressed and his hair slick to his face from combing. He was wearing tight jeans and a long-sleeved black button-up shirt that Damion had bought him. Requiem figured it would put Juni's parents more at ease if they didn't have to see his multitude of input ports. He couldn't hide all of them, not without gloves and a cap, but he could hide most of them.

"Is it time?" he asked Damion, thankfully not sounding like he was asking if it was his time of execution.

"Yeah. Ready to face the head of the household?" Damion's smile was not broad or amused.

"If you do not mind, I will abstain from answering your question," Requiem replied, stopping next to Damion, his gaze on the ground. He knew that very soon Damion would be upset. From what he'd read, it was common for the servants of a household to eat separately from the owners and guests. Requiem knew that Damion wouldn't stand for that and there might be a bit of an argument. "Do you mind if I suggest that in the next hour or so, you concentrate on… keeping your temper if I or 108 are the topic of discussion?"

"What do you mean by that?" Damion spoke slowly in a way Requiem had noted meant he was attempting to control his temper. "It's just a dinner. After which they will ignore us, I'm sure." He gave the top of Requiem's head a pat.

Requiem closed his eyes for a moment. Damion was not a man who worried about angering others. Requiem opened his eyes and released a small sigh. "Just a thought." He followed him out of the door.

They followed the smells of food and the low rumble of voices. As they walked down the expansive hallway, Damion kept one eye on Requiem, as if to make sure he didn't scurry off or one of the other servants didn't try to pull him away. Now, after Requiem's warning, Damion really was on edge.

As they came into the dining room, Juni and his father were talking, and from the way Juni's neck was turning red, it wasn't all good.

"Look, Juni's friend is here," Daulee Mathis announced in a falsetto tone. She had changed into a cream dress and put her hair up. She also wore more jewelry than before. She cut in between father and son and wrapped her arms around Damion's left arm. "Judas, this is Damion."

Juni's father had a strong square jaw, cold hazel eyes, and stood almost thirty centimeters taller than both mother and son. He was wearing the garb of a Chrysalis Corporation executive and a disapproving frown. The frown slowly smoothed out, and he nodded in Damion's direction.

"Welcome to our home. Thank you for looking after our empty-headed son," Judas quipped before stepping away. "Forgive me, but I will return shortly."

Juni's mother made an unsettled laugh as she watched her husband leave the room. "He is just off to change his wardrobe. He won't be long."

"Ah, it's fine. Am I intruding? I can go out with my Core if it would be easier," he offered but saw Juni begin to flush red.

"It's fine. It's fine. He's just being a stubborn old ass—"

"Juni! Your manners. That's your father," Daulee snapped as she tugged Damion forward.

Requiem didn't quite know what do to once Damion was pulled from him. His gaze flickered quickly around the room, and he spotted 108 standing against the wall next to the kitchen door, trying to look as small as possible. Moving quickly, he joined him there and hoped they wouldn't be noticed or be the cause of any trouble, but he also knew that wasn't likely to happen.

"What is your favorite food?" Juni's mother asked, not letting go of Damion's arm.

"I enjoy a good shepherd's pie," Damion told her, looking more on edge than before.

"What is that?"

Juni spoke up. "Damion, they want the Cores to eat in the kitchen, and I told my father no, but I…."

"I *do* disagree with sending them away," Damion said simply, leaving it at that.

Requiem let out an inaudible sigh. He had tried to warn Damion. 108 turned toward him, worry and slight fear in his gray eyes before he returned his gaze to the floor. Requiem stepped out from the wall, bowing his head as well.

"We do not wish to create any discord in this household or between family members. We go where our Fighters wish, though." Requiem said loudly enough for all to hear his emotionless voice. He turned toward Daulee. "Shepherd's pie is a dish made with ground lamb, peas, onions, with a mashed potato top and baked in the oven."

Juni's shoulders deflated after Requiem's words, and Requiem watched as even Damion's fight leaked out of him.

The universe seemed intent on pointing out how different they all really were in life and the fact that he, as a Core, could see how much the argument was causing ripples and the Fighters couldn't, or wouldn't, admit it, proved that once again.

"I think you two should pick out some food from the kitchen and enjoy it in my room. If that is fine with you, ma'am," Damion suggested.

Damion obviously didn't want the Cores to sit around with strangers gawking at them and have to deal with their disapproval.

"That is a wonderful idea," she exclaimed, tugging Damion forward toward the table again.

"As you order," Requiem replied softly. It was true that he didn't want to be there, didn't want to deal with Juni's prejudiced parents. But he also didn't want to leave his Fighter, and a look over at 108 told him that he agreed.

"I will take them to the kitchen and walk them back," Juni said in the tone more of a reprimanded child than an Alpha Fighter.

Requiem sent a look back at Damion, but Damion didn't catch it. After that, he directed his gaze back to the ground and let Juni lead him and 108 out of the dining room.

Damion

ONCE JUNI and the Cores had gone, Daulee started talking to try and cover up the awkward moment. Damion let her steer the conversation since the woman seemed to be enthralled with the sound of her own voice. He pulled out her chair and offered her a seat. He hoped to, at the very least, come off as polite.

Judas entered the dining room as Damion took his seat across from Daulee.

"Damion." The patriarch of the household sat down at the head of the table, putting Damion on his right and Daulee on his left. "Tell me about growing up on Mars."

Damion worried he had taken Juni's seat and contemplated how to move without being rude. "I doubt there is much I can tell you which you would find interesting, sir."

"I'll let you know when I'm not interested. Now, your family are miners, correct?" Judas turned to a servant and asked for drinks to be served.

"Yes." Damion had a suspicion Juni's father knew more about his background than Juni did. "As far as we know, our family has always been on Mars. Mom, for some reason, couldn't trace one member back to Earth."

"Few people can." Judas folded his hands on top of the table. "Have you heard the stories about how we began to branch out from Earth? During our expansion there were a number of groups who opposed the dangers and science behind our colonization of each planet. Some of those radicals even attacked the Earth's remaining genealogy center."

"Radicals generally have good points but are quieted by the side with the bigger guns." Damion interjected.

"I do not see what point they were attempting to make by destroying centuries of genealogy records." Judas's voice was pitched low, ready for another rebuttal.

Daulee jumped into the conversation. "Do you have brothers or sisters?"

"Yes. A brother and a sister."

Her smile was vibrant and filled with a familiar warmth. "Your mother must be truly happy."

Damion shook his head and leaned back, allowing a suddenly appearing servant to fill the wineglass in front of him. "Yes. It's hard work, but Mom always seems to try and brighten our spirits and keep us out of trouble."

"Your father told you to enlist."

"No." Damion corrected Judas's assumption. "He did not want me to go, neither did Mom. It was the right choice for me and my family."

Juni's father picked up his glass and began swirling the red liquid around. "You are one of those who sends home nearly half of his pay."

"Yes, sir." Damion picked up his glass, but he forwent the swirling before drinking the wine. He was sure the beverage cost at least half of his monthly earnings. Hell, the room he was given was bigger than his whole home on Mars, and the vid took up an entire wall. And Damion wasn't even counting the bathroom and another smaller room that was used for visiting servants.

"That is very generous of you." Daulee had not moved a muscle to drink the wine.

"I don't have kids, or a wife, or anything to spend money on while I'm in the Corp." Damion shrugged and wondered where Juni had gone.

"Do you not worry about needing money once you leave the Alphas?" Judas's tone was amused.

"No. I'll probably die in service before I get to spend everything I get to save. Alpha pilots have a ten-year shelf life at the best." He should have picked his words with far more tact as he regretted them the moment he saw Juni's mother's painted eyes grow wide.

"Good thing, then, that we're the best!" Juni interrupted the words that were about to tumble out of Daulee's open mouth. "We have the Corporation's best Zodiac ships, and we have Cores to help us not blow up."

He put a kiss on top of his mother's head before sitting next to her. "Besides, the Corporation hasn't had a really tough fight in a long time."

"You've barely been in the service and already putting yourself in danger!" Daulee's voice bordered on a screech.

"Calm down," Judas snapped at his wife. "He picked this course, and you supported it despite my reservations. That negates any complaints you may have now, wife."

Daulee's mouth snapped shut and her happy smile faded.

"Gods damn, Dad, tone down the disapproval for ten minutes." Juni tossed up his hands.

Damion was regretting coming to Juni's home. The level of his discomfort was rising by the second.

"The only thing I approve of, at the moment, is you having enough skill to even warrant selection into the Alphas. Despite the dubious report on how that came about."

Damion cut in. "Dubious? The process is simple. A Core is assigned to a Zodiac ship and if that ship has no pilot then the Core chooses a pilot. We had an opening in the Zodiac fleet because a pilot took a position as a sergeant at the Fleet Academy a week before. And Juni is a great pilot."

"Yes. I am aware of the Zodiac Cores' functions as I manage the Lunar Core program. I am more aware of their abilities than either of you. To be entrusted with such a valuable commodity is a great gift. I hope neither of you squander it."

Damion doubted Judas Mathis had any idea what Requiem could accomplish. Damion also knew Judas held the same view on Cores as the majority of people. Commodities. Computers. Soulless shells made to serve and nothing more.

"Dad, shut it. We know what our Cores are worth. We'd only be Betas if it wasn't for them. And you don't work with the Cores, Dad, you deal with the program's accounting. You might manage numbers, but we fly with Cores. We know what we have." Juni's hands became fists on top of the table.

"I hope you do, for your mother's sake. It would break her heart to lose you because you were too busy showing off rather than doing your duty. After your contracted time expires, I expect you to return home as promised." Judas waved a hand toward the servants, and they brought food to the table.

Damion saw the vein in the back of Juni's hands bulge, a sign of his anger. "All I promised was to consider what I wanted to do."

"As your friend said, the life span of most Alphas is ten years. By the time your contract comes up, you'll be nearly six years in. Reenlisting back into the Alpha squad is a death sentence," Judas snapped.

Daulee's hand shot out and caught Juni's raising hand before she spoke in a trembling tone. "Let's enjoy dinner."

Damion wondered if his own mother held the same concern and worry over him as Juni's mother did for his friend. He could tell Daulee wanted the conversation to end, not due to where the argument was heading—to a full-blown verbal war—but because of the talk of Juni's life being in danger.

Judas cleared his throat. "Yes. Let us."

Damion silently prayed to the goddess Eleos that the food was good and they avoided any more talk of Cores and death.

Damion was happy when dinner was over. He was even happier that he could get out of the tension-filled apartment. Juni's parents didn't seem like bad people, but they were definitely not normal working citizens either. At times Damion hadn't been sure if he was being complimented or judged.

Requiem

"Remember to lock the door and don't let anyone in," Damion told Requiem as he got ready to leave.

Requiem was sitting on the large bed, but at Damion's words, he stood up and followed him to the door. "As you order. Enjoy yourself."

"Try and watch out for each other." Damion squeezed Requiem's shoulders. "And don't worry. We'll be back in a few hours."

"I will not worry, and we will remain here together so that there are no separate incidents," Requiem replied, keeping his gaze lowered. "I will inform you if there are any problems."

"I hope there won't be." Damion ruffled Requiem's hair.

Damion stepped outside the room and met Juni at the front door. Even the normally happy Juni looked stressed and ready to drink. They headed out together.

Requiem slowly closed the door after them, locking it securely by typing in the code Juni had given him. Afterward, he placed his hand over the panel, changing the code to something only he would know. He turned back to the room, his gaze falling on 108, who was standing next to the bathroom door, looking as lost as Requiem felt.

Requiem indicated a seat, silently telling 108 that they should sit down. He then proceeded to turn the vid screen to a technical programming station, where they could try and lose their minds in new information.

Chapter Fourteen

Requiem

IT WAS past 3:00 a.m. when Damion came back with a heavily inebriated Juni.

"You are too damn loud," Requiem heard Damion warn as they neared the guest room door. "And I've had to practically carry you through the streets to your parents' house, you laughing idiot!" Damion did not want Fighter Juni's parents to hear their son so drunk.

Requiem quickly rose from his chair and went to the door. 108 was asleep on the sofa and had been for a while, leaving Requiem to make sure no one disturbed them. There had been someone outside the door at one point, causing a few nerve-racking minutes for Requiem as the person knocked a few times, sighed, and then left. But that had been all.

After he keyed in the pass code, the door slid open to admit the Fighters. 108 awoke the moment the door opened and Juni's drunken voice filled the room.

"I don't know why those girls were so damn prissy!" Juni looked at the two Cores and waved. "Hi!"

108 quickly and easily took Juni from Damion as if he had to do this type of maneuvering often. As soon as he had Juni balanced correctly, he started down the hall toward the inebriated Fighter's room. All without saying a word.

"I have to start picking better, or at least smarter, company to keep." Damion sat down in the nearest chair and began to take off his shoes, asking Requiem, "How was your night?"

Requiem stayed within the doorway, watching 108 and Juni walk away, his gaze trailing Juni's hand as the Fighter slid it down 108's back and grabbed his ass. 108 looked at Requiem for a long moment, nodding at him to say it was all right, before they disappeared into the bedroom. Requiem let the door slide closed, keying the lock.

"Uneventful," he finally replied, walking over to Damion and kneeling down to help him take off his shoes. He tried to ignore the smells that surrounded Damion: scents of alcohol, sim tobacco, and a fragrant perfume. "Yours?"

"It started out fun." Damion rubbed his eyes, not even objecting to Requiem's help. "Then the girls became crazy, and Juni drank more, and in the end we got lost."

"Crazy? Lost?" Requiem asked in a monotone, pulling off Damion's socks and putting them neatly inside the boots before tucking them under the chair. He stood and began to pull Damion's shirt off, getting him ready for bed. "So you did not have a relaxing experience?"

"Nah, it was fine until I had to carry Juni back." Damion let out a rusty chuckle. "Made me feel sixteen for a few hours."

"I am thankful, then, that you had a pleasant time." Requiem folded the shirt neatly and put it in the laundry chute. He crossed the room and retrieved a glass of water, handing it to Damion. "You needed the relaxation."

"Let me guess—you were bored." Damion had a smile on his face that didn't go away. "It was fun seeing Juni get smacked."

"I was acceptable," Requiem replied and then tilted his head, confused at Damion's obvious good mood. "Why was Fighter Juni struck?"

"Because he tried to make a pass at a lady who was with someone already." Damion laughed. "Twice! I was more afraid of the boyfriend showing up." Damion drank some water and then took a deep breath. "Definitely high-scale bars here."

"I see. For a Fighter who was once praised for his observational skills, perhaps he should stay in a Zodiac and not on the ground." Requiem stood to the side of Damion's chair in case there was anything else he needed to do. "Will you be going out again?"

"Tonight? Hell no." Damion shook his head. "Right now I think sleep is the best thing for me to do. Also, Juni was on his second set of shots for the night and in our second bar. After that I was burnt out."

"I did not mean this evening." Requiem took the empty glass from Damion's hand and set it to the side so that he could pull Damion to his feet. Damion might not be as drunk as Juni, but he was still somewhat inebriated. "So the alcohol impeded Fighter Juni's observational skills?"

"Alcohol impedes a lot of shit and then makes you feel like you're ten times bigger and stronger than you actually are." Damion walked over to the bed slowly. "As for going out again, I'm not sure. I think Juni had planned on giving us the five-star tour tomorrow."

"If my observations of Fighter Juni's personality are correct, I can assure you that he will attempt to convince you to go out again." Requiem held on to Damion's arm to help him, but he was not expecting Damion to flop on the bed facedown, pulling Requiem with him. Letting go of Damion's arm, Requiem sat up, sighing imperceptibly. "What happened to the women you were with?" he asked, merely to keep Damion awake while he tried to get him into the proper position for sleep so that Damion didn't wake up with a kink in his neck in the morning.

"They went on their way." Damion rolled onto his back slowly and let out another sigh. "Just didn't work out. Dancing was fun, though. It's been ages since I danced with anyone."

"What did not work out?" Requiem asked, undoing Damion's belt so that Requiem could take his pants off and leave him in his boxers.

"First, I refuse to pay for sex even if Juni was all up for the thought, and second, I was worried where we'd take them. I don't know if they have love hotels like they do on Mars."

"Love… hotels? I do not understand." Requiem put the pants down the laundry chute and then maneuvered Damion around so that his head was on the plush pillows. Requiem tugged on the blankets to free them from under Damion's heavy body. "Explain, please?"

"You know, places that you bring someone to have sex for a few hours," Damion said matter-of-factly as he lifted himself enough to allow Requiem to pull out the blankets. "Never heard of them? Really?"

"There is much that Cores are not informed of and are encouraged not to learn. Anything pertaining to sex is one of those subjects," Requiem replied, pulling the blankets over Damion as soon as he got him into place.

"Don't worry, I doubt we'll ever be going to one, and neither of us can afford a Countessa."

"Why would we ever go to one? And what is a Countessa?" Requiem slid off the bed, going to his bags of clothing so that he could change into his sleeping clothes.

"You know… the legalized prostitutes." Damion closed his eyes, and his voice began to fade. "Hmm, Requiem?"

"Yes?" Requiem undressed from the clothes Damion had insisted he wear on Lunar, before changing into a pair of sleep pants.

"Come here for a moment." Damion reached out to pull him closer.

Requiem had gotten his pants on when Damion's large hand wrapped around his elbow and pulled him back onto the bed. It was a common feeling, Damion pulling him constantly off balance. He sat up, turning so that he was sitting on the bed, facing Damion, the man's hand still wrapped around his bare arm.

"It may just be the alcohol, but I don't think I'm that drunk. And yet I still can't get you out of my head," Damion admitted in a slurred voice. "What does that mean?"

Staring at him, Requiem swallowed in what he could only guess was *nervousness*. "I… do not know what it means." But he knew how Damion felt. Requiem could not stop thinking about his Fighter either. Being around Damion was the only time he felt safe, real even. "Perhaps the reason is merely that we are in each other's presence nearly all the time. So when I am not there, you feel like I should be because I am generally with you. I am sorry if I inadvertently came in between you and your evening."

"It's not just about being together." Damion pulled Requiem a bit closer. "It's about the attraction."

Damion's motions effectively pulled Requiem's arm out from under him, making him fall back so that he was lying next to Damion. "You believe that you think about me often because… you are attracted to me?"

"I don't know what I'm feeling other than I want to kiss you again." Damion slowly leaned closer to Requiem and then hesitated.

Requiem was too shocked to stop him even if he thought it was a bad idea. He didn't mind, but the last time Damion had done something like this, Damion had regretted it immediately afterward. He was about to say so, but by then Damion's soft lips were on his own and Requiem couldn't say anything at all.

Requiem kept his eyes open, not knowing if he should close them, as he pressed his lips back against Damion's. Originally, it was out of curiosity, but once the soft flesh was on his own, a warmth filled his body, making him feel… *complete*. Wanted. Needed. And that was a large thing that he had been looking for in his life-event, though he hadn't realized it until that moment.

Damion's eyes were closed as he kissed Requiem. His hands clenched for a moment before he pulled away. He opened his eyes and smiled at Requiem. "Thanks."

"You are welcome," Requiem replied softly, a bit of wonder in his voice. "But… why? If it is okay to ask, that is. Last time you did this, you immediately regretted it afterwards. Despite my assurances that I did not mind. Why do it again?" He could feel Damion's hand tighten and then loosen on his arm, as if the man were restraining himself.

"I don't fucking know," Damion answered. "Because you've been raped before? Because we're two guys, and I've never been with another man. Because it just seems like a really bad idea even if I can't help myself wanting it."

Damion paused a minute, his lips pressed tight before he continued. "I should have drunk more."

"Why would drinking more have had any effect on your decision?" Requiem pulled his arm free and slid toward the edge of the bed, his long legs dangling over. "You've already explained to me the difference between rape and consensual sex. With you, it would not be rape. You are too… good-hearted to ever force me to do something I do not wish to do." He moved off the tall bed and stood. "As for the other reasons, I do not have any answers for you. That is obviously something you need to work out yourself."

"I've been trying," Damion said as he appeared focused on Requiem's lips. "Sorry. I know this must be confusing for you as well."

"I must admit, it is rather confusing, yes. And I still do not understand how drinking more alcohol would have helped the situation, but I have a feeling you are in no position to answer that either." Requiem walked to the entrance of the servant's room, where a cot had been made up for him, out of Damion's sight. "Once you understand your own mind, let me know, so I can be relieved of this confusion. For now, get some rest. Sleep well."

After having given the orders for once, Requiem shut off the lights. Perhaps everything that had happened since Damion returned to the room would make more sense once Damion was sober. However, Requiem was confident of one thing. Damion was nothing like Morales or Requiem's other previous Fighters. If Damion had wished to go further, it would have been more than acceptable to Requiem.

Chapter Fifteen

Sunday August 21, 454 MC
0536 GMT
Damion

DAMION HAD fallen into a fitful sleep. He missed the days when he could drink all night and sleep like the dead until the next afternoon. What finally woke him up was Juni. Juni's loud, annoying voice screaming into his ear and shaking him harder than a Saturn meteor strike.

"Wake up! I need to talk to you!"

"For fuck's sake, what is it?" Damion smacked Juni's arms away.

"I, uh, I had a lot to drink," Juni babbled, suddenly shy and quiet with eyes that looked at everything but Damion.

"Yeah, and?" Damion scrubbed his face and looked around for his Core.

Requiem had been the one to let Juni inside. He followed Juni into the bedroom and winced as Juni proceeded to wake his Fighter in a way that wasn't very pleasant.

Damion was still blinking blearily. He saw Requiem placing a glass of water and a dose of Clear Head on the bedside table while Juni was still babbling.

"How drunk would you say I was?" Juni asked in a shaky voice.

Damion gave Juni a befuddled look after thanking Requiem for the water and pill. "Pretty drunk, but not enough to puke on yourself. Close, but not that close. Why?"

"I… well…." Juni licked his lips and looked nervously between Requiem and Damion.

Damion had a headache, but he wasn't brain-dead. He could tell Juni was uncomfortable with Requiem around, which was odd in itself because usually he didn't mind blurting out his heart in front of the Cores. "Will you go check on 108, please?" Damion asked Requiem with a gentle smile.

Damion noted Juni's refusal to look directly at him. Requiem frowned slightly, a mere pursing of his lips. He nodded. "As you order."

Requiem

REQUIEM LEFT the room quickly. It was barely six in the morning, GMT, but the servants of the household were already up. He kept his gaze down, hoping that no one would stop him. No one did as he reached Juni and 108's room and knocked gently on the door, waiting for 108 to answer. When 108 didn't after a few moments, Requiem keyed the door open and slipped into the dark room.

His gaze immediately fell on 108, highlighted by the bathroom light as he stood in the doorway of it. All 108 was wearing was a pair of boxers that appeared hastily tugged on. His body was taut with tension.

Requiem walked over and gently grasped 108's arm. 108 didn't resist as Requiem pulled him back into the large bathroom and pushed the door closed behind them.

Getting 108 under good light so he could see him better, Requiem looked over the dark skin, assessing his physical condition. Those steel gray eyes looked slightly glazed, and 108's full lips looked to be a combination of reddened, fuller, and maybe a little bruised. There were bite marks dusting 108's neck, shoulder, chest, and sides. He knew humans called those marks hickeys. Requiem turned him to see if there were any other marks, any signs of abuse, and saw none.

He finally met those nervous eyes with his own. "Did Fighter Mathis hurt you?" he asked softly.

108's eyes widened slightly for half a second before he shook his head. "No," he whispered in a hoarse voice.

"Did he rape you?" Yet again, Requiem received a shake of 108's head. "Was it consensual? Did you want to?"

A pause and then a slight, barely perceivable smile and a nod. Requiem responded with his own nod, releasing 108's arm. "Are you acceptable?"

"Very" was the husky response.

And now it was Requiem's turn for a widening of eyes and a tilt of his head, a moment's contemplation. "Good. My Fighter sent me to check on you. Not only to make sure if you were in an acceptable condition, but also because Fighter Juni would not converse with him while I was in the room. Do you need help getting dressed?"

"No. Thank you," 108 replied and then looked down. "I require a shower."

"Then do so. I will go back. Contact me if you have need of me."

"Very well."

Requiem left, even more confused than he had been before he went to sleep.

Requiem

"I THINK I fucked 108," Juni blurted out only seconds after Damion took his pill.

Damion sputtered and coughed, likely gagging on the pill he had just swallowed, followed by the sound of his cup crashing down onto the nearest surface. "*You what?*"

"I woke up and we were naked and he looked, you know, how women look after you screw them all night long… and hard." Juni swallowed audibly after he squeaked out the confession.

"You bastard!" Damion grabbed Juni's shoulders.

"Wait! Wait! I didn't mean to!" Juni threw his hands up to ward off the intended beating. "And he didn't look, you know—hurt or anything."

"He is not," Requiem said from the doorway, having overheard them as he entered the room. "He is perfectly acceptable." He paused for a moment, thinking back to his encounter with 108. "A few bite marks, and he is walking a bit differently, however."

Juni turned red and began sputtering. "I-I can explain, I mean, I don't need to really, but I—"

"For the love of the fucking Earth! You're a complete idiot." Damion let Juni go and sat back with his head in his hands. "You came back quick," he told Requiem.

"There was no need to remain. Once I was assured that 108 was not harmed nor forced to do anything against his will, I returned. He was planning to take a shower when I left, and I expedited my return so he could do so. He did not need my assistance. If you wish, I will wait out in the sitting room until you have further need of me." Requiem turned away as soon as he finished speaking, to spare Juni the embarrassment of having to face him. He walked to the side of the room and began to pull out their clothing for the day.

"No, no just… get ready for the day." Damion waved a hand, and he appeared unable to look at Juni. "I should have drunk more."

"Huh?" Juni sat up and gave him a confused look. "But… what do I do?"

"What do you mean 'what do you do'?" Damion glared at him. "You better not screw around or I'll kick your ass."

"Screw around? What? Are you saying I have to date him?" Juni sounded scared, his eyes wide and his voice high.

"Do not hurt him," Requiem insisted before he could help it. He snapped his mouth shut, clenching his jaw from anything else he might say. His gaze flicked from Juni to Damion, unnerved if he may have crossed a line he shouldn't have.

"I won't… yet," Damion said, still giving Juni a heavy stare as Juni said at the same time, "I didn't plan on it."

"I was speaking to Fighter Mathis," Requiem told Damion. He held the folded clothing against his chest as he sat on the edge of the bed. "If I may speak freely?" He paused, his eyes flicking to Damion before turning his gaze to the comforter. "108 did not mind what you did, not at all. He said it was consensual. 108's life up until this point was full of unpleasant experiences, and he does not view this one as such. It does not… please me that you seem not to remember the experience, but I do not see why it should not happen again if you both choose. Just… do not hurt him. Physically… but emotionally as well."

"Did I just get relationship advice from a Core?" Juni quipped.

That earned him a firm smack to the back of his head from Damion.

"Ow!"

"Listen to him," Damion said. "It's not good you had drunk sex with 108, but now you have to take responsibility for it. Got it?"

"What a vacation," Juni whined, rubbing his head.

Requiem gritted his teeth, keeping his mouth shut before he told Juni that if he didn't want to deal with the situation, then he shouldn't have caused it. "You need to get some more sleep, Damion. As does Fighter Mathis. It has only been approximately two hours and twenty-seven minutes since you arrived back from your night out. And I am sure that 108 needs the rest as well."

Juni huffed. "I'll stop by the kitchen and tell them we won't be needing breakfast, then do my fucking best to avoid my mother and father so I don't have to explain anything. Just get up when you want and come to my room, and we'll eat out." Juni sounded less harried than when he had first arrived, but he also sounded almost saddened now.

"Don't be a complete idiot and try and pretend it didn't happen," Damion warned.

Requiem's gaze flicked up to Juni and then back down. "He did not mind, Fighter Juni. You have been the first person to ever touch him with kindness. He trusts you, and not only because you are his Fighter. He trusts you as a person."

"Thanks." Juni gave Requiem a small smile. "See you two in a few hours."

Damion watched him trudge off. "That, I should have seen coming."

"I do not see how you could have," Requiem said, pushing Damion so that he was lying back down. He pulled the blanket up to Damion's chin. "I advise getting some more rest. The Clear Head will only work for a little longer without true rest."

Requiem slid off the bed to stand, but Damion reached out and caught his hand. "Where are you going?"

Requiem's gaze moved from Damion's grip up to his face. "Back to bed myself, if that is all right with you?"

"No. Sleep here."

Requiem paused a moment, his gaze on Damion's hand again. "As you wish," he finally replied, sitting back down on the bed.

Damion wrapped one arm around him, looking so happy that Requiem didn't say no. Closing his eyes, Damion took a deep breath and then let it out. "If I had been as drunk as Juni, that could have been me, and that wouldn't be fair, would it?"

"To whom? You are the one who keeps saying that you wished you had been more inebriated all evening," Requiem pointed out, relaxing against Damion's warmth.

"I don't know." Damion's voice sounded pained.

"Forgive me for saying so, but I must admit that you are more confusing than you claim me to be at times."

"I think that's because of the emotions I'm plagued with, and you're simply confused by them."

"I will not suggest ignoring them, for that is how we got into a disagreement last time." Requiem sat up, his gaze lowered so that he focused on Damion's neck. "Do not worry about 108. When I saw him, he was… content, or as happy as our type can be. I feel as if he finally found some semblance of peace in his life."

"How do you feel about it all?" Damion reached out to gently tip Requiem's chin up.

Requiem appeared to honestly think about it for a moment, keeping his eyes from Damion. "I am… content with it. I am pleased that 108 is finally becoming his own person instead of the tool he was before. He is beginning to think for himself, to make his own decisions. And Fighter Juni's exuberance and kindness are what he needs, even if they are vexing to you at times."

"It's because he doesn't use that thing called a brain unless he's flying," Damion grumbled and then continued in a stern voice. "Look at me, dammit! You're making me feel bad."

"I did not mean to," Requiem replied softly, fighting the hold on his chin.

"Then just come out and say what is on your mind!" Damion let out a frustrated sigh.

"I feel that I have already said everything I wanted to say." Requiem's hand rose to grip Damion's wrist under where he was holding his chin. "Everything else is… too confusing to form into complete thoughts."

Damion let go of him. "Maybe sleep would help both of us."

Letting out a soft sigh, Requiem nodded, releasing Damion's wrist almost reluctantly. "As you wish."

Sometimes Requiem was so frustrated by how he was unable to describe what he was feeling inside. So vexed that he was never taught the words that corresponded with certain emotions, making it impossible to explain things clearly. Because he was feeling more and more every day. More things that he did not understand.

"Damion," Requiem finally whispered after a long silence. "Are you still confused? Still trying to come up with an answer?"

"Answer? I know what I want." Damion groaned in apparent frustration, "I sound like a cliché. I wonder what you want."

"What… I… want?" Requiem sounded, yet again, confused. That was one emotion, feeling, that he could definitely identify and he was becoming displeased with it. "I am meant to want whatever you do."

Damion shook his head. "That isn't the same thing."

Requiem shifted, moving under the covers with him. The chill finally got to him. He lay alongside Damion, soaking in his warmth. "How do you know it is not?"

"I, uh, don't?" Damion pulled him closer

"Exactly. Nor do I know what you want since you did not previously know what you wanted yourself. So how do I know whether you would like me to stay here with you, or whether you'd like me to leave and go sleep somewhere else?" Requiem asked quietly, his head on Damion's chest, his eyes hidden by his hair. He himself had no idea what he was saying, didn't really know what he wanted besides Damion's warmth, kindness, and tenderness. He would do anything to make Damion content. He paused, licked his lips, and swallowed down another feeling he couldn't identify. "I want whatever you want, Damion. Not only because it is my place as a Core to think this way but because I want you to be happy, content, and would do anything to have you be so."

"That makes me happy, except that isn't you saying you're ready to have sex either." Damion sounded disappointed.

"Is that what you wish?" Requiem asked almost inaudibly. "I… do not know anything about sex in the definition you've given me."

"It's… I don't know. It's sex." Damion groaned. "It can be great, really great, but not if both people aren't into it."

As Requiem leaned up, he balanced himself with a hand on either side of Damion's shoulders. "Then what do you wish for? You put your mouth on mine, but each time you regret it or wish you were more inebriated. I cannot tell you what you want, nor can I tell you what I want, for I do not quite know what you speak of when you say 'consensual.' All my experiences were not, so how am I to know? I have nothing to draw a logical conclusion or hypothesis from."

Requiem was confused, frustrated, and tired with the whole situation.

"Just… tell me when you want to have sex," Damion said quickly.

Blinking, Requiem looked down at him, and frowned a little. "I… do not understand. How does one make these types of decisions?

How does one know when it is time to do so? Is this what you wish for me to do?"

"That is sort of the problem I'm having," Damion grumbled.

For the first time, Requiem made a small growl of frustration. Bending his arms, he pushed into a sitting position. "If you cannot even understand it, how am I, a Core, supposed to? You are the one with emotions. The one who can understand them, know what they are. You are the one with the answers. I do not see how I am supposed to know these things and make even a plausible theory out of it." He sighed, turning his face away. "This is probably why the Corporation kept us from learning about them. In the end, computers and the system are easier to understand. More rational."

"For once I agree with you." Damion sat up as well. "Look, that is why I haven't made you have sex with me, all right? I know it's supposed to be one of your functions, but I don't want you to feel forced or obligated. I wished I had drunk more to give me more false courage to go through with it, but I can't risk you reverting back to the way you were."

"That is no longer an option," Requiem replied, suddenly very tired. "The way I have become since I chose you is something that will not go away. It is a result of not eating full portions of the supplement." He said those words in his normal tone, but it was obviously casual, almost flippant. "And you have rarely forced me to participate in something I was not willing to do in the first place."

"Then come over here and kiss me, but only if you don't mind me taking things to the next level," Damion dared lowly.

Requiem looked at him for a moment, his head tilting to the side. He honestly didn't know what would happen if he did as Damion ordered. But as much as Damion didn't think it was, it was that, an order. So he leaned over and pressed his lips to Damion's, curiosity and maybe a little unknown fear filling his head. Not of Damion—never Damion—but of where this experiment would lead.

Chapter Sixteen

Damion

DAMION WAS shocked that Requiem had actually kissed him. He knew this would change things, but no matter what happened, Requiem would always be his Core. The last of his moral barriers broke as he placed a hand on the back of Requiem's head and began kissing him—*truly* kissing him. Damion slipped his tongue between the trembling lips while he dragged the thinner man even closer. He was fully aroused and not too hungover to know exactly what he was getting himself into. He had never had full-out sex with another man. There had been drunken nights of experimentation in boot camp, but never penetration.

As Damion tucked Requiem under his body, he kept kissing him and threading his hands through the silky hair. It was as if a dam had broken and every hidden desire that Damion had felt for so long was bursting forth.

Requiem seemed shocked when Damion's tongue entered his mouth, and he began to pull away. Damion curled his fingers through his hair, impeding him. Hesitantly, Requiem slid his tongue along Damion's, gently exploring his mouth. Requiem slowly placed his hands on Damion's rib cage.

Damion moved his lips from Requiem's, down his pale neck and chest. He didn't know what would please Requiem, so he licked at the left nipple first, waiting for a reaction.

Requiem jumped slightly at the touch. "Strange," he mumbled. He moved his hands from Damion's side and back to the bed. "This is unexpected."

Damion gazed down and saw Requiem finally start to respond. Damion lightly scratched his nails down Requiem's pale sides as he kissed his way back up his chest to those waiting lips. He tried to ignore the lost look on Requiem's face. He supposed this was different from Requiem's other sexual experiences because those times were rape—and this wasn't. He hadn't ordered Requiem to have sex with him. The problem was that Damion wasn't sure *what* to order him to do.

Damion rocked his hips down into Requiem's, needing the friction of the silken pale skin. His cock was now hard as steel and aching for any sort of stimulation.

"New. Never felt this before." Requiem's eyes widened as Damion's hardness slid against his own, separated by mere cloth. Damion's mouth and body held him gently against the soft bed beneath them.

"My body. Warmth. Sensations." Requiem gasped.

Damion's nails on Requiem's tender sides, his mouth on Requiem's chest, neck, and lips—everything caused his Core to tremble.

"You okay?" Damion asked, feeling Requiem shiver as Damion began to pull down Requiem's sleep pants with gentle but needy tugs.

Requiem licked his lips and nodded, and the eyes that met Damion's were wide and filled with ever-changing emotions. "It is… interesting. And also very perplexing," he finally replied, his hands still gripping the bedding beneath him.

"Not scared?" Damion had pulled the pants down and was about to touch Requiem's shaft when there was a knock at their door.

"No, not scared." Requiem's head slanted in response to the knocking, yet he did not appear worried. "I think the emotion could be identified as *nervous*, but I am not sure."

Damion tensed as there was another, more persistent knock.

"Do you wish me to answer it?" Requiem asked. "This is an unfortunate interruption."

"No, no just…. Gods damn it, yes!" Damion got up from the bed and headed to the bathroom. "Just… find out who it is, but give me ten."

Requiem

"As you order," Requiem said, suddenly cold from the lack of Damion's warmth as he left the bed.

Requiem took a deep breath, settling his body back into its normal state, and sat up. He blinked, seeing something odd. His penis was… well, doing something interesting that it had never done before. As he watched, it slowly seemed to… deflate, going back to the state that he knew was normal.

"Huh," he mumbled.

Hearing the banging on the door again, he slid off the bed and pulled his sleep pants back up. He walked to the door and spoke the unlock code to allow it to open, tilting his head slightly as he saw a dark-eyed, bedraggled Juni at their door. Again.

"Fighter Hawk is in the bathroom at the moment," Requiem said, lowering his gaze.

"Damn it." Juni pushed past Requiem and walked quickly into the room. "Hurry up, Damion! I need to talk to you."

No words came out of the bathroom, only a deep grunt.

Requiem keyed the door closed behind Juni, letting out a silent sigh at the other Fighter's back before moving into the room as well. "May I get you anything?" he inquired softly.

"No, no." Juni shook his head, tapping his fingers against his leg in impatience or nervousness. "I just need to talk to Damion for a moment."

The bathroom door slid open and Damion appeared, looking equal parts pissed and exhausted. "What?"

"You tired?"

"What!" Damion's dark eyes filled with fire.

"I mean, do you want to leave now? I mean, I can't relax." Juni fidgeted, rocking from foot to foot.

Requiem looked up at Damion and stepped back. He had never seen Damion look that angry before, except with Arkin, and that had been a different kind of fury. Arkin had been a feral, deadly, cold anger. This… this was blistering, somewhere along the lines of intent to strangle Juni, and Requiem was relieved that it wasn't directed at him. At least, he hoped he didn't cause it.

"Perhaps, Fighter Juni, it might be a more logical idea to walk around your home. Fighter Hawk is very weary and not feeling all that well," he suggested quietly. "Unless what you need to speak of is of high importance?"

"Go to your room and deal with your Core and wash up. Don't come back to this room for at least another three hours or I swear on my Zodiac I will beat you with the closest object I have available," Damion said in a very low voice.

"Uh… right. Okay." Juni backed away from him with trepidation.

Requiem stepped away from Juni and Damion, then ordered the door to open before Juni ran into it. Once Juni had left, Requiem gave a lock command and then he stepped back against the wall, watching Damion warily

"He—he, I will kill with my own hands one day," Damion growled, clenching his fists at his sides. "If he wasn't competent in a Zodiac, I would wonder why he even joined."

Requiem stayed silent, continuing to watch Damion and keeping his back to the wall. Damion calmed down slowly. The rapid rise and fall of his chest ceased, and the flush of his face faded, but he was still angry and tired, and Requiem didn't know where this anger had come from. Didn't know if he had caused it or if Juni did, and he didn't understand why Damion was so upset. So he stayed there, remained quiet, and waited.

Damion looked up. "What?"

Requiem opened his mouth to lie, to say that nothing was wrong, but his voice wouldn't work. He could not lie to his Fighter. "Why are you so upset?"

"Because he disturbed us. Because… because I just had to jack off in the bathroom like an embarrassed teenager with his mom at the door." Damion sat on the bed. "Aren't you frustrated?"

Requiem stayed where he was, his gaze following Damion. "So… you are not angry with me, then? I did not upset you?" He ignored Damion's question and decided he would ask later what this phrase "jacking off" meant.

"No, no." Damion shook his head quickly.

"So you were merely angry at Juni for… stopping us?" Requiem tilted his head to the side.

"Yes." Damion sighed, his shoulders slumping forward. "It's two steps forward and five steps back."

"I do not understand. Was there a time constraint I was not aware of?"

"It's hard to… keep it up, and even harder to get the mood back." Damion tried to explain, his hands circling in the air in front of him with useless motions.

Finally pushing away from the wall, Requiem walked over and slowly, hesitantly sat next to his Fighter, thoroughly confused. "I am sorry. I really only comprehend half of what you are saying, and I have a suspicion that asking you to explain will only result in you becoming more frustrated."

"It's not your fault, okay? I'm sorry. I guess you didn't have a problem with getting it to calm down, huh? I kinda figured you wouldn't." Damion gave him a weak smile.

"Getting what to calm down?" Requiem asked with a slight frown, thinking, then connecting the dots. He opened his eyes wider. "Do you mean my penis?" Requiem asked bluntly, looking down to his lap. "I must admit, I was very intrigued. Are you saying that is supposed to happen? It has never done that before."

"Damn." Damion covered his face with his hands. "Why am I not surprised you can say that so easily?"

"Did I say something wrong?" Requiem asked, reaching out to grasp Damion's wrist lightly.

"No." Damion laughed. "I just can't shrug off a huge woody as easy as all that. And I can't say… *penis* without being reminded of the health book they pass out at the clinics."

"But that is what the organ is called," Requiem replied, realizing he was beginning to get a headache from the confusion. "Besides, I have already informed you that the chemical in the food Cores eat prevents us from experiencing sexual stimulation. Because 108 and I have begun to eat less than the prescribed daily amount, it is beginning to have certain effects on our bodies. Personally, it was unexpected that I reacted at all."

"I know that's what it's called, but most of us don't call it that." Damion wrapped his arms around Requiem and rested his head on the top of his Core's.

Requiem was silent for a moment, thinking, and then realizing he was uncomfortable in his current position. Moving slightly, he slipped out of Damion's warm arms, trying to decide how he could attain optimal relaxation. He sat back down, but this time across Damion's lap. "There are other names for it?"

"Uh, yeah. Slang. When you can plug in again, just look for them," Damion suggested as he wrapped his arms back around Requiem. "Better you learn that way."

"As you order," Requiem replied quietly, laying his head on Damion's shoulder and closing his eyes. "There is much I do not understand. I thought I understood a large amount, but I suppose there is still much I have to learn."

"You know a lot, Requiem. More than any other human when it comes to computers and the systems, but when it comes to everyday life, you are a bit behind, and that's only because of how you were raised." Damion brushed his hand over Requiem's hair.

"I was not raised, Damion. I was grown and then created, molded if you will. But I would not use the term "raised" in connection with my upbringing." Requiem wrapped his naked arms around Damion, soaking in the warmth. It seemed he was always cold unless Damion was holding him.

"All right, sorry, I didn't mean to upset you." Damion sighed. "Want to try to sleep a few hours again?"

"You did not upset me. I was merely correcting your misconception." Requiem nodded. "Sleep, yes. As you wish." He began to slide off Damion's lap, already regretting losing the warmth.

"Come back here," Damion grumbled, grabbing his arm. "I want you to sleep next to me."

"I will not disturb you?"

"No, not at all." Damion tugged Requiem forward again.

"Very well," Requiem replied wearily, falling wherever Damion pulled him, suddenly too tired to move himself anywhere else. Cocooned in his Fighter's arms, Requiem had never felt so safe and protected or fallen asleep so quickly.

Chapter Seventeen

Tuesday August 23, 454 MC
1117 GMT
Requiem

"EVERYONE READY to go to the temple for offerings today?" Juni asked, walking right into Damion's room.

Requiem had examined Damion's increasing agitation in conjunction with Juni's and 108's sexual activities. The more apparent sex they had, the more verbally disparaging Damion was toward Juni.

"Think the Goddess would listen if I asked her to strike you mute?" Damion smirked.

"Might I suggest using duct tape instead?" Requiem came out of the bedroom with Damion's shoes and placed them on the floor next to his feet. "It is an ancient invention but still very effective to this day." He opened his mouth to say more, then realized that what he was going to say might not be appropriate, so he closed it. Requiem believed that duct tape was more effective than sending prayers to a force that only existed in the collective minds of worshipers looking for an answer. An answer they eventually pulled from their own thoughts but insisted came from a higher power. He did not believe it was plausible.

"You would miss me," Juni said rather proudly.

"Sure I would," Damion answered dryly. "We're ready. It should be interesting seeing a well-funded and established temple."

Requiem reached out and gently grabbed Damion's wrist. "Is it proper for 108 and me to attend?"

"Yeah, I don't think it will be a problem." Damion looked to Juni for confirmation.

"They'll just think you two are servants." Juni's smile slipped some. "But it is beautiful."

"If you believe so," Requiem stated, reluctantly letting go of Damion's arm.

"Just stay close." Damion's common mantra came out naturally.

"There's a speeder outside waiting, so let's go!" Juni clapped and rushed out of the room, probably to collect 108.

Requiem followed Damion out the door. He had read about the temples and had to admit to some curiosity about them. But it was still more than a little nerve-racking to be leaving the sanctuary of the room.

Damion put a comforting hand on his shoulder. "You don't have to be so worried. Nothing happened the other day when we went out and looked around the neighborhood. The only difference is we're going a bit farther in."

Not saying anything, Requiem placed his hand briefly over Damion's before letting it drop. Damion had been so busy looking around at the tall, beautifully structured buildings that he had not seen the looks of contempt and curiosity that he and 108 had received from passersby. Contempt from the locals, curiosity from the servants walking around.

Unexpectedly, the Cores had one ally within the house in the form of Matha, the head servant of the Mathis household. Matha had been the person outside their door the first night while Juni and Damion were out, apparently checking up on the Cores. Since then, she had discreetly left them sweets and other things when she delivered their clean clothes every morning. When they saw her in the halls or when she came to tidy the rooms, which the Cores kept nearly immaculate, she favored them with a smile and a wink. Requiem had been wary of her at first, as he was with anyone except for Damion and a few others, but 108 had assured him that she meant them no harm. He had begun to thank her, which seemed to please the middle-aged woman greatly.

They walked outside, where a fancy and expensive-looking speeder waited beside the curb. Requiem knew Damion appreciated speeders, having seen him watching them in vids and remarking on the look of them. This one had a highly polished metal exterior and the silence of its engines was impressive as the transport hovered about thirty centimeters off the ground.

"This yours?" he asked his friend while appreciating the black-tinted windows.

"Nah, my dad's. They refuse to buy me one since I wrecked one when I was fifteen." Juni grinned. "It wasn't my fault."

Damion let out a snort of disbelief. "Of course it wasn't. Who's driving?"

"Me of course!" Juni announced, running to the left side of the vehicle.

"We won't make it to the temple in one piece." Damion gave Requiem a wry grin.

"He has yet to run into the *Zeus* during sims, and a Zodiac is much more difficult to control than a speeder," Requiem replied. "He is within the top class of Alpha Fighters. I am not concerned. Although, I would be even less concerned if you were piloting." With a faint smile to Damion, he slid gracefully into the back seat.

At Juni's command, 108 sat in the passenger seat next to him. Luckily the darker Core slid his seat up, enabling Damion to stretch out his legs. Damion had a moment to look at the red-lit digital controls before he lurched forward.

Juni sped off into the city abruptly, making Damion grab on to the door handle. "You drive like a madman."

"I drive like I have a purpose. Right now my purpose is to make it to the temple in under ten minutes." Juni chuckled almost maniacally.

Damion gave his friend a peculiar look. "How far is it?"

"About twenty minutes away!"

Juni laughed at Damion's groan.

Requiem was intrigued by Damion's death grip on the door handle with one hand and the near crushing grasp on Requiem's with the other. Damion was tense.

Excessive velocity did not bother Requiem, nor the thought of death in a speeding vehicle. Perhaps the slight worrisome feeling was because Damion himself did not have control over the vehicle, because Requiem had seen Damion's love and need for speed in the way he piloted a Zodiac. Requiem moved his free hand and placed it over Damion's as he moved his gaze from Damion to out the window, watching the buildings pass in a blur of motion.

Juni made it to the temple in a little over eleven minutes, and Requiem wondered how the local law enforcement hadn't pulled Juni over. He tried to shake off that feeling as he looked at the immense temple through the window of the speeder.

"This is just one temple?" Damion asked.

"The largest one on Lunar. Modeled similarly after the Parthenon in ancient Greece," Requiem said quietly, looking over the large building.

There were two levels on which worshipers could watch over the ceremony. Cylindrical columns surrounded them and gave the illusion of infinite height—an elaborate illusion, since Requiem had calculated that the ornate ceiling was approximately 60.9 meters above the altar. Each architectural embellishment had been gilded. Gold reflected from the hovering light fixtures that circled the columns, shining onto the marble floors and giving the temple what Requiem would define as *grandeur*.

Damion was still shocked speechless as Juni led them inside the temple. Afternoon prayers had already started, but they weren't the only group running late. He kept hold of Requiem's hand.

His grip on Damion tightened, his knuckles white with the pressure he was exerting. As soon as they entered the temple, with its lines of benches, his gaze lowered to the marble floor. Too many eyes on them, on him and 108. Damion had asked him to wear a sleeveless button-up shirt that left his arms bare and the ports on them exposed for all to see.

Requiem could feel his heart beating faster, audible to his own ears as Damion gently directed him onto a bench seat near the center of the temple. Requiem slid along the marble seat, the thick velvet cushion making it bearable to the backside. He stopped next to 108, who had seated himself before Requiem.

Damion and Juni had put the Cores between them while they sat and listened to the priestess.

Requiem kept his head down and his mouth shut throughout the service. Most of the time his hands were in his lap, clenched tightly together. The few times he did venture to look up at 108, the other Core looked enraptured by what the priestess was saying, her voice reaching everyone just by using the acoustics in the expansive building.

The center of the ceiling above the priestess opened in a perfect circle, letting bright sunlight in. It was an impressive sight, but it was also functional since during major holidays, a large bonfire would be needed. The shrine had two white candles that had the names of the god and goddess carved into them. Today's offerings were for Artemis and her husband, Ares. The first candle, representing Ares, was larger than the second—Ares was a god of far more import in this temple. A procession began from the back of the temple to the front. The priestess's voice rose as the chanting filled the space around them. Two large men passed, dressed in red robes, and one held a large gold chalice filled with red wine, which he stood on the altar in front of Ares's candle. The second placed a sheathed dagger next to the bowl.

Another procession began for Artemis, this one with two women dressed in white. The younger woman bore an armful of yellow and white flowers. Wildflowers, Requiem believed they were called. The older woman held a small replica of a bow and arrows. As those were placed, there was another eruption of chanting from the crowd.

Gaze flickering down to 108's hands, Requiem saw 108's fingers wrapped around Juni's wrist. Juni's hand had settled on the inside of 108's upper leg, merely resting there, looking as comfortable with its placement as 108 was with having it there.

Requiem turned back to his hands, closing his eyes again. He came to the conclusion that he was inexplicably afraid of people in general, or at least the majority of people he didn't know. He couldn't even listen to the service; he merely sat there.

Damion was watching the ceremony closely until he glanced over toward Requiem, and then he reached up to gently ruffle the back of his hair. Although Damion was enraptured with the service, Requiem felt out of place.

Requiem looked up at him and saw the swift, comforting smile Damion gave him before he looked back to the priestess. Damion's warm hand was still there on the back of his neck, and it seemed to channel confidence into Requiem's body. It was then Requiem became aware that no matter what, Damion would be there for him. Would protect him from the swarms of people around him even if it meant Damion's death. He was Damion's… not his property, no. But *his*. His to protect, to take care of, and watch over.

That, out of everything, allowed Requiem to relax and look up and listen to the spoken words.

Damion only took his hand away when the ceremony came to an end and people began to empty their pockets of money for donations. Young boys and girls stood holding silver bowls at the exits. He leaned over Requiem and asked Juni in a low voice, "You leaving anything?"

"Nah." Juni shook his head slowly. "Not today."

"Really?" Damion sounded shocked at his friend's response.

"I leave mine at another, smaller temple across town." Juni shrugged and looked around as if he was expecting to see someone.

"Which temple?" Damion asked.

Now that the ceremony was over, Requiem lowered his gaze once again. He had attempted to keep his head raised, but once the ritual was over, people started looking around at him and 108. Cores were rarely seen off their ships, and those who owned personal Cores wouldn't dream of bringing their "servants" to temple. So seeing not just one, but two in a place as common as a temple sparked people's curiosity.

Leaning back in his seat so that Damion could talk over him, Requiem felt a small, warm, slightly damp hand run over the port on the back of his neck in tentative curiosity. Somehow he kept from jumping and turned partially to look over his shoulder. A young child with brilliant green eyes stared back at him in open fascination. The little girl now sucked on her hand, stuffed in her mouth, that had tentatively touched Requiem's port, a wondrous smile that only a child could make formed around it. Requiem stared at the child, and the child looked back unabashed.

Until a large hand gripped the wrist of the mouth-implanted hand, pulling it out and away. Requiem looked up, ready to defend the child who was so roughly handled, only to find a matching pair of green eyes set in an adult male face frowning disapprovingly down at him.

"Mind your eyes and keep them off my daughter, servant," the man spat, tugging the child down the row. "Come along, Asrith," he told her in a tone that was no warmer to the tiny girl.

Asrith looked back over her shoulder at Requiem, waving with a small smile as she was dragged away, pattering her small feet swiftly to try and keep up. Haltingly, Requiem raised his hand and waved back.

"That was unbelievably rude." Damion glared at the man's retreating form. "I can't believe he's in this temple acting like…. Never mind, yes I can."

"Hey, don't start a fight here," Juni said in a serious tone for once. "My father would kill me."

"I won't." Damion sighed. "We done, then?"

"Want to go down a way and stop off at the smaller one for Ares?" Juni offered.

"Sounds good."

"Do not concern yourself with it. I am used to it," Requiem whispered to Damion, feeling his body still tensed for a fight. He placed a cool hand on Damion's forearm to placate him. "It does no harm."

"She was only being curious, and he acted like you were a dirty piece of trash." Damion was upset. "Let's just go."

"Follow me," Juni said, slipping out of the bench to the left.

Requiem didn't want to explain to Damion that, to the man, he *was* dirty. He was an abomination—a hybrid of man and technology that just wasn't natural to the normal population. Core popularity had lowered considerably the past decade and they were not looked upon favorably or with anything but general disgust. He followed 108 out of the row, waiting there for Damion to exit before falling in beside him, his gaze once again on the polished marble floor.

Damion went with Juni and was happy to get out into the fresh air. "I'll admit that it's an awesome sight, Juni. The priestess was also very good and she didn't bore me at all, but…."

"A little too snooty for your taste?" Juni smirked and didn't sound a bit upset about what Damion thought about it.

Requiem and 108 kept silent and close to their Fighters. While Requiem's head was down, his hair covering his eyes, 108 kept looking around with open curiosity.

"Let's jump in the speeder. I think you'll like the next temple a bit more." Juni slipped into the driver's side of the transport again and Damion slipped in the back with Requiem.

"Like I have a choice, since I really don't know where we are to begin with." Damion chuckled.

"Sure, sure." Juni made sure the Cores were in before speeding off.

Chapter Eighteen

Requiem

REQUIEM FINALLY lifted his head, looking out the window as he took Damion's large hand in his so that Damion could use it in place of gripping the door handle. The city was beautiful, from its tall, ancient-style buildings to its glittering atmospheric dome that simulated daylight while still showing the stars through a hazy glow. You could even see Earth like a beautiful blue-and-white gem decorated with starlike pricks of light still on the planet in the distance.

"We are going to another temple?" Requiem inquired softly, not looking away from the window.

"I want to take you to one that I usually drop by when I'm home." Juni seemed excited.

"Is it to the sex goddess?" Damion was half-joking, half-serious.

"No!" Juni laughed.

"There is a goddess specifically for sex?" 108 inquired in his soft voice. 108 hardly ever spoke above a whisper as it was.

"Not really just for sex, but more for romance. Or it's supposed to be, but there are people out there who hope the more they give, the better their sex life will become." Damion grinned. "Do you need that, Juni?"

"Fuck no!"

"Fighter Mathis's sexual lifestyle has already improved 100 percent since arrival on Lunar," Requiem said in a clinical voice, his gaze still not leaving the blurring scenery. "It is not probable that he would be able to go over that percentage. Only lower it."

Juni's ears turned red at the unexpected jab from Requiem. "Hey!"

Damion was too busy laughing to make any response.

Finally turning his head, Requiem blinked as he looked toward the now nearly crying Damion. "Did I say something incorrect?"

"No, no you're right, and that's why he's pissed." Damion wiped away the few tears that had escaped.

"Bite me," Juni grumbled as he shifted in his seat, uncomfortable at the teasing. "Not like you're getting any."

Requiem's gaze flicked from Damion to Juni and then back again. He opened his mouth to say something, thought better about it, and then turned his gaze back toward the window.

Juni drove a good long time through the town. Suddenly the decline in status of the area became more apparent. The Chrysalis Corporation liked to boast on the vids that poverty did not exist in the Corporation's main settlements, but that wasn't always true. They only hid it a lot better than the countries of long ago.

Juni stopped in front of a small store that sold clothing. "We have to walk the rest of the way."

"Where are we going?" Damion looked around at the dilapidated area of town. "You actually hang around here?"

"Yeah, some of my best friends came from this side of town." Juni shrugged and took 108's hand.

Requiem exited his side of the car, looking around briefly before closing the door. It was definitely much different from the area they had just left. The ancient buildings were still there and it appeared no one had taken care of them in over a hundred years. Buildings were dull with dirt, crumbling with disuse, and decorated with paint in ways that were obviously not a part of the original design. Trash littered the streets, and the smells from it, as if an air circulatory had been broken for a while, reached his nose.

Requiem walked around the speeder to stand next to Damion, his gaze lowered but not fixed on the ground anymore.

Juni walked forward with a purposeful look on his face. "Just stay close."

Damion had told Requiem that when you went into a part of town such as this, it was best to not act like you were a tourist. If you looked out of place, you became a target. Unfortunately, Cores would always look out of place, except on the *Zeus* or other Corporation ships. Even the people who could afford their own personal Cores kept them out of sight from the general public.

Requiem discreetly looked around from under his hair, sticking close to Damion's side as they walked. "Is not the main source of acquiring income in this area contracting jobs to maintain the biosphere protecting the city?" he eventually inquired.

"You need the right supplies to do that and money to buy those supplies." Juni's jaw clenched. "Sometimes there just aren't enough funds. If they can't bid on jobs, they can't file for wages for hours worked."

"What brought you down here when you were a kid?" Damion appeared as curious as Requiem about how Juni, a man with a strict father and money, ended up in a desolate part of one of the most luxurious settlements in the solar system.

Juni shrugged casually. "Mom lost me in a shop uptown once. I started walking around because I was young and dumb, and I was mad about something and ran off, wanting to be by myself. I found my way here."

"You're lucky you didn't get killed. I can't believe your luck." Damion shook his head.

"The inhabitants of these types of social areas tend to see those of your monetary caliber as invaders," Requiem agreed quietly.

"You mean as assholes? You're right." They finally stopped outside an older temple. "Ready to meet some real believers?"

Requiem lowered his head even more, gripping Damion's wrist. To him, the word believer in correlation to the word religion was the same thing. He found it all fake. Just something for people to blame when things went wrong, yet when things went right, they praised themselves and then, maybe as an afterthought, their respective gods. Religion, to him, was a crutch. There was no proof that gods existed, and the religion in high favor had changed over the centuries.

Requiem knew from research that the multiple-deity platform that Damion and Juni believed in was first established thousands of years ago when Earth was the sole habitable planet. Requiem looked up briefly, absorbing everything before looking down again. A monotheistic religion took over power for nearly four millenniums after converting the original polytheistic believers over several continents. When men began reaching beyond the Earth, the polytheistic belief structure took control once more and the monotheist believers were silenced. The details were lost to time, but Requiem had complete access to the Corporation's libraries. He did not understand why humans would fight so hard over disembodied spiritual ideals. Over the course of a hundred years, most monotheists were converted, by either force or choice, and the few that remained kept their beliefs hidden.

So what was the truth? According to Requiem, none of it. But he wouldn't say that. It meant too much to Damion, and Requiem wouldn't take that faith, that *belief*, away from his Fighter when to do so might cripple his abilities. So he stayed silent and followed him through the crumbling doors.

Inside this much smaller temple, people filled the seats. They weren't just sitting there staring; each person was talking to the next. Some were trading goods, while others looked like they were getting medical care. It was a day of worship in other places on Lunar, but here, it was not only a day of worship but also a day for the less fortunate to come and trade, barter, and reach out for help from their community.

Even if those who could not find open seating were all in the aisles, the dais was still empty. They still respected that area for the God Ares and meager offerings were set there.

He was still gripping Damion's wrist, partially standing behind him but analyzing at the same time. "This is not just a temple. It is a community in truth."

"Yes. People who live within approximately forty-five kilometers around here come here every day of worship to find help and to pray." Juni gave Damion a small smile.

"This reminds me more of home." Damion returned his friend's smile warmly. "Ares would be proud."

Despite the sense of close community, the generous feel of the area, and people surrounding him, Requiem lowered his gaze once again. They were outsiders. Not only that, wealthy-looking outsiders, and unless something else clued these people in, they would be treated as such soon. While Juni and Damion could hold them off, 108 and Requiem only had rudimentary self-defense training.

"Let's go talk to the priest." Juni took 108's hand and headed through the crowd.

"You okay?" Damion asked Requiem.

"I am acceptable. Merely wary." Requiem reluctantly released Damion's wrist as he realized how tightly he had been gripping it.

"It's okay. If Juni says it's safe, it has to be." Damion reached up and ruffled the soft white hair. "Not everyone wants to hurt you."

Requiem arched into the warm touch like a cat in a beam of sunlight. "I am aware. It is not something I am used to. I am attempting to implement that knowledge while we are here. But I have found I am... *uncomfortable* while in the presence of large groups of people. It is making it a bit difficult. I will attempt to not disturb the rest of your worship."

"You're fine. You're not disturbing me." Damion sighed as they followed Juni. "I just wish… I wish I could show you how to enjoy yourself."

"Enjoy myself?" Requiem parroted. "I do not understand. Please explain."

"Just enjoy being alive. Enjoy meeting people—real people, not the people who rais—made you or the other Cores, and more than just Juni and me. Don't you ever wonder what we're fighting for?"

"It is not my intended function to think beyond what I was created to do. The circumstances in which I have been required to do so have led to several unfortunate events." Requiem looked at Damion from the corner of his eye. "I am merely to perform as I was ordered to do by the Corporation."

"I guess you're right, sort of." Damion had a look that meant he didn't like Requiem's answer, but he also didn't argue about it at the moment.

"Juni." An older man's voice boomed over the low murmur of the temple.

Requiem found the man who had spoken. He had salt-and-pepper hair, with warm but tired eyes. It was apparent by the hard lines of age and the swelling in his knuckles that he had spent a lifetime in service to the temple and to Ares, but he still had a regal bearing, the red-and-gold robes around him clean, although ragged around the ends.

"Hello, Hisano." Juni laughed. "I brought friends."

"I see that." Hisano looked over at Damion first, then at the Cores. "Are you going to introduce us?"

"This is one of the men in my Alpha fleet, Damion Hawk, and his Core, 47. And this is my Core, 108," Juni announced proudly. "I wanted to show them around."

People in the temple were curious why this man's attention was focused on them. He had a red sash around his neck with a ram embroidered at the ends. Requiem lowered his head even more and stepped behind Damion. Both moves were not just out of respect to an Elder of the community and temple, but also to keep himself from the gaze of the man and to prevent offending him.

"I have heard of the Cores, but to be honest, this is my first time seeing one up close." Hisano still had a small smile.

"They're not like the vids and rumors make them sound." Juni looked fondly over at 108. "Though they don't socialize very well."

"Your temple is wonderful." Damion changed the topic. "It reminds me of mine back home on Mars. I'll admit to not going to a full service in years. I don't make it a priority to visit the one on ship either. Maybe I need to fix that."

"Ah, I knew you didn't look like a local-born," the Priest said but not in judgment. "Are you taking care of our little Juni?"

"Little!" Juni sputtered.

Requiem took a chance and lifted his gaze, looking around Damion's shoulder at the older man. It was obvious that Hisano had seen many harrowing years. The man would be in charge of all of the temple upkeep and would probably also work at his own trade to supplement what the temple failed to gather in donations. Requiem estimated him to be in his early forties, but a hard life had him looking a rough sixty. In a time when a regular citizen's life span had extended to nearly 120, and maybe even longer, it was interesting to see. Long life was obviously only for those who held more influence, not for those who worked harder for a living.

Damion shrugged and laughed. "He's a handful and a bit clumsy day to day, but he's someone I trust with my life inside a Zodiac. He wouldn't have made it to the Alphas if that wasn't true."

"Thanks, I think." Juni grumbled. "108 still likes me even if you all abandon me."

"Core 108 is bonded to you. Even if he did not have a personal attachment to you, he could not help but to agree with you," Requiem said softly before he really thought about the consequences—something very unlike him.

"Thanks!" Juni's frown deepened and his face fell slightly. "Then I truly am alone."

"Stop pouting." The priest reached out and gave the top of Juni's head a light smack. "You have many friends. You're someone people have a hard time disliking."

"That's true." Damion laughed warmly, patting Juni's shoulder. "You are rather popular."

Realizing that he had said something to upset Juni, Requiem bowed his head once again, slipping back behind Damion. 108, on the other hand, was looking at Juni, emotion in his eyes as he squeezed Juni's hand in a way that could only mean comfort.

"Does this one not speak?" The Priest looked at 108. "I guess it doesn't matter. Why don't you all sit and visit with others for a short time?"

"Is there anything I can do?" Juni's spirits suddenly seemed to turn upward.

"There is always work that can be done." Hisano chuckled and began to walk away with just a pat to Juni's shoulder.

"Now what?" Damion asked, looking back at the small but well-cared-for altar.

"I usually walk around and talk and see if there is anything I can do to help, but you don't have to." Juni looked at 108. "Neither do you."

"I will stay with you," 108 said softly, never one for many words.

Requiem moved up so that he was standing next to Damion, his gaze discreetly following Hisano's form. "If Damion wishes to help, I will stay."

"Couldn't hurt to stay around and help a few people. Might be an old lady or three we can carry something for." Damion grinned and followed Juni into the crowd.

Requiem looped a finger through a belt loop on the back of Damion's jeans, letting Damion pull him forward so that he wouldn't get lost in the crowd. He didn't particularly know what he and 108 could do to help, but if Damion asked, he would do anything he could.

Juni sat and began talking. The man could talk to a wall or any stranger. That was one part of him that Requiem found surprising and odd. Before Damion could get far in his conversation with an elderly woman, Juni had sold out their services to help two couples by stopping by in the next few days and mending broken farming equipment. Damion admitted he had no clue how to fix the farming equipment, but the farmers had manuals, and the Fighters had Cores who were able to read the booklets efficiently.

Requiem had swiftly taken a manual from Damion's limp fingers. Damion had admitted being a bit lost by the technical jargon it contained. Requiem and 108 quickly flipped through it, talking quietly to each other about the "mysteries" it contained.

108 gave a slight frown, looking at Requiem and shaking his head.

Requiem replied with a nod before looking up at Damion through his bangs. "This will not take long. Definitely not the two days Fighter Juni supplied as a time frame. I will be able to repair the more intricate damaged equipment, while 108 can repair the exterior. I theorize that it will only take about three hours if the descriptions of the problems they are having are correct."

"Three hours?" Juni's jaw hung open

Damion scratched the back of his head. "I guess it's worth some fresh fruit, then."

"If they approve, I can also administer some improvements that will increase their speed, and therefore their revenue, by approximately 20 percent," Requiem added with a look to 108, who nodded.

Damion laughed as he looked at them. "And you said you wouldn't be able to help."

Requiem blinked up at him. "We are not helping, merely doing what we were created to do in a minimal capacity."

"You're *helping*." Damion ruffled Requiem's hair affectionately, his smile warm. "I'm proud of you."

Juni smiled at 108, waggling his eyebrows. "You want to try some of that ice cream I talked about the other night?"

"Sweet cold item?" 108 questioned.

Requiem sighed under Damion's warm hand. More than likely he would do anything for the warmth of that hand. "When would they like us to begin the repairs?"

"I have their location. We'll show up after breakfast tomorrow. Doing good work will help bring us favor with the gods." Juni stood up. "I'm going to tell Hisano we're leaving."

"You want ice cream?" Damion asked Requiem.

"What is ice cream?"

108 looked over at him. "Juni says it is something sweet."

Requiem turned back to Damion, looking down sheepishly. "You did claim that you would let me try different types of treats while we were here."

"If Juni's buying, you should ask for some." Damion grinned. "It's a bit expensive out here and better quality."

Requiem looked up at him for a moment and then lowered his head again, shaking it before changing the subject. "When we go to help the farmers tomorrow, we are going to have to bring some medical supplies with us for precautionary reasons."

"Precaution? What are you going to do? Set me on fire?" Damion looked worried.

Requiem gave Damion a look on the brink of being sarcastic. "I believe that you came to terms months ago with the fact that I was not going to terminate you. Why would I change my mind now?" he said in his normal monotone, but he hoped Damion caught a hint of the "dumbass" he had implied.

"Ha-ha." Damion laughed nervously. "Right."

"You slackers ready?" Juni came up with a smile. "What's so funny?"

"Absolutely nothing," Requiem replied. "Other than, after everything, my Fighter still apparently believes that I am going to attempt to terminate him one day." Requiem started walking through the crowd toward the temple doors, weaving through the mass of people like a river around rocks, effectively leaving Damion behind. He heard Juni's astonished comment.

"I think he just dissed you and walked out." Juni's voice was shocked.

"I noticed," Damion grumbled, but Requiem heard him following.

Requiem had known that Damion would follow him. They always went hand in hand even if, as then, Requiem didn't want them to. But that didn't mean Requiem should stop walking. He just could not conceive why Damion would have said that unless he still believed that Requiem would terminate his life one day. It seemed that the trust Requiem felt did not go both ways.

"Requiem, hold up!" Damion caught Requiem's wrist. "Please. What has you so mad?"

Requiem didn't turn around to look at him, merely continued to walk until Damion's grip made him come up short. "I am not mad, nor can I be. I have merely been enlightened and found it distasteful and against what I had believed to be true."

"Could you talk in a way that doesn't make my head hurt for a moment? I was joking. You know, *sarcasm*?" Damion tried to look him in the eye.

Requiem refused to oblige, keeping his gaze straight ahead and away from Damion's. "Fighter, you were not joking. You were nervous, worried, and slightly alarmed when I suggested bringing medical supplies. I meant for me. While it may seem that my eyes are always on the ground, my attention is not."

Now he looked at Damion, his eyes and features blank. "I informed you at one time that there was an extremely slim chance that I would ever kill you, and since then, very quickly, it became no chance. But you seem to have not come to that same conclusion, nor apparently do you remember saying at one point that if the Commander gave you orders to terminate me, you would do so. I had theorized that now, even if the Commander ordered you, you would not terminate me. Your recent reaction has caused me to rethink where I placed my trust."

"Terminate you!" Damion's face reddened with anger. "What goes on in that head of yours is beyond my comprehension. I said what I did because I was worried about being accidentally maimed by one of Juni's ideas, and then you take it to heart and subsequently imagine me murdering you in your sleep."

"At this point, it has nothing to do with that fact. Your reaction to my asking that specific question was merely the catalyst that brought us to our current predicament," Requiem replied calmly, the only way he ever replied, or spoke, or communicated. Even with Damion's fury staring him directly in the face, he didn't back away. Nor did he attempt to futilely twist his arm out of Damion's grip. He met Damion's gaze without flinching. "And affirmative—terminate. You claimed at one point in time that if the Commander ordered you to kill me, and only then, would you do so. And no, you will more than likely never understand what goes on in my mind, just as I will never understand what goes on in yours. What it comes to is that you do not trust me."

"I trust you with my life." Damion's voice held equal parts fury and hurt.

"Then why were you nervous? Why did you react the way that you did, even if you proclaim it was in jest? You even asked if I was going to set you on fire." Requiem shook his head, finally lowering it. "Do not answer that. It is not important." He looked up, but again turned his gaze away from Damion, down to the grimy sidewalk. "If you do not mind, please let me go."

Damion let go of Requiem's wrist, but he didn't look happy. Requiem noticed Juni and 108 watching from near the temple entrance. Juni had a shaky smile as he looked from Damion to Requiem and then back again.

Juni cleared his throat before waving. "Time to go."

Requiem continued on his walk to the speeder in silence, waiting outside the hatch for Juni to unlock it, and then sliding in. He immediately diverted his attention out the window, his hands in his lap, his face blank.

"Ice cream?" Juni offered.

"Yes," 108 said softly.

"I am interested. It sounds intriguing," Requiem agreed from the back, still looking out the window.

"I know the best place. They ship the frozen milk from Earth once a month." Juni's voice had its excitement back.

"Is that what this ice cream is made out of?" Requiem inquired, his tone of tight interest.

"Well, yes, that and sugar." Juni sped back toward the more aristocratic part of the city.

Damion attempted to deflect some of the uncomfortable air in the car. "I cannot believe all the perks you've had while growing up here, and you're still not an asshole. Or at least not a gigantic asshole."

"Thanks, thanks for that." Out of the corner of his eye, Requiem noted that Juni did not pull his gaze from the road while he made a rude gesture with his left hand at Damion.

Damion shook his head. "You're welcome. Now, this ice cream stuff. How good is it really?"

"It's worth the drive and the price—that much I can guarantee."

"Then I think it's what we all need." Damion sighed.

Chapter Nineteen

Friday August 26, 454 MC
1731 GMT
Requiem

THREE DAYS later they arrived back on the *Zeus*. And for those three days, ever since Requiem had told Damion that he thought Damion didn't trust him, Requiem had shown no emotion. He had reverted back to the person he had been when they first met. Only answering when a question couldn't be avoided, keeping his gaze down to everyone, sleeping on the cot in the servant's room—becoming the typical, mechanical Core. Any time Damion touched him, Requiem moved away as soon as he could.

Requiem opened the door to their quarters for Damion from behind him and keyed the lock. He moved across the room in silence, placing his small duffel on the floor of the closet before unzipping it and unpacking the clean clothes within.

Damion looked over at him and sighed. "Happy to be back and able to plug in?"

"While rudimentary and not completely engaging, I was about to do so to some extent on Lunar with the console and also with the farmers' machinery," Requiem replied, circumventing the true question without lying or really answering it.

"Damn it, can't you just give me one fucking straight answer?" Damion exploded.

"What specific answer would you like me to give you?" Requiem replied calmly, finishing with the clothes and collapsing the bag for storage.

Damion threw his duffel against the back wall and marched the two steps over to Requiem, grabbing him by the shoulders, giving him a hard shake. "A real one, not one that's fabricated!"

Requiem's head snapped back from the force, but he still managed to keep his gaze from meeting Damion's. "The word fabrication in this scenario means a lie, and I cannot lie to you.

Therefore what I said was true." He focused on the collar of Damion's shirt. "If you wish to hear something different, please let me know and I will do my best to accommodate you."

"I don't want you to say something just to accommodate me!" Damion gave him another shake. "Be your own fucking self! The one that you were before that stupid trip to the temple."

Requiem was silent for a few moments, completely still, his gaze unmoving from Damion's neck. "I do not know who that person is anymore," he finally replied, this time quietly. "At some point it became unclear. Perhaps it was when I finally met you. Or perhaps it was when I stopped taking the supplements as frequently as I am supposed to. Or even, perhaps, it was when I became unsure of where our trust in one another stood."

"I told you I trust you! What do I need to do to convince you of that? Why won't you believe me?" Damion wrenched Requiem's chin up.

Even with his head tilted up, his eyes raised, Requiem refused to meet that dark gaze, no doubt burning with fury and hurt so real that Requiem imagined he could feel the heat on his face. His head hurt, and he was getting a headache. He wanted to believe Damion, wanted to believe in his Fighter, but he had seen his face. A question, so innocent in the presentation, had caused Damion to become suspicious. And that had caused an emotion that Requiem had sense-identified as hurt. Pain, deep in his chest, almost betrayal. It had been too much for him to handle at the time, and now he was merely confused.

"I do not know," he finally whispered. He pulled off one glove and then the other—gloves he had worn since they had worked on the farmer's equipment. Since he had shoved his hands into the wires and made them obey his will—an ability that only he had.

Finally, he looked into Damion's eyes for the first time in three days, raising his fingers at the same time. Fingers that were red and blistered, seeping, and in some places bleeding, from where the blisters had popped. They were thin stripes all over his fingers. Angry red lines. "But in the end this is why I inquired about medical supplies, because I knew that this would be the result. Instead you thought, even for a nanosecond, that it was because I would hurt you. That is why."

"What the hell?" Damion dropped his grip on Requiem's chin and took his hands in his to inspect them. "Why didn't you tell me about this?"

Requiem pulled out of the touch, clenching them into fists, not acknowledging the pain as more blisters popped. If Damion looked closer, he would see thin white scars of similar shape and size following comparable patterns over his fingers. "It was not important. I took care of them. And you are avoiding the main issue."

"No, I'm not. You don't trust me enough to tell me you're hurt! You don't trust me not to kill you! I offer you my life, and it's not good enough!"

Yet again Requiem was silent, his gaze boring into Damion's for a moment until he dropped it once again. "You are correct in some aspects. My fingers do not hurt and are superficial injuries that I am used to. They are not an issue. What you are correct about is that yes, it is good enough. You have ownership of my life, so it does not matter whether or not I trust you with it. You have offered me your life, and that is enough."

"I don't know if you just agreed with me or not, but first I want to get your hands bandaged. Do we have what we need to wrap them, or should I hang my head as we go to Medical and wait to get yelled at again for taking poor care of you?" Damion took hold of Requiem's hands and frowned sadly at the angry lines. "How didn't I notice this?"

"There are sufficient supplies in the restroom, on the top shelf of the closet, in the back." Requiem's angry-looking fingers curled in Damion's large hands. "You did not notice because I chose not to let you. I have had much practice hiding my injuries and brought my gloves with me in the event that such a situation arose."

"Fuck," Damion cursed and went to the restroom. "Don't keep anything like that from me ever again. If you get hurt, tell me."

"As you order. I did attempt to warn you beforehand," Requiem said quietly, walking over and sitting down on the edge of his capsule. "What happened to my fingers is not really an injury, though, and does not hurt that much. I am used to it." He caressed the side of the capsule.

"Give me your hands." Damion ordered as he came out of the bathroom with the supplies—gauze and rapid-gel. He began applying the gel and wrapping the worst of the blisters. "Don't agree with me unless you agree."

Even though pain flashed up his arms, Requiem didn't wince or make a sound. "As you order."

"Stop fucking saying that! I'm not ordering you. I'm asking you. There is a big difference."

Requiem fell silent, keeping his gaze on the hand that Damion gently worked on. In truth he didn't know what Damion wanted from him. Damion told him to be himself, yet when he was, Damion didn't want that either. So Requiem kept his mouth shut and his head down.

"There. How does it feel?" Damion asked.

"Acceptable. Thank you." Requiem opened and closed his right hand to check the maneuverability of his fingers.

Damion brushed his fingers over Requiem's cheek. "Why do you look like that?"

Requiem shrugged, sighing softly as he held on to the capsule beneath him, his eyes closing slightly from the warmth Damion's hand gave off. "I do not know."

"Requiem. Look at me. Tell me what you are feeling." Damion tugged him away from the pod by his arms.

As he was pulled to his feet, Requiem dropped his hand to brace on the capsule beneath him, tried not to cling to the inanimate object he had missed so much. He did look at it for a moment before slowly turning his head and lifting his gaze to the man holding him by the arms.

"I do not know what I feel. I do not know these emotions and what they mean. What I do know is that I do not know what you want from me. You tell me to be myself, yet even when I am, you do not seem to agree with it." He licked his lips, lowering his gaze for a moment before he forced it to meet Damion's again. He continued to explain what he'd been thinking for a while. "I do not even know who I am anymore, so I do not know how I can expect you to know what you want from me."

"Being yourself is what you were doing before you got mad at me," Damion explained. "Don't you agree? Saying what was on your mind?"

"I did not get mad. I was… I believed perhaps I had misunderstood you or you did me. You knew I would not attempt to kill you, and when you reacted in an unfavorable way, I was…." Requiem's face twisted in confusion. "I think perhaps the emotion is *hurt*… maybe betrayal. I do not know. That you did not trust me as I thought you did. And how do I know that was truly who I was before? I was not feeling before. I do not like this… this feeling. I do not like emotions."

"I'm… I'm sorry I thought that if you had your emotions back, you'd be happy. You'd be able to be happy." Damion looked disappointed in Requiem's reaction. "I'm sorry if I made a mistake."

"Fighter, I have never had emotions. They began feeding me a supplement to repress them immediately when they obtained me from the breeding tube. They have never been a part of my life, and now that I have begun to have them, I do not know what I am dealing with." Requiem shook his head. "There is nothing for you to be sorry for. You did nothing wrong. Except, perhaps, by misunderstanding me."

Damion had a small smile on his face. "You were angry, but that's okay, and I really don't blame you. I shouldn't have made such a stupid comment, but honestly, I didn't mean to insult you."

"It is in the past now, and we now understand each other a little better. That is all that is important." Requiem's gaze once again slid from Damion's face and down to the floor. Old habits were exceedingly hard to break. "But in the end, I still do not understand what you want from me. You perplex me. I chose you because I knew you would not be like other Fighters, but I did not realize how different you were."

Damion laughed quietly. "Is that a compliment or a complaint?"

"Neither. A conundrum." Requiem ran a bandaged hand through his hair. He froze for a moment as he lowered his arm and then continued the movement. That was odd. He couldn't remember ever really doing that before, even when his hair was in his eyes. Shaking his head slightly, he raised his gaze back up to Damion. "But you never answered my question. What do you want from me? What do you expect of me? I do not understand it."

"I expect you to be you. To yell at me, to trust me. And I'll trust you. I promise. I want you to be the human you really are. Not a machine." Damion pulled Requiem closer, tilting Requiem's head back so that he could slant his mouth over his, kissing him.

Requiem blinked in shock as he was jerked forward, causing him to lose his balance and catch himself against Damion's chest. He froze for a moment, not sure what to do, but then sighed as a feeling of warmth radiated from his lips, causing him to relax against Damion's form. This was… *nice*, pleasant.

When Damion eventually pulled away, Requiem looked up at him and licked his lips, tasting Damion on him. "If I am going to continue to have these emotions, I will need to learn what they are. As in the definition of each feeling. If I am to be both human and machine, this is something I must acquire. I must be careful in my investigation when I am in the system so that I do not alert the Creators. Is there a possibility that you could advise me in these matters?"

"I'll try." Damion raked his fingers through Requiem's hair, pushing the silky tendrils away from those large blue eyes. "You describe them, and I'll try and give you a label."

Requiem's head tilted back with the movement of Damion's hand, his eyes sliding closed for a moment. "They are difficult to describe other than... *weight*, in my chest. Hot, cold, tight, fast, slow— I do not know."

"That's the hard part of being human. I want to show you more. I have this, this *need*, this lust inside me." Damion pulled Requiem closer, wrapping him in his arms. "Do you like me touching you?"

"You touching me?" Requiem tilted his head slightly to the side, his arms bent and pinned between their bodies. He thought about it for a moment, thinking about how any time Damion touched him, it made him feel... "Warm. You always make me feel warm. Relaxed, I suppose, when you touch me. What does that mean?"

"It means you enjoy it." Damion turned his head, slanting his mouth over Requiem's to kiss him again as he gently caressed Requiem's sides.

Requiem's clenched fists splayed against Damion's chest, then uncurled as contentment spread from Damion's lips over his body. It was true. He was never more relaxed than when Damion held him, not even in his capsule. He had never thought that he was constantly cold until Damion came into his life and taught him warmth.

"Enjoy? Is that word not connected to... *happy*? Perhaps *content*?" he asked curiously, his lips moving against Damion's.

"Yes, it's when you're very pleased." Damion kissed down Requiem's neck.

"Interesting," Requiem whispered, licking his lips again as Damion's feathering touch on his skin caused his heart to speed up, pounding in his head. "Is that why you touch me? Because you enjoy it? Because you are pleased with me?" He paused for a moment, astounded that Damion couldn't hear his heart trying to get out of his rib cage. He reached down to one of Damion's hands, gripping it loosely and placing it flat over the left side of his chest. "What does this mean? Why did my heart accelerate?"

"You're excited." Damion tugged Requiem's shirt up and moved his hand along Requiem's pale skin and then took his wrapped hand and put it to his own chest. Requiem could feel Damion's equally pounding heart. "Me too. Touching you, thinking about you, makes me go mad. I want to have sex with you, but if I do… I want you to like it."

"Excited?" Requiem said softly and actually shuddered as Damion's warm hand moved to his bare chest, resting over one of his ports. "Why does excitement, touching, and thinking about me make you go mad? You seem perfectly sane to me."

His bandaged fingers curled against Damion's chest. But after a moment, curious to see the difference, he moved his hand—not quite away, but he slid it up and under Damion's shirt to rest once again over Damion's heart. The tips of his fingers were exposed above the wrappings. The bare touch against naked skin made the warmth increase throughout his body, causing him to tremble again. "If we participated in sexual activities, it would be different than what I have experienced in the past. That alone would make me… like it. Is that what you would like to do?" He tilted his head again, meeting Damion's gaze.

"Oh yes, I'd like to," Damion said hoarsely, the words sounding caught in his throat. He audibly swallowed, shifting to ease the pressure in his pants. "I even bought some lube, when Juni wasn't around, of course, so it won't hurt. At least from what I read, it shouldn't too much."

"Lube?" Requiem replied, confusion sparking in his eyes, almost unconsciously sliding his hand down Damion's chest to his stomach, resting his fingertips there. "You are… is it *nervous*? You are nervous. Unsure."

"I'm nervous," Damion admitted and began to slowly undress him as if he were unwrapping a long-awaited recreational pass. "But I want this as long as you don't object."

"I do not." Requiem lifted his arms so that Damion could slide his shirt off. "We did not go to completion last time because of being interrupted, and I am still just as curious. Perhaps even more so now. I have already placed a voice lock on the door. Would you like me to cut off the option for communication so that no one can access the vid screen?"

"Can you do that from here?" Damion had let go of Requiem, already beginning to take off his own pants, hopping on one foot in his eagerness.

"Not as of right now. I am working on distance control, but I would need to implant a receiver, and I have not done enough research yet to be comfortable with doing so. At this point I still need tactile stimulation with the system," he replied, his arms loose at his sides as he watched Damion.

"Ah, yeah, sure. Then go ahead." Damion nodded and then stood up to open his bag. He brought out the lube he had bought on Lunar.

Requiem walked over to his capsule, smoothing a hand over the edge of it before reaching in and grabbing a jack, pulling it out, and turning around so he could plug it in at the base of his skull. He let out a long, relieved sigh as the system appeared before him in greens, blacks, and pulses of white skittering across his inner eye. He could get lost in this homecoming, but Damion was waiting for him.

He temporarily severed the communications output so that no one could vid in, and with minor regret exited the system. Taking a deep breath, he opened his eyes and pulled the input jack out of his port, letting it retract back into the capsule. He blinked blearily for a moment, clearing his vision before looking at Damion. "What would you like me to do now?"

"Take off your shirt and boxers and get on the bed," he told Requiem as he moved to the bed and sat down.

Chapter Twenty

Requiem

WITHOUT SAYING anything, Requiem did as he was asked, unbuttoning his pants and taking them off along with his boxers, leaving everything on the floor. He walked over to the bed and sat on the edge, looking at Damion expectantly. "Why do you still want to have sex when you are nervous about doing it?"

"It's because there's excitement and anticipation mixed in with the apprehension. This will be completely new to me. Been a long time since I was a beginner in bed." Damion pulled Requiem toward him slowly. "I want to kiss you again."

"Why apprehension?" Requiem asked, his gaze searching Damion's face. His heart sped up again when Damion grasped his arms, and Requiem leaned toward Damion. "If you want to kiss me again, why do you not do so?"

"I don't want to hurt you," Damion said, before he kissed Requiem anyway.

Requiem leaned into the kiss, into the warmth, sighing softly at the comfort contained in it. He really liked this kissing thing. It made him feel… good, safe. "I trust you not to hurt me," he said against those lips before pushing his against them. "Trust in yourself as well."

Damion rubbed his palms up and down Requiem's arms and back, skimming the occasional bump of a port.

Not drawing away from Damion's lips, Requiem shifted closer so that his bare leg was touching Damion's own, his torso twisted so that he was facing him. Damion's hands left a trail of goose bumps on his skin. Hesitant yet curious at the same time, Requiem parted his lips, his tongue running a line over Damion's bottom lip before withdrawing slightly.

Damion let out a small groan, slipping his tongue between Requiem's retreating, parted lips. He reached down and began to stroke Requiem's soft penis.

Requiem gasped, a sound that was almost a squeak. He tore his lips from Damion's and leaned back. He looked down at his lap where Damion was doing amazing things with a part of Requiem's body. A part that Requiem had perceived as only good for one thing. The motions Damion used caused an interesting, pleasurable feeling to race through Requiem. "I do… I do not understand."

"It's about feeling good. This feels good, right?" Damion swallowed audibly.

"Good… yes… I do find it… appealing." Requiem was unsure of his words or what exactly he was feeling, but he… liked it. "I have been grasped there before, but it has never felt like this. In the past it was uncomfortable, and occasionally painful."

"This shouldn't be those things either, it should all feel good."

Damion leaned forward to kiss Requiem again, keeping up his movements over Requiem's slowly hardening shaft. He was already erect himself.

Requiem was still looking down, astonished at his growing organ, when Damion kissed him, effectively distracting him. He parted his lips, moving a tentative hand up to twine his fingers around a strand of dark hair. The heat, the pleasure in his body, just kept building. His skin tingled with warmth, and he felt he needed something… something *more*, but he didn't know what it was. He noticed he felt weak and the arm he was supporting himself on was trembling, but he couldn't care. It was all intriguing.

Damion gently urged Requiem down onto his back, still stroking, still kissing. He began to move his hips against Requiem's thigh, the soft warmth of skin over muscle pleasant, then leaned away to catch his breath.

Requiem looked down to his thigh as he felt a wetness against his skin. After reaching down, he ran his fingers with a featherlight touch along Damion's hard shaft to the tip. He stroked his forefinger over the slit before bringing it up to his gaze and running the sticky liquid between his thumb and finger.

"You are leaking. It is wet and sticky. This is normal? I have cleaned it off of me before from previous encounters with Fighters, but I did not know it was normal."

"Y-yes." Damion tucked his head into the crook of Requiem's neck, kissing lightly and licking. "It's what happens when you're feeling good. It's called precome."

Tilting his head to the side, Requiem let his hand drop, but this time it landed on Damion's waist in a tentative touch. Closing his eyes, he realized he was breathing rapidly as if he had run kilometers. His other hand was still in Damion's hair, and Requiem grasped those strands tighter as Damion's hot mouth on his neck caused him to quiver. Damion's hand on his now erect penis continued to send warm flames licking through his system, flames that seemed to build higher. It was almost… frustrating. He was feeling something growing within him, building.

Damion looked down at Requiem's leaking cock. "Have you ever had an orgasm?"

Silent, Requiem stared into Damion's wide eyes. He shook his head. His bandaged fingers trembled against Damion's waist. He was trying to contain something, trying to hold himself together. And it was the truth, the heat threatened to explode out of his skin, and he was slightly… *afraid* of it. He had never felt this way before, and he didn't know if it was normal, if this was how it was supposed to be during sex.

"I'll let you come first, and then we can try to loosen you up." Damion gently kissed Requiem's lips first and then down his body to his erection. He stroked faster, using the precome as lube before giving a tentative lick to the side of Requiem's hard shaft.

"What do you mean by loosen me—?" A strangled gasp cut his question off as his fingers dug into Damion's hair. The wet, hot heat of Damion's mouth on his most sensitive parts caused the fire to flare, roaring through his body. A low moan escaped Requiem's throat as he breathed out, the unfamiliar sound surprising him.

Damion gave another few licks to the now very hard shaft in front of him. "Not too bad. I hate to admit it, but I've become disgustingly well read over the last three days. I want to show you how good it can feel. I want you to experience pleasure, sex, all of it."

Requiem closed his eyes, swallowing down the whimper creeping out of his throat. His whole body trembled. He couldn't contain the pressure he was trying to hold in anymore. His whole being was tense except for his legs, which twitched out of his control. "Damion… I do not know this feeling. Pressure," he said in halting breaths, pausing for a moment before continuing. "I think I am *afraid*."

"Don't be. It's okay, you can come. I promise you it will feel better than anything you've ever felt before."

Damion rubbed his left hand over Requiem's lower stomach while his right resumed stroking, faster than before. "Touching another man, like this, I never knew it would make me this excited. Happy."

"Come? I do not know what you mean. Come where?" Requiem managed to get out before Damion's hand increased its speed further, inflaming the burning that had started around his groin and increased throughout him. Requiem couldn't hold it in anymore—he wasn't strong enough—so he gave up and hoped that whatever happened didn't kill him.

For the first time in his life, Requiem orgasmed. His mouth opened in a silent scream as he went rigid, his fingers twisting in Damion's hair as the most amazing, blissful feeling burst through him from head to toe. He heard a roaring in his ears and saw white bursts behind his closed eyes. It was… wonderful.

Requiem nearly convulsed under Damion and covered Damion's hand in pulse after pulse of sticky, thick release.

Requiem's hands slid from Damion's hair to the bed as his chest rose and fell with soft pants. Eyes wide, fixed on the ceiling, he continued to twitch every so often. His skin had flushed from heat and exertion and a shock of his hair was plastered to his sweaty skin. All of those things, nearly every single one of them, were new to him. And it was overwhelming.

Damion leaned forward, putting a soft kiss on Requiem's parted lips. He stroked his clean hand over Requiem's cheek. Requiem's thoughts lingered on his… lover's… lips.

"Turn over, please," Damion urged.

Requiem's eyes eventually came back to focus, meeting Damion's for a moment. Then he nodded and shakily sat up. The liquid pooled on his stomach caused him to pause as he stared at it. He looked up at Damion again, mild confusion filling him, but he didn't say anything as he turned, getting on his hands and knees and lowering himself so that he lay back down on the bed on his messy stomach.

Damion began kissing the skin around each port. He counted them in a low voice. He started at the base of Requiem's spine. Four were along his spine, and that wasn't including the one at the base of his skull. Damion put a long kiss to the port at the back of his head. Damion moved to Requiem's arms, splayed out to his sides. There were two in each of them as well, one in the biceps and another in the forearms. One behind each ear, in the back of each thigh, and each calf. And these were just the ones on the back of his body. "What's this?"

Requiem felt Damion brushing his hair aside over the line of inking on the back of Requiem's head he would never have seen before. The faint, long tattoo of writing was normally hidden in his hair.

"When did you get that?"

Requiem turned his head to the right, content to stare at the wall by his capsule. "I was marked when I was brought into the Corporation. The tattoo reads 'Chrysalis Corporation—Core #11023052-47.'"

Simply put, it basically said "Property of the Chrysalis Corporation." Under the tattoo there was a small, shallow divot in his skin, about the size of a protein tablet in diameter. "All Cores are marked in a similar way."

"I see." Damion sighed and placed a kiss on the mark before rubbing his hands up and down Requiem's sides. "I'm going to try and prepare you so I can… well, so I can fuck you."

"Affirmative," Requiem replied quietly.

Even though the warmth from his orgasm had turned his body to jelly, Requiem somehow tensed, becoming as taut as a violin string. This part—this was the part he wasn't sure about. Every time it had hurt—horribly so—and there had been blood. Damion assured him there was a difference, and so far Damion hadn't lied to him. But out of everything, Requiem always remembered the pain.

"I'll try and do this as best as I can, but this is our, well, *my* first time."

Requiem heard Damion open up the small tube and squeeze out some of its contents. Then Damion smoothed his fingers down the crease of Requiem's ass before pressing one finger against his tight entrance.

"No, it is both of ours," Requiem whispered into the pillow, where he'd turned his head to keep his face hidden. His whole body sang with tension, even more so with the gentle, slippery brush of Damion's digit against his opening. "I do not count what others have done to me as anything except an uncomfortable memory."

"You mean rape." Damion sighed. "I need you to take a breath and try to relax."

Requiem gave a brief look of disbelief over his shoulder before he buried his face. But he did as Damion asked, closing his eyes, taking a deep breath that raised his upper body, and releasing it slowly. While doing so, he concentrated on easing all his muscles. He focused his thoughts on how much he trusted Damion. How safe and secure he made him feel. How Damion had never hurt him and never would on purpose. That, more than the breath, helped him relax.

Requiem could feel Damion moving one finger in and out a lot easier now. He suspected Damion would need to get two, if not three, fingers inside to stretch him.

"If it starts to hurt worse, let me know. It might be… uncomfortable at first," Damion said.

Requiem buried his arms under the pillow, cradling the soft material so that it fluffed around his face. What Damion was doing did burn somewhat, but it didn't hurt, per se. Requiem had felt a lot worse. Damion's finger inside him was gentle and hesitant. He was trying his best, his honest best, not to hurt Requiem, and Requiem appreciated it. He nodded to let Damion know he had heard him, but otherwise kept silent.

"It will be all right." Damion rubbed Requiem's lower back as he slowly pushed in a second finger. He sounded unsure whether he was telling Requiem to keep him calm, or himself.

"I am aware. I trust you" was the muffled, strained reply Requiem managed from the pillow. He had tensed again at the invasion of the second finger but relaxed after a moment. It burned. Yes, it burned, but yet again it wasn't too uncomfortable.

"You doing all right?" Damion asked.

"I am acceptab-*aaahhh*!" Requiem moved quickly. He knew he was quite flexible for a Core, and in less than a quarter of a second, he had put his hands under himself and pushed up, effectively bowing his back so that he could look over his shoulder at Damion. One moment he had been concentrating on keeping relaxed as Damion slowly moved his fingers in and out of him, the next those fingers touched something in him that caused an intense wave of pleasure.

"That it?" Damion chuckled at Requiem. "All right, I'll try and focus on that since it seems to loosen you up more."

"What…?" Requiem looked from Damion's face to where his fingers were buried in him and back to his face again. "What was that?"

"It was your sweet spot, um, your prostate." Damion's voice was laced with happiness.

"I still do not understand so much," Requiem said with a soft sigh, warily lying back down.

"That's fine because neither do I." Damion focused on hitting that spot inside Requiem's body a few more times before pushing in a third and final finger. "Does it hurt?"

Requiem trembled as sweat dripped down his back from trying to contain his gasps and not squirming under Damion's efforts. At Damion's question, he shook his head rapidly before he buried his face again. So many sensations he had never experienced before. More pleasure than he had felt in his entire life. The only thing that compared was jacking in, and that was pleasurable because of the freedom it represented. But this… this was different.

Damion was able to move all three fingers easily now. "I am going to enter you now. I can't wait another minute." He pulled his fingers away.

Requiem sagged back onto the bed as soon as Damion's fingers left him. His torso rose and fell against the mattress from the rapid panting muffled by the pillow. Sweat slicked Requiem's hair to the back of his neck. All that, and the only true pain he felt was where his member was caught between his stomach and the bed, since he lay completely flat, his legs splayed out. It was a pleasurable pain, but pain nonetheless.

Requiem glanced over his shoulder to see Damion slicking his penis with a shaking hand.

"Raise up on your knees," Damion instructed and waited for him to do so before guiding the tip of his cock to the greased entrance.

Requiem didn't know how he felt, having his ass in the air with his torso still partially on the bed, his face buried in the pillow. But he did as Damion asked, feeling very exposed. His whole form trembled in both fear and anticipation as he felt Damion's penis nudge against him. Lifting his head from the pillow, he looked back over his shoulder, wondering what Damion was going to look like when he entered him. Requiem had never cared before, in the past just waited for it to be over. But this time he was curious because it was Damion.

Damion slid into Requiem's body. "Fuck. So warm, soft." He pushed forward centimeter by centimeter.

Requiem couldn't help but release a gasp from the burning pain of Damion stretching him even further. He turned back around so that Damion couldn't see his face. Damion's penis was not small, and even with being prepared, it burned. But not as bad.... No, he could deal with it. This time he didn't feel the pain of his skin tearing or the warm trickle of blood down his leg—none of that. Damion was gentle, sliding slowly into him, and while it hurt, it was bearable. Sucking in a deep breath, Requiem raised his upper body, reaching for a shelf that was part of the bookcase embedded in the wall instead of a headboard. He gripped it tightly, letting his head hang down.

Once Damion was fully inside Requiem, he paused before he finally asked a whispered question. "Are you all right?"

Requiem let out the breath he was holding in to keep from whimpering, nodding at the same time. "I will admit that it is not comfortable, but it does not hurt too badly. I suspect once you start moving, it will be fine." His arms were trembling from gripping the bookshelf so tightly.

"Good." Damion moved slowly at first. His thrusts were hesitant. The slow play of pushing his erection in and out of Requiem's body was causing Requiem *frustration.*

"Is there a problem?" Requiem inquired.

"I don't want to hurt you."

"You will not." Requiem trusted Damion, and not just in sex but in all other decisions. "Do what pleases you."

"If I hurt you too bad, you'll say something?" Damion's voice was deeper from arousal.

"I will report if there are any unbearable sensations." Requiem whispered.

Damion didn't wait a moment longer and began thrusting his hips in and out of Requiem at a fast pace, as if unable to stop himself or take it slow.

Requiem couldn't keep a gasping scream inside, and he tilted his head back as he squeezed his eyes shut. The first few thrusts burned like a hot poker up his spine, but after that... after that it wasn't so bad....

In fact, it was good. Really good.

Requiem let his head fall back down, his hair hanging in his eyes as he gasped. He strained not to move. Every time Damion pushed into him, he lurched forward and only his grip on the shelf helped to keep him in place. Eventually, what he really wanted to do was push back, to help Damion find that spot inside him that

Damion's fingers had found, but he forced himself to stay still, not sure if Damion would appreciate him doing so.

Damion's hands shook as they rested on Requiem's hips. "Being inside you and knowing you want it makes this amazing." He moved his hips as he spoke. "You can move too. Please, for the love of the gods, move!"

Requiem looked back over his shoulder again and any words he might have said were lost as he saw the blissful look on Damion's face. Requiem had never taken stock in physical appearances before, but Damion, he realized, was beautiful. Especially with his face flushed with color, his brown eyes bright with… with *heat,* was the only thing Requiem could think of, but it was a side of the man that he liked. And then his mind scattered in a wave of overwhelming ecstasy as Damion's movements inside his body shifted over that place Damion had called the sweet spot. Requiem couldn't help pushing back in reaction, turning back to the bookshelf with a wheeze.

"Shit," Damion said. "So tight. Good. Fuck."

Requiem couldn't control his voice anymore, couldn't control the sobbing that spilled forth from his mouth. In the past he had been able to make no sound, no cry of pain, anything. He prided himself for keeping his silence even if it displeased the Fighter he had been paired with, who had raped him. But this… this was nothing he could control. It felt so good every time the head of Damion's penis ran over that unknown place inside him. He could feel himself as he was before, his own need hard and weeping, almost painfully so as the sounds of skin on skin slapped in the air.

Damion reached around with a fumbling hand and found Requiem's penis and wrapped his palm around it. "I'm going to come inside you."

He shuddered under Damion with his head thrown back as a whimper slipped from his throat at the heat of Damion inside of him and the pressure of Damion's strong, callused hand around his erection. Too many sensations—touch, smell, sound, and even the dryness in his mouth from his panting breaths and hoarse cries. It was overwhelming, so much so that tears combined with sweat on his face.

Even with all that, there was only one thing Requiem could reply. "Where else would you come, besides inside me?" It was the least he was able to say as he pushed shaky arms against the shelf, thrusting himself back onto Damion.

Damion didn't answer—he either couldn't or wouldn't. His hips were snapping forward fast and furiously until he gave one last thrust. Requiem's channel clenched hard around Damion's cock, taking all he was able to offer.

It was an interesting sensation for Requiem, being able to feel Damion fill him. It made him... *happy, content,* even with his own hard, near-painful ache. Feeling Damion shudder, hearing him gasp, grunt, and let out a long groan as he released inside of Requiem. Even the tight, certainly bruising grip on his hip made Requiem feel content that his body had given Damion such pleasure. But the grip of Damion's other hand—the one wrapped around Requiem's need, still sliding back and forth with the motions of their bodies—was what gave Requiem true pleasure. For the second time in his life, and that night, he came.

This time he couldn't keep in the quiet scream, his back bowing at a near impossible angle as he spilled onto the bed and Damion's hand, pleasure ripping through him.

Damion rolled to his side, taking Requiem with him. He reached around with a sweaty arm and hugged Requiem tightly to his chest. "Fuck, that was good. Intense."

Requiem didn't have the strength to do anything but fall with him. His lungs were moving rapidly, panting air out between parted lips. He couldn't speak, couldn't do anything but lie boneless in Damion's arms. His eyes were heavy lidded, open, but he couldn't seem to focus on the opposing wall.

Damion let out a long sigh. He sat up a bit and looked at Requiem's face. "You felt good too?"

Somehow Requiem found the strength to roll his eyes toward Damion. He tried to speak, stopped, licked his lips, and swallowed before answering in a hoarse voice, "I am definitely feeling... *good.*"

A grin split Damion's face. "Great. Good." He lay back down.

Once Requiem caught his breath and didn't feel so much like jelly, he rolled over in Damion's arms so that he could look into his smiling, peaceful face. Requiem ran his bandaged fingers tentatively over Damion's tan skin to reach those smiling lips. He concentrated on the smile for a moment, wondering at it. "This makes you happy?"

"Of course. Sex always makes people happy." Damion held up a finger and quickly added. "Consensual sex, that is."

Requiem twitched his lips in a brief copy of Damion's smile, except much smaller and quicker. "It is all right, Damion. I know the difference now. I knew what you meant." His hand dropped as he looked up at Damion through his bangs. "I suppose my question was not clear enough. I meant does sex with *me* make you happy? You prefer the female sex, so why participate in it with me? Is the reason that females are not readily available on the *Zeus*, or is there some other explanation?"

"I don't know. I mean, I've never gone all the way with another guy before, but you… you I just wanted. Let's say I figured we had to be compatible."

Quiet for a few moments, Requiem eventually raised his head so that he was looking Damion full in the face and not through his hair. He reached out and stopped, curling his hand in on itself for a moment before he reached out to Damion's face again. He merely ran his unbandaged fingertips over the smooth skin, wondering.

"May I… may I ask you? Could you please… kiss me again?" Requiem didn't know why he asked, but he knew he liked it. It made him feel warm, safe, wanted for himself and not as a Core.

"Not a problem. You don't have to ask. If you want a kiss and we're alone, just take one."

Damion pulled Requiem close and pressed his lips against Requiem's once again. He looked pleased at Requiem's desire for more.

Requiem let out a long sigh, one hand pinned against Damion's bare chest while the other lay curled against his cheek, allowing him to feel Damion's jaw move as they kissed. It was… nice.

Damion pulled back after a few minutes. "You feeling okay?"

Blinking, Requiem nodded, taking his hands back almost abruptly, thinking he had done something wrong. "Affirmative." Then he thought about it for moment, squirming slightly. "Although I admit that I may require a shower."

"You didn't do anything wrong." Damion chortled and sat up. "Even if I could go for another round, I don't think you'd be able to walk tomorrow."

Requiem watched him, shifting into a sitting position as he tilted his head, his brow furrowed in confusion. He didn't notice it, but each day he suspected more and more emotion showed on his face, in his body language, and not just his eyes. "Another round? I do not understand?"

"Having sex again. Sorry, it's slang." Damion sniggered again. "I forget myself at times."

"You… can do that? More than once in one day?" Requiem inquired curiously as he slid to the edge of the bed. He was covered in sticky fluids, seemingly all over, and they were starting to dry and become a little itchy.

"Oh yeah, but I wouldn't recommend it because from what I read, it can get you a little more than just sore." Damion gave him a wry grin. "At least not until you get used to it more."

"You would want me again?" Requiem asked, surprised. In the past, the two Fighters who raped him only performed the action once. It was painful, but thankfully quick. After that, they would either roll over and go to sleep or throw him away in one fashion or another. Never had they used him more than once or twice. He really needed to get used to the thought that in all ways, Damion was different. Requiem had come to the conclusion that the Fighters had believed that if they raped him more than once, they would fall into the stigma of being labeled a homosexual.

"That was my plan until… until, well, until we've had enough of it." Damion scratched the back of his head, looking embarrassed.

"Have you had enough sex?" Requiem inquired simply, pushing up from the bed to stand, then turning around to look at Damion. Requiem tilted his head. He ignored the sticky fluid that seeped out of his stretched hole and down his inner thighs.

Damion shook his head frantically. "No. Hell no."

Requiem kept his icy gaze on Damion's face for a few moments. He wanted to take a shower, but he also wanted to experience more. Wanted to feel good again. "Then why do you wish to stop now if you haven't had enough?" He really was a bit confused.

Damion blinked. "Because if we do it again right now, then tomorrow you might hurt."

"I am used to pain. And you want to," Requiem said with a casual shrug, wondering what the issue was before he turned and walked to the bathroom, intent on a shower.

"Wait." Damion stood up quickly, following him. "You want more?"

Requiem had already turned the shower on and was pulling a clean towel out of the closet. "Any hypothesis that needs to be proven takes several experiments before the testing is complete and a conclusion is made." He didn't look at Damion, instead putting the towel on the counter before turning back toward the now steaming shower.

"You could have just said you didn't mind letting me fuck you again even if it meant having a sore ass tomorrow." Damion walked into the bathroom behind him. He turned Requiem around and kissed him deeply, eagerly.

If Damion didn't have such a grip on him, Requiem might have fallen backward into the shower. His eyes were wide as Damion's lips met his, hot and demanding. But they soon slipped closed, his pale body melting against Damion's tan one as his lips, tongue, and teeth responded in kind.

It took a few moments before Requiem heard an external pounding through the rush of the water in the tub and his own distraction. Reluctantly he pulled away slightly, his lips still touching Damion's. "Someone is at the door."

"*Damn it*," Damion cursed, grabbing the towel Requiem had placed on the counter to wrap around his waist, trying to hide his hard-on. "Whoever that is better be here to warn us the ship is under attack."

Chapter Twenty-One

Friday August 26, 454 MC
1821 GMT
Damion

As Damion opened the door, Juni's frowning face was the exact opposite of what Damion wanted to see. "What!"

He was aware of Requiem in the bathroom, listening.

"You weren't answering your vid, so I got concerned!" Juni spat. "And then your door was locked, so I wanted to make sure you were okay. Gods, sorry for being a friend. What's got your pants in a twist?"

"You seem to have this ability to always know when I'm about to have sex!" Damion spat in return before he could stop himself.

Juni stared at Damion in rare stillness, his eyes wide, mouth open from where his jaw had dropped. After a few silent moments, his face stretched into a lecherous grin. Then he got a glint in his eyes before purring, "And where the hell did you find a girl so soon after getting back from leave, huh? That's quick work."

"I didn't." Damion rubbed his face with his left hand, since his right was holding the towel up.

Juni blinked, the smile fading slightly as he took in Damion's state and then looked over Damion's shoulder to the crumpled and dirty sheets. His eyes flicked back to Damion, widening. "Where's 47?"

"In the shower." Damion's smile was tight and tense as he stared at his friend. "Look, either come in or not, but let's not talk with you in the hallway, okay?"

Juni seemed to waver between the two options. "Is… just…. Gods, is 47 okay? Just answer me that." After he realized what he was insinuating, Juni rushed on. "Not that I think you've hurt him, I don't! I know you never would, but he was so upset with you. It just seems like a weird turn of events. I, out of everyone, have no room to judge."

Damion groaned and wanted to smack Juni, but instead he just nodded. "He's fine. We're fine. He… I…. We just resolved our issues."

Juni snorted, rolling his eyes. "Is that what they're calling it nowadays?" he drawled, but then went pale at Damion's glare. "I'll just—" He smiled, pointing over his shoulder with his thumb and backing away slowly. "—leave. You kids have fun now." And with that, he ran.

"Going to kick your ass, you spoiled idiot!" Damion yelled out the door before heading back to the bathroom. He was instantly saddened when it looked like Requiem was already finished. "Done?"

Requiem looked up, blinking through the hanging folds of the towel draped over his head. "Showers do not take that long," he replied with a very brief, small, and awkward smile before continuing to dry his hair.

Damion sighed, unwrapping the towel around his waist. He had felt arousal with many of his sexual encounters, but giving in to a desire he had wanted to fulfill for so long had made the moment amazing, and he wanted a reprise. "I was hoping you would wait."

"For what? I am still here, am I not?"

Requiem put his towel on the counter and tilted his head slightly. Damion could see faint bruises that still showed starkly against the pale skin on Requiem's hips and neck. Requiem took the towel from Damion, folding it neatly next to his own.

Damion shook his head, "You know, to have sex again. It was Juni at the door thinking we had suddenly died."

"Generally sex requires the participation of two people. Therefore I had no choice but to wait for you since you were not here. If I had gone somewhere else, then that would have implied that I did not wait for you. Yet I am still here."

"Yes, but now we can't have sex in the shower because you're done with the shower. I mean—Never mind." Damion shook his head in frustration. "I guess you're not interested anymore. I'm going to kill Juni."

"Sometimes you make absolutely no sense, despite your high intelligence," Requiem said, with a shake of his head. He walked over to the shower and turned it back on. He turned to Damion, tilting his head slightly. "You need to take one as well, correct? There is no need to terminate Juni."

"I could have also had sex again, and if Juni hadn't come here, then I would have gotten it," Damion pointed out as he stepped into the spray of water.

Requiem merely looked at him for a moment, almost in disbelief. "Your test scores and IQ tests rank one of the highest in the Corporation, did you know that?"

"They do?" Damion shrugged. "I guess that's why I got into the Alpha program quickly."

"Affirmative. So I am intrigued by how someone so intelligent can be so dense at times," Requiem said with a brief smile and a shake of his head. Reaching into the shower with a slightly shaky hand, he gripped Damion by the back of the neck with a mere press of fingers, leaning in to kiss him. He gave a brief brush of lips against Damion's before pulling away. "I am being clear now, yes?"

"Yes. That I understand." Damion dragged Requiem under the spray and began kissing him as he had wanted to before being disturbed. He was suddenly squeezing Requiem's tight ass and grinding their hips together.

Instantly soaked again, Requiem wrapped trembling arms around him, moaning in a barely audible tone against Damion's mouth. He choked on a gasp when Damion grabbed his butt tightly, rubbing their needs together.

Damion kissed across Requiem's jaw and down the pale column of his neck. He was so worried about hurting or scaring him that he failed to take his usual initiative when it came to having sex. And while Requiem was trembling a bit in nervousness, he was also tilting his head to the side to give Damion more access to his neck. Requiem's hands gripped Damion's shoulders as he tried to keep his balance on the slippery shower floor.

Damion bit his way up to Requiem's ear. His fingers delved into Requiem's ass cleft, teasing his entrance. When his teeth reached Requiem's ear, a tingle raced through him and he suspected Requiem felt the same as he gasped and pulled away slightly, bringing soaked, bandaged fingers to his ear in wonderment. Requiem looked into nothing for a moment before looking up at Damion's face.

Damion could see his confusion. "I was just trying to get you aroused," he explained as he looked down at their mutual erections. "I figure it's more fun if we're both hard."

"I understand your actions. I just do not understand my reaction," Requiem replied hesitantly, his fingers still touching his ear. "My… when you bit my ear it…."

"It felt good? It made your body respond?" Damion chuckled and pulled Requiem's fingers away from his ear. "Everyone has sensitive, erogenous zones. It's nothing to be worried about."

"If you say so," Requiem said hesitantly, his hand wrapping around Damion's.

He looked back up into Damion's eyes for a moment before he leaned in to lay a light kiss on Damion's lips. A bare, feather touch of skin.

"That feels nice." Damion laughed softly, a mere rumble in his chest. "Want to go back to the bed since we might slip and fall in here?"

"I… like it when your lips turn up like that," Requiem said instead of responding to Damion's question. His fingers ran over said lips before moving to the left side of his own bare chest, over one of his ports and his heart. "It makes me feel warm here. It is perplexing."

"That's just your emotions making your heart clench. It happened to me when we were in bed." Damion pressed two fingers against Requiem's entrance.

"It… did? Why?" was all Requiem was able to get out before he gasped, his body clenching around Damion's pressure. He managed to relax, though, and ended up against the wall. "Sorry," he mumbled.

"It's okay." Damion turned off the water and pulled away. "Let's go to the bed."

"Will we not just end up having to wash again?" Requiem asked confusedly.

"Probably, but it's better than me not paying attention and one of us slipping and falling." Damion was used to sex with girls, and he wasn't sure if they would need more lube. The fact he was now willing to do this with another man no longer worried him. He desired Requiem. He wanted to have sex with him. The kissing seemed to make Requiem pliable. Damion felt like a teenager, but the lust was tinted with the need to protect.

"You are right. It would not be good if we have to take a trip to Medical for something we could have prevented." Requiem stepped out of the shower, grabbing his still-damp towel and handing Damion his own.

"Don't need that yet." Damion bent down with a bark of laughter and picked Requiem up, almost like a princess. Requiem actually squeaked as Damion lifted him up and carried him into the room to drop him onto the bed with a bounce. Before he could recover, Damion's mouth was on him and Requiem grasped his shoulders tightly. They were both dripping with water and messing the bed up more than it already was, but Damion just didn't care as Requiem's spread legs rubbed against the outside of his.

Damion trailed his lips back to Requiem's ear, since that seemed to really get his attention. He started nibbling at the lobe and then gently swirled his tongue inside. Damion was already hard just from this simple foreplay. He was happy to find every part of Requiem that elicited a shiver or a moan.

Damion spent the next two hours exploring Requiem again and again, until they were both near unconsciousness.

They never did make it back to the shower.

Chapter Twenty-Two

Saturday August 27, 454 MC
0547 GMT
Requiem

CORES WERE not supposed to have the ability to dream. They were purposefully given a chemical to shut down the visions seen during REM sleep. But while Requiem slept, he dreamed. For the first time that he could remember, he saw pictures in his mind that didn't really make sense, but they were there all the same. Flashes of images in color and black-and-white, pictures made of electricity and flashing pulses of moving light.

No, the dream didn't make much sense, but there was one thing, one person, that appeared in each sequence, and that was Damion. Requiem's partner, Fighter, and now lover.

Requiem woke with a sharp intake of breath, his muscles twitching in an attempt to sit up, but he found himself unable to move with Damion's weight on him. Requiem looked over at Damion's sleeping, peaceful face. Damion, whose arm was currently wrapped around Requiem's waist, keeping him where he was. Requiem ran gentle fingers over Damion's face, and Damion merely smiled in his sleep, rubbing against those fingers for a moment before settling back down.

Slowly, carefully, Requiem slid out from Damion's grasp and out of the bed, standing with some difficulty due to a slight pain in his lower back. He winced, then let a brief smile touch his lips as he limped over to his capsule, sitting down on the side and sliding into it. He sighed in relief to feel the familiar machinery embrace him. The dream had disturbed him, and he had been a bit overloaded with too many new emotions and physical stimuli within the last few hours and needed something normal.

Closing his eyes, he keyed in his code to activate the capsule by feel alone, gasping softly as the jacks slid into his ports. Letting out a long breath, he relaxed into the system and back into sleep, to a place where he hoped the dreams would not follow him.

Damion

DAMION AWOKE and looked up to the clock and noticed it was only thirty minutes from the time they were supposed to be at the hangar for briefing. He expected to find Requiem next to him, but Requiem's side of the bed was cold and empty. He sat up, a bit worried, and frowned when he saw Requiem plugged into the capsule.

Damion watched as Requiem released the jacks with a twitch of his fingers, gasping as they unplugged from his system, his back slightly bowing in response. After a moment he sat up, blinking blearily until he focused on Damion's disapproving look. He gave him a small, tentative smile that seemed apologetic and embarrassed at the same time.

"I dreamed," Requiem said quietly, as if it explained everything.

"Huh?" Damion wasn't completely awake enough for that sentence to make any lick of sense to him. "You had a nightmare or something?"

"I do not know the difference between nightmares and dreams," Requiem replied, sitting up and then stepping out of the capsule to move over to the bed. After a moment's hesitation, he sat down in Damion's lap, wrapping his arms around him. "I have never dreamed before. It was unsettling."

"Dreams don't always make sense. Sometimes they're just random. Some people believe they're messages from the gods." Damion hugged Requiem's smaller body close, not wanting to leave their room. They had to go to the briefing and face the world as Fighter and Core. He wanted to stay in this room and exist just as Damion and Requiem.

"I do not believe in the gods." Requiem laid his head on Damion's shoulder. "We have patrol duty in approximately one hour."

Damion groaned as he looked back up at the clock. "Yeah, you're right. I guess we both need to shower and dress."

Requiem nodded, sliding off Damion's lap. "There were some unidentified rebel ships in the area approximately two days ago. They have not been seen since, but alert status has been raised." He tilted his head. "Did you wish to take a shower first, or would you prefer me to?"

"Let's just take one together, and I promise to behave this time." Damion stood up and watched Requiem closely to see if his Core seemed hurt at all.

Requiem was limping a little, but not enough that he seemed to notice as he walked to the bathroom. "What do you mean behave?"

"I won't start anything." Damion laughed as he followed Requiem. "Like a few hours ago."

"I understand." Requiem turned on the shower and cranked up the heat. He always took his showers near boiling. Damion noticed the slight frown on Requiem's face, and he cataloged it under *disappointment*. "If we participate in sexual exploits," Requiem said, "drawing on an average of all our times to come to coitus the night before, then we would definitely be late."

"Good way to put that!" He let out a bark of laughter, then calmed when he remembered why Requiem was unnerved.

"Do you remember anything about your dream?" Damion asked as he scrubbed Requiem's hair.

Requiem sighed, leaning into Damion's hands. "Affirmative, but only a few things. It took place in many different areas, but you were always there. It was perplexing."

"Yeah, sometimes I'll be dreaming I'm back at home, then other times at places I've never visited but only seen on vids." Damion shrugged. "Do you have to go to the capsule every time that happens?"

Requiem's head tilted and Damion could see the wheels turning as Requiem thought about the question seriously for a moment. "I do not know. I have never had a dream before, and I felt… I felt like I needed something familiar to ground me."

"I guess you have to do that to feel better." Damion urged Requiem to rinse out his hair.

Requiem tilted his head back under the water and quickly rinsed out his hair before grabbing soap and pouring it onto a washcloth. He started washing Damion's back. "You are upset?"

"I just got used to you sleeping next to me, so I figured you would be there when I woke up. I'd just rather you stay next to me."

Requiem's hands paused in their washing for a moment before resuming slowly. "I cannot say that I can all the time. Unfortunately I do need to plug in daily while on the *Zeus*. I am not saying that I cannot sleep in the bed, but I do need to jack in so that they can monitor me while I rest at times. So I may only occasionally sleep in your bed."

Damion let out a deep sigh of resignation at Requiem's need for the capsule. "All right. I get it."

Damion washed off the soap and heard the fifteen-minute warning from the other room. "Slave drivers."

Requiem stepped out of the shower first. He grabbed a towel and handed it to Damion before getting one for himself. "We only have approximately seven minutes to get ready if we are going to arrive in time."

"No problem." Damion quickly toweled off his hair and then went to pull out some clothing.

Requiem was a bit quicker at it, pulling up his uniform and zipping it up to his neck. He grabbed his passkey and put it in the arm pocket, then made sure that all the holes in the suit matched up neatly with his ports. There was a reason that a Core's uniform was tighter than a Fighter's was: so they didn't have any problems with jacking in. He sat on the edge of his capsule and waited for Damion to finish.

Damion fastened his belt and combed his fingers through his wet hair. "All right, let's go before we get yelled at our first day back."

Nodding, Requiem moved to the door and called for it to open—and then stopped. Blocking their way were four men from the *Zeus*'s security team, and they did not look happy.

The one in a lieutenant's uniform stepped forward, blocking the doorway even more. "Core 47, I am Lieutenant Niles. You are to come with us. The Creators would like to see you," he demanded, his dark eyes serious and unkind before he turned them to Damion. "Your patrol is canceled for the day because of his absence. You will be confined to quarters." He turned, motioning his hand for one of the other men to walk into the room, before he turned back to Damion. "Collins will make sure you do so." He grabbed Requiem by the arm and began to pull him into the hall.

Requiem looked back at Damion for a moment, his eyes sad and even a little fearful. He acted like he knew what was going to happen next. His lips formed the word "good-bye."

"Wait! Hey! What's this shit about?" Damion rushed forward, trying to take Requiem back.

The man already in the room—Collins—came out of nowhere and punched Damion in the stomach, pushing him back into their quarters. The leader turned, still gripping Requiem's arm. "Fighter Hawk, I suggest you do not make this any worse for you than it already is. The Creators discovered last night that you've broken the rules concerning Core 47, and as a result, his programming is unraveling. They've become aware of the fact that he is not eating all his supplements and therefore will become useless to the Corporation unless something is done about it. This is your one warning, Fighter Hawk. If you continue to let this happen, you will be dishonorably discharged for corrupting and tampering with the Corporation's property."

"That's bullshit! He's fine! He is the best!" Damion stood up and thought about fighting his guard dog but stopped short, wondering if they would take it out on his Core. A cold fear filled his veins. "If you would only let me explain! I told him to do it! It wasn't his fault!"

The Core in question, his *Requiem*, stayed silent. He seemed to know it wouldn't do any good. He stood there with his head bowed and gave in to the inevitable.

"Of course it was your fault! They are not blaming 47, merely fixing him before he becomes too broken to keep conscious. The Creators will return him to you in ten hours. We expect you to keep your fucking mouth shut, or I'll have Collins here shut it for you. End of discussion." And with that, he walked out, dragging Requiem away by the arm.

Damion took a step forward, and that same annoying body blocked his way. He was so angry. He was also so afraid. He hated waiting. At least they wouldn't hurt Requiem—he hoped.

Collins stood in front of the door, turning to flash a key card over the console next to the door that would override Damion's voice commands. After that, he walked over to the small table, grabbed a chair, and dragged it in front of the door to sit on, then crossed his arms with a snide grin on his face.

He was smaller than Damion, but had more upper-body muscle. For a quick moment, Damion considered whether or not he could take him down and determined Collins would give him a challenge in hand-to-hand. Damion would have to use a weapon. He then considered whether attempting to escape would be his best bet to help Requiem.

"So, Hawk, we're going to be here for at least five hours together. We should get to know each other."

Collins cut off Damion's train of thought and stared at him with empty, almost dead-looking brown eyes.

"No offense, but you're keeping me here against my will while they go and 'fix' my Core." Damion tried not to sound like a complete ass, but it was hard to achieve.

"Hey, it's your own fault. Be happy they're fixing him," Collins said as he stretched and linked his tan, callused fingers behind his head. "Generally when a toy or a tool gets broken, there are two different ways to go about it. Fixing it or throwing it out. Be happy they're doing the former and not wiping him and plugging him into the system."

"He's too damn good to be wiped," Damion said through clenched teeth as he attempted to calm his temper.

"Mm, yes, but sometimes you have to throw out the good with the bad when a Core becomes a liability and can't be controlled. And that's what the creepy scientists are afraid is goin' to happen. Especially with 47, who's shown way the fuck too much independence since he arrived on the *Zeus*. And that was before he stopped taking his thrice-daily dose of gruel."

Collins closed his eyes until they were mere slits, watching Damion closely through them. "You'd actually be doing both of you a favor by doing what they tell ya. Either you do, or you get booted and he gets a complete mind-wipe and plugged into the ship. Nothing more than a breathing machine until he dies. And let me tell you, the plugged Cores are fucking creepy. They just lie there, eyes wide open, cords coming out of every orifice and beyond and just… breathe. That's it. They don't move or nothing, just lie there, staring."

"Are you trying to freak me out? Because all you're doing is pissing me off!" Damion snapped and kicked the back wall of his room. "He was fine! He's good because he is different from other Cores. He's faster and smarter. They say we can basically do anything we want with them, and now they're pissed because I did."

"Ah, anything within the rules. Anything that doesn't ruin the precious balance of man, machine, and slave that they've made the Cores into. Your Core was starting to feel emotion. There were even signs of dreaming. Both big no-no's. They aren't supposed to feel, and dreaming is unnecessary. They're supposed to be good little automatons unable to disagree, fight back, or go against orders."

Collins paused, opening his eyes and leaning forward so that his elbows rested on his knees, his hands dangling between. The guard's dark tan complexion was a striking contrast to the pale green material of his uniform. "Why do you care anyway? He's only a Core, yet you're freakin' the fuck out."

"He's *my* Core! Mine," Damion growled as he stopped pacing and looked at his jailor. He was getting a hunch the guard was holding something back. "How do you know so damn much about them anyway? Who are you exactly? You're not just some infantryman."

"Easy there, Hawk. You just sounded like you pissed on the kid in a territorial dispute like a dog would a tree." Collins put up placating hands as he leaned back in the chair. "And yeah, I am just some infantryman. Doesn't mean I always have been, though. I was once an Alpha. I've been told my Core is now plugged into the bridge. Went crazy one day and killed a Creator and a doctor. So he was wiped, and I was shoved down to the bottom of the barrel for not reporting the changes in him."

Damion frowned but still refused to meet former Fighter Collins's eyes that were just as lifeless as some of the Cores' were. A doll's glass eyes, shiny but devoid of emotion. "Why wouldn't they just let you be rechosen? If they let Arkin have Core after Core, why not you?"

Collins shifted, pulled out a pack of soothe cigarettes, and handed them to Damion. These were like the Stim Cigs Damion enjoyed at times for a jolt of energy, except these of course were to help calm a man down. Damion took the pack but wasn't sure if he wanted to use one of them or not. Collins's eyes were focused on the ceiling. "Because I didn't want to be rechosen after they took 162. Not only that, but my Core already went crazy and I'd known something was up beforehand, even had a part in it, but didn't say anything because I didn't want him taken away from me. Why would they let me have another one after that? Nah, I'm better off, and I don't want another Core besides 162."

Damion sat down finally and turned the pack of cigs around in his hand. "All I wanted when I joined was to do anything but work in a dead-end Corporation job. Then they give me status, but with strings attached. Req—47, he's the best. I'll be the best with him if they'd just leave us alone and let us fight."

"They ain't gonna do that, though. They don't see much point in having something they can't control. If they control the Core they can, in some way, control you," Collins said. He looked at Damion for a moment, seeming to weigh him. "You care too much for 47, and by the way, I caught that. You named him, and that just proves my point. They don't like it when you feel more than partnership and trust in your Core, and you have gone above and beyond that." He looked over at the mussed bed, nodding his head at it. "And I'm not just talking about that."

"There's nothing wrong with *that*." Damion's anger and nervousness returned. "They expect us to use them like that, and I can call him anything I want. They expect us to trust the Cores with our lives. Of course we're going to become attached."

"Actually most Fighters don't become attached. No more than they would to a pet, anyway. Why would you make friends with your computer? You trust your Zodiac to keep you safe, but you don't have sex with it." Collins paused, looking up at the ceiling. "Well, there was this one guy in basic…." He shook his head. "But that's another story. And yes, you might argue that many Fighters do that with their Cores, and it's true. It is another of their supposed functions that I see as nothing better than whoring them out."

He got up, turned his chair around, and straddled it, looking intently at Damion. "The difference is that some Fighters actually care when they fuck their Cores. Others, it's like masturbation with a warm hole. Big difference."

"They're human. They're not just pets." Damion probably had thought of Requiem like a pet at first. He had made sure he was fed and safe but hadn't cared past that, really. Until the weeks passed and he saw how aware of his surroundings Requiem was compared to other Cores. "He came different. He has never been like the other Cores. He never will be, and I can't treat him like a computer when he's not one. Didn't you fuck your Core and feel something? Or were you disregarding his emotions completely?"

Collins was quiet for a few minutes. "I loved 162. He was unstable at times, but I did love him. It wasn't either of our faults, what happened. He was taking his daily regimen of mush, but… it always made him a little squirrelly afterwards. Paranoid even, and his sleep patterns were horrible. It wasn't until I took him off the gruel that I realized he was having a reaction to it. The reason he snapped and killed that Creator and doc was because they gave him a full dose of it, undiluted, straight into his bloodstream. It was too much and he shattered, his mind just went into overdrive, trying to get to me, but I was in Medical, unconscious with an injury. He defended himself against the Creator who was going to wipe him. The doc was going to take him, take us, away and he fought back so he could make it to Medical to find me."

There was pain in his voice—deep, old pain, but it was there.

"That's what they're going to do to your Core. Except they'll probably give him a bigger dose and do some other stuff. But...." He looked at Damion with something akin to pity in his eyes, but also deep understanding. "He won't be the same. I warn you that. But at least you'll get him back—this time."

"What do you mean he won't be the same?" At that moment, Damion wished he had a bottle of whiskey from home.

"The heavy dose of serum will wash away any semblance of emotion, of personality. Tactile functions will be dulled. He'll be the perfect little zombie again. 47 might still remember everything from before, but he won't understand what he was feeling. And I think on some level he will still have those emotional connections, but he won't be able to figure them out. Just like those who are plugged in, he'll be trapped within his own mind or behind the haze of chems in his brain."

"Are you trying to cheer me up? You're doing a really fucking swell job." He couldn't believe all the work he'd done with Requiem would be washed away so easily. "Why didn't you try and take your Core and run?"

"Hey, I'm just trying to give you a heads-up here, not be Miss Mary Fuckin' Sunshine." His gaze traveled toward the floor. "I never had an opportunity. It all happened so fast. He snapped, killed the creeper and doc, and they swept him away. I wasn't even conscious. Found out about it afterward.

"After they're wiped and plugged in, they have them locked up tight. Only higher-ups and the creepers are allowed to see them, and if your Core is one of them in there, then you never get to see them. I don't know if 162 is even alive anymore or ever plugged into the *Zeus*. I was told and shown two different stories. But the ones who are plugged in, well some of them just… die. Shut down and die."

He inhaled and blew a few smoke rings before continuing. "Besides, even if I had the opportunity, we wouldn't get far. Cores have a tracking device implanted into the back of their heads, straight into the gray matter. The Corp can find them anytime, anywhere. And shut them down with it as well. It sends out a pulse that fries their brains to jelly. It's so if they're ever taken in battle, the rebels won't be able to access or keep the Corp's property. So there's really no point."

"Would you want to know if he was still plugged in?" Damion asked slowly, wanting to find out more from someone who had been in his position before.

Collins thought about it for a long moment. "I don't know. I don't want to think of him lying there brain-dead. I think I would prefer if he were actually dead. I wouldn't want him to be trapped like that. He would wish for death instead. I know that."

"If my Core was here, he could find out. He can do anything inside the system," Damion stated proudly, even if he felt sad. "He killed three Fighters before choosing me."

"You mean he chose you before killing three other pilots," Collins said with a snort. "I heard about that. Hell, everyone heard about that and thought you'd end up just like the others. But once I heard the whole story, I knew he wouldn't kill you. The only reason your Core is not with my 162 is because of his advanced abilities with the system. On the one hand, he's a valuable commodity that the creepies want to let grow and see what he does, what he learns, what he can manipulate. On the other hand, they don't want him to grow independent or have too many individual thoughts about anything other than the system. If he does continue to push them, they'll put him in the category of being a liability and wipe him. They won't like it, but they figure there will always be another."

Damion grumbled as he felt the beginning of a headache born of stress at the unfair situation. "They can't take him away."

Collins stood up. He opened the small fridge and pulled out two beers, popping them open as he walked back and handed one to Damion. "Can't really do anything about it if they choose to." He sat heavily back in the chair, sipping the brew. "Do you love your Core? Or are you merely protective?"

"He's mine—of course I would be protective. I've put months of work into making him happy." Damion wasn't sure if that meant love, but he knew Requiem was more than just important to him.

"So basically, an incestuous big-brother complex," Collins said with a shrug of his broad shoulders and took another drink. "So you ain't gonna do anything about it if they decide taking him would be the best bet all around." Damion noticed Collins said these probing words while watching Damion carefully. "Just get a new Core. It ain't love, so it isn't that important."

"What the fuck is your problem?" Damion spat through clenched teeth, his eyes narrowing in anger. "He isn't *replaceable*! He isn't a machine! Just because you gave up, doesn't mean I'm going to!"

"And I'm just wondering how you think that isn't love?" Collins said with a small sad grin around the mouth of his bottle. "For the record, I didn't give up. I never had the opportunity to do anything other than let it happen. I was unconscious when he was taken, and anything else would have been suicide anyway and that wouldn't have helped him either."

Damion took a swig of his drink, trying to wash away the bad taste in his mouth. He wasn't sure if it was his anger or his fear that had him choked up at the moment. It may have even been Collins's words making him feel confused and panicked. "I just want my Core back."

"Understandable. And they'll return him—this time. But the question is, what will you do when they do?" Collins focused intently on Damion.

Damion pulled the beer away from his lips and gave him an incredulous look. "What do you mean? Even if they numb him up, he will still be my Core."

Collins rolled his eyes in exasperation. "That isn't what I meant. I've given you examples of everything they do. After your Core comes back, are you going to follow their rules or attempt to get the Core who you know and appreciate back and therefore face the possibility of losing him permanently?"

"I don't have a choice." Damion dry washed his face. "I can't tell you what I have planned. I just met you. I don't know if I can trust you." More than he had already, anyway.

"Very true. And good call. I just wanted to get you thinking about other options." Collins finished off his beer and tossed it in the trash.

"I grew up on Mars. I know you can't trust anyone in uniform." Damion sat back down and wondered why they would even let a man who had a Core taken away guard him. A grand plan to show Damion how powerless he was in the face of the Corporation's power. "The next few hours are going to suck."

Collins laughed, a short bark that sounded husky from disuse. "Both very true points. Got a pack of cards?"

"I packed a deck when I was shipped out, but I haven't used it in a few weeks. Juni sucks at poker and my Core just counts the cards." Damion went back to his duffel to look inside, wanting to bolt. Wanting to track Requiem down and make sure he wasn't being hurt. But he couldn't do any of that, and he needed more than one beer to take his tension away.

Collins stood up and grabbed the table, putting it between their chairs. "No offense, but if they happen to check on us and don't see my ass planted in front of the door, they'll pull me, and I can assure you Miles don't give a shit about you or your Core. I'll do what I can to pull the full shift instead of splitting it with the asshole." He reached into his uniform jacket and pulled out a flask, setting it on the table. "Here, you need this more than I do right now. Mostly because I don't suck at poker and you're going to need it to soothe your pride."

"Big talk from an infantryman." Damion sat down and put the deck on the table. "You want to use real credits or ration vouchers?"

Collins turned his chair back around to a proper position and sat down once again. "We'll start off with the vouchers. I hoard my money like a dragon hoards gold, and I'm rather reluctant to give it up. You wanna deal first or shall I?"

"Aren't you a little old to believe in dragons? Next you'll say there are aliens hiding behind the sun." Damion opened the deck and began to fold the cards while looking at the flask.

"What? You didn't get that memo? Well, aren't you in the fucking dark ages?" Collins used a pinky finger to push the flask toward Damion. "Go again. Take a swig right now. I promise it ain't poisoned. Well, not in the literal sense. Shit will take the hair off your balls, but it won't outright kill you."

Damion took the flask and tipped it back, letting the liquid hit his tongue. It was smooth at first, but then his entire throat felt as if it had been set on fire. Goddamn Uranian whiskey was easy to pick out because it took all of Damion's strength not to cough up the acid eroding his throat. "Not bad." He couldn't hide the wheeze.

He put the flask down and began to deal the cards, unable to say another word for the next few minutes. He was almost scared to take a drag from his smoke in case his entire body lit on fire from the inside out.

"You're tougher than I thought. You can still talk," Collins teased blandly, looking at his cards.

For the remaining time, they played cards, drank, and generally tried to keep Damion's mind off what was happening to Requiem. Collins managed to keep the whole shift, despite the regretful growls from Miles, who had been looking forward to goading Damion to do something stupid—that was what Collins told him, and Damion knew it was possible.

Eventually Damion had to lie down, his head swirling from the strong liquor, while Collins dozed with his back against the door.

The ten long hours passed and began to creep into the eleventh before Collins started to frown at the clock in the room. It was only then that the door beeped, asking for the unlock code. Collins stood up, straightening his uniform, before passing his card over the panel to unlock the door.

Chapter Twenty-Three

Damion

"LOOK ALIVE, Fighter."

Damion rolled off the bed and stood up straight, keeping his mouth shut, even though he wanted to tell the man to go to hell. He tried to look past Collins, hoping to see Requiem.

Requiem was brought in by two men. They were not the same men who had taken him away. They held him up on either side by his arms. His head was bowed and his toes dragged heavily even as he attempted to walk. Damp hair plastered his head, shaping paler than usual skin, which was saying something. The lieutenant followed behind, his lips pursed in a frown as he kept sharp eyes on Damion. He flicked his chin to Collins and then the door.

"Remember what I said," Collins shot a look full of pity at Damion as he saluted the lieutenant and then left. The two others took Requiem to the capsule, lifting him roughly into the pod before letting him slump back. His ice blue eyes were glazed and only half-open as the men left him and went out the door.

Damion rushed to Requiem's side and pulled him forward into a sitting position. "What did they do? Are you okay?"

Requiem blinked blearily at Damion. His arms were limp at his sides, and a bruise colored the bend of one arm with a trickle of blood still trailing down. His skin was chilled and damp, and the pads of his fingers appeared wrinkled, signifying he had been submerged for a long time.

"I am acceptable, but weary" was all Requiem said, his voice monotone, cold, and husky as if it had been misused at length.

"Fuck." Damion picked him up carefully and carried him to the bed. "You look like shit. Have you even eaten in the last few hours? I bet you haven't."

Requiem had wilted. It was obvious he didn't have control over his muscles yet.

"My stomach was emptied for the procedure, so no, I have not. I am not in need of sustenance at this time. If you wish me to, I will consume my rations."

"You're back to talking like a machine." Damion sighed as he wrapped Requiem up in all the blankets he owned and leaned him back against the pillows. "I'll get you some water. If you haven't had anything in your stomach for a while, you might get sick if we push it."

"As you wish," Requiem replied. "I would also be quite acceptable in my capsule if you do not prefer me in your sleeping space." His voice was weary and his eyes still half-open. He looked content to remain on the surface of the bed.

"You really are acting different." Damion hated both himself and Collins for being right. "You know I want you with me. Don't you remember what we were doing here less than a day ago?"

Requiem blinked very slowly, and Damion could almost see the gears working in his mind. "I do apologize, but I do not have much recollection for a segment of time ranging for approximately two weeks. I have retained some pieces, but a significant portion is not present."

"*What?*" Damion's voice rose. "*How can they do that?*"

Requiem blinked again through soggy strands of hair, his head tilting slightly in the familiar birdlike motion, except jerkily this time, like an unoiled robot. "How can who do what, sir?"

Damion punched the air above and in front of him, fighting off the very men in his mind who had done this to them. The moment his fists stopped moving, he screamed, his voice cracking in the process, "Take away your memories!"

"I am not privileged to that information," Requiem said, starting to tremble despite the layers of blankets around him.

"It can't be permanent. Maybe it's a side effect?" Damion asked Requiem, struggling to keep hope alive inside himself.

"I am concluding that you mean a side effect of my procedure. I do not know."

Requiem wasn't able to keep his head up anymore and let it fall back against the wood of the recessed bookshelf with a low *thunk*.

"Requiem…." Damion sighed and pulled him more centrally onto the bed and tucked him in tightly. Once finished, he sat on the edge, hands folded and dangling between his knees, thinking and trying to control his urge to find the person responsible and commit homicide.

Then it dawned on him.

He was the one responsible for everything going on at the moment. He was the one who pushed Requiem to eat real food instead of his rations, and he was the one who initiated sex that Requiem actually enjoyed.

It was his fault.

Requiem finally seemed to stop shivering, and perhaps it wasn't just because of the blankets but because of Damion's presence. Requiem watched him through hooded eyes for a few moments.

"You do not seem completely acceptable, and I hypothesize that it is because I do not have the knowledge you require. Is there anything that I might do to assist you?"

Damion sighed, rubbing his face as he tried to hide his despair. "Just go to sleep. I can only pray you remember everything when you wake up."

"I have displeased you. I apologize."

Requiem's mechanical tone was softer in repentance. Slowly, and with obvious effort, he sat up and struggled out of the blankets before moving off the bed and shakily walking toward his pod. Despite Damion's insistence that he wanted Requiem to sleep in the bed, Requiem seemed almost compelled not to. His eyes glazed again as he wobbled across the room.

"Where in Hades are you going?" Damion asked, more than a little pissed off as he watched his Core—or the person who used to be his Core, because the man in front of him was just a shell.

With visible effort to keep himself on his feet, Requiem turned around to look at Damion. "You ordered me to go to sleep. I am required to use my capsule to do so."

"No, you don't. You've slept in my bed for almost a month. Now get back into bed and sleep." Damion tried to control his temper, to remind himself that it wasn't Requiem's fault that he was like this. Damion couldn't take his fury out on the exhausted man. So he added a "Please."

Requiem merely stood there for a moment, beginning to tremble. He looked to be fighting an internal battle that had him panting with effort. His eyes squeezed shut, jaw clenched, as he fought the compulsions placed upon him. Slowly, carefully, shakily, he took a step back toward the bed.

"Stubborn fool, even brainwashing you doesn't change that," Damion said fondly as he stood and picked up Requiem once again, dropping him back into bed with a little less finesse than usual. He began to wrap Requiem in the blankets, cocooning him in soft warmth. "Stay."

Requiem was still breathing heavily. The sweat on his body was just making him shudder, and his skin looked feverish as he watched Damion with heavy-lidded, exhausted eyes. "Was ordered by you to stay. Was ordered by the Creators to jack in. I will admit I do not know what to do."

"You're supposed to listen to me. You're my Core." Damion looked at Requiem straight on, his stern expression allowing no resistance to his orders. "Let me deal with those assholes. They've had you jacked in for hours already."

Suddenly Requiem's pale hand was out from under the blankets, fingers held gently against Damion's lips. He was fighting another internal battle, and it showed in his eyes, his teeth chattering as he spoke. "I r-request that you do not s-speak of anything that you wish not to be repeated back to the Creators."

"I can't even trust you not to tell them everything now?" Damion's voice was filled with hatred, and then immediately it changed to overwhelming sorrow. "Where did you go? Are you even still in there?" He spoke in a soft, broken voice as he finally realized that Collins had been telling him the complete truth—Requiem was different. More 47 than Requiem now.

Requiem's gaze met Damion's tortured one. "I do not know how to properly answer that question" was all he could reply verbally. However, tears gathered and slipped down his cheeks. Just a few before they ceased, seemingly never noticed by Requiem. His mind and what he could say, what he could remember, were wrapped in chains, binding who he truly was.

"I'm sorry. Just get some rest." Damion gently brushed the wet cheek with a slightly trembling hand. "I'm sure you've been through hell."

"There is no need for you to apologize. It is my lack of information that is at fault." Requiem slipped farther into the blankets, letting the warmth wrap around him, dragging him toward the abyss. "As you order."

"As I order," Damion mumbled as he watched his Core—his lover—slip into oblivion.

What the hell was he going to do? Everything they had just gone through was wiped. *Everything.* A part of him still felt the need to lash out.

His pondering was interrupted by an insistent banging on the door to his quarters. "Damion! You in there? Fuck, man, answer the damn door!" a familiar voice demanded, tinged with fear and worry.

Damion went to the door and flung it open. "Stop screaming! Gods, you're worse than a yowling cat."

"Well, if you had seen Security guarding your best friend's door for most of the day, you'd be howling like a cat too," Juni spat uncharacteristically, quickly walking into the room past Damion and then whirling around to meet him eye to eye. "What in the gods' names happened?"

"They took him." Damion quickly closed the door and waved a hand toward the occupied bed. "They took him, wiped him clean, and now, now he's back to the way it was when we first met. He doesn't remember anything."

Juni's gaze took in the sleeping figure in the bed before looking back to Damion with a stunned expression.

"Fuck. I mean... shit.... Shit." Juni couldn't manage to articulate more than that, running his fingers through his hair. "What do you mean by anything? You mean everything or...? And why did they take him? It just doesn't make any sense."

"I don't know. They just showed up." Damion sat down on the foot of the bed almost bonelessly, looking at the ground without truly seeing it. "All I can think of is that when he jacked in last night they somehow found out. They said they knew he had a dream. Knew he hadn't been taking his full ration of supplements."

Grabbing a chair, Juni dragged it to sit in front of him. "He dreamed? 108 hasn't done that and he hasn't been taking the supplements as frequently either. Although he also jacked in last night." Juni was quiet for a moment before shrugging slightly. "I know it's a pain in the ass, but can you just start from the beginning again? He's bound to remember something eventually."

Damion pressed the heels of his hands into his eyes, which were burning with the threat of tears. "From the beginning? Fuck, Juni, it took months for me just to...."

Juni didn't push him to complete that sentence. "So what are you going to do? What are your other options?" he asked quietly, trying not to disturb Requiem's sleep. "I know if it was 108, I'd be goin' fuckin' insane right now, trying to figure this shit out."

"I fucking don't know, okay?" Damion's hands clenched over his forehead. "I've been warned that if it fucking happens again, I'll be dishonorably discharged. They'll take him and plug him into the main system!"

Juni looked at him with his mouth open wide for a moment before it shut with a click of his teeth. Cursing under his breath, he stood and began pacing. "And if you find a way to take him away, they'll just find you both." He was silently saying Damion was damned either way. "Well fuck, D. You're the smarter one out of the both of us, and if we can't figure this out, we're screwed." He turned to Damion before he could protest. "And yes, I meant both of us. I'm not letting you deal with this shit alone. Not only are you my best friend, but eventually they'll come after 108 and I just…. That can't happen. I'm sorry, Damion."

"If they haven't picked up 108 yet, maybe there is something he's doing differently when he goes into the capsule, and maybe that can help us." Damion was thinking out loud, reaching for anything that might help his situation. "But you can't get involved. I'm sure they're already watching you and him closer now as well, since we're known to hang together."

"I'll talk to 108, see what he can tell me, but the hell with just abandoning you and 47! I don't care if they know we hang out together. I'm not going to just desert you guys, and I know 108 will feel the same," Juni insisted.

"We can't trust him." Damion looked toward his sleeping Core. "Requiem… he said that everything I say to him would get reported back to them. I don't know how long that will last or if he can even fight it."

Juni was silent for a moment, pity and anger apparent in his normally jovial features. "The fact that he was able to warn you is proof enough that he's trying to fight whatever sick fucking compulsions they put on him." Juni's gaze flickered to Requiem, who was in a deep sleep. "Maybe you can't trust what you say around him, but always trust that he'll be fighting. I've seen that in him more so than 108. 108 was beaten down over time, but 47, he's always been a fighter."

"108 had Arkin, that would be hard for any Core to recover from, and I still don't understand why they let that man have a Core to begin with." Damion ran his fingers through his short hair. "I just don't know what to do or where to start."

"I really don't have any advice for you there, man. You know 47 better than anyone, so only you would know how to bring him out. But then you have the problem of still needing him to eat the sludge. It has to be a balance of getting his personality back but not the emotions that would trigger the scientists noticing." Juni shrugged. "I'll help you any way I can, but I don't envy you figuring that out."

"I don't envy the reflection you have to put up with every day in the mirror," Damion muttered with a small smirk.

"Here I am! Offering you whatever help I can, and you go and insult me? See if I ever offer you anything ever again." Juni rolled his eyes and shook his head before pausing. Then "Wait a minute…. *Requiem?*"

"Hm? Oh, nothing." Damion got up and tried to think of something quick to change the subject. "I need a stiff drink."

"If that's what it takes to make you explain why you named your Core, and Requiem of all things, then get completely plastered," Juni stated dryly while watching him. "And make me one while you're at it."

Damion went over to his fridge, picking out the last of his beers. "Look, I don't know why I did, I just did. And so what if I did?"

Juni put up his hands in a placating gesture before taking the offered beer. "Hey, I'm not judging. Just curious."

"I just can't see them as computers. I mean I can, but not him." Damion sat heavily back down on the end of the bed. "Do you love 108?"

Juni nearly sprayed his beer all over Damion but managed to just cough as he choked on it instead. "Do I *what?*"

"My guard said that if I named him, then that meant I loved him, but I don't know, man." Damion frowned at the few beer droplets that had managed to get free, covering his shirt and part of his arms.

Juni stared at him a long second before turning contemplative. "What I feel for 108… well, I've never really experienced true love in that way, I suppose. I have love for my parents and others, but not romantically. But I guess yeah, I love 108 in a way. I don't really know what that way is yet, but I guess it's love."

"We can't run, but I need to find a way to get Requiem back to normal. I can't treat him like a robot, but now I can't even treat him like…." Damion tossed back the last of his beer.

Rubbing his face, Juni sighed. "Can't even treat him like what?"

Damion frowned. "Like the person I took to bed just hours ago, because they locked that part of him away."

"Just because it's locked away doesn't mean it's not there," Juni replied with a shrug and then a swig of his beer. "If you treat him differently, if 47 is still in there somewhere—which I'm sure he is—perhaps treating him different will just make it harder for him to be himself again. It may make him bury it further."

"How did things get so fucked up so quickly?" Damion scratched the back of his head in frustration.

"Because it hit you like a brick." Juni finished his beer and threw the bottle in the trash with a clank. "How the hell were we supposed to know this could happen? We thought the Cores were ours, not something that could be taken away or changed so easily."

"I should have known better. The Corp owns every part of the explored galaxy. Their ownership includes the Cores and people such as you and me." Damion shook his head again. "He warned me."

"Who warned you? 47?" Juni frowned in confusion.

"He said that they would know if he wasn't taking his supplements, but we had stopped those before we left for leave, so I thought…." Damion wasn't sure what he thought. "I guess it was the dream."

"They never really stopped," Juni mumbled as he chewed on his thumbnail. "I know both he and 108 were still eating at least a cup of the stuff a day when we were on leave. 108 still does, but I wonder if 47 stopped for some reason."

"I-I don't know." Damion realized he hadn't been paying attention. His stomach knotted, and a torpedo of guilt hit him square in the chest. "I'll ask him when he wakes up."

"I hate to ask, but will he remember?" Juni inquired around his thumbnail, his expression pained.

"I… don't… *know*," Damion said again. "Guess it doesn't matter now. I'll just have to find a way around it or deal with him being a robot."

Juni stood, putting the chair back by the table. "My only suggestion right now is to have faith in 47. He's tougher than you think, but he's going to need your help in whatever way you can." Juni squeezed Damion's shoulder tightly. "Get some sleep. I'll talk to 108 and see if he can help at all."

"Thanks, Juni." Damion gave his friend—his closest and only friend on this fucking ship—a smile. "Ask 108 to look up a guy named Collins too. He's ex-Alpha."

"Ex-Alpha? That must be an interesting story. Will do. Get some rest, and I'll hopefully have some info for you tomorrow before patrol." Juni waved a hand over his shoulder as he left.

Damion watched him leave, feeling alone even with Requiem behind him. He wasn't sure how long Requiem would rest, but hoped when he awoke, things would be better.

Chapter Twenty-Four

Thursday October 13, 454 MC
1131 GMT
Damion

ABOUT SIX weeks later, the *Ares* pulled onto the flight deck after completing another patrol circuit, although this one had not been as uneventful as the previous ones. The *Ares* had run into a few rebel fighters, obviously doing a patrol of their own. It hadn't taken long to take them out, with a few quick maneuvers on Damion's part, and an activation of the Barrier on Requiem's.

Despite not being like his former self, Requiem had still finished his adjustments of the Impulse Barrier. He told Damion that as long as he didn't overdo it, it didn't drain him. They had left the rebels floundering with disabled ships and reported them to the *Zeus*. After the rebels recovered, they would be discreetly followed by a small group of Betas to see where they went. Hopefully they would lead the *Zeus*'s pilots to their main battleship.

But that wasn't Damion and Requiem's job. Their job was over for the day, but it seemed like it was never done, as if there was an endless battle going on. Not between Requiem and Damion, but between Requiem and the hold the Creators had on him. Unfortunately, every time Requiem opened his mouth, it seemed to infuriate Damion just because Requiem wasn't who he used to be—wasn't who Damion wanted him to be.

"If you do not have any other immediate plans for me, I wish to complete some final adjustments to the *Ares*. Would that be acceptable?"

Damion sighed as he pulled off his helmet and ran his fingers through his dark, sweat-damp hair. "Yeah, if that's what you want to do, go for it. But don't leave the hangar until I can get back from the mess hall." Even if Arkin was gone, Damion didn't like Requiem walking about by himself. He was even more afraid now that it wouldn't be another Fighter taking him, but the Creators or the Commander.

"As you order, Fighter Hawk. Would you prefer for me to go get your meal before starting work?" Requiem asked as he slid down the ladder to the flight deck floor.

"I can get my own tray, and I need to get your gruel." Damion eyed Juni who was exiting the *Hermes* a little farther down the walkway. "Just stay by the Zodiac until I get back."

Damion couldn't relax around his Core, not like before. He couldn't be sure that Requiem had broken the compulsion to report everything to the Creators. And every time he had the thought to reduce some of Requiem's supplements, he worried guards would show up during the day and take Requiem away permanently.

"Juni, can you send 108 over to help 47?" Damion wanted to talk to his friend alone and without feeling 108's judging gaze on the back of his skull.

Juni blinked at him before looking over at Requiem. He frowned, nodding in understanding, before his gaze turned to 108 and his mouth curved into a warm smile. "Do you mind?" he asked his Core. 108 gave him his own brief hint of a smile before shaking his head and walking to Requiem. Juni joined Damion in his trek down the hall to retrieve food.

Damion stopped to look back at the Cores. Requiem was already on the ground, opening a hatch in the belly of the Zodiac, when 108 joined him, sliding in gracefully to the side. Requiem gave 108 a nod of greeting, silently accepting his help as he pointed out a problem with the wires. 108 seemed to immediately understand and scooted out from under the ship to retrieve a few tools. Damion turned his head away from the scene and continued walking.

"What's up?" Juni asked as soon as they were out of earshot of the Cores.

"I think I might do something very stupid if I have to face this version the Creators sent to me for much longer." Damion pushed his fingers through his hair. "I can't figure out what to do with him, and he's back in his pod every night. I think I'm going crazy."

"Just don't do anything that might get yourself or 47 killed. Or result in him being taken away from you."

Juni's gaze flicked worriedly over him. Damion could only imagine what he looked like. Death: dark circles under his eyes, hair that needed cutting, and definitely more bone than body because he wasn't eating enough. The situation with Requiem was tearing him apart.

"I'm sorry that the info that 108 dug up didn't help." 108 had confirmed Juni's thought that Requiem had pulled back on taking his supplements shortly before they returned from leave, while 108 continued to take a minimum dose of his. Requiem had gone approximately twenty-four hours taking bare minimum levels of his supplements. Damion didn't know how 108 had escaped the Corp's notice while Requiem had not. But then, Requiem was much stronger in the ways of the system than 108, although he had started to teach 108 before the Creators changed him. "What did you have in mind?"

"I can't fucking gauge what I can do because every time I think he's starting to remember, I'm dead wrong. The moment I even think about cutting back his gruel and he even cracks the slightest smile, I'm jumping at shadows and he's taken the full dose before I realize it." For a moment Damion thought about going below decks and picking up a girl just to have some reaction.

It might not have been so hard if they had wiped Requiem clean of every valuable memory. Knowing that Requiem could remember some of what he and Damion had gone through, their first flight, the trip to Lunar, and that Requiem admitted he had flashes of memory of the kissing but couldn't feel a single emotion in reference to it was what caused Damion's heart to ache and his fury toward the Creators to burn brightly.

"That still doesn't answer the question of what crazy idea you might be getting into your head." Juni stated what they already knew, which was that they were all caught between a rock and a hard place. "You ever think maybe it's a possibility that Requiem is protecting you? That perhaps he is aware of what's going on and has decided not to fight just so that you won't get hurt?" He sighed. "I know that's a crazy idea, but I'm fishing for anything at this point."

"He could fucking tell me that he remembers something at least," Damion ground out. "I actually thought about going home. Asking for that discharge and going home to go work security at the mines."

"You would leave 47?" Juni asked in a startled tone. "I didn't think you would want to give him up, but if you've thought about it, why haven't you?"

Damion dragged his nails over his scalp in frustration. "I can't give him to another Arkin, and right now only we can do the Barrier.

No, I can't leave him. He needs me as much as I need him. Hell, only he can perform that maneuver, and he only do it with me. So what would they do if he refused to work with someone else and started killing again?"

"Wipe him, more than likely," Juni said reluctantly, looking at Damion out of the corner of his eye. "Take apart the *Ares* and figure out how he did it. There are many things they can do. Or… or you could take him with you," he suggested in a barely audible tone. "But the only problem with that is that they'd find him, unless you somehow removed that tracking device."

"It's hopeless." Damion let his head fall back against the wall of the elevator. "Fucking hopeless, and you know it too. Let's just get our food."

Juni kept his mouth shut after that. Damion knew he was simmering with anger and frustration to the point that it was almost visible.

They made it down to the mess hall, and it seemed Damion's temper would hold out for the day. Until one of Arkin's ex-lackeys decided today was a good day to poke fun at Damion's recent decline in flight scores. At that point Damion tossed the food on his tray over his shoulder and used the metal as a deadly weapon.

"Oh shit! D, *stop!*"

Juni dropped his own tray and scrambled over the table to try to grab Damion before he could bring the tray down on the other Fighter's head. But he just wasn't quick enough. He winced at the loud clang of metal on skull. He grabbed Damion's arms before he could do it again, but by that time the damage had been done and Arkin's lackey had sprung back up, wobbling, with an upper cut that caught Damion's jaw and threw him back into Juni. From there it turned into a full-blown brawl.

Fifteen minutes later found Damion rubbing his bruised jaw as they stood against the starboard wall in the mess. The security force had guns pointed at all their bellies. Damion could see the Commander approaching, and he was pissed. Damion knew he was already on the officer's shit list. He could feel the suspension coming on just by looking at that glare.

"Sorry," he mumbled under his breath to Juni.

"Better be," Juni growled out of the corner of his mouth. "I hope you feel better now." And then he sighed, wincing from bruised ribs. "If I don't end up in the brig with you, I'll make sure to watch over 47 until they release you."

"Hawk. I should have fucking known." The Commander's voice bellowed throughout the mess hall, causing several others to wince. "I heard you started this little shindig. Congratulations, you won a night in the brig. Maybe more, if I'm lucky." He nodded to a few of the Security officers, and they immediately grabbed Damion by his arms and pulled him out of the mess hall.

One of them was Collins, who took in Damion's appearance and gave him a sad shake of his head before looking forward again as he pulled him to the elevator.

"Still pissed that you couldn't kill me by accident, Commander?" Damion gave Collins a sloppy grin. "And Arkin died jacking off in his room."

Collins rolled his eyes and then sighed as the Commander's grin widened and he gave Collins a nod. Collins gave Damion a nearly imperceptible shrug and an obviously apologetic look before his fist came out of nowhere and connected with Damion's face.

"Keep it up, Hawk. I can do this all day," Commander Sandrite said smugly.

Damion staggered a few centimeters and his ears rang for a second. "Not what your wife said the other night."

"That's real funny, Hawk, I can just add it to your list of infractions here," the Commander drawled as Collins punched Damion in the ribs following the nod the Commander gave him. "But I suppose you would try and find sex anywhere now that your Core has stopped whoring out for you."

Damion coughed, and his knees did almost buckle that time, but he leaned against the elevator wall to help keep him up. "You trying to live through my sex life? That's a bit sad, Commander."

The guard on the other side of Damion tightened his grip on his arm to keep him standing.

"Oh no," the Commander said. "My sex life is just fine. I don't need to live through your nonexistent one. At least my partners can react. I think you'd have better luck fucking a hole in the wall than your Core. The wall might have more emotion. Or do you have the Core fuck you?"

As the elevator doors opened, Collins tightened his grip on Damion's arm in warning.

"You have every right to be scared of him," Damion muttered under his breath.

"What? Be scared of a doll?" The Commander snorted as he led them toward the containment cells. "Why would I be afraid of him? Especially after they reprogrammed him, making him into a good little toy." Stopping in front of a door, he called for it to open with a higher code clearance, and after three beeps, the door unlocked. Collins and the other guard dragged Damion inside and dumped him onto a hard cot before exiting, slipping past the Commander.

"You have to wonder, though, what might happen to your little Core while you're in here," the Commander said in a musing tone, then gave a satisfied grin. "Not that you'd be able to do anything normally, but now you won't even be there to protest when the Creators retrieve him this evening and you won't see him go." He closed the door with a light laugh, leaving Damion in darkness except for a small barred window in the door. "Have a good night's sleep," he said through that opening.

Damion began kicking uselessly at the door. He knew it wouldn't do any fucking good, but all the anger bled out of his actions as he screamed into the empty cell. He wasn't scared, just pissed. As he crumpled onto the cot, he thought about praying for the first time in years.

Chapter Twenty-Five

Thursday October 13, 454 MC
1214 GMT
Requiem

47 KEPT pace with the security team in front of him. Requiem. The morning after his return from the Creators, Damion had reinforced the designation "Requiem." Forty-one days had passed since then, and he had come to a decision he preferred the Requiem designation far better than 47. His entire memory was an unorganized memory-code sequence. Requiem had been able to string together a chronological pattern of those memories, but there was a gap between what he was able to recall and what Damion would mention as the *emotional connection* behind those memories.

Requiem kept his head down from the time Security came and retrieved him until they brought him to the Creators' facility. They informed him his trips to the Diagnostic section in the Medical Bay would be more frequent. There would also be unannounced escorts. Requiem had calculated the trips varied in seven- to ten-day patterns. He continued to keep his gaze lowered even as they lifted him and set him in a chair similar to his own on the *Ares*. Except with this one, they strapped him in by his ankles and wrists. It was only once they left that he dared to look up cautiously from under his bangs.

He didn't know where Damion was, but he knew that if Damion had been available to get in the way, he never would have been brought here. He was merely intrigued and mildly curious as to where Damion was. If Damion had gotten himself into a situation he could not return from… well, there wasn't much sense in continuing to exist. And it was either end his life or be wiped, which he didn't agree with. He would not continue to be as he was now, trapped within his own mind. Except worse. Much worse.

Requiem's gaze fell upon a woman sitting in front of a console, the glow from the machine haloing the Creator in a white light, which silhouetted them in the dark room. Something within Requiem started to struggle, tried to get away, even if his body merely blinked and continued to watch.

The Creator stepped out into the light holding a multitool in one hand and a media pad in the other. The pad scrolled information as she bent down and momentarily used the multitool to flash a light in Requiem's eyes. "47, report physical status."

"Acceptable. Although semiweary from recent patrol, still at 87 percent physical capacity," he said in a monotone voice. He didn't even wince away from the light in his eyes, although his pupils contracted to pinpoints and then back once the light was retracted.

"Your recent sessions have reported normal once again. Your intake of supplement has also been back to normal. It is all acceptable." She looked over to the media pad. "We are still unable to replicate the Barrier you use during your flights. I require you to give us the entire schematic to the *Ares* for the modifications you've performed, including the technology for that Barrier."

"Understood. I must report that retrieving the data in full will take approximately one week. Additionally, the Impulse Barrier has yet to be completed. I am still modifying it." Inside, Requiem was grinding his teeth in frustration. He didn't want them to have it yet, not until it was complete. Not until he could make it so that it wouldn't injure other Cores. "The Barrier still requires modification in the power supply, and I have yet to design a way so that it will not affect Cores in other Zodiacs if they come within range of the Pulse. It is not a weapon that can be used in close formation with friendly Zodiacs."

"Understood. You have seven Earth-side days to deliver those schematics. Your performance has increased and your compliance improved." She tucked the multitool into her white coat pocket and gave 47 a smile that contained no warmth, merely approval that the tool was working correctly. She pushed back a long piece of brunette hair as she looked at the scrolling information displayed on the screen to her right. "Exemplary. Report now on your Fighter's recent decrease in performance."

That was a subject that Requiem really didn't want to talk about, and warning signals flared in his brain. He would have to be careful. "Fighter Damion Hawk has of late become increasingly agitated due to lack of sleep and correct nutrition. While he is still one of the most successful Fighters, these combined points have decreased his reaction time."

"Those reasons are unacceptable explanations for a decrease of 43.4 percent in performance for an Alpha Fighter." The Creator sighed and put the pad down on an instrument tray to her left. She looked up, obviously monitoring not only 47's facial response, but also physical response. "If his performance decreases even further, we cannot overlook a potential liability to the fleet. If Fighters cannot adapt, they are useless."

She walked over to the monitor to the left of 47's head and punched in a short code. "I am supplying you now with a list of other choices. You have the right to choose another. You have possibly outgrown your Fighter, making him useless to us. A replacement would be the right choice."

Requiem inhaled sharply as a jack entered the input in the back of his skull. The system came up faintly, names and test scores rolling through. But he didn't pay attention to them.

"Fighter Damion Hawk is the best. I will remain with the best and work with him to put him back on the path toward improvement. I will succeed within ten Earth-side days to get him back to full capacity." The thought of choosing another Fighter nearly made him physically ill, but he managed to keep all his levels steady to not disrupt the monitoring process.

The Creator's lips tugged slightly downward. "I see that your stubbornness still has a hold on your decisions. Do you truly believe you can get your Fighter to improve? His scores have fallen off dramatically in the last three weeks. It is a bit illogical to try and fix what is beyond repair."

"Nothing is impossible," Requiem said, the words coming out like the mantra they were for him. "If it was illogical to try and fix what appeared to be beyond repair, would not I have been wiped already?"

"I believe your last invasive treatment here has done wonders for most of your flaws. As I have said before, your recent activities show that you have been performing above average and you're developing into one of the finest Cores this fleet has produced. You will bring us much knowledge to improve not only *Zeus*, but other fleets."

"It is enlightening to know that I am improving to be better than my previous state. It is what I strive for," Requiem answered truthfully.

"Yes, and you do deserve the best. A Fighter who gets himself thrown into the brig due to a testosterone brawl of no significance is not the best and is not for you." She showed him on the monitor that Damion had been taken into custody for the next twenty-four hours.

"I waited for and then chose Fighter Hawk because he is the best," Requiem said. "The best reaction time, the best with weapons technology, the best with hand-to-hand, and his IQ scores are well above average. From my understanding, every human has a period of time in which they are what is called 'off.' I believe, at this point in time, that Fighter Hawk is merely off his normal path. I will attempt to work with him to get him back to his normal levels."

"I do not believe this is the most logical course, since he is the reason you went off your supplements to begin with, but we will give you the time you request. If, at that point, his performance is still suboptimal, then we will have him removed from the *Zeus*." She turned around and called over a younger male assistant. "Now we will check your implants."

Requiem nodded while internally breathing a hesitant sigh of relief. "All seem to be operating at full efficiency," he stated as the assistant undid the straps tying him to the table. Once ordered to, he sat up, letting the assistant unzip his uniform to slip it off his torso.

"I saw a change in the receiver in the back of your skull and your tracking chip. Perhaps your use of the Barrier is affecting it. We must make sure you do not have any flaws." She turned back with another tool, this one similar to an input jack with a sharp pointed end and a wireless receiver at the other end. "Sit forward."

Requiem did so, tilting his head forward so that the Creator could have better access to the input jack in the back of his skull. He braced for the unpleasant sensation, wincing as he was rewarded with a sharp jab.

"Good. Now hold still." She held the probe with one hand and typed with the other. "You have also been spending increased time with 108. Report on his well-being."

"Acceptable. Fighter Mathis is a good addition to the Alphas, and it was a logical course of action for 108 to choose him. 108's previous Fighters were very violent, with abuse and rape causing him to lose efficiency. Bonding with Fighter Mathis has increased his performance and also his ability to speak out when he has an idea or question. I have been helping him to expand his abilities." Requiem held stock-still, not even blinking as he reported. The Creator knew all the information. Requiem knew she was asking in an attempt to see if she could elicit any response in regards to 108.

"Interesting." The Creator pulled out the probe and moved down to the next port in his spine. "Has your Fighter influenced 108 or Fighter Mathis to disobey protocols?"

"Negative," Requiem answered without hesitation, only flinching at the disagreeable pain in his spine.

"You are to report if Fighter Hawk tries to influence other Fighters in any way against protocols. You should follow your Fighter's requests, but you must follow our orders." She pulled the probe out and handed it to the assistant.

"Understood," he replied reluctantly. He didn't sound hesitant, but internally he roiled in confusion and mental distress. He was bonded to Damion. Damion was his Fighter. He had always been taught to follow his Fighter's orders above all others, but now he was told to follow the Creators' above his Fighter's. His mind was torn, but it was definitely leaning more toward his Fighter, and that confused him even more. He would receive brief flashes of memory. Those memories were vague flashes of kisses to images of them in the *Ares*. They were momentary, and they perplexed him. When Damion touched him, Requiem had sensations of calm and sadness. He could not deny he felt a deep trust in his Fighter. But none of this showed on the readout or in his face and body.

"Excellent." The Creator was quiet through the rest of the exam. If anything, she was thorough, not allowing him out of the Diagnostic section before finishing what she determined necessary.

"Am I acceptable?" he asked as he pulled his uniform back on.

"I believe your positioning chip has shifted slightly. It does not pose a problem at this moment. We will monitor it. Your ports look fine. Are there any upgrades you determine you shall need to improve the Barrier?"

Requiem thought about it for a moment, running through schematics in his mind. "I was thinking of implanting a suppression device. When the Impulse Barrier runs through the auxiliary power supply, it begins to drain the energy from my body. I would be able to hold it longer, releasing a larger pulse, if I could temporarily ignore the drain on my systems. Therefore I was thinking of a device that would allow me to do so."

"To cut off your link to the Zodiac's supply would be quite difficult. I shall try to run a few tests and determine if a device would be possible without cutting you off from the entirety of the Zodiac."

She typed furiously on the media console. "I will know more once you give us the schematics of the Barrier."

"I am not speaking of cutting me off from the Zodiac's supply, merely deadening my senses on control," Requiem explained. "This allows me to use the Impulse Barrier but sustain less damage. As well as when I acquire any injury while inside the *Ares*, whether it's an electrical backlash or direct physical damage, I won't be distracted by pain and can continue to perform."

"Interesting," she said again. "I will look into it for you. You are exemplary."

"Thank you. I strive to be the best for the Corporation and the fleet." *And for Damion*, he added silently as he nodded. "Do you have need of me for any longer?"

"You should report to your room for the remainder of Fighter Hawk's detention." The apparent disapproval for the Fighter was clear in her tone.

"Understood." Requiem slid off the table onto slightly shaky feet. Relief rushed through his system for the mere fact that she hadn't thought to put him in the immersion tanks for this session. "Do you wish me to go on my own, or is there a reason I do not understand that you sent Security to bring me before?"

"It was for your protection, of course." She waved a hand in dismissal. "Certain precautions should always be made."

"Might I ask what I would need protection from?" He tilted his head, perplexed.

"From your Fighter." She turned and narrowed her eyes in suspicion at him.

Requiem blinked, now completely confused. "My Fighter? Is that not a change from the general populace thinking I was going to terminate him? What do you base this on? I am merely questioning for my own knowledge, so that I may know what to look for if you feel I am in danger. That way I may report it." He really wanted to know.

"He has become unstable. His actions also pose a threat to your well-being. If, say, he would be foolish enough to try to leave with you, that would be a grave mistake."

"Understood," Requiem replied after a moment's thought. He gave the Creator another bow of his head. "I will depart now." And he did so, quickly and efficiently moving through the door and out into the hall.

All he wanted was to sit down and think, but instead he walked to the elevator to get to his room. Inside, he was panicking. He needed to talk to Damion now, but that wasn't possible since Damion had ended up in the brig. Requiem knew Damion was becoming more volatile each day, but he didn't think he would be illogical enough to actually get himself in serious trouble.

When he finally arrived at his room, he unlocked the door with his verbal key code, but caught movement out of the corner of his eye. Turning his head, he saw Juni standing about three meters away with a container in his hand.

"108 told me they had released you. Are you all right?" Juni asked, searching the hall to make sure they weren't being watched.

"I am acceptable."

"D's in the brig," Juni said after a moment, looking at him to gauge his reaction and physical well-being.

"I was informed. What did he do?" Requiem asked.

"Cracked one of Arkin's old lackeys over the head with a metal tray." Juni gave a snort and shook his head.

Requiem's own headshake was nearly imperceptible. "That was illogical given the current situation, but I cannot say I know what else Damion could have done. They have the potential to be as abusive as Arkin himself."

Juni let out a half laugh. "No shit." He placed the container in Requiem's hands. "Here's your mush. Thought it would be a good idea not to miss a dose or else they'll take you away again. This time permanently, and that would just plain kill D. Let me or 108 know if you need anything. We'll be here as fast as we can."

Requiem took the container, looking at it for a moment before raising his gaze to meet Juni's. "I acknowledge and appreciate your concern. If I have need of anything, I will let you know. Have a good evening."

"Yeah, you too. Take care." Juni said, moving away and back down the hall.

Requiem moved into the empty quarters, trying not to notice the lack of his Fighter. He placed the container on the table and sat down on the bed. And for a long time after that, he merely stared at his rations, thinking.

Chapter Twenty-Six

Friday October 14, 454 MC
0900 GMT
Damion

DAMION WALKED back to his room with two things on his mind. First, he needed a shower, badly. He smelled like the ass end of a Mercurian workhorse. Second, he was tired. He hadn't been able to sleep the entire time. He was worried about Requiem. Even if Requiem wouldn't miss him, and the doctors and the creeps would keep Requiem safe for the most part, they could also take him away or wipe him again.

Requiem looked up, his ice blue eyes locking on to Damion's face as soon as he walked into the room. Damion could tell Requiem had showered and changed into a new suit. He was happy seeing Requiem sitting on the bed instead of inside his capsule.

"You're still in one piece." Damion gave him a small, sad grin. "What, not plugged in? That's not like you." He pulled off his shirt and winced at the ache in his ribs. "Fuck if Collins doesn't have a big fucking fist."

"You are hurt. Your ribs are bruised, as is your cheek, and you have blood on your mouth," Requiem said. It sounded less like a report and more a slightly surprised observation. Damion didn't miss the fact Requiem ignored his words. He stood from the bed and walked to the bathroom, returning with a wet washcloth, and began to methodically, but gently, clean the blood from Damion's face.

Damion stood still, eyeing him closely with slight suspicion but also a smidgen of hope. The sudden change in Requiem's behavior shocked the shit out of him. This was the closest thing to emotion he had seen from his Core in weeks. "I'll live."

"That was never in question. Your body will take much more damage than this before it shuts down." Requiem finished his task and put the washcloth in the laundry chute. There he paused, his back to Damion, his head down in obvious thought. "You have been emotionally unbalanced as of late. I have come to the conclusion that this was the reason you ended up in the brig."

"Emotionally unbalanced?" Damion let out a bitter snigger, angry with himself for even having the slightest bit of hope. So much for thinking that Requiem was showing more emotion. "Not surprised you'd put it that way. I'm going to grab a shower."

"As you wish," Requiem replied quietly, sitting back down on the bed.

Damion walked into the bathroom, not saying another word. He tried to never get his hopes up when he saw a flicker of emotion in Requiem. In the past, every time he saw it, or thought he saw it, he would get hopeful, but it was dashed away soon after. Requiem was safe, and for all of Damion's bitching and stress about the situation, that was the most important fact to him.

After he washed, he stepped back into the room, tossing all the dirty clothing and towels into the laundry chute and pulling out some fresh underwear.

"They wish for me to choose another Fighter," Requiem said behind Damion's bare back.

"What? Oh. Didn't take the bastards long." Damion ground his teeth, not turning to look at Requiem. Requiem would ask too many questions if he saw the anger in Damion's features. "What do you want?"

Damion hoped he wasn't wrong when he heard anger in Requiem's voice as he answered.

"I want you. I chose you. But if you do not improve in the next seven days, they will remove you from the *Zeus* and they will have what they want. Me without a hassle." He seemed strained, almost in pain as he said these words; it was as if he was fighting against a wall.

"You actually give a damn?" Damion turned in amazement before quickly striding over to Requiem and grabbing his chin to stare into his large blue eyes. "Do you even care if they terminate me?"

"Of course I do," Requiem replied without hesitation, looking confused. Damion had begun to wonder when Requiem trembled if it was against the barriers in his mind, against the brainwashing and compulsions.

"But you still don't remember anything, do you?" Damion let the pale chin go and sat next to Requiem on the bed. "You told them everything, and they told the Commander everything. Do you know how much that makes me not trust you? It kills me not being able to tell you things." Damion pulled at his shaggy hair. "Damn it, I almost wish I could just leave and take you with me."

At those words, Requiem put his hands over his ears as if he could block out what Damion had just said. "Do not say that," he hissed, his trembling increasing as sweat appeared on his brow. "I... have tried my best... to circumvent them. Telling them half-truths. But I... have been given... orders to tell them if you propose... exactly what you just did." His words were stilted, obviously forced past a compulsion. "I am sorry that I do not remember what you wish me to, but it is difficult... to be in between two sets of orders—yours and theirs. I try to follow the ones I want to... the ones I feel are right... which are yours. But there is only so much... that I can fight."

Damion pulled on Requiem's right hand, tugged him closer so he would pay closer attention to Damion's words. "Then make your choice, and stop being their slave."

"It is not as easy as you say." Requiem's hand curled around Damion's, squeezing it tightly as he attempted to make a fist. "They created me. My loyalty is to the Corporation, but... it is also to you. I do not understand. I have never been this.... I have never been between loyalties before. But... they own me. And if I do not do what they wish, you will either be discharged or terminated, and I do not know what they will do to me."

"I'll protect you," Damion growled in frustration, his fingers tightening around the thin wrist in his grip. "Why can't you believe that?"

"I do believe you, and while nothing is impossible, it is improbable that you will be able to protect us both from the Corporation." Requiem withdrew his touch from Damion and wiped the sweat off his face with his sleeve. "They believe you will hurt me. That you are too volatile right now and are a threat to my well-being."

"I would never hurt you. I'd like to put a bullet in a few of their brainpans, but not you." Damion got up just to take Requiem by the shoulders and push him down on his back on the bed. "But I don't know what to do. How can I help you if you just tell them everything? You were pissed when you thought I didn't trust you not to kill me, yet here we are back at the beginning. Would you kill me now? If they told you to terminate me?"

Requiem fell back on the bed easily, pliable. "Terminate you?" he whispered, confusion showing in his eyes for a moment before it disappeared again behind the wall. "If they… ordered me…?" He was struggling against something, that much could be seen in the way he trembled and the sweat dripped down the sides of his face. "N-no… I could not. Would… not."

"You'd disobey them to save me?" Damion grabbed Requiem's wrists and pinned them above his head. He gave the thin wrists a squeeze as he continued to look down into Requiem's icy eyes.

"I… would… terminate myself to keep you alive," Requiem forced out through panting breaths.

He was obviously confused as to what Damion was doing, but didn't fight him at all.

"Say it out loud. You obey *me*, not them. Say it." Damion put his left hand on Requiem's forehead, still holding the shaky wrists to the mattress with his right.

"I… do not…. Please." Something was tearing him apart. His eyes rolled in their sockets, not able to focus on Damion. "I… yes. You" was all he was able to say, to promise.

"Again. Again." Damion leaned closer, sharing the warm breath Requiem panted between them. "Say it again."

"You," Requiem croaked out. He whimpered behind his teeth, his arms straining against Damion's steel-like grip as they attempted to come down and cradle his head. And then something snapped, a barrier broke, and Requiem let out a long sigh, his body relaxing and the pained expression on his face disappearing. "I obey you," he whispered.

"Good." Damion swooped down and pressed a bruising kiss against Requiem's lips. His left hand curled into pale white hair while the right grasped the back of Requiem's neck.

Requiem inhaled through his nose, as his lips were apparently otherwise occupied. He was confused, and his eyes conveyed it. His arms stayed where Damion left them, his fingers twitching, wondering what they should do.

"I want to have sex with you," Damion said as he pulled his lips away and looked down into Requiem's confused face. "Do you understand?"

Requiem continued to stare up at him for a few moments, his gaze flicking back and forth over Damion's face. "We have… done this before." It was a statement, but it sounded more like a question.

"We did it for about twelve hours straight." Damion showed the first signs of happiness and amusement in almost two months. "But you really don't remember it, do you? I wish you did—maybe this would be easier on you."

"I am sorry." Requiem sounded sincere as he slowly lowered one hand so that it touched Damion's face and his smiling lips, in what looked to be rediscovery. "I wish I could, just so you were not… *unhappy* anymore."

"You've taken the right step. Just show me that you want me more than them." Damion leaned down and began to kiss him again, but this time he also started to unzip the Core's attire. This time the kiss was slow instead of the predatory need from before. He licked Requiem's soft, supple lips before delving inside the hot recesses of his mouth. He slid his tongue alongside Requiem's, teasing it with his own before they twined together in a slow dance.

Requiem's hand fluttered from Damion's mouth to his cheek. It was a complete change from the personality he had shown for the last few months, since the last time he had seen the Creators. He pulled away from Damion's lips abruptly.

"I… can-not. If I… if my levels become erratic, against what they wish them to be, they will discharge you, make you leave the ship. The Creator is already suspicious and wanting me to choose another Fighter unless your levels improve. If mine become unstable, or fall, they will immediately blame it on you. Damion, so far I have done my best to hide things, to circumvent the rules, but it has not been enough. We are in danger, you especially."

"See, right there." Damion sat up, lifting him up a little so that he could pull Requiem's arms out of his suit. "That's what I want. For you to think for yourself. You're not back to normal yet, but it's enough to make me happy for now. As for the Creators, I don't care about them or their rules. You're mine. You admitted that the last time we had sex, and I'll make you admit it again."

"I… implied… that?" Requiem sat up so that the suit fell down around his waist. "If you do not care, then you will be terminated. They are a force to be reckoned with. I do not understand how you plan to go against them."

"You're the one who always goes on and on and on about how nothing is impossible." Damion hurriedly stripped Requiem naked as he spoke, moving Requiem as he worked. "And to answer your question, yes, you did fucking say it, and don't call me a liar. It pisses me off that you can't remember as it is, so you'll just have to trust me."

"Nothing is impossible, but there is improbable," Requiem stated, having lain back down on the bed while Damion removed his boots and the rest of his clothing, throwing it all to the ground. "I was not going to call you a liar. I feel that you would not lie to me. But… I do not know what to do about remembering. Yet I feel I must try something, since it seems to make you volatile that I do not."

"Wouldn't it piss you off if they were able to take me away and strip my memory of you? Of everything you worked on to make me better? To make me happy?" Damion growled, kicking off his boxers while reaching for the lube that had lain forgotten all this time in the bedside table.

"I… do not know. I do not understand how to be… pissed off, as you say." Requiem obviously thought about it for a moment. "It would make me…." His brow furrowed in a flash of confusion. "Uneasy? I would work to help you remember."

"That's what I've been trying to do without getting us in trouble, and it hasn't been fucking working. This is the first time you've even acted like you give a damn." Damion tossed the lube onto the bed and then gripped Requiem's hips, urging him more into the center of the bed. "Weeks and weeks, all I could do was remember how great it was to have you to myself, and then they took you away. You're mine. You're mine, and yet they took you away."

Requiem's body was pliable to Damion's commands, as if he was going through the motions but still not noticing what exactly was going on. "The Creators," he mumbled. His gaze flicked about, seeming to be looking for something, except it was probably internal, inside his mind. "The submersion tank. Needles. Light. Burning in my veins from chemicals." Each word murmured as he was beginning to remember. "They created me. Own me. Control me. But I…." He winced, unable to finish the sentence.

"No, fucking gods be damned, they don't! *You* control you. You are a human, and you're my Core." Damion roughly pushed Requiem back down onto the bed and pressed another insistent kiss against his muttering lips. Even if Requiem didn't remember, Damion did, and he knew what he had to do to get him to respond. If he had to start from scratch, so be it, but this time he wasn't going to use kid gloves. No, he wasn't holding back, since he knew Requiem had liked it and asked for it before. Nothing was going to stop him from reclaiming what was his.

Chapter Twenty-Seven

Requiem

DAMION'S WARM lips stifled mumbled words and Requiem froze for a moment against them before instinct and familiarity took over and his lips moved against Damion's in a near primal dance. Requiem's twitching fingers lifted to hesitantly cup Damion's face.

Damion kissed down Requiem's pale, tender neck. He closed his lips around Requiem's flesh and sucked hard, using his teeth every so often to raise blood to the surface of Requiem's pale skin.

A shocked, deep inhale was the only response Requiem could give. Interesting, but still familiar feelings shot through him, originating from his neck but driving the sensation of hot pleasure to his groin every time those teeth bit gently down on him. His hands moved from Damion's face to his shoulders, almost fluttering over the tan skin. His mind was torn in two. One side, the side of him that was loyal to the Corp, that was dependent on the chemicals and the supplements, that side was surrounded by walls and compulsions. The other side was just as loyal—maybe more so—to Damion. The person he had fought for, killed for already, the only person who seemed to truly care about him.

Damion moved his mouth lower to Requiem's right nipple. He laved it for a few moments before lightly biting the pert nub of flesh. He reached between them while his mouth was busy, took Requiem's shaft in hand and began to stroke.

"Damion—" Requiem had been about to tell him to wait, but the hand around his flaccid organ interrupted him, stifling his words in a strangled gasp. His fingers tightened on Damion's shoulders in shock.

"You like it." Damion chuckled darkly, reaching farther between Requiem's legs to tug on the soft sac of his scrotum.

"I do n—*ah!*" Requiem couldn't seem to get out a full sentence, his body jumping at the skilled fingers on sensitive parts. "I do not understand," he finally managed to squeeze out. "And I do not know if my body can react the way you seem to want it to."

"You're feeling good, that's all I can ask." Damion licked at Requiem's slowly bruising neck, savoring the taste of the pale skin. "Turn over."

Once Damion was out of the way, Requiem did as he was ordered and moved to his hands and knees. He knew that this was what Damion wanted. Looking back over his shoulder, he watched what Damion would do next.

Damion opened the lube, spreading a generous amount over his fingers. He rubbed Requiem's small ring of muscle with a single digit before slowly pushing it into Requiem's body. "I am going to put it here. Where you're tight and hot."

"A-affirmative," Requiem replied hesitantly, but he didn't tense against Damion's probing finger. He realized that while his mind did not remember what they had done together in the past, his body must have, because it was acting on its own.

Damion moved his finger in and out quickly. "Breathe, Requiem, then it won't hurt as much."

Requiem hadn't noticed until then that he had been holding his breath, and he let it out in an easy rush. "This feels... familiar," he managed to say past the tightness in his chest. His body was remembering things with shivers of past pleasures and current ones spawned by Damion's subtle movements inside him.

"It should." Damion quickly added a second finger and twisted them. "It will burn and hurt at first."

"But... not like in the past, where I bled. Only a little this time?" Requiem looked over his shoulder to speak, intrigued by the excited and dark heat in Damion's eyes.

"I will do my very best to not hurt you." Damion kissed the pale left shoulder as he pushed the two fingers deeper inside Requiem's clenching body, finding that small circle of nerves to tease.

That got Requiem's attention, and he hissed in surprise, letting his head fall forward and his forehead brush the pillow. He fisted his hands in the sheets on either side of the soft pillow as he tensed, clenching around Damion's fingers. "What is...?" He paused, a flicker of memory brightening and then dimming. "Sweet spot," he mumbled.

"Yeah, it's a sweet spot." Damion pulled his fingers out, and Requiem again watched him pour more of the shiny, slick lube on them before he pushed in three digits. "Don't hold your breath."

Requiem released the air trapped in his lungs again, trying to relax, but every time Damion's fingers caused pulses of dull pleasure to speed through his system he tensed. Soon he was panting, rocking back against the digits unconsciously, wanting more.

Damion withdrew his fingers one last time and slicked his cock with the remaining lube on his hand. "I want to hear you say that you will only obey me." He pushed the purple crown of his engorged cock against Requiem's hole.

Trembling with some unknown emotion, Requiem looked over his shoulder as he felt the pressure against his entrance. His mind was torn again, flitting back and forth between duty and what he wanted, *who* he wanted to obey—which was Damion. But then there was his training, his loyalties to the Corporation. They told him to obey his Fighter, but they also said that their orders took precedence over the Fighter's when there was a disparity. While the headache didn't come back, confusion warred within him. Muddled thoughts and decisions slipped from his reach. "Damion…," he whispered, hearing the indecision and struggle apparent in his voice.

"Tell me." Damion gave a hard thrust, driving himself deep into Requiem's body in one fast push of his hips.

Requiem's head fell as he let out an involuntary scream of pain. Blazing fire flared throughout his whole body, causing him to tremble. Even though Damion had mostly prepared him, that first thrust was a bit too much. Requiem had had worse, much worse, but the pain still settled in him as a throbbing burn originating from his anus and traveling up his spine. "You. I obey you!" Requiem forced out, the words a sob.

"Tight! Damn it, relax a bit." Damion stopped moving, no doubt because Requiem's body was clenching in spasms around him. "It won't hurt for long."

"I… apologize." Requiem shivered, his fingers clutching at the sheets beneath him even more, wrinkling them in a tight grip. He attempted to relax around Damion's penis and eventually ended up with his torso on the bed, his ass high in the air.

Damion rubbed his hands up and down Requiem's heaving sides. "Are you really sorry, or are you just saying it because it fits the situation?" He pulled out partially only to immediately push back inside. "I want you back. I want you to remember what I remember. I want you back."

"I truly am sorry. I do not wish to upset you," Requiem said right before his breath caught in his throat. He hiccupped around the sudden gasp as pleasure flared through him. The head of Damion's cock continuously rolled over that spot inside him, causing a wondrous feeling to spread through his body, pushing back the pain.

Damion's right hand squeezed Requiem's hip with enough force that Requiem was sure he was going to leave marks peppering his pale flesh.

"You won't obey them. You'll only obey me." Damion brutally snapped his hips forward again. *"Say it."*

Requiem cried out from the mix of pleasure and pain, his hips shying away from the harsh grip of Damion's fingers. "You ask me the same thing they ask!" he insisted while gasping for breath, trying to make Damion understand that it was something he couldn't promise. "I cannot lie to either you or the Creators. I must obey both."

"No, you have a choice. You're not a slave." Damion leaned down and bit into the patch of skin between Requiem's neck and shoulder, making another claiming mark on his Core.

Gasping, Requiem unconsciously tilted his head, allowing Damion better access to his neck. He felt pressure near his groin and knew that the unexpected was happening. Despite all the chemicals in his system, he was getting an erection.

"You can be free and still trust me. You can be free and not listen to them. You can be free and listen to me without being a slave." Damion nuzzled the love bite.

"Yet you ask me to obey only you, as do the Creators." He cut his words short as he planted his hands under himself, pushing his torso up again in pleasant surprise as further glorious feelings sparked through his body. "How is that not a definition of a slave?" His last words ended in a quiet groan.

"Now you get fucking mouthy," Damion growled and moved his mouth to bite Requiem's ear while his hips moved faster.

Whimpering, Requiem trembled at the hot breath and the arousing sharp pain in his ear. Sounds of panting filled the space around them, emerging from both men equally. "I do not mean to be. It was merely an honest question."

His words were broken, interrupted by silent cries. His eyes slid closed, his lips parted as harsh breaths escaped him. Requiem moved to brace his hands against the wall under the bookcase, pushing him back against Damion, pushing Damion farther inside so that Requiem could feel the head of Damion's cock deeper than he'd been penetrated before.

"For someone who doesn't remember, your body definitely does, because you want more, I can tell. And you're feeling good. Just like I promised." Damion reached around and grasped Requiem's hardening erection, giving it a stroke.

An involuntary cry left Requiem's lips, but he choked it off as quickly as possible. Damion's rapid stroking increased the amazing feelings filling him, and his arms trembled with exertion as he pushed back against Damion's thrusts that led him into Damion's callused grip. Requiem's body felt like it was bathed in sparking fire and increasing pressure that originated from his groin and spread throughout. "Damion…," he breathed out, not able to say any more.

"*Fuck.*" Damion groaned and began to thrust deeper, harder, even faster.

The sounds of skin slapping on skin, sighs, moans, and grunts overwhelmed Requiem's ears while other feelings overwhelmed his mind and body. The heat was building higher and higher in his groin and his breaths came in hurried gasps, exhaling almost as soon as he could breathe in. Damion's hand on his cock followed the pace of his pounding into Requiem, occasionally stuttering as he was overcome with pleasure, but still constant. White spots began to appear behind Requiem's closed eyes, and he let out a soft whimpering moan.

Damion let out a loud roar of completion, emptying his pleasure into Requiem's tight passage. He slumped forward, letting go of Requiem's shaft to put his arms out to the sides so that he wouldn't collapse onto Requiem's shaking body.

Requiem let out a soft moan as he felt Damion filling him. Hot, wet semen flooded his insides to the point that no more would fit. It bubbled out of him around Damion's cock, dripping down his thighs and slicking his tight sac. Damion's breath on his neck and his sweaty, slicked skin sliding against Requiem's back caused him to shiver more, along with the heavy weight still hanging between his legs that dripped his wantonness onto the sheets. He didn't say anything, merely panted as the sparks on the inside of his lids faded away with the lack of stimulation.

"That feel good?" Damion slipped his still half-hard cock gently out of Requiem's come-filled channel and rolled to his side, giving him a perfect view of Requiem's raging hard-on. "Want help with that?"

Nodding, Requiem collapsed back on his haunches, still holding himself up with his elbows as his whole body throbbed with neglect. He distantly felt Damion's pleasure leaking out of him even more and onto his thighs, making his skin slick.

"Come here." Damion pulled Requiem toward him with a soft touch. "I'll jerk you off but I want to see your face when you come."

After falling on his side, his back toward Damion, Requiem immediately but shakily flipped onto his back so that he could comply with the Fighter's orders. His breaths were still coming out quickly, but not as much as before as he started to cool. He opened his eyes.

"Tell me how you feel." Damion reached down and began to stroke the slightly curved erection. The precome and sweat made Requiem's firm flesh a little slippery, plus lube always seemed to get everywhere.

Requiem let out a choking gasp, his eyes fluttering closed and then opening again as his lips parted in a pant. "I… do not… know."

"Yes, you do, just think about it for a minute." Damion moved closer and began licking Requiem's neck, pressing his thumb against a thicker vein.

Requiem ended up pressing his hands against Damion's chest; not pushing him away, but there was some pressure against Damion as Requiem squirmed. "I… hot, g-good. Pressure and heat," Requiem finally responded between pants and low moans.

"It will feel even better here in a few seconds." Damion increased the movement of his hand. He stopped talking and started to bite whatever skin his mouth could reach.

Requiem realized that he would soon be covered in bruises and red-rimmed bite marks, but he didn't really care. That increased, fiery pressure was back and the pleasure-pain from Damion's teeth nipping sharply at his skin only made him more sensitive. He couldn't help his squirming or the moans and whimpers that escaped his parted lips. The pleasure was growing more and more intense.

"Damion…."

"I think you like it because the pain reminds you of jacking in."

Damion spoke as he pulled his lips away from Requiem's skin to look down at his face. Damion's large hand engulfed Requiem's cock. Requiem glanced down. The shaft in Damion's touch strained purple with need.

"Just let go and come," Damion rasped.

It seemed as if that was what Requiem was waiting for—a command. At Damion's words he did let go, letting the roaring heat overwhelm him and the white spots take over his vision as his mouth opened in a silent cry. He clenched the sheets as his muscles went taut, ejecting his pleasure over his chest and Damion's hand.

Requiem's head fell back, panting, eyes glazed, his body twitching in aftershocks. He merely lay there for a few moments, unable to speak as random sparks of pleasure flitted through him, occasionally making him twitch. Eventually he let his head slip to the side, his gaze meeting Damion's as he licked sweat from his lips. "I will hold on to the memories this time," he said quietly.

"You had better make that promise worth your life, because I can't do this shit again," Damion said in a warning tone. He could not lose Requiem again and not lose his mind. The idea frightened him more than death.

"I do. I cannot lie to you, Damion. If I say something, it is the truth. I will fight to hold on to these memories. That would mean defying the Creators, and for that they would terminate me. So yes, it is worth my life." He sat up, managing not to wince as the endorphins slowly disappeared, letting him know about every ache and pain all over his body. "You say that you cannot do this again, but you do not think about where I have been. While you have been dealing with the Core that I am supposed to be, I have watched you from within my own mind slowly slip away from what I know you can be." He didn't look at Damion as he said these words, and all of them were hard to get out.

"What the hell is that all about?" Damion reached out and grabbed Requiem's upper arm, "You think it was easy on me? I don't know what you were going through because you didn't tell me!"

"I did not say it was easy for you. I know it was not, but there was nothing I could do." Requiem concentrated on the end of the bed, his eyes wide and unblinking. "And I could not—cannot—tell you. A barrier was broken tonight, which is the only reason I am able to speak to you as I am doing now. But I do not know how long it will last. I am telling you what I can, while I can."

"You mean if I had just thrown you down and fucked you into tomorrow, then a lot of this shit between us could have been averted?" Damion shook his head.

"No, it was not that specifically. It was a combination of you ordering me to obey only your orders, and the Creators demanding the same."

"I swear the gods have a sense of fucking humor and lately it's at our expense. What now? Are you still going to report everything I say to the Creators?"

"My inability to follow either of those commands, since they contradicted each other, is what eventually loosened the compulsion." Requiem was very aware of Damion's tight, bruising grip on his arm. "I do not know what happens now."

Damion tossed himself back against the bed, letting his arms fall to his sides. "You are a fucking handful."

Requiem was silent for a moment, his gaze slowly shifting to his hands in his lap. "Do you wish to be free of me? I could do as the Creators ask and choose another Fighter if that is what you wish."

"I'm only going to say this probably about ten more times in the next few hours, but you're mine. As much as I don't want you to be a slave to them, I also want you to be your own person again. That isn't saying I can help my own… need to have you. I had thought about leaving and just starting over back on Mars." Damion's laugh was not amused, only tired. "I even thought about stealing you away like some really bad cheesy romance novel and trying to survive, but don't ask me how I thought I could make that work. What I know is we're together in this huge mess. If they take you away again, I'll probably go mad and kill a room full of Creators before going down."

Requiem looked over his shoulder at him. He didn't say it, but they both knew the Creators would take him away again at one point or another, and then they would both end up dead. It was only a matter of time. Requiem's personal mantra—nothing is impossible—could only go so far and stand for so much. Without saying anything, Requiem lay back down, ignoring the mess on his chest and stomach and what was on the bed in favor of curling his cold body against Damion's warm one.

"Cat got your tongue?" Damion turned on his side and draped an arm around him. "We'll figure this out. As long as you keep fighting them, we can work on hiding in plain sight. At least for now."

"What is there to say? I may only do so much with the constraints on me," Requiem mumbled into Damion's chest. "I will fight as long as my mind can hold out. But I cannot make promises that I do not know if I can keep. That would be too close to lying."

"They don't seem to take you away if I'm around, except that one time after you had your dream." Damion brushed back Requiem's hair. "We just have to cut your supplements back, but you can't stop taking them altogether this time. 108 has been taking only half his doses and they haven't caught him yet. But I don't know why, and neither does Juni."

"I do not think that is wise at this point in time. We are already under suspicion, and if we go even slightly against regulations, it will merely increase suspicion and we cannot afford that type of scrutiny at this time. We must not give them any reason to bring me in for another session." Requiem sat up, slipping out of the warmth of Damion's arms. "May I take a shower?"

Damion laughed. "Why do you want a shower if you're going to get dirty again anyway?"

"I am?" Requiem blinked slightly over his shoulder at Damion.

Damion sat up and wrapped his arms around Requiem's chest, pulling him close. "I want to do it again, don't you?"

Requiem's eyes slid closed as he shuddered slightly at the heat of Damion's skin against his back and around him. "I would... not be averse to the idea."

"You could just say 'Yes, Damion, I like your big dick.'" Damion laughed and turned Requiem around so he could kiss him once more. "Never want to take this for granted again."

Damion's lips stopped Requiem before he could respond. He arched his head back so that Damion could reach his mouth, and let out a sigh of contentment as Damion's warm tongue slipped past his lips to battle with his own. Slowly, he slipped long fingers through Damion's hair and stopped at the base of Damion's skull and held him.

When Requiem removed his hand from Damion's hair at last, Damion placed Requiem back down to the bed again, all the while trying to kiss him, running his hands up and down Requiem's body.

Warmth filled Requiem from the connection of their mouths, warmth he only ever felt when Damion touched him. He placed hesitant palms on Damion's ribs, his fingertips tightening and relaxing against the muscled flesh.

"You feeling good?" Damion asked as he pulled away for air, staring down at Requiem.

"Feelings… emotions…. You taught me them once… did you not?" Requiem thought his fingers had a mind of their own as they played over Damion's skin.

"Yeah, took me months, and in a day they were all stripped away." Damion dipped his head down to bite into the other side of Requiem's neck, opposite from the mark he had already made.

Requiem let out a choking cry, his fingers biting deep into Damion's sides in shock and pain. But for some reason that pain sent a shot of pleasure straight to his groin. It was brief, but there, as he squirmed under Damion's grip.

Damion licked at tender areas and up Requiem's neck. "Go ahead, make a little noise."

"I… cannot." Requiem panted as his neck throbbed in remembrance. "At least, not much. We are taught to be silent in our pain, so as not to disturb our Fighters or the Creators. It is something that is bred into us very young. I let some out when I am with you, but the rest is hard."

"I am telling you that you're free to make as much noise as you want or need to." Damion gave a little tug to Requiem's hair.

Requiem merely looked at him for a moment and nodded. Damion didn't understand that it was something that he just couldn't do, that he had been taught for as long as he could remember not to, and he was punished when he did. When he screamed, yelled, or cried, he was punished because it was a sign of emotion and emotion made you weak. But he let Damion know that he understood he had permission. He just wouldn't use it.

Requiem leaned up and pressed his lips against Damion's, hesitating as he ran his tongue along the lower lip.

Feeling Damion's startlement, Requiem immediately pulled back, looking up at him, searching for disapproval. "Did I do something wrong? I apologize if I stepped over a boundary."

"No, you were fine. You can do that again any time you want." Damion's grin spread from ear to ear in happiness. He moved so he was between Requiem's legs, spreading Requiem's long limbs apart.

"Acknowledged," Requiem replied softly before doing so.

Requiem liked this thing called kissing. It made him warm inside, made him feel wanted for himself alone: for more than just his mind, his abilities, or even his body.

Damion began to stir once again. His hands trailed down Requiem's smooth skin to his firm ass, giving it a squeeze.

Following Damion's movements with half of his attention, Requiem bent his knees so that they were planted on either side of Damion. The movement raised his ass just a little off the bed, allowing Damion whatever access he wanted. Remembering how Damion liked to hold him, with some hesitation Requiem wrapped his arms around Damion's body. He held him loosely in case Damion did not like it. He could let go right away if he had to.

Damion rocked his hips forward, but his hot flesh never penetrated, only slipped along the cool, sticky skin for the first few moments. Their rush to claim each other had been mostly sated during their first round.

Damion finally reached down and guided his erection to Requiem's entrance. When Damion rocked forward this time and entered him, the warmth contrasted with the coolness of Requiem's skin made Requiem's heart ache. As Damion pushed himself deeper and deeper, he kept kissing Requiem and swallowing his silent moans.

Requiem's arms tightened around him as soon as Damion was inside, an instant reaction to their connection. This time there was no pain, only pleasure, as he had already been stretched by their previous activities. This time his moan was muffled by Damion's mouth, tongue, and hot need. Requiem trembled with immediate pleasure, curling his toes into the mattress beneath them.

But it wasn't the same. He wanted more somehow, so he shifted to try to find it. Only when he wrapped his legs around Damion's waist did he find it, and he had to pull away from the devouring kiss to suck in enough air to gasp as Damion slipped deeper into him.

Damion pushed his fingers through Requiem's hair, his hips surging forward. It was perfect.

Requiem's eyes were hooded as they met Damion's, idly intrigued at the suddenly softer expression on Damion's face. He wondered what it meant for a moment, until the hard heat sliding in and out of his body ran over that perfect spot inside him and he closed his mouth quickly, with a click of his teeth, to hold in the scream that threatened to spill out. It felt so… *good*. He knew—somewhere inside him—he knew he had felt this before and was still amazed that something could feel so pleasurable.

Damion's hips kept moving as if he were trying to elicit more noises from Requiem. This was what Requiem had needed the last few months, even if he hadn't known it. This man right here in his arms and wrapped around him.

Hesitantly, since he wasn't quite sure what he was doing, Requiem moved his hips to meet Damion's, increasing the noise of their slapping skin. He was also curious about what might get an increased reaction out of Damion. Raising his head, his hot pants falling sporadically on Damion's lips, he lightly grazed his teeth along the lower lip while clenching his body at the same time.

"Damn!" Damion screamed and his hips snapped forward more forcefully. "If you do that too much, I'm going to come too soon."

Requiem let out an involuntary squeak at the driving force inside him, gasping to catch his breath. "But is that not what you wish to do?" he asked in a shaky voice. His skin was warm and he was aroused, he could feel sweat trailing over him as they moved together. He appreciated hearing Damion yell out like that. Not in anger or harshness but because he felt good. It had a different tone that made Requiem's skin crawl with pleasure.

"I guess you have a point." Damion groaned and let go of Requiem's hair, placing his palms on the bed to give himself more leverage. "Touch yourself."

"Touch myself? Where?" Requiem looked up into Damion's looming face that dripped drops of salty water onto his skin, causing him to shiver even more. He unwound his arms from Damion's broad shoulders and slid his hands over Damion's neck and chest to grip the muscular arms braced around him.

"Your cock." Damion chuckled as he gently touched it in encouragement, then licked his lips, angling his hips in the way that made Requiem scream. "Do you know how unbelievably gorgeous you look covered in sweat and sex?"

Damion's movements and instinct proved to be correct as Requiem let out a short, soft scream, his head tilting back into the pillows as he arched slightly off the bed. Panting harshly, he did as Damion ordered and brought a shaky hand to his erection, wrapping long fingers around it, causing him to jump as his ecstasy increased. He bit his lip against a groan. Damion's thrusts into him caused Requiem's erection to move in and out of the circle his hand created. Remembering what Damion had done to him earlier, he moved his hand, copying those movements to produce spectacular results.

"Requiem." Damion's voice was near reverent as he kept thrusting, moving harder and faster. He leaned down onto his elbows to capture Requiem's lips in a sloppy kiss.

Requiem very nearly purred into his mouth as pressure built within his body—that familiar, wondrous, heated pressure that licked throughout his system from his groin to his toes. His hand began to move faster along his need, sweat and dribbling precome making the movement slick and smooth.

As Requiem clenched him tightly, Damion didn't hold back his voice or stop the assault until the bunk's mattress actually began to move from the wild thrusts. Damion's arms began to shake, his heart beating nearly out of his chest as he pressed into Requiem.

After releasing his free hand from around Damion's arm, Requiem moved it so that his fingers tangled in pitch-black hair, grasping the back of Damion's head. The pressure became too much, sending tingling ecstasy throughout him and causing him to let out a soft, choking scream. His body clenched around Damion as Requiem came for the second time that night.

Damion's hips moved until he was spent and his release pushed deep inside Requiem once more. Finally Damion rolled to his side, while Requiem still clenched his hand in Damion's hair.

Chapter Twenty-Eight

Requiem

DAMION LAUGHED once he caught his breath. "Guess I need a haircut."

Requiem shivered, hiccupping in surprise as Damion pulled out of him abruptly and rolled to the side. Sticky wetness already began to leak out of his hole and onto the sheets. As soon as he realized it, he released Damion's hair, letting his arm drop bonelessly to his side. "I apologize," he whispered in a husky voice, bringing his hand into view in front of his eyes, watching through unfocused eyes the result of his own passion trail down and web through his fingers.

"You have nothing to apologize for. It was fantastic." Damion chuckled as he watched Requiem. "You really that fascinated?"

Requiem turned to meet Damion's gaze and his vision came a bit more into focus. "I would not say that it is fascination. It is nothing I have ever felt before, and it is… intriguing," he attempted to explain, not really understanding it himself. He understood the human body and that the purpose of ejaculation was primarily for procreation, but he had never been told that it could feel so… exquisite.

"*You* are intriguing." Damion rolled onto his back before sitting up and picking up his underwear. "Here. It isn't much, but it will do."

Requiem took a moment to study Damion's body, momentarily focusing on Damion's tattoo. Their uniforms covered most of their bodies and Damion rarely wore anything that did not cover his upper biceps, so it wasn't often that he saw the ink. The design was unique with the wings emerging from Earth, making complete sense. Chrysalis: a beautiful, changed being breaking out of its cocoon.

Looking away, he took the fabric and cleaned his hand and eventually his chest and stomach. The time spent wiping the inside of his legs was quick—most of it was on the sheets now anyway. "You will need new sheets. I cannot foresee you resting comfortably on all this moisture," Requiem pointed out.

"We can worry about that after morning meals." Damion took the soiled boxers and tossed them back to the ground. Wrapping his arms around Requiem, he gave him a slow and passionate kiss.

Requiem sighed, curling his body against Damion's. This kind of kiss was… nice. He never knew there were different kinds of kisses. He had appreciated the hot, lustful ones. The ones that were demanding of his mouth, taking what they wanted, which he accepted with definitely no protests. But this one was warm, and it heated his skin from head to toe.

"I never thought kissing another man would make me this fucking happy, but here we are." Damion smiled as he rested his forehead against Requiem's.

"Do you ever regret that I am not a female?" Requiem asked, his nose touching Damion's.

"Not really. It may have made it a bit easier in the beginning to accept all of it, but now I really can't get you out of my mind."

"I am… a distraction?"

"Yeah, you can say that, but not in a bad way." Damion shrugged. "Don't worry."

Requiem thought about it for a moment. "Do I distract you when you are piloting or fighting?"

"Not usually, only since this shit with the Creators started the last few weeks." Damion made lazy patterns over Requiem's skin with his fingers, marveling at the toned muscles and silky texture.

Requiem trembled at the featherlike touch, goose bumps appearing on his skin. "As long as that is all, it is fine. And as long as your levels improve over the next week, else they will force me to choose a new Fighter, which would not be acceptable. Then we would be in trouble because we would have to figure out something immediately."

"Don't worry about my performance." Damion frowned and propped his head up with his hand. "We need to find a way to fool them so they don't pick up on your changes again."

"I do not know how I will go about it. I am still taking full supplements and jacking in for rest. I do not know if they will notice my personality change otherwise. Honestly, I do not remember how they realized it previously, so I cannot hypothesize a theory." His eyes closed under Damion's gentle fingers.

"I hate the way you react while on those damn supplements," Damion grumbled and tugged on Requiem's hair. "Cut back on them."

Requiem went silent, wincing from a pain in his head that wasn't from the tug on his hair as he fought against a compulsion in his mind. "I do… not believe… I can. Contradicting." His brow furrowed as a dull headache developed toward the back of his skull.

"Yes, you can. I know you can do anything. That is what you say all the fucking time. You're the best, and nothing is impossible." Damion let go of Requiem's hair and pulled him in for another kiss.

Requiem gave a quiet "umph" against Damion's mouth. His eyes came back into focus. Sighing into the kiss, he slowly raised his hands and gently placed them on both sides of Damion's face, merely cradling it with his fingertips as if he were afraid to touch him completely.

Damion pulled back only slightly, and they were so close it was hard to focus on anything but Damion's nose.

"You can do it," Damion said.

"It will put us both in danger when I am collected again in seven days. They will see that my supplement levels are not at full and discharge you. We cannot take any risks. I am not saying it is impossible. I am saying it is illogical." Requiem spoke in a forced voice, his gaze meeting Damion's.

"You are just stubborn." Damion sat up and moved away from the bed. "I don't want to put you in danger, but I can't stand it."

Once Damion got out of bed, Requiem sat up and put his feet on the floor. "Then you must make a decision. A decision that I cannot know about, so you must merely implement the decision without informing me. If the Creators ask me questions, I can circumvent them to the best of my abilities, but if they suspect something, they will continue to ask until there is no other way but to answer them." He watched Damion's back as he walked over to get some water.

Damion groaned. "How do you make everything tilt on its axis ass-backwards in a second? You could just lie."

"As I have told you frequently, I cannot. Even if I attempted to, they would know that I am doing so. Whether it is by body language or my vital signs. While I can control my heartbeat and reactions to an extent, the Creators do not use topical means of studying them. They use our ports, and the tools they use can sense even the smallest fluctuation."

"Then make the computer tell them what you want them to see. You can do that, right?" Damion returned and handed him a bottle.

"For that to happen, I either need to be jacked in to tell them or at least have a tactile connection, and unfortunately it is obvious when I merge with the system." Requiem took the bottle. For a few moments he thought about the problem Damion had put in front of him. "But that would be a way to hide some aspects when I am jacked in to the pod. I should be able to mask myself there. Create a loop with a few random variables to make it seem live." His last words trailed off in a mumble as he stared at his pod, thinking.

"You are not plugging in for another few hours." Damion growled. "You can wait to play while I am out tomorrow."

Requiem tore his gaze away from the pod, blinking at Damion in confusion. "If I do not plug in today, no amount of circumventing the system will help us because they will merely come and take me. They are already cautious about letting me near you because they suspect that you will attempt to take me off my supplement or harm me out of frustration. They do not want me hindered from perfecting the *Ares*. If I do not plug in to rest, they will assume the worst and use it as an excuse."

"Then just plug in long enough to report that I needed you for physical satisfaction. They can report that to the Commander."

"The Creators do not report to anyone. They merely oblige the Commander by giving him reports when he requests them." Requiem took a long pull of water, emptying half the bottle. "But if that is your command, I will do so." He stood, placing the bottle on the table as he walked over to his capsule.

"Don't take too long," Damion said gruffly.

"As you wish." Requiem slipped into the capsule, lying back against its supports. He opened up the console panel on the edge of it and pressed his fingers into the lighted divots. A second later he gasped, his eyes widening for a moment as his spine bowed slightly before everything went lax and his eyes closed as he dove into a world of darkness, racing lights, energy, and information.

Requiem remained in the capsule for a little over an hour. During that time he created a loop, taking samples from scans of his vital signs and mental patterns for the last two weeks and rearranging them through the pulses. It was a fairly simple job, but extremely tedious because he had to hide what he was doing from the current scan. At the same time, he was receiving information about the next day's assignments and other news. It all required his mind to be in three places at once, so when Requiem finally extracted himself from the system, his eyes fluttering open as he took a deep breath, he was tired.

He remained in the capsule for a few minutes, trying to remember how to breathe normally as he blinked blearily, processing the information he had received.

"You okay? You eat recently?" Damion picked him up gently in his arms, turning toward the bed. "I don't want you in that damn capsule any longer than necessary," he grumbled.

Requiem gasped as Damion lifted him. The input jacks were still plugged in to his ports and pulled painfully. "Wait!" he choked out as the cables started to pull, one hand scrabbling at Damion's chest while the other reached for the capsule. He managed to quickly flip open the console and touch the scanner. Requiem gave a little hiccup of a whimper again as the chords automatically unhooked and retracted from his ports after he gave the command. Once done, he sighed in relief, sagging a bit in his lover's arms. He licked his lips, swallowing, his mouth dry. "When the cables plug in, they flare out, hooking into the input ports. Unless I key in and retract them, they can potentially rip out the ports."

"That would have been good to know. You hurt?" Damion looked to see if he was bleeding.

"No, I do not believe so. They merely pulled mildly. I am acceptable." Requiem rubbed at the port in the base of his skull.

"I'm sorry." Damion watched him for a few minutes after putting him on the bed, then handed him a fourth of a protein bar.

"There is no need to apologize. You did not know." Requiem looked at the bar and took it cautiously, then chewed on it slowly. "I need to go down to the mess hall and retrieve my supplement. Even if I do not want to eat all of it, I still require what it contains." One hand on the back of his head continued to massage the abused port. "Additionally, I received some news and our orders for tomorrow. Patrol has been increased to a higher status as the President of the Planetary Worlds, Jasper Barlett, will be arriving on board for an inspection in four days' time at approximately 1300 hours."

"That is the very opposite of fun." Damion shook his head. "Means everyone will be sucking up, even the Commander. I can go get your gruel if you want."

Requiem thought for a moment as he finished off the rest of the bar. "I apologize if I am overstepping my bounds, but do you think it is wise for you to go alone? The event that occurred yesterday was more than likely a setup by the Commander to get you in confinement. I do not know, but I hypothesize that if you are seriously reprimanded one more time, it will not matter if your scores improve. They will take you away from me."

"That would make you sad?" Damion grinned. "I promise not to get into a fight. Besides, I want you safe in here behind a locked door. Also, you might be too sore."

"To walk? I am not the one they are attacking at this moment," Requiem said, tilting his head slightly. He assessed his physical situation. "I will admit that I am feeling the effects, but I am still acceptable."

"I can get your meal and be back in ten minutes." Damion ruffled the top of Requiem's head. "You just stay here and relax like a normal person for that time."

"If that is what you wish, I will do so." Requiem leaned up against the wall to the side of the small bed.

Damion found pants and a shirt along with his boots and headed out to the mess hall. "Lock this room down and no one enters unless it's me."

Requiem nodded in response as he watched Damion walk away.

As soon as Damion left, Requiem slipped back into the capsule. Working with speed, he jacked in, slipping into the security system to watch Damion. He wanted to make sure that there was no security team released to collect either himself or Damion and that there was no danger lurking around the corner for him.

Chapter Twenty-Nine

Damion

DAMION MADE it to the mess hall to retrieve their lunch and requested an extra ration for the evening, along with Requiem's supplement, so that he wouldn't have to leave their quarters later to retrieve more food. Even if he wanted to throw the gruel out, he knew he shouldn't, so he didn't, but damn, would it have helped his mood. He felt like people were watching him, and it made his skin crawl.

After Damion used the door chime, Requiem opened it for Damion so that he didn't have to shuffle the trays.

"Oh, you're still up? Figured you would fall asleep." Damion looked around the room.

"I do admit that I am weary, but I wanted to make sure that you returned without any issues." Requiem locked the door after them and went back to sit on the edge of the bare mattress. He was still naked, obviously not seeing any point in getting dressed. *Clever man.*

"You worry as much as I do." Damion laughed lightly as he sat beside him after placing the trays on the table.

"I am merely cautious," Requiem replied, looking toward the food.

"What's wrong?"

"Currently nothing is wrong, other than the obvious encompassing problems. But for now, nothing." Requiem turned to look at him.

Damion shook his head. "All right, why are you staring at the food?"

"Because in general I do not find enjoyment in consuming it. However, I know I must do so to keep energy in my body. It is merely the effort of getting up and doing so that I am debating at this time."

"You seemed to enjoy it while we were on leave." Damion sighed as he gave a light tug on Requiem's soft hair.

Requiem looked at him for a moment, then stood up slowly, walking over to the table and sitting down. He picked up his spoon and began to eat his tasteless meal.

"IT'S REALLY all gone, huh? All our private moments." Damion had asked too many times, but he still couldn't believe it. He sighed, rubbing his eyes as he mentally wiped his last question away to ask another. "What will our job be while the President is here?" He didn't want to think about the pain in his chest at Requiem's lost memories. "Hopefully just patrolling around the ship?"

"Far patrol in the outreaching sector for eight-hour shifts. Eight hours on and off for the tenure that the President is here."

"Eh, could be worse." Damion shrugged, concerned with more than what their patrol was. "What time do we have first round?"

"In approximately ten hours," Requiem stated, taking his disposable tray over to the trash receptacle.

"And you don't want to sleep in the same bed as me?" Damion didn't like the idea of Requiem sleeping in the pod but didn't want to make him stay awake in bed with him just because Damion wanted him there, because then Requiem would be sluggish when they flew out.

"I have already checked in for the day and given my explanation for being absent. In approximately two hours, I will be seen as plugging in to the capsule for the rest of the day. If you wish, I can remain with you." Requiem turned around to sit on the edge of the pod.

"You figured out how to do that already?" Damion was shocked at the expediency with which Requiem had figured out how to arrange the system.

"I programmed and activated it when I was jacked in earlier. It will not stand up to intense inquiry, but it will hold under surface scans." Requiem ran his scarred fingers almost lovingly over the white metal of his pod.

"Then come over here and help me fall asleep. These fresh sheets need to be softened by some activity." Damion wanted Requiem away from that evil machine and closer to him. He was hoping more human contact would help him remember—would help him become less machine.

Requiem gave the capsule one last caress, then moved and sat by Damion. "I do not know how I can help you fall asleep. What do you wish me to do?" His head tilted to the side.

"You're being far too innocent. It makes me want to dirty you up more," Damion said with a chuckle before tugging Requiem closer and pressing their lips together for a deep kiss.

Requiem quickly gripped Damion's shoulders in shock as Damion pulled him close. Damion felt Requiem's lips on his own and let his tongue caress inside Requiem's mouth, tasting him. Requiem let out a long sigh, relaxing slightly after the grab, but he was in an awkward position with his torso twisted sideways toward Damion. After a few moments, Requiem climbed into Damion's lap, kneeling on either side of his thighs without breaking the hold on his mouth.

Damion moved his palms to slowly rub up and down Requiem's pale sides, up his prominent spine, and over the bumps of his ports. The skin was soft and now marked from Damion's teeth and hands. It almost felt like things had never changed, as if the last few horrible months had never happened and that Requiem still remembered what they had shared.

Requiem framed Damion's face with his long fingers. His chest and stomach strained toward Damion as they kissed, his fingertips lightly pressing against Damion's jaw.

Damion moaned happily as he trailed his right hand down Requiem's back, his finger dipping between the firm globes of flesh to caress over the sensitive hidden entrance of Requiem's body. Requiem sucked in a deep breath that Damion hoped was one of anticipation. He shivered and pulled away from Damion's lips, licking his own that now looked swollen and slightly raw.

"I still… do not understand these feelings," Requiem murmured, looking into Damion's eyes.

"Me neither at certain moments, but it feels good, so they can't be too scary." Damion made slow circles around the slightly inflamed clenched opening with his fingers, mildly amazed at how quickly Requiem had tightened up again. "We only live once anyway."

"Perhaps. But there are studies that have shown that there is a possibility of life after death," Requiem replied in shuddering breaths, his eyes fluttering open and closed as he raised himself up on his knees a little to give Damion better access.

"Think if we died, we could be reborn as poor farmers on Mercury?" Damion grinned warmly.

"Anything is possible." Requiem replied with his normal mantra, running his fingers through Damion's thick hair.

Damion just snickered as he kissed Requiem's neck and slipped a finger into the dry, tender hole.

"Can you reach the lube?" Damion asked before biting the bruise he had placed on Requiem's neck earlier, making the mark on the pale skin darker so that it would last even longer.

Requiem stifled a short cry and gave a shaky answer. "I do think I can manage if you release me."

"You want me to release you?" Damion let out a low chuckle that was almost sinister in sound.

Requiem tilted his head away to look at him out of the corner of his eye. "It would be required if you wish me to retrieve what you requested."

"I want to fuck you again, so do you think it's needed?" Damion abandoned his pursuit of the long stretch of neck and bent his head to lightly bite a soft, pink nipple.

Requiem attempted to reply but choked on the words, his tones turning into a soft, almost inaudible moan as he moved his hands to Damion's shoulders. His movements caused him to rub even closer to Damion's erect penis. "If you require it, I will retrieve it. It is up to you how you wish to enter me. I am merely stating that I cannot reach it unless you loosen your grip on me."

Damion eased his hold on Requiem's hips but continued his assault on the soft skin without a word, only willing to concede to releasing one hold.

Requiem sighed, looking reluctant to pull away from their hot, wet pleasure, but Damion had asked him to do something and he needed to do it. Leaning around Damion, he could barely reach the tube Damion had requested. He fumbled it for a moment with the tips of his fingers before gripping it and sitting back up straight, holding it out to him.

"Have you ever prepared yourself before?" Damion asked, not taking the tube. His breath caused Requiem's skin to pebble with goose bumps wherever Damion exhaled.

Requiem blinked, looking down at the lube and then back up at Damion. "Prepared… myself?"

"Put your fingers inside?" Damion knew Requiem probably hadn't, but it excited him more to ask the question and hear his innocent answers.

"Inside…. You mean like you have? No, I have not. There was no need to," Requiem said perplexedly. "Until you did it, I had never had fingers inside my body before."

"I want you to try it." Damion took his hands away from caressing the smooth skin and the slick interior walls of Requiem's body, leaning back on them instead, with a large grin on his face, so that he could watch.

Requiem looked at him for a moment, his expression unreadable. Finally, he looked down at the tube, flipped open the cap, and squeezed some gel onto his right fingers as he had seen Damion do. "You will guide me? I have not done this before."

"I want you to push your fingers inside, then stretch yourself by twisting your fingers just a little bit." Damion licked his lips unconsciously, watching his lover in a hungry, predatory way.

"As you wish." Requiem put the tube to the side on the bed and placed his left hand on Damion's hip to balance himself as he rose farther up on his knees, still straddling Damion's thighs. Making sure his middle finger was well lubed, Requiem twisted his upper body to reach his hole and slowly slid the finger inside his hot, tight canal.

"How does it feel?" Damion asked, his gaze switching from Requiem's face to his hand, watching Requiem's finger slowly disappear inside what he knew to be a clenching starburst of tight muscles.

"Intriguing," Requiem mumbled in response as he pushed the digit farther in. He rocked his hips as he appeared to be exploring the sensations. He slipped a second finger inside himself, arching as he pushed the fingers as far as he could reach. Requiem gasped as he brushed some sensitive spot inside him, scrabbling with his free hand to grab Damion's wrist so that he didn't fall.

"Found that spot, hm?" Damion chuckled as he wrapped his hand around Requiem's semihard shaft and began to stroke.

Damion gripped Requiem's slender erection, sliding up and down, and Requiem let out a small, involuntary whimper. After a few moments of this, he pushed a third finger inside himself. He seemed not to notice anything beyond the good feelings building within him, not even when he began to ride his own fingers.

"Ready for me?" Damion asked. He had grown achingly hard just from watching the sexy man in his lap please himself. He was going to explode from the erotic sight if he didn't sheath himself in Requiem's body soon.

"If you wish." Requiem's voice sounded breathy.

He removed his fingers, but Damion determined only to let that emptiness be temporary. He could feel Requiem's heart pounding.

"Where would you like me?" Requiem gasped.

"Right where you are above me, just move down." Damion let go of Requiem's cock to grasp his own at the base and hold it steady. "I want to watch you ride me."

Requiem braced himself with his fingertips on Damion's hard stomach, raising himself up and positioning himself over Damion's cock until Damion lifted it to bump his waiting entrance. Requiem slowly lowered himself onto Damion, sighing as he was filled once again. It must have still burned him a bit, but Damion knew it would be replaced by good feelings, like his own.

"Feels so damn good…." Damion moaned, his eyes partially closing as his head tilted back in bliss.

Requiem slid down him, ever so slowly, taking him in millimeter by millimeter. He didn't stop until Damion was deep inside him. Pale hands slid to brace himself against Damion's chest as Requiem panted quietly, his glazed eyes on Damion's pleasure-filled face. "What do you wish me to do now?"

"For the love of the Goddess, move!" Damion lifted his hips to thrust upward into his lover's clenching body.

Gasping at the movement, Requiem obeyed, using his knees and thigh muscles to ride Damion's length. A quiet moan escaped his lips as he moved, slowly at first, and then with increasing speed, his body tightening around Damion.

"Yes, yes, just like that but a little faster." Damion tried to match Requiem's movements, but it was difficult since he wasn't sure what to expect from him.

Requiem, as always, silently complied with Damion's order. His hair already stuck to his face with sweat. Damion changed his angle slightly until his cock slid repeatedly where Requiem wanted it, and

Requiem cried out. He slapped a hand over his mouth to stifle it, losing his rhythm a little bit since he had lost half his balance.

"Don't do that. I want to hear you." Damion thrust his hips up harder.

But Requiem kept his hand where it was, despite Damion's orders. His next scream was stifled the same way as Damion slammed up into him, causing Requiem's head to tip back in pleasure, eyes squeezed tight.

"Put your hand down! It's an order!" Damion growled through clenched teeth, frustrated by Requiem's lack of vocal reaction.

It went down immediately, but Requiem looked at him with widened eyes, his pace faltering. Damion had never spoken to him that way before, ever. He had never truly given Requiem an order or even asked him to do anything in that tone before.

Damion couldn't help the overwhelming glee that filled him from watching Requiem obey him so quickly. He reached out to squeeze the already bruised hips, helping his lover find the proper rhythm once again, while he kept his own hips moving.

Requiem's hands clenched into fists. He trembled with the effort to keep them down and away from his mouth as he followed Damion's movements, matching them with speed and urgency.

"Fuck. You feel so good." Damion groaned as he looked down between them where the sloppy, wet sounds were originating. He was hard enough to hurt, and seeing his cock pushing into Requiem's tight body was making it difficult to not come too soon.

Requiem didn't speak then, only panted. He let out a small cry as Damion shifted and hit that spot inside of him again and then continued to do so repeatedly. Requiem whimpered every once in a while when Damion went really deep.

"I'm going to come inside you again." Damion didn't know why he had to tell Requiem. It made no difference, but he wanted to say the words, needing to tell Requiem that he was claiming what was his again.

Requiem only groaned in reply, shuddering at Damion's words. "As you wish," he finally said, his voice rough. "I do not think I am going to be able to contain it much longer." His fingers gripped Damion's wrists with nearly bruising force.

Damion focused on his orgasm, since there wasn't much else to focus on when his head felt like it was going to explode, his vision blurred and his entire body nearly convulsed in pleasure.

When Damion started to fill Requiem with hot spurts, it finally tipped Requiem over the edge. He let out another quiet scream, his nails digging into Damion's wrists as his knuckles turned white from their grip. His release spilled over Damion's chest and stomach. Gasping, Requiem let go and fell forward onto Damion, planting his hands flat on the bed on either side of Damion, his head bowed as he panted, trembling.

"Fuck, that was good." Damion weakly moved his arms around Requiem and hugged him close, not minding the sticky mess he was pressing between their bodies.

One small tug was all it took for Requiem's shaky arms to give out on him, and he collapsed against Damion. Requiem's whole body shook in the aftermath. He moved his hand up so that he could run his fingers through Damion's hair, nodding in silent agreement.

"Now we can take a proper nap." Damion smiled lazily in blessed satisfaction.

"That would be agreeable," Requiem mumbled with a yawn. "If you wish, perhaps I could take a shower at some point in the foreseeable future?" Damion could see his passion sliding out of Requiem and onto the newly replaced sheets. The fluids from earlier had long ago dried on Requiem's skin in crusty patches.

"We both should take one before duty, yes." Damion smiled. "Good sex is messy."

Requiem let out another long yawn. He slid onto his side but kept Damion's hold around him, cuddled up widthways across the bed.

Damion grinned as he watched him. "Comfortable?"

"Affirmative," Requiem replied, managing to find a clean spot on Damion's chest to lay his head.

"We'll get cold here soon and then itchy, and then we can shower and I suppose get a few more minutes of sleep. But until then I'm taking a nap." Damion chuckled, hugging Requiem and feeling sated for the first time in months.

"We could take a shower now and then have uninterrupted sleep until we have to get ready for patrol," Requiem suggested. His eyes had already closed, though, but he must also be itchy.

"Will I have to hold you up?" Damion asked, not really minding.

"I believe I will be able to hold my own weight. It will not be necessary."

"Right. Fine. A warm shower, then a few hours of sleep." Damion moved upward slowly, not wanting to jostle his lover too much.

Requiem sat up, sliding to the edge of the bed and then standing. Or at least he attempted to stand. He ended up falling back down to the bed when his legs wouldn't cooperate. He frowned slightly at his weak limbs, tilting his head a little. "It seems that I have some unforeseen difficulties."

Damion laughed at him, "Yeah, well, it's to be expected, and I did warn you. Doesn't matter." He walked over and helped Requiem off the bed, then across the room to the bathroom and into the shower stall. Damion didn't want him to fall and hurt himself and end up sent to the labs so quickly.

"Yes, you did. I apologize for not taking those warnings seriously." Requiem clung to Damion's arm to keep himself standing.

"It's fine. Having you need me is kind of nice." Damion smiled warmly at him.

Requiem looked up. "I always need you. How is now any different?"

Damion felt a warm spot in his stomach burn itself up to his chest. "Really?" The single word was rusty and almost a squeak.

"You do not believe me? I informed you that I could not lie to you, and I have reminded you of that frequently." Requiem tilted his head back so that the hot water ran through his hair.

"It's nothing. I believe you." Damion was silent for a few minutes, focusing on washing himself and Requiem, as well as investigating the growing emotions inside him.

"Ah—" Requiem said after a minute or two. His eyes were closed. "—but you can still lie to me. It is acceptable. You are not required to tell me the truth."

"I want to tell you, and I want… I want you to be free of the Creators, of the Corporation." Damion sighed as the spray bounced off his body.

Requiem turned Damion around, returning the favor by washing his back. "If you want to tell me, then do so. It is not so difficult to tell the truth. But if you do not, then do not." He was silent for a moment, washing Damion's skin gently with the washcloth. "Damion, I will never be completely free. I am property of the Chrysalis Corporation. Only when I am at your side can I act like I truly am."

"You will be free one day," Damion said with a conviction he wholeheartedly felt.

Pausing in his washing, Requiem stood still before beginning his task again. "Anything is possible."

Damion laughed softly. "Right, and you keep saying I'm the best."

"You are, and you will reclaim that title once your performance goes back to acceptable levels." Requiem reached around Damion to put the cloth away and turned Damion around again so that the chemical wash could rinse the soap off him.

Damion quickly rinsed off, then pulled Requiem in for a deep kiss, letting his tongue slide lazily over Requiem's, exploring his hot mouth. "Just give me a day."

Requiem fell against him. His eyes widened in astonishment for a moment but then closed. He melted into the warmth of the kisses. "I will give you ten," he finally stated. "Even though you will not require them."

"You're at least sounding a bit more normal. A bit." Damion reached for a towel. "You done?"

"Affirmative." Requiem casually wrapped his arm around Damion's waist. "Before I told you I chose you, and for a little time after that point, this was not normal," he said after a few moments.

"True, our lives have changed a lot." Damion was happy to rub the towel over Requiem's skin, appreciating the marks he had left all over Requiem's neck and chest.

Requiem winced slightly as Damion rubbed over his hips. He looked into the mirror across from him and Damion saw him abruptly halt in his walk when he saw the numerous love marks that peppered his skin. The most prominent were on his neck and hips.

"I would even say drastically," Requiem said drily.

"You just like sex," Damion teased, pulling the towel away from Requiem to dry off his own skin.

"I do not quite see how that statement fits into the current topic of conversation, but yes, I do not oppose the process. Especially when it does not give me large amounts of pain." Requiem ran his fingers through his hair, patting it down. "Additionally, the fact that you appreciate it most thoroughly adds to the... *pleasure* of it."

"It definitely is pleasurable, but you like it too." Damion tossed the towel aside and bent down to pick up Requiem. "This will be faster than just limping to the bed."

Requiem threw an arm around Damion's neck for balance as Damion lifted him off his feet. "You seem to receive enjoyment from being able to carry me since you do it so often."

"Makes me feel useful." Damion put Requiem down on the bed. "Want underwear?"

"You did not feel useful before?" Requiem wore a perplexed expression. "And no, thank you. Unless you would like me to put some on."

"I just felt that outside the *Ares* you really didn't need me for anything." Damion shrugged and pulled out a pair of boxers for himself.

Requiem was quiet for a moment. "I will admit, in the beginning perhaps, before I met you, that was all Fighters were useful for. Cores are created to help the Fighter, not the other way around. But it soon became a need for companionship that I did not have to keep myself guarded through. I could... speak my mind at times and not have to worry about repercussions." He frowned, a mere quick downturn of his lips. "I did not expect to agree with my Fighter, even one that I choose specifically. It was a pleasant surprise. The ability to agree and the warmth."

Requiem seemed to be having difficulty finding words.

"I think that is the nicest thing you've ever said." Damion sat down next to him and ruffled his damp hair.

Blinking, Requiem looked at him. Requiem's head remained tilted as he crossed his legs on the bed. "I apologize if I am not a pleasant person. I do not know how to express myself since I have been encouraged not to. Emotions are still confusing when they do become apparent."

"I didn't say that to make you feel bad, but compliments from you aren't normal either. You're not a bad person, but you can be a pain in the ass." Damion's sigh sprang from the well of miserable frustration inside him. "Maybe it is me who isn't the nice person."

"It did not make me feel... *bad*. And you are a nice person. One of the nicest."

Requiem still sounded a little confused with the conversation. Damion was amused at his reaction. "I guess we are in agreement that we like each other."

Requiem ran his fingers through his damp hair, still appearing confused. "I agree that we are in agreement." A yawn forced its way out of him. "May I request that I rest now?"

"I think we both need to sleep." Damion lay down and made room for Requiem as well.

After a moment, Requiem curled his naked body against Damion's so that he was between him and the wall. He was used to sleeping in an enclosed space, so it was probably easier for him to relax there instead of on the edge of the bed where he had nothing cradling him. He laid his head on Damion's shoulder.

"Sleep well." Damion closed his eyes after hugging Requiem close, liking the feel of the smaller man in his arms.

"You as well," Requiem replied softly.

Chapter Thirty

Tuesday October 18, 454 MC
1331 GMT
Requiem

REQUIEM HEARD Damion sigh as they made yet another circle around the *Zeus*. They would alternate between three flight plans for today. Damion had been making sure to do each flyby perfectly to prove his worth as a Fighter.

"Bored?" he asked Requiem.

"I do not know what you mean by bored," Requiem replied from his chair, scanning something only he could see. He was patched into the navigation unit and also the scanners, doing complete 360-degree sweeps of the area.

"This is not as fun as even doing stupid sims," Damion grumbled. "Two days ago I wouldn't have minded an assignment like this, but it's just boring."

"Incoming ship. Midrange. 99.9 percent possibility that it is the President's ship, the *Olympus*," Requiem reported.

"I suppose we should watch it dock, then."

Damion banked the Zodiac to the left and a few other Zodiacs and his Beta unit followed his lead. Ever since Arkin's death, the rest of the Fighters had slowly deferred to Damion, making him the squad leader.

"Incoming transmission from the *Olympus*," Requiem stated in a mechanical tone.

"This is the flagship *Olympus*. Requesting escort to the *Zeus*."

The *Zeus* replied quickly. "You're cleared for approach and escorts are flanking your ship."

Damion grinned, listening to the communications. "I guess we're the flanking ships."

"They are also requesting us to guide them in. The *Olympus* nearly exceeds our docking bay parameters, and they are sending me coordinates to help straighten out their approach," Requiem told him.

"Let's hope their pilot didn't have a few beers before duty." Damion held his course steady along the *Olympus*'s starboard side.

Requiem paused for a moment, thinking quickly. "Suggest doing an audio guidance instead of an intrasystem."

Damion muted his outgoing comm link to other ships. "You want me to what? Are you plugged in a little too tight?"

"My inputs are perfectly acceptable and running at full capacity," Requiem replied, and there was a hint of an eye roll in his voice. "I am merely suggesting this course of action for the reason that it will bring up your performance numbers and also bring you to the President's attention. They will not be able to do anything to us if you are in the President's notice. I will guide you."

"You are a sneaky son of a bitch. Let's hope they don't crash." He flipped on his comm and hailed the President's ship. "This is the *Ares* requesting that you allow us to guide you in."

"Permission granted, *Ares* Fighter. Flagship *Olympus* will follow your lead," the pilot replied immediately.

"They will not crash," Requiem assured Damion, taking a deep breath and concentrating his view and navigation on the ship, pulling up schematics and calculations in the system. "Inform them that they need to shift 2.54 degrees to the port side in order to remain centered. They must achieve this with approximately 3.1 meters on either side of the ship for clearance, and 5.18 meters center on the top and keel of the vessel."

"*Ares* to *Olympus*," Damion said as he reopened the comm. "Your majestic vessel is going to be a tight fit, and we need you to go two and a half degrees port. Use the Corp symbol in your cross hairs if you can."

"Roger, *Ares*," the pilot stated, and then continued in a mumble that obviously was not supposed to be heard. "Bloody hell, simple peaceful mission, they said. Just pilot the flagship, they said. Didn't tell me that dockin' the bloody ship was going to be a square peg, round hole situation."

"He is still one degree off course and the stern is fishtailing too much. If he continues on this path, he will be able to get the bow of the ship in, but the stern will clip the *Zeus*. Advise that if he continues in this manner, we will have to do a four-point grappling guide." Requiem's fingers twitched as he moved through a schematic of the *Olympus* and continued to see measurements rise and fall in calculations.

"*Ares* to *Olympus*, you're still not lined up right. If you are having difficulty, we will have to assist." Damion turned off his channel for a brief second. "For fuck's sake, they put a newbie in charge of piloting the President?"

"Roger, *Ares*, I'm having trouble with the starboard rear thrusters. Attempting to correct now."

The pilot's tone was tense.

Requiem immediately zeroed in his sensors to the thrusters, his teeth clenching slightly at what he saw. "Code Red advisory for manual lead-in! Rear thrusters have a vapor leak and need to be shut down immediately or risk sparking a blowout. Repeat, advise to shut down rear starboard thrusters and throw out four-point line for manual guidance!" His fingers gripped onto the arms of his chair as his eyes flickered back and forth through the system only he could view.

"*Hermes, Dionysus, Athena*." Damion opened up the channel further. "We'll need to grapple onto the ship. *Olympus*, please shut down your rear thrusters and let us help you in."

"Belay that!" the Commander's voice came over the comm. "Everything looks fine where we are sitting. You're overreacting, *Ares*."

Damion circled around and passed Juni's *Hermes*. "Commander, they could blow an engine if they don't. They have a leak."

Requiem let out a near-silent growl, took a deep, shuddering breath, and closed his eyes. He crossed through the communication circuits and momentarily slid into the warning systems for the *Olympus*. He could feel the *Ares* drawing on his personal energy for the boost, but continued to work instead of activating the auxiliary power bays. They would need them for their thrusters if they were going to successfully pull the much larger vessel.

Finding a short in the *Olympus*'s alarm systems, he rerouted it so that it was once again attached. He was momentarily intrigued at the way the short had been created, almost purposefully, before retracting himself fully back to the *Ares*. He partially returned to his own mind in time to hear the pilot of the *Olympus* vocalize over all channels.

"Negative, Commander Sandrite. The *Ares* is correct. Our alarm systems just went off informing us of the vapor leak in the thrusters. Damn observant, *Ares*. If that blew, then not only the hull of the *Olympus* would have been damaged, but probably the *Zeus* as well."

There was a pause. "Rear thrusters have been deactivated. Permission to anchor granted. Coming in fast, so accuracy is a must."

"As long as *Hermes* isn't sleeping, we should be fine," Damion quipped even as he was focusing on deploying his tether.

Juni laughed as he flanked Damion. "Can't sleep with you buzzing over my fucking head."

"Deploying in ten seconds. Mark," Damion announced.

Requiem sent out a call to the three other Zodiac ships for the Cores to link up. If all four Cores were perfectly attuned, the tethers could be released simultaneously and with maximum accuracy if they were all synchronized over the schematics in the system. All gave their silent agreement and a grid appeared, overlaying the schematic, a perfect square with the points reaching from Core to Core.

"Core sync complete. Accuracy at 99.9 percent, pending all five ships stay on current course and await deployment," Requiem stated out loud. His voice was cold, mechanical, and distant as he was too engrossed in the system and the link to even notice his body's failing energy.

"Four… three… two… one…. Deploy," Damion announced. "The power cells in the *Ares* are acting funny—the levels dipping, then rising quickly back. Requiem, what the hell are you up to now?"

"Attachment complete. Core sync deactivating," Requiem said instead of replying. With a shuddering breath, he pulled out of the link and more into awareness. "I am doing what is necessary."

"Attachment completed flawlessly. Good job, Alphas. Lead us in," the *Olympus* pilot said with obvious relief, and cheering could be heard in the background.

"Bullshit, you're doing that fucking thing you do when you make the Barrier," Damion hissed in a low voice. "Just stop it before one day you end up dead."

"*Ares*, set thrusters at minimum burn to pull starboard aft 4.78 degrees, *Athena* required to guide from the aft side. *Hermes* needs to set thrusters at maximum burn to pull starboard rear 10.33 degrees to correct fishtail. *Dionysus* required to guide from the port side," Requiem advised instead of replying to Damion's warning, bringing up the schematic in the systems again to watch for when everything hit zero mark.

"*Ares*, is everything okay? It sounds as if your comm system is muffled. Do we need to switch leads?" the *Olympus*'s pilot stated. They must have heard Damion's hissing outburst even if they couldn't understand what he had been saying.

"Everything is fine, *Olympus*," Damion quickly answered. "My Core is just moving us around so we don't ruin that pretty paint job of yours."

"We'd appreciate that, and so would the taxpayers," the *Olympus*'s pilot joked.

Requiem waited until everything was on zero and aligned before speaking again. "Perfect alignment, still two meters too far to port. Advise that the *Ares* and *Hermes* go into full thruster burn on mark to pull the *Olympus* into alignment. Also suggest that interior grapples are put on standby to attach to the nose of the *Olympus* to bring them in once the *Olympus* is in place."

"Get that, *Hermes*?"

"How can I not?" Juni sounded amused. "I feel like the Cores are flying this thing in instead of us."

"Mark," Requiem stated loudly so that it would be heard throughout the comm system. He felt the ship vibrate with the sudden burst of fuel, the hull groaning with the effort of pulling the much larger vessel. Feeling the *Ares* falter, he realized that he had taken too much of the auxiliary energy when he reactivated the alarm system on the *Olympus*. Taking a deep breath, he fed the *Ares* his own energy to keep the thrusters burning. "Thruster shutdown in three... two... one... down."

"Have the interior grapples deployed," Damion ordered.

About a second later, the sound of metal hitting metal and mechanisms attaching echoed throughout the area.

"Deployment and attachment complete. *Olympus* is being pulled in. Docking successful. Thank you, *Ares*. See you onboard."

"Guidance grapplers have been released and retracted," Requiem reported weakly and then sagged into his chair. "We are being requested to dock before going back out on patrol."

Damion disengaged his grapple and turned off the communication link. "Requiem."

Requiem heard him unbuckle his harness and turn around in his seat. This made it possible for him to reach back and tug Requiem's hair.

"What the hell did you do?"

After failing once or twice, Requiem eventually sat up. He was still connected to the system, so he could only turn so far in the chair to look at Damion before the cables tugged at his input jacks. "In what capacity do you mean?" he asked wearily, swaying a bit in his seat.

"What the fuck did you do to drain yourself this time? Damn it, if you keep that up, one day I swear you're going to die. Stop it."

Damion gave another small tug to his hair.

Requiem winced slightly at the persistent pulls before sighing and lying back down in his chair, his arms shaking as he lowered himself. "I had to enter the *Olympus*'s systems to trigger the alarm for the rear thrusters. I cannot be 100 percent positive, but I am 91.5 percent sure that it was shorted out on purpose. That leads me to the conclusion that perhaps the vapor leak was not an accident either." He took another long breath. "To support my jump into the flagship's systems without draining power from the thrusters, the *Ares* needed to take some energy from me. But it was still not enough. Because we were on patrol beforehand, there was not enough energy to complete the maximum burn that we required to pull the *Olympus*, so I gave more of my energy to complete the process." He paused again, his voice already having grown rough and quieter from the effort of speaking. "I do what is necessary, Damion, for both of us. If we had failed in any of those tasks, we would not have been able to complete what we have done."

"Then someone else could have done it." Damion turned back around in his seat and flew them into dock.

"Then the purpose of the whole plan would have been lost. The *Ares* and its Fighter have been put into a spotlight, and it is hard not to notice at this time. You even managed to maneuver around the Commander's attempts to discredit you, and instead he was discredited himself." Requiem paused. "Docking at level two, slot fourteen is available and has already been approved for use. I did what I had to do to keep us safe. I did what my purpose is. I am sorry if you do not approve. I will be fine."

"I don't approve of you risking your life for something as inconsequential as the President."

Damion sighed and flew them into dock.

Chapter Thirty-One

Requiem

As THE cockpit opened, Damion crawled out first and nearly had to pick Requiem up out of the Zodiac.

"If you reach the correct conclusion, I was not doing it for the President, I was doing it for you." Requiem leaned heavily against Damion once they reached the catwalk platform, unable to even hold his head up. "Our actions have put us in the notice of the President and have discredited the Commander. I did what was necessary, and there was no risk to my life."

"You don't know if there was risk to your life, and if there was, you wouldn't care anyway. Damn it." Damion lifted Requiem's chin to look at his lover's face. "Don't make me take you to the doctor."

"As long as I do not allow the *Ares* to drain my energy completely, I will not be terminated," Requiem stated patiently, his gaze staying on Damion's chin as was appropriate for a Core in a public area. "And it would be illogical to take me to the Med Bay where I would merely be brought back under the attention of the Creators."

"You are a handful." Damion sighed and let Requiem's chin go so that his head could fall forward once again. "Can you walk?"

Requiem thought about it for a moment, taking stock of his current status. "How far do you require me to travel?" he asked hesitantly. "And what type of impression do you wish to give for the President, his pilot, and his security? They are disembarking now."

"Why are you so worried about the President? I doubt the Commander will send us back out, or if he does, it won't be for the next five hours." Damion sighed. "Just… sit and rest."

"We are assigned to do outer patrol for the next five hours immediately. The only reason we were ordered to dock was because the *Olympus* requested it." Requiem continued to lean heavily against Damion's side, his head resting against Damion's shoulder, eyes closed.

"Why would the *Olympus* request it?" Damion sounded confused. "But I'm happy we can escape the Commander's wrath for a few more hours, even if you need to rest."

"Unknown, but my conclusion is that they wish to thank you for your quick thinking and assistance."

"I requested it because I wanted to see who was behind the Zodiac who detected the potential threat to my vessel." A tall, darkly tanned man walked down the catwalk, followed by a small group of personal guards.

"Uh…." Damion snapped his slack jaw shut and turned to try to salute while attempting to hold Requiem up.

Requiem forced himself to wake up a little and pushed away from Damion to grab on tightly to the railing behind him, keeping his gaze on the ground. He tried to hide the fact that his whole body was shaking with fatigue and attempted to keep from sliding straight to the ground. Damion needed to stand on his own for this, receiving the attention and singular accolades that went along with it.

"How did you do it?" the President asked, looking at Damion more than his Core, as was usual.

"It wasn't me. My Core is the best on the *Zeus*. Perhaps in all of Chrysalis Corporation." Damion lowered his gaze in respect for the man's position.

"The Core did detect it, but you were the one who flew us to safety." The President looked right at Damion and almost through him. It wasn't a harsh gaze, merely judging, assessing.

"And it took three others as well. We wouldn't have been able to do it without the *Hermes*, *Athena*, or *Dionysus*."

"The malfunctioning thruster was not an accident. That vapor leak and the shorted-out warning system were both purposeful," Requiem whispered, his voice pitched only for Damion's ears. "The President has an enemy on his ship who wishes him harm."

"Does he have something to say?" The President frowned as Commander Sandrite entered the walkway and quickly marched up to them on the catwalk, the President's guard tensing at his angry expression and quick steps.

"My Core believes it was an assassination attempt," Damion answered.

"That's preposterous," the Commander growled. "He has no way of knowing if that is true. We are sorry for this Fighter's rash assumptions."

Requiem sighed and took a deep breath, gripping the railing tightly as he forced his body to stand up straight. His gaze was still directed toward the ground, but he was no longer trying to hide himself. "There was evidence of the warning system connected to the rear thrusters being sabotaged. I was required to reroute the circuits so that the alarm would sound. The failure was too clean to be a malfunction—something that I have only seen internally that resulted from cut wires. I suspected and have come to the conclusion that the leak is also the result of a manual disconnect. More than likely a person of ill intent released the lock on the fuel inject site." He was loud enough now for everyone to hear. He caught himself again as his legs decided they didn't want to hold his weight anymore and he began to slide toward the ground. Requiem desperately used his arms to hold himself up. "If the Commander suspects that my abilities do not extend that far, I respectfully request that he receives a report from the Creator in charge of my caretaking. She should be able to correct your misinformation."

"You impudent little—"

The Commander flushed with fury, and he might have even raised his fist to Requiem if it hadn't been for Damion standing between them. The Fighter glared at the Commander, a dark look that made the Commander's men put hands on their weapons.

Years of conditioning caused Requiem to wince away from the Commander's threat.

"He's never wrong. He's the best. Excuse me," Damion said in a low voice before turning and picking Requiem up under his thin arms, ignoring Requiem's slight jump of shock.

Requiem had been concentrating so hard on the potential threat from the Commander that Damion's movements caught him unaware. Requiem quickly relaxed into the warm arms once he realized it was Damion. Ignoring everyone else, Damion carried him up the ladder and into their Zodiac. "Just rest here."

"Is there a problem with the Core?" the President asked calmly from outside the *Ares*.

Requiem gently gripped Damion's arm as he turned to leave him in his chair. "I would suggest telling him the truth. It will not hurt our situation and will discredit the Commander more."

"He's just tired," Damion answered quickly, loudly enough to be heard through the hatch.

"These two are nothing but trouble," the Commander interjected yet again.

"My Core uses his own body to fuel the Zodiac's power at times," Damion explained as he climbed out of the ship. "He's never been wrong."

"So you're saying that 47 was completely right in killing his previous Fighters in cold blood? How interesting," Commander Sandrite said.

In the ship, Requiem closed his eyes and winced as he listened. That, as they said, was not good.

"It was self-defense since you wanted him dead," Damion said.

"I wanted him dead? Is that what you think, you insubordinate asshole? That it's my fault your broken toy killed those men?" the Commander growled.

"Gentlemen, please," President Barlett interrupted. "Whatever may have happened in the past, I owe this Fighter and his Core my life and the life of my crew. If it wasn't for the *Ares*'s Fighter, then things might have ended differently."

By this time Requiem had pulled himself up to the hatch and was watching from there, clinging onto the edge with one arm, the other out of sight. Inside the ship, his hand wrapped around a wire attached to the gun turrets that had silently turned, aimed toward the Commander without anyone noticing. He didn't have much more left in him, but he would use the rest of the energy his body contained to protect his Fighter.

"Sorry, Mr. President." Damion bowed his head slightly. "I have five more hours of patrol to do, and I should let you go."

"Well good luck to you. Safe flying and gentle skies, Fighter. I will make sure to speak with you later, and I know my pilot wishes to have a word with you as well. He's busy doing repairs at the moment. I thank you again for your assistance." The President turned to the Commander. "And I believe you have a tour awaiting us, Commander Sandrite. Shall we continue?" His voice was gentle but definitely held some contempt on the outskirts of it. The Commander nodded, and with a final glare toward Damion, he turned and led them away.

Juni silently walked up behind Damion with 108 hiding in Juni's shadow. "Damn. You want to be killed?"

Damion sighed and tugged at his hair with both hands. "Shit, shit, shit."

Requiem released the cable he had been holding on to, and it fell to the floor of the Zodiac with an audible *thump*. "Presently, I believe we have the President's protection. But when he departs in five days' time, that will go with him and it is very likely we will be in danger."

"Are you okay? What the hell are you doing there?" Damion asked as he looked up at the ship.

"The Commander is going to demote you at this rate," Juni said worriedly as he followed Damion's gaze to the *Ares*.

"I was merely preparing, and once the danger had passed, I accidentally let go of the cable. That is all." Requiem slid back into the Zodiac. Unfortunately his legs had stopped giving him the time of day and he slid straight to the floor. Sighing softly, he leaned against the inner hull. "Luckily, Damion's scores are on our side. Unless he drops again, the Commander would not be able to demote him."

"He's pretty sure about that, but he could still try to kill you. Anything you can do to help?"

Requiem heard 108 reply. "Presently I have no suggestions. But I will attempt to think of something."

Damion scrambled back into the *Ares* and helped Requiem into his seat. "You just love to drive me insane."

Requiem clung to Damion until he was placed into his seat, sighing in relief as he sagged into the chair. He raised one hand, running it lightly over Damion's cheek. "I apologize for causing you so much strife. I do not mean to."

"It's okay. This time it's my big mouth that has gotten me more notice than you had anticipated." Damion ruffled the top of Requiem's head. "You can sleep while we fly around, and I'll be bored."

Juni spoke again. "You did good out there too."

Requiem was glad to hear Juni praise 108. "108's sync was flawless. 491 and 362 had some difficulty, but there was no hesitation. It was quite an excellent connection, and he held it with me. If he had not, it might have fallen apart," Requiem said softly, his eyes already starting to slide closed. His hand slipped down Damion's arm to grip his hand, holding it tightly. "I do not like leaving you without a full range observation, but I do not believe I can help you at this time. Please wake me if any anomalies occur."

"Yeah, if I see a UFO, I'll wake you right up." Damion smiled as he stood up and climbed out again. "I want to burn out and get away from the Commander and everyone for a few hours, but I could use some water."

"You don't want to leave your poor baby alone, huh?" Juni laughed warmly. "All right. I'll get you your water ration for the ride and be back in five."

"Damion, I will be acceptable if you wish to proceed with a break," Requiem said weakly, struggling to stay awake long enough to depart. "We have a window for takeoff in approximately ten minutes."

"I'll be fine for now. I'm not leaving you alone."

"Your worry is unfounded." Requiem mumbled just loud enough for Damion to hear. "No one would bother me while I am in the *Ares*."

"Like hell." Damion waited outside for Juni to return. After some minutes, Damion spoke again. "Thanks."

"The Commander is showing off every nook and cranny. It will take days at this rate." Juni snickered. "I don't think the President's face moves much either."

"Damion, two minutes," Requiem announced, still clinging to wakefulness by the tips of his fingernails. He wouldn't feel completely safe until they launched.

"I know." Damion climbed the ladder and leaned down into the ship to grab his helmet. "Juni, he's going to be out for a while. Could you please have 108 keep an ear out in case there are any orders from the Commander to send us trouble?"

"Will do," Juni replied. "Have a safe patrol."

"Are you certain that you do not need me to relay information?" Requiem asked, his eyes still closed, his trails through the systems sluggish.

"You're fine, just rest."

Requiem dimly heard Damion jump into the pilot's seat and initiate takeoff protocols with a few taps to the control panels. He called the command center for permission to leave the *Zeus* and then took off for, hopefully, a quiet five hours.

Having no choice but to take Damion at his word, Requiem mumbled, "I am sorry," before letting the darkness take him.

Chapter Thirty-Two

Damion

DAMION WAS happy to finally be docking, and also to hear that the Commander was still far up the President's colon and not paying any attention to the Fighters, Damion, and Requiem. He unbuckled and turned to wake Requiem up.

Even after five hours of sleep, Requiem had difficulty waking up. It took Damion shaking him several times for him to even open his eyes and blink blearily at him. And then another minute or two before he could jack out of the system and sit up, rubbing his face.

"You're going to eat and then head right to bed," Damion grumbled as he helped Requiem down the catwalk.

While not leaning on Damion as much as before, Requiem held on to him for balance, as he seemed a bit dizzy and groggy from his nap.

"As you wish," Requiem mumbled.

Damion walked him back to their room, helping him sit on the bed before unzipping his flight suit. "Stay here and sleep, in the *bed*, until I get back."

"May I ask where you are going?" Requiem crawled onto the soft mattress.

"To get food." Damion smiled warmly. "And something to drink."

"Okay." The exhausted Core was already drifting back to sleep. "Be careful."

"Always."

Damion left and met up with Juni in the elevator down to the mess hall. The lights within showed the floors flashing by as they plummeted nearly twenty floors.

"How is he?" Juni asked, leaning up against the wall.

"Drained to the point of imitating the walking dead." Damion sighed, attempting to rub the fatigue out of his eyes. "How you doing?"

"Oh, I'm just peachy. I left 108 in the room keeping an eye on the Commander."

Juni paused for a minute as the doors opened, and then they walked out.

The mess hall corridor was always busy. It was the only place where all the crew from different sections of the massive ship could mingle. No one ever mingled unless they were family, though. Military stuck with military, and science heads stayed with their own kind, as did the civilians.

"I asked him about the whole ship-draining shit. He's not sure how it's done, and I don't want him learning how to do it. But from his observations, it shouldn't do 47 any harm. Unless he lets it go too far. And then it's a possibility that it'll stop his heart. Just thought you should know."

"You mean you don't want my Core rubbing off on yours?" Damion chuckled softly, but it lacked any true humor. "I actually don't blame you one bit."

"No offense, D. 47 is amazing as a Core, and his abilities… fuck, I still can't believe some of the shit he can do. But he's insane in his sanity, if that makes any sense. And he's willing to do anything to get the results he wants. Even risk death." Juni shook his head. "No. I'm too fond of 108 to lose him. So no, I don't want him learning what 47 can do."

"No offense taken." Damion sighed again. "At times I wish he was a bit more normal. It would stop me worrying so damn much. Of course, if he was different then he wouldn't be so great."

Juni shrugged, opening up the mess hall door for his friend. "If he wasn't who he was, he would still be the Creators' puppet, 108 would probably be dead, and you and I would still be Beta pilots instead of Alphas. Damned if you do, damned if you don't."

"When did you get smart? Taking 108's supplements?" Damion teased as they stepped in line.

Snorting, Juni rolled his eyes and shook his head. "Nah, I just got tired of 108 giving me the look. The look that says in no uncertain terms I'm being a dumbass. Let me tell you, for someone who doesn't have many emotions, that guy can do scathing rather well." He picked up two trays, handing one to Damion.

"Really? No offense, but 108 could impersonate a rock." Damion saw someone looking at them from the catwalk above. "Oh Gods, here too?"

"He does that to put you in a false sense of security," Juni replied and then looked at Damion, following his gaze up. "What's wrong?"

"I can feel the Commander's squinty eyes anywhere." Damion lowered his head and hoped not to be noticed. "Does the President really give a damn what we eat?"

"He would if he tasted this shit," Juni mumbled, wrinkling his nose at the plate placed on his tray. "I'm not quite sure if this is supposed to be spaghetti or bloody brains. Let's just get our food and the gruel and get out of here ASAP. You don't need to be in that asshole's view any longer than necessary."

"I agree with you again. Damn, this has to stop happening." Damion grabbed his tray and the supplement for Requiem before following Juni out.

"108 will warn us if they decide to intercept," Juni said, stepping back into the elevator and hitting the button with his elbow. "You know it isn't going to stop. It's only going to get worse once the President leaves."

"Yeah, great, and in five days the Creators want Requiem back on the table to dissect, and the Commander wants me replaced." Damion growled in frustration. "Going to be a shitty week."

"No, it's going to be a great week. It's the weekend that's gonna suck," Juni corrected as they stepped out of the elevator and into the corridor. He was silent for a few minutes as they walked. "What are you going to do, D? There ain't a lot of options, but you know you have my help if you need it."

"I don't want to get you involved, but thanks for being willing to throw your cushy life away." Damion was only half joking.

Juni rolled his eyes. "Oh, shut the fuck up. You know I'd help you in a heartbeat. Shit would get really boring without you here. Besides, if they don't have you to pick on anymore, who says they won't come after me? It's simply self-serving to help you." He hit the button for the door with his elbow, a really handy body part if your hands were full. "Now go wake up your Core. Maybe cuddle a little. Might do you some good. See ya." He turned and entered his room.

"You're a nosy ass!" Damion shouted after his friend, and then sagged against the wall for a moment. Fuck. What was he going to do?

As his mind was reeling with ideas, good and bad, he arrived back at their room and put the tray down on the small table. "Requiem?"

Requiem lay on the bed on his stomach, pressed against the wall, with his arms wrapped around a pillow and his face buried in it. One blue eye opened, blinking blearily at Damion as if he couldn't focus on him. Inhaling deeply, Requiem sat up, letting the breath out slowly and rubbing his eyes. Luckily, it seemed easier for him to wake up now and he appeared a little more rested.

"Wow, don't look so happy." Damion walked over and helped him stand up. "Let's get you out of that."

A little steadier on his feet, Requiem let Damion remove his rumpled flight suit. "I apologize for resting so long. I did not mean to," he finally said, his voice hoarse from misuse.

"It's all right. If you stopped trying to be a battery, it wouldn't happen so often." Damion helped strip his lover out of the suit and then ruffled his hands through Requiem's soft hair just to make himself feel better.

Requiem closed his eyes slightly at Damion's touch, blinking blearily as he was suddenly standing in just his boxers. "I have to come up with a way to add another energy output on the *Ares*. There is not enough room to do so at this time where it would be sufficient."

"It's because you keep trying new shit." Damion pulled him in for a kiss just because he wanted to feel his lover's warmth against him and to make sure Requiem was truly all right.

Not completely balanced yet, Requiem stumbled into him, catching himself with his hands on Damion's chest as their lips met. "I need to test my boundaries."

"One day you'll end up dead, then where will I be?" Damion let out a soft sigh, leaning his forehead against Requiem's. "Then I probably will end up dead as well."

"Not dead. You'll be free," Requiem replied quietly, stepping away from Damion and sitting down at the table, pulling his bowl toward him.

"I think you overestimate my intelligence." Damion sat across from him and started on his food.

"I do not understand your statement," Requiem replied, his spoon pausing in its scooping of food.

"If you died, I don't think I'd be long for this world, so to speak." Damion shrugged, tore off a piece of his protein bar, and held it out to Requiem.

Requiem's icy blue gaze watched Damion as he slowly took the sticky piece from his fingers. "Please explain," he requested, nibbling on the sweet food.

"If you died, I'd probably find the person who did it and kill them." Damion wondered where his meaning was being lost.

"Why?" Requiem finished off the last of the bar, licking the stickiness off his fingers slowly. "Why would you not just leave? What if I were terminated through no fault of anyone but myself? There are too many variables for that answer to be acceptable."

"That is the computer part of you talking," Damion pointed out. "Not the human part."

Taking a bite of his supplement, Requiem shook his head. "Describe my inquiries whichever way you wish. They are legitimate questions. Why would you go after whoever terminated me if that was the reason for my death? Why would you not leave and go where it is safe?"

"Because I'd be pissed." Damion growled in frustration, trying to figure out how to make Requiem understand, but knowing it was unlikely that he would get the concept. "There isn't any logic to it, just impulse."

Requiem chewed for a few minutes, eating the rest of his meal and processing what Damion had said. "I do not understand, nor do I think I ever will. I apologize for that. I wish I could." He finally stood and disposed of his dishes.

"It's fine. It's part of you being on the supplement." Damion sighed again, running his fingers through his hair. "If I died, you'd just go to another Fighter."

Pausing for a moment, Requiem walked over and sat on the bed. "I do not believe so. Not of my own volition. The logical conclusion is that they would wipe me, and then there would be no more me."

"You're extraordinary, and they'd keep you around long enough to figure out what makes you tick." Damion got up and brought the water with him as he walked to the bed and sat down next to Requiem.

"That does not involve keeping me as me. What you call my personality would not be needed as far as they believe." Requiem shifted farther back on the bed, leaning against the wall, horizontal across the mattress.

Damion took a sip of water and then offered it Requiem. "That scares you?"

Taking a sip, Requiem tilted his head as he thought about it. "I suppose that is what you might call it. I do not know. I am not… *afraid* of death, but I am wary of being trapped within my own mind." A tremor ran through him almost imperceptibly. "I did not like it before, when they took away my ability to remember and feel, and it will be worse if they wipe me completely."

"We'll try our best to die in a blaze of glory, then, instead of letting them choose our fates." Damion felt like he needed a drink of something stronger than water.

"I would prefer not to be terminated at all. I have too many experiments to run, and death would be an inconvenience."

Requiem was completely serious as he leaned against Damion. Damion laughed, shaking his head at him. "What a goal to have in life!"

"What other goal is there? I have my duties to the Chrysalis Corporation, my experiments, and now you. My experiments I hold for myself, although my Creators require that I report to them any of my findings."

"I just wanted to not die of a breathing disease from mining." Damion grinned and pulled Requiem close against his side. "Now I'm thinking about dying trying to sneak you out."

Requiem eased into Damion's warmth, wrapping his arms awkwardly around his waist. "Sneak me out? No, do not tell me. They are going to try their best to extract as much information out of me in six days' time." He buried his face in Damion's neck.

"I can't think of anything else other than stealing the *Ares* and hoping they don't shoot us down too quick." Damion squeezed him tightly.

Getting his arms free, Requiem moved away a little, clapping his hands over his ears. "No more, Damion!" he insisted. For the first time his voice rose slightly above soft monotone. "Do not tell me. I have already explained their ways of getting information out of me, and I do not want to be the cause of your strife any more than I already am."

"I don't care!" Damion tugged him close again, looking him in the eyes. "You're mine. I have to trust that you'll fight them. If you don't fight them, then it won't matter. I'm dead either way."

With his arms pinned away from his ears now, Requiem clenched his hands into fists. He flicked his gaze over Damion's face, confusion rampant in his expression. "I do not know why you care so much. Why do you not just let me go? Let them have me and leave? If you do not go back to Mars, then go somewhere else." He shifted and ended up in Damion's lap.

"Because I can't, I just can't." Damion gave him a rueful smile. "I'm stupid, I suppose, or crazy. All I know is that I can't leave you. It makes no damn sense."

"You are right. It is completely illogical." Requiem blinked, and Damion felt the tension leaving him as Requiem eased against him. "Excuse me for this, but I am… *glad. Relieved,* I suppose you would call it. I… do not want to… I do not want to be separated from you."

It was obvious that this confession confused Requiem as he directed his gaze away.

"Good." Damion turned Requiem's chin toward him and kissed him warmly once again.

He tightened his arms around Requiem, never wanting to let him go.

Chapter Thirty-Three

Requiem

REQUIEM DIDN'T know why, but every time Damion kissed him abruptly, it caught him off guard. It had happened so often now that he should've expected it at any point, but he hadn't, and so he inhaled sharply through his nose before relaxing even more in Damion's lap. He kissed his… lover back slowly, still getting used to the feeling of having someone this close to him, of having someone want him in a nonmalicious way. And he was also getting used to… *caring about* someone. He hypothesized it was caring. He didn't have any other explanation for his thoughts or the warm feelings in his chest.

Damion pushed his fingers through Requiem's hair again, pulling away to look at him. "I want you. Are you okay enough for this?'

"Want me?" Requiem blinked, his head tilting to the side. "In what capacity?" He still wasn't used to Damion's terminology or *slang*.

"To have sex, you innocent idiot." Damion looked amused by Requiem's confusion.

"I am not an idiot. It is not my fault when you use terminology that I am not familiar with," Requiem countered. "And I am acceptable. I no longer feel as if I need to rest immediately."

"What about your backside?" Damion ran a finger lightly over a bruise on Requiem's neck.

There was slight pain from Damion's fingertips on his skin, but it only helped to remind Requiem how he received it and an involuntary shiver followed the movement. "It is also acceptable."

"Then let me get the lube while you take off your shorts." Damion smiled, pressing another quick kiss to his lips.

"As you wish." Requiem slid off Damion's lap and stood up. He removed his boxers, placing them on the chair, and then stood there, waiting.

"Why are you just standing there?" Damion removed his own clothing and grabbed the tube from the nightstand.

"I do not know where you would like me."

"On the bed, of course." Damion shook his head. "You are far too innocent."

Requiem decided that Damion's words didn't need an answer and sat down on the bed, moving to the center of it.

"You like having sex with me, right?" Damion asked as he watched him move over the bed.

"Affirmative. I find it pleasurable and… warm." Requiem looked up at Damion, approval in his eyes. "Why do you ask?"

Damion sighed, crawling toward him. "I just wanted to make sure you liked it because I have a feeling you would let me do it even if you didn't."

Thinking about it for a moment, Requiem reached out to run his chilled fingertips against Damion's cheek. "Affirmative. I would if it would make you happy. But I would also be truthful about it since I cannot lie to you. I find the experiences involved in having intercourse with you most agreeable. I apologize if you did not get that impression."

"I figured the way your eyes rolled back into your head might be a sign of pleasure." Damion leaned down for a kiss, and his lips curled in a slight smile.

"Then why did you ask?" Requiem inquired in a mumble before being silenced by the welcome lips. He left his hand on Damion's cheek, curling his scarred fingers against the warm skin as his eyes slid closed.

"I like to make sure."

Damion went back to kissing Requiem breathless while stroking his naked body, his tongue exploring every crevice of Requiem's mouth.

Requiem inhaled sharply through his nose, abandoning Damion's skin to thread his hand through the black hair on the back of his neck. "I think you are merely reaffirming for your own satisfaction."

Damion ignored Requiem's answer and focused instead on a patch of his neck. "I want to cover every centimeter of your pale skin with love bites to show everyone that you're mine."

Gasping, Requiem tilted his head to the side to give Damion more room to work. His fingers tightened in the hair he was already gripping as a sharp pain beelined for his groin, causing him to squirm involuntarily under him.

Damion licked Requiem's neck. "You get so hard from a little bit of pain."

"I do not understand it. I generally do not appreciate pain, although I can push it aside. I have never received *pleasure* from it before." Requiem focused on the ceiling as he concentrated on the hot, wet warmth of Damion's tongue soothing the sting in his neck.

"Because this is me and this feels good to you." Damion lightly bit Requiem's clavicle while his hand moved between them to take hold of the half-hard member between Requiem's legs. "See."

Requiem jumped slightly at the bolt of pleasure that sparked through his system as Damion wrapped around him. "I see the results. I just do not understand how they come about," he stated, a bit breathless. It was then that he noticed something. Thinking back to the times before when they had sex, there was an increase. "Each time we have sex it feels different. Stronger. More…. My body reacts more, feels more." He sounded perplexed by this admission as he skimmed his hands down Damion's neck and shoulders.

"I like that." Damion grinned. "Now spread your legs apart so I can prepare you."

"But I do not understand it," Requiem said again as he did as Damion asked.

Damion spread the thick, slick substance over his fingers. "You don't have to."

"Yes, I do. Everything needs an explanation." Requiem watched Damion's face as he gripped the man's upper arms.

Damion chuckled. "Just live with the knowledge that sometimes there is not a damn good explanation." He slipped one greased finger past Requiem's tight entrance and into the heat of his channel.

"But that is not knowledge. That is the absence of—" Requiem gasped before he could finish the sentence. The slight burn of the finger entering him trailed up his spine.

"That is acceptance," Damion whispered, kissing Requiem and quickly adding a second finger.

Requiem's low, soft moan was muffled by Damion's lips and tongue. Requiem's blunt nails dug into Damion's muscular arms as his legs twitched and he squirmed. In these moments, his body took control, knowing what it wanted even if his mind hadn't completely caught up.

Damion worked on stretching Requiem's muscles while they kissed slowly, his tongue simulating what his cock would soon be doing.

Requiem skimmed his fingers over Damion's skin, along his shoulders, down his arms, and eventually running featherlight over his ribcage and sides. He continued to move his hips, pushing Damion's fingers deeper into him even as his tongue ran along Damion's and his teeth nibbled experimentally along Damion's lower lip. He felt hot, his skin sensitive and needy.

Damion slipped in a third finger, this time pushing deeper and rubbing the inner walls of Requiem's channel.

Letting out a small, surprised cry against Damion's lips, Requiem shuddered underneath him. He had to pull away, suddenly unable to breathe. Requiem wasn't one to beg—he never had, in fact, as a matter of personal pride. But that self-promise shattered as his need flared and he writhed wantonly. "Please," he whimpered.

"Please take the fingers away or please do that again?"

Requiem managed to pry his eyes open to focus on Damion's face. He shook his head, not understanding what he wanted, just knowing that he wanted, needed more. His lips felt raw and swollen, his skin hypersensitive, his body throbbing, and his cock almost painfully hard. All he knew was that he wanted Damion to make it better, to deal with the pulsing of his blood and the fire under his skin. And he didn't know how to tell him that.

Damion pulled his fingers out of Requiem and spread the lube over his own throbbing shaft. "Raise your knees more," he ordered, his voice deep as it often became during sex.

Requiem bent his knees with his feet flat on the bed. He watched Damion with hooded eyes, his chest rising and falling rapidly with silent puffs of air. In that moment, seeing Damion's tan skin flushed with heat, his dark eyes glittering, Requiem realized that he considered his Fighter to be what was commonly known as handsome. Visually appealing. He had noticed it before but never really acknowledged it. He always knew that Damion was attractive on the inside, his intellectual mind and fiery spirit, but never paid much attention to the wrappings. Now noticing, this pleased him.

"What's that grin for?" Damion asked as he began to push his way inside Requiem.

"I did not know that I was, as you say, grinning—" The end of the sentence trailed off in a strangled cry. With the scrambling fingers of one hand, he clutched at Damion's hip, while he covered his mouth with the other as his body bowed.

It hurt, despite being prepared. The pain of being stretched in such a way burned its way up his spine, but at the same time it was *wonderful. Pleasant*, because he knew it would get better. It would feel *amazing* soon.

Requiem moved his hand so that his lips could meet Damion's. Damion braced himself on his forearms and leaned down to kiss Requiem again before he began moving slowly. Requiem moved to grip both sides of Damion's hips, grasping tightly as their tongues slid along each other's hungrily. It soon turned good, amazing even, but didn't quite reach where Requiem needed it. Shifting, he moved his hands up to Damion's waist and wrapped his legs around Damion's hips. His heels dug into Damion's ass, urging him on.

Their bodies were honest, remembering how they liked it and where. Damion's left hand curled into Requiem's hair while he pulled his hips back halfway and then surged forward with enough force to please both of them.

Requiem let out a soft cry, his head tilted back, eyes squeezed shut, panting mouth open. With each thrust, Damion managed to run the head of his cock over that sweet spot inside him that made him catch his breath in ecstasy. His body clenched around Damion as Requiem tensed from the sparks shooting through his veins.

Damion found another spot of skin to mark with his lips and teeth while his hips continued to thrust into Requiem's willing body. Requiem's muscles squeezed him tightly every time he pushed inside. There was no hesitation to Requiem's movements or moans. Damion found the bruised, tender flesh behind Requiem's ear, right next to a port, and worked it with his mouth and teeth.

Biting down on his bottom lip to stifle another cry, Requiem quivered at the feeling of Damion's hot mouth and sharp teeth on his skin. He skimmed his hands over Damion's back until they reached his shoulders, and then he hooked his fingers over them, gripping tightly. He buried his face in Damion's neck while still giving him access to his flesh.

Damion focused completely on the act. The sound of flesh against flesh echoed throughout the room, and sweat mixed with the precome from Requiem's cock trapped between them.

With Damion thrusting into him hard and fast, along with Damion's muscled abdomen rubbing against his need, Requiem was quickly approaching completion. The pool of heat in his groin built to near volcanic levels and little cries were muffled by his teeth and Damion's neck.

Damion let out a loud cry as his orgasm tore through him, his hips moving as he pushed his seed into Requiem's open body. "Yes!"

Requiem followed him into oblivion, muffling his own low cry by biting Damion's shoulder. He dug his fingers harshly into Damion's shoulders as his mind exploded into whiteness. He trembled and twitched, his muscles tightening around Damion, milking him as he came violently all over their chests and stomachs.

"Gods," Damion gasped, and he almost crushed Requiem beneath him as he sank down.

Requiem didn't care, not really noticing the heavy weight on top of him, because he was clinging to it. He released Damion's shoulder, saving it from his teeth as his head flopped back onto the mattress. He closed his eyes. He was having difficulty catching his breath and he was unable to deal with muscle control any longer. His legs had unlocked from Damion's hips and fallen back down to the bed.

Damion licked his lips and slumped to the side, wincing a bit and causing Requiem to gasp as Damion slid out of him. "Damn, it's like my skin is on fire."

Requiem let his arms drop to the bed. His body still twitched occasionally, trying to regain control over his muscles. "I am having a similar feeling," he replied in a hoarse voice, his gaze focusing on the ceiling lazily.

"Good." Damion grinned from ear to ear and ran his fingers through the mess on his stomach. "Shower?"

"A distinctly appropriate solution." Requiem shifted—or at least attempted to. In actuality he only twitched. "Unfortunately I have to report that I do not believe I can currently move." Tiredness settled over his limbs, threatening to drag him into an abyss, but he fought against it. He blinked, his gaze trailing over to the comm screen as it beeped twice for an incoming internal transmission.

"Who the fuck is trying to get us?" Damion muttered as he sat up with a groan.

Juni's name flashed across the screen, an icon of a cartoon face with a big grin flashing next to it for his signature.

Seeing it, Requiem sighed and looked away, closing his eyes at the same time. It was quite extraordinary, the perception Fighter Mathis had. At least this time he was calling after instead of before or during, otherwise Requiem was sure it would not have been pleasant for 108's Fighter.

Damion grabbed his discarded underwear before sitting down and opening the transmission. "Do I have to start tucking you into bed?"

"What the hellll-lo, was I interrupting something?" Juni's cheeky grin appeared on the screen as he viewed the state Damion was in, his gaze trailing to a spot of fluid on Damion's collarbone.

"One day I'm going to interrupt you and see how amused you are," Damion warned, giving him a glare. "Did something happen that you're bothering me?"

"Mmm, that would have to involve 108 and I being in the room," Juni corrected with a sly grin as he looked to something—or someone—off screen. A low snort was heard and then the sound of a door closing. Juni laughed softly, looking back at Damion. "I was going to see if you wanted to go to the officers' bar on level two for a few drinks while 47 slept, but I'm guessing that he wasn't that tired. So I'll retract that and let you go have more messy fun."

Damion flipped off his friend. "I'm going to shower, and then I'm going to sleep and hope that I won't have to patrol with your lazy ass tomorrow."

"Oh, you cut me to the bone." Juni dramatically placed a hand flat to his chest over his heart. "Too bad, so sad. We're running paired doubles tomorrow. You're stuck with me allll day—0700 hours. And I will torture you. Oh yes, I will." Insane laughter could still be heard as Juni cut the video feed and only ended when he shut off the vocal.

Damion let out a long sigh. "At least I won't fall asleep at the helm." He got up and looked over at Requiem. "You need help to the shower?"

Prying open one eye, Requiem looked at Damion. Taking an internal account of his body, he reluctantly nodded. "I apologize, but I do not believe my muscles will hold me in the appropriate position to walk at this time."

"All right." Damion bent down and pulled Requiem's arm over his shoulders and then helped him to the bathroom.

"Thank you," Requiem whispered. His legs shook with each step, feeling like wonderful warm jelly. He ignored the feeling of Damion's seed exiting his body and sliding down his legs.

"Just lean against the wall for a second." Damion helped him back against the cool tile of the bathroom wall before starting up the shower.

"I apologize that I am such a burden to you," Requiem said softly after a few moments. The steam from the shower caressed his skin in a pleasant way.

"You're not a burden." Damion pulled him forward again and into the shower stall, which was barely big enough for both of them. He held Requiem close as he began to wash Requiem's bruised, weary body.

Requiem sighed blissfully as the warm water and Damion's hands soothed his tired body. He rested his head on Damion's shoulder and closed his eyes, letting himself be taken care of. "I appreciate that you attempt to say otherwise, but it is not the truth. If it were not for my presence in your life, it would be much simpler and not nearly so dangerous. But I thank you for it."

Damion started on Requiem's hair. "I don't think there is a simple way for a Fighter to live."

A brief moan began behind Requiem's lips before he caught it and cut it off. He sighed in contentment as Damion's strong fingers massaged his scalp, easing the headache that had started to creep up into his temples. "Perhaps not simple, but simpler."

"Again, I deny that statement, but I think you'd argue with me 'cause you have to be right, always." Damion gave a tug to Requiem's soapy locks and then nudged him under the spray.

"I deny that statement. I do not claim I am right. I merely make suggestions that you can take under consideration if you wish." Requiem couldn't get out any more words as the steamy water poured over his head, rinsing out his hair. He leaned against the wall, enjoying the heat and Damion's grip on his arms keeping him upright.

"Let me just wash quick and we'll get you back to bed."

Damion sounded amused at Requiem's lethargy—probably because he was the cause. Requiem leaned against the cool tile wall of the stall and closed his eyes, keeping quiet. He felt he might fall asleep right then and there and used the chill against his back to keep himself awake.

Damion finished showering quickly and then turned off the water before grabbing them both towels. "Here, dry off before you catch a cold."

"I have never caught a 'cold.'" Requiem took the towel, his brow furrowed minutely as he dried off.

"Well, you can get one from not taking care of your body," Damion explained as he bent down and picked up Requiem again, carrying him back to bed.

Requiem wrapped an arm around Damion's neck, clinging to the damp towel. "Is catching a cold a euphemism for becoming ill?" His words slurred with exhaustion, and he was hanging on to consciousness by his fingernails.

"So damn smart." Damion laid Requiem down on the bed and quickly covered up his damp body with the top sheet. "Jack in tomorrow to appease the assholes downstairs before we head out."

"As you command," Requiem replied with a yawn, turning on his side. "Do you wish for me to wake you an hour before launch?"

"Thirty minutes." Damion crawled into the bed and sighed as he pulled up the extra blanket for himself before hugging Requiem close. "If Juni starts singing tomorrow, I want you to order 108 to knock him out."

"I am fairly sure that 108 would not require an order from me to make that decision if it is for the good of all."

Requiem snuggled closer to his… *lover*—such an odd term—and quickly gave himself to sleep.

Chapter Thirty-Four

Saturday October 22, 454 MC
0935 GMT
Damion

THE NEXT few days passed calmly. Damion was more unnerved from the lack of attempts on his life than anything else. They would do their patrols and come back without incident. It seemed Requiem's looped playback was working well enough since there had been no more surprise visits. And the Commander hadn't poked his nose in either.

According to Juni and 108, the President had also showed casual interest in Damion and Requiem. If the President was around and Damion and Requiem happened to pass by or be in the same place, he watched them until they were gone.

Patrol was also easy and passed without incident. There were a few times where it seemed something was on the edge of their radar, but nothing showed up or it left when the scan was expanded, so they never figured out exactly what it was. There had been an extensive diagnostic and physical check of the *Olympus*. There was no indication who sabotaged the ship or when it occurred in the reports. They were also scheduled for outreaching patrol for the day the President left—the day before the Creators were going to come and retrieve Requiem.

Damion sighed as he dressed for their last day of patrol. The flight suit was a comforting cocoon in which he felt powerful and sure, and things made sense when he wore it. "What are you going to tell the Creators when we get back?"

"I do not know," Requiem replied quietly as he zipped up his flight suit. He sat on the edge of the capsule to pull his boots on. "I believe this is the type of situation that I can only deal with without preparation. I have until tomorrow to decide."

"Damn it." Damion felt his anger and aggression return all at once in the span of one heartbeat. "Just tell them everything is fine."

"The answers depend on the questions, Damion. I am not allowed to report until ordered to." Requiem stood, looking at him. "The

Creator's and my agreement was based on your scores. They have improved. Therefore I will not be forced to choose a new Fighter. Beyond that I do not know what to expect."

"What about the Barrier? The one you can't even do without almost blacking out?"

Damion didn't like the idea of Requiem handing that over to the creeps. It was more than just dislike—it was fear. The fear of his Core being taken away for more experiments and never being seen again.

"I must give them the schematics if they ask, but I am the only Core who can transfer energy to the Zodiac and therefore power the Barrier if the auxiliary power source gives out. They want it for the fleet, but it will be useless to them unless I can figure out a way to demonstrate to them how to power it efficiently." Requiem tilted his head as he explained it, watching Damion.

"It won't stop them from experimenting." Damion was furious just from the mere thought of the numerous Cores who would die trying to be batteries. He hated thinking about them taking Requiem from him and using him for their tests. Requiem never thought about the consequences for himself.

"Nothing will stop them from experimentation. Short of termination, that is." After a moment's hesitation, Requiem walked over to stand in front of Damion, looking up at him. "What would you suggest for me to do?"

"You wouldn't like my answer." Damion put his hands on his hips as he looked down at Requiem. He wondered if those big eyes would suck him in completely one day. Perhaps they already had. Sure seemed like it.

"Would not like, or should not hear?"

"I'm pissed that you probably shouldn't hear it." Damion hated not being able to trust Requiem, not completely.

"Very well. Shall we depart? We need to be at the hangar in approximately four minutes and ready to launch in ten."

"Might as well. Maybe we'll see what keeps setting off the sensors." Damion grabbed a few extra protein bars to snack on during the patrol. He despised being hungry, and Requiem seemed displeased by his whining, so it was better to take a snack just in case.

"Our main objective today is to secure the *Olympus* as it makes its departure. We will be in the outermost quadrant. Once they pass us, they have an hour's flight before they meet up with their own security force, which was delayed and is now en route." Requiem opened the door for Damion and followed him out, keying the lock before they began to walk down the corridor to the elevator.

"Why the hell are we the only ones going? Didn't someone just try and blow the guy up?" He couldn't believe they would just let the President skip off without his full entourage.

"The President overruled the Commander's suggestion to wait. The reason was not in the status report," Requiem answered. "We will be out of the *Zeus*'s range, enabling us to test the *Ares* in open space without direct observation."

"It's still boring." Damion shrugged. "But I guess it's better than target practice or Juni's stories."

"It will give us both time to think, as well as attempt to discern what is on the edge of our sensors in that immediate sector." Requiem keyed the elevator and they stepped in, pushing the button for the flight deck.

"Probably debris." Damion didn't fully believe his own words but was unable to think what else it might be. "But debris doesn't usually move away."

"Precisely." Requiem walked out of the elevator, waiting for Damion, then following him toward the flight deck. "Nor does debris move in a way that could be construed as evasive. Debris goes in a straight line. It is intriguing."

"You like trouble," Damion teased him. The last thing either of them needed was to be more intrigued or find intriguing enemy spies.

"In actuality I try to avoid any sort of confrontation. It does not seem as if confrontation avoids me." They approached the door to the dock.

"You could say that," Damion scoffed, opening the door and walking toward the *Ares*.

"I just did."

Requiem looked at him briefly, his brow slightly furrowed. He looked back at the lock console on the side of their Zodiac. He keyed in their code and the hatch on top of the ship opened, the ladder rolling out to the floor. He waited for Damion to board, climbing in himself once Damion was inside the *Ares*.

Damion slipped into his seat and pulled on his helmet before starting the *Ares*'s power-up sequence. "Diagnostic report?"

Requiem sat in his chair, jacking in quickly as the chair eased back to a half-reclined position. He quickly went through each of the *Ares*'s systems. "Diagnostic complete. *Ares* running at 99.7 percent. Approved for launch."

"Engaging engines and awaiting bay doors to open." Damion switched channels on the comm. "Juni, you're not fucking sleeping over there, are you?"

"So what if I am? You probably had a later night than me," Juni replied, as chipper as always.

"If I did, it's because I have more stamina."

"Screw you, Hawk, I have stamina."

"Says the guy who once passed out while screwing his girlfriend."

There was sputtering over the comm from Juni, along with chuckles from the other Alphas eavesdropping.

"Engine heat pattern at maximum output. Bay doors expanding. Ready to launch in fifty-three seconds," Requiem reported.

Damion initiated the ship forward and led the other Alphas and a squad of Betas out into silent space before the *Olympus*. "Let's start scanning."

"Deep space scans initiating. Radar, heat, and echo sensors all activated." Requiem's voice came through the speakers of the Zodiac. "I have scanned through the *Ares* itself, the sensor output, and schematics of the other Zodiacs. Area clear for a 160-kilometer radius."

"We'll do a circle around, then swing back to help the escort for the *Olympus*." Damion turned the craft around. He made sure to push the *Ares* quickly as swinging around the *Zeus* was no small feat. The expansive battle cruiser was a gleaming metal beast, a testament to all the power of the Corporation. The entire ship appeared seamless. The hard lines where the sides flared out and the lower hangar protruding from the underside of the *Zeus* made the ship look massive. The main gun on the front was enormous and had the ability to decimate cruisers and smaller fighters in one blast.

"Affirmative," Requiem stated. "Expanding sensors to maximum output."

Damion did his circle of the *Zeus* and swung back just in time to see *Olympus* leaving the docking bay very slowly. "This is *Ares*. We're all clear. This looks like another boring day, folks. We'll take the aft side of the *Olympus*."

Damion switched the comm off, a habit he had started since Requiem came back altered. "We could just fly away, you think? How far would we get before they realized we were running?"

"We would not travel this far before we would be fired upon and terminated," Requiem's true voice said from his chair. "And I cannot leave the Chrysalis Corporation. I will not betray it."

"Yeah. We can't betray them to be happy," Damion growled, looking at his gloved hands on the controls.

"No, I cannot. Even if I did want to, when they found out, I would be terminated. The tracking device implanted in my skull would shut down my internal systems," Requiem explained. "May I request that you stop speaking of such things as it will make it more difficult when the Creator questions me tomorrow?"

"I can't help it." Damion sighed as he looked out at the *Olympus*. "If I don't talk about it, then I just want to shoot something, and right now that might not be a good idea. Alpha Fighter Hawk, why did you shoot upon the President's flagship? Sorry, sir, I was thinking about the white-coated creeps wiping my Core and taking him away from me forever."

"Perhaps a visit to the recreational range might be in order when we dock," Requiem suggested. "Approaching one-kilometer mark. The rest of the fleet is breaking off. At the request of the *Olympus*'s pilot, *Ares* will continue as guide to the *Olympus* to the edge of the zone."

"We'll come around the *Olympus* and move ahead of them once everyone is out of our way." Damion flipped the outgoing comm open again while letting out a sigh. "See everyone back on the *Zeus*."

"I'll have a brew cracked and waiting for you," Juni promised as the other nine Alphas moved back toward the distant *Zeus*.

The Betas continued patrols around the *Zeus* as was normal.

"Path cleared," Requiem replied. "Sensors continuing at max output and sweeping. Thrusters activating to medium power to pull out of the *Olympus*'s wake and move ahead."

Damion waited for the Zodiacs to pass before pulling forward and dipping under *Olympus* to get ahead of the flagship. "Should only be about twenty minutes away, then we'll be able to let your hand go, *Olympus*."

"Thanks, *Ares*."

"No problem. Doing our duty."

As Damion communicated back and forth with the *Olympus*, Requiem concentrated on the sensors.

"Something is out there, just on the edge of my scans, but I cannot quite be clear what it is. It is the same anomaly we have been seeing for the last four days. I have checked the sensors several times to see if there is a malfunction, but they are working perfectly."

Damion slipped off his helmet so that he could scratch his head and roll his neck. This was boring. "You bored?"

"Bored? I do not believe so."

Damion watched the empty, star-filled space in front of him. The expansive nothing they were floating in was less frightening than the mines back home. Such a large space, and they didn't have any part of it to themselves. He gave a full-body shake as he tried to get back on task. "Why couldn't the President's security force just meet us at the *Zeus*?"

"It is for security and space reasons. That many ships in the vicinity would be a flight hazard. Additionally the ships reported that this early departure by the President coincided with their engine maintenance window. Since they are unable to perform long-distance flight, they are watching for rebels or opportunistic assassins to make sure there will be no incidents between passage." There was a pause. "Something just zipped across my scanner, Fighter Hawk. It is too slow to be a comet or something of that nature. It was just on the edge of the sensors. I would like to recommend secondary alert status and have the *Olympus* increase their scanner range."

"All right, if you want, but don't get me excited over nothing." Damion pulled his helmet back on and contacted the *Olympus*.

"You usually do anyway, where I am involved," Requiem replied over the intercom, his normal expressionless tone sounding exceptionally dry.

The *Olympus* replied that they didn't see anything out of the ordinary. They might have said more, but their comm systems went out. Requiem gasped as an invisible wave flowed over the *Ares*. It abruptly knocked out the *Ares*'s communication systems.

"Comm system terminated by an outside source," he reported in a tense voice. As soon as he finished speaking, the sensor system went haywire, showing unknown vessels flying in at high speed. "Incoming! Approximately thirty unknown hostiles."

"Rebels, more than likely. Can you contact the *Zeus*?" Damion spun the *Ares* into a roll over the top of *Olympus*, taking on a defensive position. "Can we talk to the President's ship at all?"

"Negative. All comm systems have been severed by a pulse of some kind." Requiem's eyes flickered rapidly, concentrating on keeping all the ships in sight. "Incoming on the starboard side and aft, three vessels. Suggest evasive tactics and to lead them away from the *Olympus*."

"Then we better make ourselves worth following!" Damion rolled the craft again and opened fire on the enemy ships, trying to piss off the attackers as much as possible. He figured taking out one craft and disabling the other was a good start.

"They seem to be ignoring us and avoiding firing on the *Olympus*. They are leaving half their numbers to surround the *Olympus* but are not attacking it," Requiem reported. "The other fourteen vessels are following the *Ares*."

"What the hell are you doing back there, sleeping?"

As good as Damion was as a Fighter, pilot, and shooter, the rebels seemed to be dodging their fire along with firing at them. But with Damion's erratic movements and their wide attacks, it seemed the rebels weren't trying to hit them. Taking a deep breath, Requiem closed his eyes, charging up the Impulse Barrier.

Damion grumbled as he saw his panel flicker for a moment. He disliked Requiem at times for this very reason; his Core was preparing to initiate the Barrier. "Can't you, for once, just have a bit of faith that I can get us out of a situation on my own?"

Damion's teeth ached at the first direct hit to their shields. The jar was nothing for now, but he knew they couldn't take many direct hits and live. He wasn't lying down and taking it, but there were just so many. Since the enemy was clustered together, at least it was easier to hit many of them at the same time before dropping down or up above the debris he left in his wake. *Just so many of them.* His starlit sky faded under a blanket of metal and fire. "Fuck."

"Eighteen more enemy craft coming from the port bow along with a larger vessel. Odds of it being their main battleship: highly probable," Requiem reported as the Impulse Barrier slowly pulled energy from the auxiliary energy pack.

Damion knew it was enough to power one small burst that would disable approximately ten enemy ships with how tightly packed they were. Anything stronger would start to pull from Requiem himself.

"Probability of the *Ares* escaping the battle with the use of the Impulse Barrier is low. Without it, it is… not impossible, but highly improbable. They are not shooting to kill at this time. They are attempting to disable our shields."

Another hit rocked the *Ares*, punctuating his point. Klaxons sounded throughout the small interior, red lights flashing warnings as text scrolled across the screen. "Shields are down to 33 percent. I have concluded that they mean to capture us along with the *Olympus*, more than likely for information. This cannot happen." He paused for a moment. "One of us must survive and escape to alert the *Zeus*."

"*One?*" Damion was getting pissed at the computer statistical bullshit that his lover was spewing. Damion wasn't shooting at the ships to capture them, only to kill at this point. "Screw you, Requiem! We both get out of this or we both die! There is no other option."

"There is an infinite array of options. This one is merely the most likely to work," Requiem replied. "Activating the Impulse Barrier. Going offline for approximately ten seconds."

With his work and practice with the Impulse Barrier over the past few months, Requiem could activate it quicker now. A familiar whine sounded through the *Ares*, almost too low to hear before it rose to a high pitch and then exploded into a bass thump that ranged outward from the *Ares*, disabling the rebels around them.

Some of them stayed out of range, just far enough for the blast to be unable to reach them.

"Charging. The *Ares* has approximately one minute before the enemy vessels come back online. More incoming." The disabled ships spun in uncontrolled movements, bumping into each other and crowding the *Ares* to the point where it almost wasn't maneuverable. "Larger vessel coming alongside the *Olympus* but not exhibiting any hostile action at this time."

Damion felt bile in the back of his throat as he thought of what Requiem had to endure just to use the Barrier almost every time they went into battle. This other ship wasn't some small freighter. Damion knew a battle cruiser when he saw one. "Fuck. We can't just leave the President's ship here."

He'd never get far if he just cut and ran back to the *Zeus*. If the Commander didn't kick his ass out of the Alphas, the Creators would because they'd be scapegoats. Doing so would mean he would fail in the true test of being a Fighter for the Corporation. His life was their property as much as Requiem was their toy. He didn't have a choice. Fight, kill, or be killed. Die at the hands of rebels, fighting their best, or limp back and face another form of death. "We're in this together. Don't think I'm leaving you behind."

Requiem didn't answer. "Enemy coming from all sides. Powering up Barrier. This is a decision that you must make, Damion. There are too many variables for me to go through all the options. I do not have time to analyze all of them, as I would need to do in order to make a proper decision. This will take a mind that does not need to be analytical." Requiem took another deep breath as the Impulse Barrier started to power up again, drawing power from the electric impulses within his own body through the jack. The whine increased in pitch.

"You're a real pain in my ass." Damion dipped the ship to the right a few degrees, leaving the disabled enemy behind and then raced back toward the *Olympus* and the other ship. "Hopefully when the President doesn't reach his convoy, they'll send someone and the enemy ships will be too slowed down to have gotten him far or have killed him yet."

"Incoming," Requiem reported loudly as enemy vessels suddenly surrounded them. Another shot hit their shields, rocking the *Ares* and sending sparks throughout the interior as the shields failed. Requiem let out a small sound of pain. "Shields are down. Damage to the starboard thruster. It is only at 37 percent capacity. Guidance system is also damaged and inoperable." His voice was tight as electricity crackled through the *Ares*. "Core offline for fifteen seconds. Engaging the Impulse Barrier."

The *Ares* rattled as the Pulse spread out from the Zodiac, leaving ships dead in space. But more peeled away from the *Olympus* and also exited from the larger vessel. Requiem immediately began powering the Barrier again.

"Shut down everything we don't need! I just need the engines and the weapons. Reroute everything, Requiem, even life support." By this point Damion had given up thinking they would get out of this alive. It was now time to show the rebels exactly how much damage an Alpha Fighter could do and that there were no cowards in this small craft. "Give me some shields."

"As you ordered," Requiem replied in a breathy voice.

The shields flickered back to life just in time to take a hit that would have taken out the number two power supply. The lights within the capsule pulsed and then dimmed, the only light now from Damion's operating systems and the outside lights of the *Ares*. The air within the ship grew warm, almost stuffy except for the occasional burst that circulated fresh oxygen. The life-support systems were failing and misinterpreting commands. "Shields at 46 percent, engines at full, weapons at full, life support down to 30 percent, starboard thruster leaking and at 12 percent," he reported.

"Let's see how much damage I can do to that ship."

Damion tried to get out of the other ships' way while laying fire over the battleship's hull. He turned the *Ares* around and flipped them over, cursing loudly as he realized how much harder it was to make the *Ares* respond now. He was able to lay down another burst of fire over the hull before having to break off to avoid enemy fire.

The shots only hit the large ship's shield, sending flickers of light over the dark metal. The rebels' vessel was as large as the *Zeus* and had opened a bay, slowly pulling the *Olympus* into its large underbelly. There would be no problem with the *Olympus* fitting within it. The entire hull of the *Olympus* disappeared fast as if the rebels were used to hauling large vessels inside, and quickly. All their ships split off from surrounding the President's ship, heading toward the *Ares*.

Another hit, and the shields were torn down again, sending the *Ares* into a spin.

"Engine one down. Both thrusters damaged but functional."

Red lights strobed throughout the *Ares*. "I do not understand. At any point in time, the rebels could have killed us, but they seem to be waiting, circling like Earth sharks."

Damion heard him take a deep, shaky breath.

"Activating the Impulse Barrier. The only logical action at this time is to retreat. You will have one minute to do so."

"No! You can't! *Requiem*!" Damion screamed, wanting to turn and shake his lover to make him stop but unable to take his gaze from the window or his hands from the controls for even a second. He was filled with terror for Requiem, his heart pounding in his chest with the knowledge of what Requiem was doing to himself. To them.

The whining of the Barrier filled the capsule, combining with the shriek of the alarms, the crackling of failing systems, and the smell of burning electronics. Requiem didn't stop.

"Wait! Requiem! No! *No!*" Damion screamed again desperately, but he was too late once the *Ares* pulsed outward.

Tears, along with sweat, trailed down Damion's face. The cabin began to heat up and then suddenly cooled as life support failed. The aftershock from the Pulse on the unprotected Zodiac sent pain up Damion's arms.

He looked over his shoulder at Requiem with wide, tear-filled eyes—broken, chest not moving, face in the lax expression of death, unresponsive to any of Damion's screams. All this made a fire in the pit of Damion's stomach, forming a rage that he wanted to show to the galaxy. Damion screamed futile insults, only using up more of the precious air that was already thin in their cabin, as he beat his hands bloody against the unresponsive controls.

Without Requiem to hold them, systems began to fail, powering down. The only items that remained operational were the weak thrusters and parts of Damion's flickering screen that showed him which way to retreat.

From the distance, four rebel vessels at the edge of the Pulse radius that had been waiting for this opportunity swarmed in. The sound of grips hitting the metal of the *Ares*'s hull echoed throughout the chamber as they latched on to the Zodiac, pulling it toward the large ship that had already swallowed the *Olympus*. They maneuvered easily through their comrades who remained dead in space, and they weren't taking their time. They moved with urgency.

Lastly the systems that monitored Requiem's vital functions started screaming their own alert but were suddenly silenced soon after they began as power was taken from them as well. Damion found himself heaving large gulps of air and looking at the last few panels around him that still had power. There was no escape. They would be dragged into the belly of that ship and he'd be slaughtered or tortured for information. Requiem would be dissected. He reached out to the main monitor, pressing a few buttons before inputting his personal code.

A static voice crackled throughout the cabin, barely audible. "Initialize self-destruct."

"Confirmation by Alpha Fighter Hawk, Damion Pierce. Core deceased. Override Core sequences and set to destruct in five minutes."

That gave him just enough time to say good-bye. It gave the rebels time to think they had won, and it would put them right in the belly of the battleship. Then he'd blow it all to Hades from the inside out. It might not take the ship down, but it should fuck up enough of their bay to give the President's convoy time to meet up.

There was a red pulsing light that read 04:30 on the screen above Damion's head. Damion couldn't send a wave out even if he wanted to. Who would he have called? Mom? Juni? *Sorry, guys. Finally fucked up big enough to end up spaced.*

Damion's heart began to race as the battleship eclipsed the *Ares* as his Zodiac was swallowed. *Requiem.* That one name was on his mind. Damion hurriedly took off his helmet, dropping it to bounce on the metal floor as he reached for the single pistol holstered to his right thigh.

He could see people now through the red numbers on his window.

03:24

"Why don't they just kill us?" Damion didn't want to wait for the indignant death of being shot, trapped in his ship like a fish in a barrel. He couldn't quite turn enough to reach Requiem with his safety harness holding him tightly to his control chair.

He unbuckled his safety harness, and while it was a tight fit with the top hatch of the *Ares* down, he managed to squeeze himself next to his lover's chair.

Requiem wasn't moving, nor did he seem to be breathing. His eyes were closed and his head tilted to the side. His arms had fallen off the rests in the last jolt, and the only thing that kept them there were the input jack cables.

02:15

The enemy ships pulled the disabled *Ares* through the atmospheric barrier, a glittering of silver as they did so, bringing the damaged Zodiac into the same bay as the *Olympus*. Hydraulic arms reached out, grasping the *Ares* with a jolt as the vessels disconnected their cables. The arms dragged the *Ares* into a docking plate where people were waiting at the end of the ramp.

The first thing Damion noticed was people who looked like security—men and women with various weapons—and medical technicians around a stretcher. There was also a tall woman with ruby red hair, tan skin, and a slight scowl on her face that caused the beauty of her features to appear severe. Beside her was the President, calm, cool, and collected.

Alive, and obviously there of his own choosing.

Damion's Core had sacrificed everything for a traitor. Betrayal, hate, and sadness filled Damion's chest as he saw the President standing there seemingly safe, sound, and right at fucking home. Damion looked away from the collection of people outside their view window, pressing his forehead against Requiem's, trying to will life into the man he cared most about in the universe. The one person Damion had come to truly love.

His hand tightened on the pistol grip as the strident tone of the two-minute warning echoed in the small dying ship. Damion pressed a soft kiss to Requiem's lips with his own trembling ones in a final gesture of love. "We die together. There was never any other option for me," he whispered softly against the cooling lips as he shut his eyes, awaiting the inevitable.

Saturday October 22, 454 MC

1042 GMT
In the Belly of the Titan

TO BE continued.

T.A. VENEDICKTOV is in reality two people.

A, Ariana Juno, is a full-time working single mother with a love of chai tea lattes and tumblr. When A is not working or raising two amazing children she is plotting with her co-author. A has been in the medical field for fifteen years and has a love of travel. She lives in the Midwest and has an ice cream habit which calls for an intervention. A daydreams most of the plots of the T.A. novels—daily, hourly, nonstop, which drives T nuts at times.

T is a full-time mom with a background in theater. T has traveled outside the USA to multiple countries. The main headliner in regards to editing and keeping their writing in order as well as trying to untangle all of A's random ideas. T lives in Florida with her fiancé and three human children as well as three cat babies. She's been battling Sjogren's Disease while drinking coffee and kicking ass.

The duo has been writing unprofessionally for over a decade together and hope to share their characters with the world.

Facebook: www.facebook.com/chrysaliscorp
Twitter: T.A. Venedicktov
E-mail: 29hogtiedmuses@gmail.com

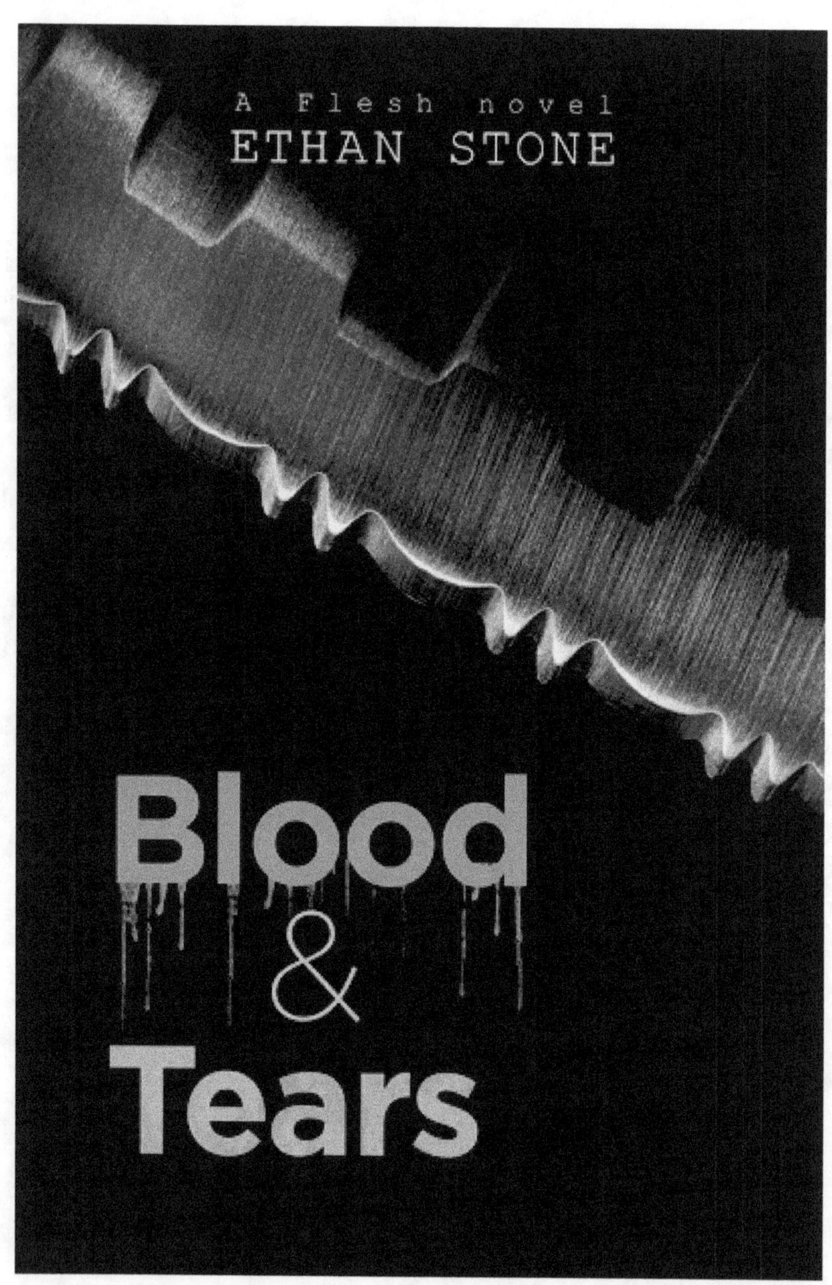

www.dsppublications.com

'TIL DARKNESS FALLS
Pearl Love
www.dsppublications.com

GNOMON

LUCHIA DERTIEN

www.dsppublications.com

www.dsppublications.com

DSP PUBLICATIONS

visit us online.

WWW.DSPPUBLICATIONS.COM

9 781634 761710